DREAMALITE

Power Crystal

Once a Star Darling has granted her first wish
and returns to Starland, she receives a very
special treasure—a beautiful Power Crystal.

BRACELETS

Wish Pendant

A Wish Pendant is a powerful accessory worn
by a Star Darling. On Wishworld, it helps
her identify her Wisher and stores the
ever-important wish energy.

Astra

Astra is a superior athlete. She excels in sports of all kinds.

She is energetic, brave, clever, and confident—sometimes too confident. Astra can be self-centered and brash at times.

QUARRELITE

Power Crystal

Once a Star Darling has granted her first wish
and returns to Starland, she receives a very
special treasure—a beautiful Power Crystal.

WRISTBANDS

Wish Pendant

A Wish Pendant is a powerful accessory worn
by a Star Darling. On Wishworld, it helps
her identify her Wisher and stores the
ever-important wish energy.

Tessa

Tessa loves good food, beautiful flowers, and luxurious fabrics. She's an excellent and creative chef. She is warm, charming, and loving.

Tessa can be stubborn and has a hard time handling change.

GOSSAMER

Power Crystal

Once a Star Darling has granted her first wish and returns to Starland, she receives a very special treasure—a beautiful Power Crystal.

BROOCH

Wish Pendant

A Wish Pendant is a powerful accessory worn by a Star Darling. On Wishworld, it helps her identify her Wisher and stores the ever-important wish energy.

Piper's Perfect Dream

Astra's Mixed-Up Mission

Tessa's Lost and Found

Shana Muldoon Zappa and Ahmet Zappa
with Zelda Rose

Disney Press
Los Angeles • New York

Printed in the United States of America
Reinforced Binding
First Paperback Edition, July 2016
Piper's Perfect Dream First Paperback Edition, March 2016
Astra's Mixed-Up Mission First Paperback Edition, April 2016
Tessa's Lost and Found First Paperback Edition, May 2016
1 3 5 7 9 10 8 6 4 2

FAC-025438-16141

ISBN 978-1-4847-8297-2

For more Disney Press fun, visit www.disneybooks.com

To our beautiful, sweet treasure,
Halo Violetta Zappa. You are pure light and joy
and our greatest inspiration. We love you soooo much.

May every step upon your path be blessed with positivity and
the understanding that you have the power within you to
manifest the most fulfilling life you can possibly imagine and
more. May you always remember that being different and true
to your highest self makes your inner star shine brighter.

Remember that you have the power of choice. . . . Choose thoughts
that feel good. Choose love and friendship that feed your spirit.
Choose actions for peace and nourishment. Choose boundaries
for the same. Choose what speaks to your creativity and unique
inner voice . . . what truly makes you happy. And always know
that no matter what you choose, you are unconditionally loved.

Look up to the stars and know you are never alone.
When in doubt, go within . . . the answers are all there.
Smiles light the world and laughter is the best medicine.
And NEVER EVER stop making wishes. . . .

Glow for it. . . .
Mommy and Daddy

And to everyone else here on "Wishworld":

May you realize that no matter where you are in life, no
matter what you look like or where you were born, you, too,
have the power within you to create the life of your dreams.
Through celebrating your own uniqueness, thinking positively,
and taking action, you can make your wishes come true.

Smile. The Star Darlings have your back.
We know how startastic you truly are.

Glow for it. . . .
Your friends,
Shana and Ahmet

Student Reports

NAME: Clover
BRIGHT DAY: January 5
FAVORITE COLOR: Purple
INTERESTS: Music, painting, studying
WISH: To be the best songwriter and DJ on Starland
WHY CHOSEN: Clover has great self-discipline, patience, and willpower. She is creative, responsible, dependable, and extremely loyal.
WATCH OUT FOR: Clover can be hard to read and she is reserved with those she doesn't know. She's afraid to take risks and can be a wisecracker at times.
SCHOOL YEAR: Second
POWER CRYSTAL: Panthera
WISH PENDANT: Barrette

NAME: Adora
BRIGHT DAY: February 14
FAVORITE COLOR: Sky blue
INTERESTS: Science, thinking about the future and how she can make it better
WISH: To be the top fashion designer on Starland
WHY CHOSEN: Adora is clever and popular and cares about the world around her. She's a deep thinker.
WATCH OUT FOR: Adora can have her head in the clouds and be thinking about other things.
SCHOOL YEAR: Third
POWER CRYSTAL: Azurica
WISH PENDANT: Watch

NAME: Piper
BRIGHT DAY: March 4
FAVORITE COLOR: Seafoam green
INTERESTS: Composing poetry and writing in her dream journal
WISH: To become the best version of herself she can possibly be and to share that by writing books
WHY CHOSEN: Piper is giving, kind, and sensitive. She is very intuitive and aware.
WATCH OUT FOR: Piper can be dreamy, absentminded, and wishy-washy. She can also be moody and easily swayed by the opinions of others.
SCHOOL YEAR: Second
POWER CRYSTAL: Dreamalite
WISH PENDANT: Bracelets

Starling Academy

NAME: Astra
BRIGHT DAY: April 9
FAVORITE COLOR: Red
INTERESTS: Individual sports
WISH: To be the best athlete on Starland—to win!
WHY CHOSEN: Astra is energetic, brave, clever, and confident. She has boundless energy and is always direct and to the point.
WATCH OUT FOR: Astra is sometimes cocky, self-centered, condescending, and brash.
SCHOOL YEAR: Second
POWER CRYSTAL: Quarrelite
WISH PENDANT: Wristbands

NAME: Tessa
BRIGHT DAY: May 18
FAVORITE COLOR: Emerald green
INTERESTS: Food, flowers, love
WISH: To be successful enough that she can enjoy a life of luxury
WHY CHOSEN: Tessa is warm, charming, affectionate, trustworthy, and dependable. She has incredible drive and commitment.
WATCH OUT FOR: Tessa does not like to be rushed. She can be quite stubborn and often says no. She does not deal well with change and is prone to exaggeration. She can be easily sidetracked.
SCHOOL YEAR: Third
POWER CRYSTAL: Gossamer
WISH PENDANT: Brooch

NAME: Gemma
BRIGHT DAY: June 2
FAVORITE COLOR: Orange
INTERESTS: Sharing her thoughts about almost anything
WISH: To be valued for her opinions on everything
WHY CHOSEN: Gemma is friendly, easygoing, funny, extroverted, and social. She knows a little bit about everything.
WATCH OUT FOR: Gemma talks—a lot—and can be a little too honest sometimes and offend others. She can have a short attention span and can be superficial.
SCHOOL YEAR: First
POWER CRYSTAL: Scatterite
WISH PENDANT: Earrings

Student Reports

NAME: Cassie
BRIGHT DAY: July 6
FAVORITE COLOR: White
INTERESTS: Reading, crafting
WISH: To be more independent and confident and less fearful
WHY CHOSEN: Cassie is extremely imaginative and artistic. She is a voracious reader and is loyal, caring, and a good friend. She is very intuitive.
WATCH OUT FOR: Cassie can be distrustful, jealous, moody, and brooding.
SCHOOL YEAR: First
POWER CRYSTAL: Lunalite
WISH PENDANT: Glasses

NAME: Leona
BRIGHT DAY: August 16
FAVORITE COLOR: Gold
INTERESTS: Acting, performing, dressing up
WISH: To be the most famous pop star on Starland
WHY CHOSEN: Leona is confident, hardworking, generous, open-minded, optimistic, caring, and a strong leader.
WATCH OUT FOR: Leona can be vain, opinionated, selfish, bossy, dramatic, and stubborn and is prone to losing her temper.
SCHOOL YEAR: Third
POWER CRYSTAL: Glisten paw
WISH PENDANT: Cuff

NAME: Vega
BRIGHT DAY: September 1
FAVORITE COLOR: Blue
INTERESTS: Exercising, analyzing, cleaning, solving puzzles
WISH: To be the top student at Starling Academy
WHY CHOSEN: Vega is reliable, observant, organized, and very focused.
WATCH OUT FOR: Vega can be opinionated about everything, and she can be fussy, uptight, critical, arrogant, and easily embarrassed.
SCHOOL YEAR: Second
POWER CRYSTAL: Queezle
WISH PENDANT: Belt

Starling Academy

NAME: Libby
BRIGHT DAY: October 12
FAVORITE COLOR: Pink
INTERESTS: Helping others, interior design, art, dancing
WISH: To give everyone what they need—both on Starland and through wish granting on Wishworld
WHY CHOSEN: Libby is generous, articulate, gracious, diplomatic, and kind.
WATCH OUT FOR: Libby can be indecisive and may try too hard to please everyone.
SCHOOL YEAR: First
POWER CRYSTAL: Charmelite
WISH PENDANT: Necklace

NAME: Scarlet
BRIGHT DAY: November 3
FAVORITE COLOR: Black
INTERESTS: Crystal climbing (and other extreme sports), magic, thrill seeking
WISH: To live on Wishworld
WHY CHOSEN: Scarlet is confident, intense, passionate, magnetic, curious, and very brave.
WATCH OUT FOR: Scarlet is a loner and can alienate others by being secretive, arrogant, stubborn, and jealous.
SCHOOL YEAR: Third
POWER CRYSTAL: Ravenstone
WISH PENDANT: Boots

NAME: Sage
BRIGHT DAY: December 1
FAVORITE COLOR: Lavender
INTERESTS: Travel, adventure, telling stories, nature, and philosophy
WISH: To become the best Wish-Granter Starland has ever seen
WHY CHOSEN: Sage is honest, adventurous, curious, optimistic, friendly, and relaxed.
WATCH OUT FOR: Sage has a quick temper! She can also be restless, irresponsible, and too trusting of others' opinions. She may jump to conclusions.
SCHOOL YEAR: First
POWER CRYSTAL: Lavenderite
WISH PENDANT: Necklace

Introduction

You take a deep breath, about to blow out the candles on your birthday cake. Clutching a coin in your fist, you get ready to toss it into the dancing waters of a fountain. You stare at your little brother as you each hold an end of a dried wishbone, about to pull. But what do you do first?

You make a wish, of course!

Ever wonder what happens right after you make that wish? *Not much*, you may be thinking.

Well, you'd be wrong.

Because something quite unexpected happens next. Each and every wish that is made becomes a glowing Wish Orb, invisible to the human eye. This undetectable orb zips through the air and into the heavens, on a one-way trip to the brightest star in the sky—a magnificent place called Starland. Starland is inhabited by Starlings, who look a lot like you and me, except they have a sparkly glow to their skin, and glittery hair in unique colors. And they have one more thing: magical powers. The Starlings use these powers to make good wishes come true, for when good wishes are granted, the result is positive energy. And the Starlings of Starland need this energy to keep their world running.

In case you are wondering, there are three kinds of Wish Orbs:

1) GOOD WISH ORBS. These wishes are positive and helpful and come from the heart. They are pretty and sparkly and are nurtured in climate-controlled Wish-Houses. They bloom into fantastical glowing orbs. When the time is right, they are presented to the appropriate Starling for wish fulfillment.

2) BAD WISH ORBS. These are for selfish, mean-spirited, or negative things. They don't sparkle

at all. They are immediately transported to a special containment center, as they are very dangerous and must not be granted.

3) IMPOSSIBLE WISH ORBS. These wishes are for things, like world peace and disease cures, that simply can't be granted by Starlings. These sparkle with an almost impossibly bright light and are taken to a special area of the Wish-House with tinted windows to contain the glare they produce. The hope is that one day they can be turned into good wishes the Starlings can help grant.

Starlings take their wish granting very seriously. There is a special school, called Starling Academy, that accepts only the best and brightest young Starling girls. They study hard for four years, and when they graduate, they are ready to start traveling to Wishworld to help grant wishes. For as long as anyone can remember, only graduates of wish-granting schools have ever been allowed to travel to Wishworld. But things have changed in a very big way.

Read on for the rest of the story. . . .

Piper's Perfect Dream

Prologue

STAR KINDNESS DAY GREETINGS

To: All My Darling Friends
From: Piper
Subject: Happy Star Kindness Day!

Happy Star Kindness Day,
A time to spread good cheer.
I'm sending this holo-text to say,
You glow, girls, all staryear.

With Love and Positivity,
Piper

P.S. Personal greetings to come!

To: Sage
From: Piper
Subject: Star Kindness Day Compliment

The first Star Darling to ride a star,
The first on a mission, traveling far.
You triumphed with your heart and glow,
Even gathering some energy flow.

To: Leona
From: Piper
Subject: Thinking of You on Star Kindness Day

The third to go to a faraway world,
You granted a wish, and energy swirled.
But on your way back to our land of light,
Your pendant turned as black as night.

"Why?" you asked, so sad and blue.
No one could answer, no one knew.
But do not fret, Leona dear,
You still rock, that much is clear.

To: Scarlet
From: Piper
Subject: Star Kindness Day Tidings

You had to leave the SD fold,
But you didn't give up, you were too bold.
You joined a mission with a regular Starling,
To prove you were a tried-and-true Darling.

But why did this happen at all?
Why did you take the fall?
Another question, another riddle,
But you stepped up to shine, no second fiddle.

You showed true grit
And even some wit.
My hat's off to you,
Glad you're back with the crew.

To: Cassie

From: Piper

Subject: An Affirmation on Star Kindness Day

Who knows what to do

When we're confused through and through?

You, sweet little Cassie, you always do.

And when you came back from a mission all spent?

The lights went out 100 percent.

But you stayed calm and cool and kept us together,

You figure things out, whenever, wherever.

CHAPTER
1

In her Little Dipper Dorm room, Piper finished her last holo-text. Then she swiped the screen on her Star-Zap to queue up all the messages. Star Kindness Day was the next day. A ceremony would be held in the morning, at precisely the moment the nighttime stars and the daytime sun could all be seen in the color-streaked sky.

It happened in the morning only once a staryear. And all over Starland, Starlings met in open areas to gaze at the sight. Light energy flowed. Everyone smiled. They exchanged positive messages then and for the rest of the starday—to loved ones, to strangers, and to everyone in between. Thoughtful compliments. Meaningful praise. Heartfelt affirmations. It was definitely Piper's favorite holiday.

At Starling Academy, all the students' messages would go out at once, while everyone gathered in the Star Quad before class. Piper checked her holo-texts one last time. She had her own holiday tradition: styling her compliments into poetry. What better way to get a loving message across, she felt, than using language that lifted the spirit, too?

That staryear, she'd worked especially hard on the poems. There had been many ups and downs for the Star Darlings. So much had happened already that year. All the SD missions—some successful, some not. So that day, of all days, Piper wanted her friends to feel good.

Finally pleased with her efforts, Piper tossed her Star-Zap onto a neat pile of pillows on the floor. She'd played around with poetry ideas for starweeks. *Should I use lightkus?* she'd wondered first.

That poetry originated from Lightku Isle, an isolated island with sandy, sparkling beaches, where the local Starlings spoke solely in those kinds of poems, spare and simple with only three lines of verse and seventeen syllables total.

How they managed this without even trying was a wonder to Piper. She herself strove for an effortless state of being on a stardaily basis. But the lightkus proved too difficult and limiting. So Piper went with sunnets, rhyming poems that could be any length and meter but needed to include a source of light.

The last staryear, when Piper was a relatively new first-year student, the holiday hadn't gone quite the way she'd wanted. She had labored long and hard over those holo-texts then, too. She'd wanted to reach out to every single student at Starling Academy. She'd wanted each student to feel good after reading her text; appreciated, even loved, she'd hoped.

She wrote one epic poem but it turned out to be so long and so serious no one bothered reading it. A hot flash of energy coursed through Piper, just remembering it. She'd felt like crying for stardays after.

This staryear, she was determined to get it right. She decided to focus only on students she knew well, and that meant mostly the Star Darlings. She tried to make the poems fun and light, too. Zippy, you might say. No one would think Piper particularly zippy, she knew. She tended to move slowly and unhurriedly, taking in her surroundings to be fully in the moment. But of course she had her own inner energy. And maybe this year she would manage to get that across in her poetry.

Piper leaned back against her soft pillow, closed her

eyes, and visualized each of her friends' smiling faces as they read her special words of encouragement. Well, maybe Scarlet and Leona wouldn't exactly be smiling. Even with her failed mission well in the past and band rehearsals on again, Leona was just beginning to bounce back.

As for Scarlet, she'd had an amazing kind of mission. After being booted out of the Star Darlings, she'd brought back wish energy and basically saved her substitute SD, Ophelia, in the bargain.

Still, it was hard to get a read on Scarlet. Piper wasn't sure what the older Starling was really thinking. One thing was crystal clear, though: Scarlet didn't like rooming with Leona. And Leona felt the same about Scarlet. Even when those poisonous flowers were removed from the girls' dorm rooms so they couldn't spread negativity, those two just couldn't get along.

Yes, there was a lot happening at the academy, and on Starland itself. That recent blackout after Cassie's mission, for instance, had thrown everyone off balance. Even the teachers weren't immune. Headmistress Lady Stella, usually so calm and serene—and an inspiration to Piper—seemed a little edgy. And the head of admissions, Lady Cordial, was stammering and hemming and hawing more than usual.

Now, more than ever, everyone needed to be centered and positive. So really, this was the perfect time for Star Kindness Day.

As Piper thought about everything, her stomach did an unexpected flip. Maybe she should send a positive poem to herself! She stretched to pick up her Star-Zap without lifting her head, then tapped the self-holo-text feature.

Piper's picture popped up in the corner of the screen: a serene, faraway expression on her face, thin seafoam-green eyebrows matching long straight seafoam-green hair, and big green eyes looking into the distance.

For the holo-photo, Piper had pulled her hair back in a ponytail. The ends reached well below her waist. Her expression was as calm as when she swam in Luminous Lake. And that was how she wanted to feel now. Centered and peaceful and wonderfully relaxed. What poem would bring her that mind-set?

Like the calm at the center of the storm . . . Piper began writing. Then she paused. What rhymed with *storm*? *The Little Dipper Dorm*, where first and second years lived!

Like the calm at the center of the storm,
Floating like a breeze through the Little Dipper Dorm.

Again, Piper stopped to think.

With dreams as your guiding light . . .

(Piper was a big believer in dreams holding life truths.)

Your thoughts bring deep insight.

It wasn't her best work, Piper knew. But it was getting late and she was growing tired. Piper liked to get the most sleep possible. After all, it was the startime of day when the body and mind regrouped and reconnected. Sure, she'd had her regular afternoon nap, but sometimes that just wasn't enough.

Piper focused on dimming the lights, and a starsec later, the white light faded to a soft, comforting shade of green, conducive to optimal rest. Piper shared a room with Vega, but each girl's side was uniquely her own.

Piper knew Vega was getting ready for bed, too. But it felt like she had her own secluded space, far removed from her roommate and the hustle and bustle of school. Everything was soft and fluid here. There wasn't one sharp edge in sight.

Piper's water bed was round; her pillows (dozens of them) were round. Her feathery ocean-blue throw rug and matching comforter were round. Even her leafy green plants were in pretty round bowls. And each one gave off a soothing scent that calmed and renewed her.

"Sleep tight, good night, don't let the moonbugs bite," Vega called out.

"Starry dreams," Piper replied softly. She heard Vega opening and closing drawers, neatening everything into well-organized groups, and stacking holo-books in her orderly way. Everyone had their own sleep rituals, Piper knew, and she did admire the way Vega kept her side neat. A place for everything, and everything in its place.

Piper reached to the floor, scooping up another pillow—this one had turquoise tassels and a pattern of swirls—and tucking it behind her head. Then she realized with a start she was still wearing her day clothes: a long sleeveless dress made from glimmerworm silk. It could, in fact, pass as a nightgown. Piper's day clothes weren't all that different from her night ones. But Piper believed in the mind-body connection—in this case, changing clothes to change her frame of mind.

Piper slipped on a satiny nightgown, with buttons as soft as glowmoss running from top to bottom. Then she misted the room with essence of dramboozle, a natural herb that promoted sweet dreams and comforting sleep. Next in her bedtime ritual came the choosing of the sleep mask. That night she sifted through her basket of masks, choosing one that pictured a stand of gloak trees.

It showed a wonderful balance of strength and beauty, Piper thought.

Finally, Piper picked up her latest dream diary. She wanted to replay her last dream—the one from her afternoon nap. Frequently, those dreams were her most vivid. At night Piper listened to class lectures while she slept, studying in the efficient Starling method. And sometimes the professors' voices blended with her dreams in an oddly disconcerting way.

Once, she felt on the verge of a mighty epiphany—a revelation about the meaning of light. *What is the meaning of light?* was a question that had plagued Starling scholars for hydrongs and hydrongs of years. And the answer was about to be revealed. To her!

But just when Piper's thoughts were closing in on it, her Astral Accounting teacher's voice had interrupted, monotonously intoning the number 1,792. And Piper felt sure that wasn't the right answer.

But that afternoon's dream proceeded without numbers or facts or formulas: Piper was floating through space, traveling past planets and stars, when a Wishling girl with bright shiny eyes and an eager expression grabbed her hand. Suddenly, the scene shifted to the Crystal Mountains, the most beautiful in all of Starland, just across the lake from Starling Academy. It was a sight

Piper looked at with pleasure every starday. But now she was climbing a mountain, still holding hands with the girl. As she led the way up a trail, the lulling sound of keytar music echoed everywhere, and she laughed with pleasure as a flutterfocus landed on her shoulder. Another flutterfocus settled on the shoulder of the girl.

"It looks like a butterfly!" the girl said, as delighted as Piper. "But sparkly!"

"And they bring luck!" Piper answered. But with each step the girls took, more and more flutterfocuses circled them. Now the creatures seemed angry, baring enormous sharp teeth. "What's going on?" the Wishling cried. She squeezed Piper's hand, beginning to panic.

"I don't know," Piper said, keeping her voice calm. "These aren't like flutterfocuses at all! They're usually quite gentle, like all animals here!" Maybe if she could say something, do something, the flutterfocuses would return to their sweet, normal ways. "Concentrate," Piper told herself, "concentrate. . . ."

Perhaps if they reached the plateau at the very top, edged with bright-colored bluebeezel flowers, the flutterfocuses would settle down.

Meanwhile, she held tight to the girl, pulling her up step by step. And finally, there was the peak, just within reach. She opened her mouth to tell the girl, "We're there," when a blinding light stopped her in her tracks.

"Oh, star apologies!" Vega had said, turning off the room light with a quick glance. Vega was very good at energy manipulation. But she wasn't very good at realizing when Piper was sleeping.

Thinking about it now, Piper wondered why the dream, which had begun so well, had turned so unpleasant. She didn't want to call it a nightmare. First of all, she'd dreamed it in the middle of the day! Second, Piper believed that even the scariest, darkest dreams held meaning and could bring enlightenment. Piper felt sure this dream meant something important.

A Wishling girl . . . a difficult journey filled with danger and decisions . . . It was obvious, Piper saw now.

"I'm going on the next Wish Mission," she said aloud. It would be a successful mission, too, since in her dream, she and the girl had reached the mountain-top. Her smile faded slightly. Well, they had just about reached the top.

"What's going on?" Vega asked groggily, hearing Piper's voice.

"Nothing," Piper said quickly. Practical Vega wasn't one to believe in premonitions or dream symbols.

Once, while Vega slept, Piper had tiptoed over to watch her face for signs of emotion as she dreamed. Vega had woken up and been totally creeped out to find Piper mere micronas away and staring. The girls generally got along, and they were friends—not best friends, but friends. And it helped for Piper to keep her sometimes strange insights to herself. She didn't want to upset the delicate balance.

Now, thinking about balance, she decided on a new bedtime visualization. She pictured a scale she'd seen in Wishling History class. It had a pan on each side, and when they were balanced, the pans were level. Adding weight to one would lift the other higher.

In her mind's eye, Piper placed a pebble first on one pan, then the other, again and again, so the scale moved up and down in a rhythm. Piper felt her head nodding in the same motion as she drifted off into another dream. . . .

As soon as the first glimmer of morning light landed on Piper's face, she opened her eyes. It was Star Kindness Day! She had a sense of expectation; something was about to happen.

She glanced at her Star-Zap. A holo-text was just coming through from Astra: LET'S ALL MEET AT THE RADIANT RECREATION CENTER BEFORE BREAKFAST.

Piper half groaned. She loved going to the rec center for meditation class, but she doubted Astra wanted them all to sit still and think deeply. Most likely, she wanted to organize everyone for an early-morning star ball game. Well, Piper could be a good sport, so she made her way to the center, only to find the place deserted.

Then Leona holo-texted: I'M AT THE BAND SHELL. AREN'T WE SUPPOSED TO HAVE A PRE-BREAKFAST BAND REHEARSAL, WITH AN SD AUDIENCE?

Immediately, the Star-Zap beeped again with a message from Cassie: NO! WE'RE SUPPOSED TO MEET AT ILLUMINATION LIBRARY!

Not knowing what to do, Piper went to the band shell, then to the library, then searched across the quad for the Star Darlings. But everywhere she went turned out to be wrong. Her Star-Zap beeped again and again, with message after message, louder and louder each time, until Piper shut it off with a flick of her wrist and realized she'd just turned off her alarm.

It was another dream.

Piper quickly entered it into her dream diary. She'd have to analyze it more, but it seemed to focus on mixed-up communications—not a good sign. Frowning, she looked toward Vega's part of the room.

"Are you going to the Celestial Café?" she called out.

Vega looked at her strangely. "Of course. It's break-fast time."

"Just making sure," Piper said. "I still need to take a sparkle shower. So I'll see you there."

The sparkle shower made Piper's skin and hair glimmer brighter, and she felt its energy like a gentle boost of power. But the dream lingered, making her feel somehow off-kilter. She couldn't shake the feeling she'd show up at the cafeteria and everyone else would be having a special picnic breakfast at the orchard, or by the lake, or anywhere she wasn't.

By then, Piper was already late. No one would be concerned, though. Piper was frequently the last to arrive. She often needed to go back to her room to retrieve a forgotten item. But sometimes it was simply because she liked to take her time. Even now she paused to add a few more notes to her diary, while the dream was still fresh in her mind. It always helped to get everything down in writing, though she could usually remember details for at least a double starweek.

Even as a young Starling in Wee Constellation School, Piper could tell her mom specifics of her dreams, right down to what color socks she wore. Starmazingly, her mom sometimes wore the same color socks in her own dreams—and their actions often matched, too.

It had been hard to make friends growing up in the Gloom Flats; there weren't many girls Piper's age. The homes were spread so far apart it didn't make sense to have a Cosmic Transporter linking houses. So Piper had always felt an extra-special close connection to her mother.

When her granddad completed his Cycle of Life, Piper and her mom both dreamed that Piper and her older brother moved in with their grandmother on the other side of town. It seemed it was meant to be. Besides, her mom and dad were busy giving meditation workshops throughout Starland. It made sense for Piper and Finn to stay with their grandma. And Piper loved her grandmother's home, a mysterious old house floozels from everything, with a musty attic filled with odds and ends and a basement that echoed with eerie noises in the middle of the night. Piper found it all oddly comforting, even if the kids from school refused to visit. But now she had more classmates living on her floor than there were Starlings in all of Gloom Flats. And at least some of them—the Star Darlings—were waiting for her at the café.

A few starmins later, Piper breezed into the dining area and slid into a seat at the Star Darlings' table. To Piper's way of thinking, their table had the best spot, right by the floor-to-ceiling window overlooking the Crystal Mountains. The others smiled at Piper. But they were too excited about Star Kindness Day to stop chattering and say hello.

Smiling back, Piper placed her order with the Bot-Bot waiter: starcakes with whipped beam. It arrived a starmin or two later, even quicker than usual. Already, the holiday seemed starmendously special.

Sage actually bounced in her chair, her wavy lavender hair flying. "I can't believe I don't have Lighterature today," she said with a giggle. "I stayed up so late writing an essay, 'Long Stardays' Journey into Light.' And I didn't even have to!" She giggled again.

Across the table, Adora nodded and mumbled something about missing Wishful Thinking class. At least Piper thought she said Wishful Thinking. Maybe she was really asking for a dishful of plinking, the delicious striped fruit that bounced like a ball, since the Bot-Bot hovered by her chair. Adora went on to say more, but Piper didn't catch a word.

She'd probably gotten some sparkles in her ear from

showering. She shook her head, and a bit of green glitter fell out. There, that was better. She was about to ask Adora to repeat herself when Clover flung her arms around her shoulders. "Piper!" she exclaimed.

Really, everyone was over the moon about this holiday, Piper thought. She dug a fork into the starcakes, then turned to Leona, who was sitting next to her.

"I'm going to race through the rest of breakfast so I can be closer-than-close to the stage for the ceremony," she was saying. Then she languidly picked up her spoon and slowly dipped it into her bowl of Sparkle-O's.

Piper sighed. Leona was being sarcastic again. She probably thought she didn't deserve compliments. It was sad, really, since before her mission Leona had lived for them. Piper believed the old saying "Don't judge a Starling until you've walked a floozel in her shoes." But she had difficulty understanding Leona's need for attention. Piper preferred to blend into the background if she could, to observe and understand her surroundings.

Tessa took a big swig of juice, then looked at the glass quizzically. "That's odd. It looks like glorange juice, but it tastes just like—"

"Mooncheese," said Piper.

"No, moonberries," said Tessa.

On the other side of the table, Scarlet stood up.

"Wish I could stay and compare moonberries and glorange juice." She gave an exaggerated yawn. "But I have to get to the quad early for the ceremony." She pulled a drumstick from her back pocket and flipped it in the air. Then she shot a look at Leona. "I'm the opening act."

"What?" Leona called after her, but Scarlet was already skipping away.

All around them now, Starlings were scraping back their chairs and starting to leave. The cafeteria took on a charged atmosphere.

"Let's all go," Piper said.

Immediately, the Star Darlings jumped up to join the stream of students heading for the ceremony. Most walked in pairs, linking arms in the Starling way. Soon the grassy star-shaped quad was filled with students looking around expectantly.

Star Kindness Day was here at last!

CHAPTER 2

Piper felt the excitement almost as if it was a real, live being, pulsing with vitality. But she sensed an undercurrent of worry as well.

Piper knew what some were wondering: *Will I get as many compliments as everyone else? What if my teacher compliments all the other students in my class, but not me? What if no one I complimented compliments me back?*

The negative energy felt strongest to her left, where Vivica stood. She was a girl none of the Star Darlings liked. Piper would be surprised if anyone truly did. But still, she was sure to receive hydrongs of compliments, since most students were afraid of her.

Moving away from Vivica, Piper edged between

Cassie and Astra. Cassie turned to Piper with a questioning look.

"What do you want, Piper?"

"Nothing," said Piper. "Why do you ask?"

Cassie stared at her. "Because you tapped my shoulder."

"Wasn't me," said Piper.

"But—" Cassie began.

Then Astra burst out laughing.

"Oh, it was *you*," said Cassie. "How can I help you?"

Astra shook her head, still laughing.

Just then Lady Stella swept up to the stage, the long sleeves of her luminous gown trailing gently behind her, and both girls turned their attention to the headmistress.

There was something about Lady Stella so right and so true that sometimes Piper couldn't look at her directly. Her sparkly aura was too intense. Scarlet skipped up behind her and settled behind a large set of drums.

Without Lady Stella's saying a word, the crowd quieted.

"Star greetings, Starlings!" Lady Stella said in a low voice that somehow carried to the far reaches of the quad. "We are about to begin."

As she spoke, professors and administrators gathered

behind her, smiling at the girls. Lady Cordial stood to the side, nodding. But even that small movement seemed nervous. She always made Piper nervous, too. Idly, Piper wondered if Lady Cordial's stutter would disappear if she learned some relaxation techniques.

"I expect throughout the day there will be compliments and positive messages galore," Lady Stella continued.

"Messages galore? Is Lady Stella so sure?" Vega, standing in front of Piper, turned to whisper to her friends while gesturing at Vivica.

"So don't be concerned if right now," Lady Stella was saying, "you don't receive as many as you'd like. In all, the good feelings and sense of well-being should be powerful, and the positive energy will last and last."

"Now please set your Star-Zaps to sensor mode, to send your holo-texts at the exact end of Scarlet's drumroll."

Scarlet rapped out a complicated *tat-a-tat-tat*. Cheers rang out at the end as, at the same starsec, each and every Starling's Star-Zap lit up with messages.

Eagerly, Piper swiped the screen for holo-text number one. The words appeared in the air directly at eye level. It was from Scarlet: YOU CREEP ME OUT, STAR-LOONY.

Piper gasped softly and read it again: YOU CREEP ME OUT, STAR-LOONY. It hadn't changed.

A wave of emotion swept over Piper, and a tear trickled down her cheek. *Shrug it off, Piper,* she told herself. It was just Scarlet being Scarlet. She'd probably written much worse to the other Starlings.

Piper went on to read the next text. Surely this one would be better. WAKE UP AND SMELL THE ZING, DREAM GIRL, YOU DON'T HAVE A CLUE ABOUT THE FUTURE, PAST, OR PRESENT. That was from Clover. That couldn't be right. The texts were so negative it was alarming.

Just then Clover strode over and gave Piper a big hug. She wouldn't be doing that if she meant the text! Piper sighed, relieved, and waited for an explanation. Instead, Clover glared at her with the force of a moonium shooting stars. "Glad to know you think I have a closed mind"—she checked her Star-Zap—"plus I'm the shallowest Starling around." Clover frowned. "Is that because I grew up in a circus?"

"No! That wasn't from me!" Piper protested. "It doesn't even rhyme!" But Clover was already hurrying off in a huff.

Piper heard a sniffle and turned to see Vega holding back tears. Vega was always so rational. What kind of compliment would get her teary? Without saying a word, Vega turned her Star-Zap around so Piper could read it: PLEASE PACK UP YOUR PUZZLES SO WE CAN GO OUR SEPARATE WAYS.

"I said just the opposite!" Piper said. "Something about our paths always merging." And she had actually commended Clover for being open-minded. The compliments had been turned inside out.

"Have you always felt this way, or did it just hit you on Star Kindness Day?" Vega asked sarcastically.

"I don't feel that way at all!" Piper practically shouted. But Vega was already gone.

Not knowing what else to do, Piper read more of her holo-texts.

YOUR HEAD IS ALWAYS IN THE STARS.

YOU SNEAK UP ON PEOPLE IN SUCH AN ANNOYING WAY.

READ A FASHION HOLO-MAGAZINE AND GET SOME STYLE.

Each and every text was insulting.

Two girls in front of Piper began to argue. "How can you call me a dimwit? I shine in every class."

"I didn't say that," the other retorted. "But why did you say I can't lift a moonfeather with my wish energy manipulation skills?"

Their next words were lost as the entire quad erupted in shouts and negative energy.

Piper pressed toward the stage, to get closer to Lady Stella. Surely just seeing her would set Piper's mind at ease. But Lady Stella was wringing her hands, distraught. "What do you think is going on?" she asked Lady Cordial.

"This is s-s-s-starmendously s-s-s-s-strange!" Lady Cordial shook her head, confused.

This situation certainly isn't helping her stammer, Piper thought.

Lady Stella closed her eyes, apparently gathering her thoughts, then stepped to center stage. "Starlings!" she called, raising her arms high. At first, the students were so caught up in their Star-Zaps and confronting one another, they didn't notice.

"Starlings!" Lady Stella called, slightly louder. One by one, the students looked toward the stage.

"Star salutations for your attention. There is a major mistake here, a mix-up of the very worst kind. Do not pay attention to these messages. Stay calm and go to your next class. Star Kindness Day will be postponed until we have figured out the problem." She smiled reassuringly. "Don't worry. Everything will work out."

Piper breathed a sigh of relief. For a starsec, she had

panicked like the others. But if Lady Stella said everything would be fine, Piper believed it.

Slowly, students began to disperse, heading toward Halo Hall for classes. Only Piper stood still, so only Piper heard Lady Stella say to Lady Cordial, "First the blackout, now this. Another wave of negative energy is the last thing we need."

Piper's heart quickened. Was Lady Stella saying there was more to this than a simple technological mix-up? That there wasn't a simple fix?

It was too much to think about, especially since Piper was still smarting from the insulting comments. You couldn't just forget about those kinds of holo-texts, Piper realized, no matter what Lady Stella had said. She knew her friends didn't always want to hear about dreams or premonitions. But did they really think she was weird and creepy? And unfashionable!

Piper's feelings were hurt, and she felt a tingle of negative energy travel from her head to her toes. Suddenly, Piper wanted to be alone. She made her way around the Celestial Café to the ozziefruit orchard.

There wasn't much time till her first class. But Dododay was the only starday that she didn't have Inner-light Meditation, and she needed to take some time to herself. Moving quickly, Piper cut through rows of pink-leaved trees to the far end, where a small garden was tucked away. There she settled in her favorite spot, under a glimmerwillow tree. Its branches hung from the top in such a way that they created a closed-off leafy room.

Sitting inside, Piper immediately felt better. The smell of the sweet glimmervines, the soft damp earth, and the quiet were just what she needed. She crossed her legs, placed her hands palm up on her knees, and took a deep breath. She closed her eyes, breathing deeply, concentrating on the air going in . . . going out. Her heart rate slowed. Her tense shoulders relaxed.

Suddenly, her Star-Zap buzzed. *Starf!* She'd forgotten to turn it off, neglecting the first rule of meditation: silence all communication devices for true peace.

Still, Piper couldn't help sneaking a peek at the screen. It was a holo-text from Vega: I'M IN WISH THEORY. WHERE ARE YOU, DEARIE?

Dearie! Piper had to smile. Clearly, Vega couldn't be mad if she called her that! Even better, she was checking on Piper, making sure everything was okay. Maybe she'd already gotten over the negative texts.

BE RIGHT THERE, Piper holo-texted back.

But of course Piper was still late. Professor Illumia

Wickes motioned for Piper to sit down with barely a glance.

Quietly, Piper slid next to Vega. "Star salutations for reminding me about class," she said in a low voice. Vega gave her a curt nod. Clearly, she was still upset about Piper's "compliment."

Piper turned back to Professor Illumia Wickes. The teacher often liked to lead rambling class discussions about the philosophy behind wishes. So being a few starmins late shouldn't really matter. Usually, students could just jump in at any point; Piper expected the usual interesting debate.

That day, though, Professor Wickes glared around the room and said, "We will be focusing on the math portion of wish theory."

Math portion? Piper didn't remember there being anything about that in the syllabus. Neither, it seemed, did anyone else.

The students looked confused. "Don't just sit there!" Professor Illumia Wickes snapped. "Set your Star-Zaps to record. You will be quizzed on the material. Tomorrow." She started tapping out a series of numbers on a holo-device, and they were projected in the air. Three hundred and forty moonium, fourteen thousand and ninety-one was the smallest.

Ooh, thought Piper. *She must have gotten some seriously negative holo-texts.*

"Now plug these numbers into the appropriate wish-granting formula. Remember, any authentic theorist takes into account the sum of thoughts—"

"And actions," said Piper.

"Go on," said the professor. "Think about the true meaning behind the numbers."

"It's not how long the numbers are, or how complicated. It's the equation that matters in the end. And how you use it," Piper finished.

"Yes, star salutations for reminding us all, Piper," said the professor.

She deleted the numbers with a flick of her wrist and words appeared in the air. "We need to remember, too, that Starlings alone cannot grant wishes. Wishers need to make their own dreams come true; our job is to guide them. Generally, Wishlings have trouble manifesting their desires—not only impossible wishes, such as world peace, but personal, manageable ones as well. We are there to help them . . . ah . . . see the light."

"Huh?" said a girl named Shareen, who wore her bright yellow hair plaited around her head. "What does that—"

"Mean?" Piper jumped in. *Really, this is a silly first-year question*, she thought. And students made fun of the Star Darlings for taking their extra class, thinking it was for slow learners!

"Basically, Wishlings need help," Piper said, using the tone a baby Starling reciting the alphabet would. She sounded sarcastic, she knew, but she couldn't quite control her voice. Usually, she was better at that, but after that morning's upheaval and her interrupted meditation, her emotions seemed to have gotten the better of her. "They first need to figure out they can, in fact, make their wishes come true, and then understand the ways to make it happen."

Professor Illumia Wickes nodded, then pushed her glasses up the bridge of her nose and walked around the room. "Can anyone think of an equation, a sum of two or more parts, that would result in the desired outcome?"

Half a dozen ideas popped immediately into Piper's head.

Vega raised her hand. "Thought plus action equals no subtraction," she said.

The professor frowned. "I think what Vega is saying is that a thought plus an action can lead to a wish coming true. But it might not be that—"

"Simple," Piper offered.

Vega glared at her. "Maybe add 'believing in yourself'

to the equation," Piper said, almost apologetically.

"How about filling in the blanks for this equation?" The teacher's words appeared in the air: FAITH + TRUST +

_____ + ACTION = SUCCESSFUL WISHES.

"Luck!" Shareen guessed.

Piper choked back a giggle. "How about patience?"

"Maybe a little bit of both," the teacher acknowledged, more to be kind to Shareen than anything else, Piper thought. "But definitely patience. Now, let's try another one." She wrote another equation:

_____ + FOCUS + POSITIVE THINKING = WISHES TAKING FORM.

"Luck?" Shareen said again.

At the very same moment, Piper answered, "Visualization. You should visualize the wish coming true and think positively for the best results." This was child's play for Piper.

A girl named Lucinda shook her head. "Why did you even say 'luck,' Shareen? Clearly, it wasn't right the first time. Why would it be now?"

"Humph!" Shareen narrowed her eyes at Lucinda. "You think I have the brain power of a glowfur, don't you?" She looked around the room. "Does anyone else think so, too?" The class began to buzz.

Piper felt her own negative emotions boil over. All

she wanted to do was continue with the class. Those equations were important! But everyone else was acting as silly as a bloombug during a full moon.

A holo-vision of Lady Stella suddenly materialized in the front of the classroom and everyone fell silent. "Star apologies, teachers and students, for this interruption," Lady Stella said. She was standing in her office, hands clasped calmly in front of her. She seemed composed, but there was still a crease of worry on her forehead.

"I'd like to update everyone on the Star Kindness Day situation." She paused. "Clearly, something went very wrong with your holo-text compliments. Indeed, the messages were most likely the opposite of what each writer intended to say. We cannot let this enmity and distrust continue. The messages have vanished, which is just as well. So I'd like to ask each student to rewrite her original compliments. Reading the true holo-words may set us on the path back to good fellowship. Continue with your studies, but remember the meaning behind Star Kindness Day." She nodded twice and disappeared.

For a moment, the room was quiet. Lady Stella's words carried weight. Piper thought that it could possibly be enough, that everyone would agree: the way to feel good again was to spread good feeling.

Then Shareen snorted. "Why bother?" She glared at

Lucinda. "It can happen all over again. And you know what? I bet those *are* everyone's true feelings, and that's why the whole thing happened."

The class exploded. "You do think I'm clumsy, so you never choose me for your star ball team!" "You weren't late that day when we were supposed to meet at the Lightning Lounge. You just didn't want to come!" "So I'm just the tagalong tail to your comet, with no mind of my own, huh?"

Professor Illumia Wickes shrugged and let everyone shout until the period ended.

"Class dismissed," she said wearily.

"Wait," said Shareen. "Is there still going to be a quiz tomorrow?"

From then on, the starday only got worse. In fact, Piper thought girls were getting angrier and meaner by the starmin, and each class was more out of control than the one before. Finally, Piper headed to Lady Stella's office for the special Star Darlings class, during last period.

Just ahead of Piper, Sage and Cassie were walking in together. But there was enough space to fit a Starcar between them.

Inside, Piper nodded to the girls who were already

there—Sage, Clover, Adora, and Leona—and sat down.

Loud voices caused them all to look toward the door.

Tessa and Gemma walked in, matching each other stride for stride, angry look for angry look. "You absolutely think I don't do my share of work at the farm," said Gemma.

"Oh, please," said Tessa. "Forget about it, Gemma. Enough is enough."

"No, really, just admit it," Gemma continued.

Right then the door slid open and Lady Stella swept in.

She stood in front of the room and smiled, seeming calmer than she had earlier. "I'm glad to see you all here, given the kind of starday we've had. I've decided to cancel the guest lecture and talk to you about what's been going on. It's very, very important for all students to get along, but it's imperative for the Star Darlings to regain positive—"

"Vibrations," finished Piper.

Lady Stella smiled. "I was going to say feelings, but that works, too. Now I'd like everyone to gather in a circle and hold hands. We will offer Star Kindness thoughts, face to face.

"Why don't you begin, Vega?" the headmistress said.

Vega frowned slightly, then nodded. She turned to Astra. "You're great at all sports. But most of all, I like to watch you play star ball."

Astra beamed. "Star salutations, Vega. And I think you are very organized and good at puzzles."

Lady Stella smiled encouragingly. "Yes, that is the way it's done. Continue, please."

Clover opened her mouth to go next. But a knock on the door interrupted the compliments. Lady Cordial stuck her head in.

"S-s-s-s-so wonderful to s-s-s-s-see everyone together after those horrid holo-texts this morning. Lady St-st-st-st-stella, I was hoping to observe the c-c-c-c-class today."

Lady Stella smiled at the awkward head of admissions. "Normally, I'd welcome you, Lady Cordial," she said gently. "I hope you realize that. But today is not the best startime. Another starday would be best."

Lady Cordial ducked her head, looking embarrassed, and began to edge away.

"By the way," Lady Stella added, "I obviously don't think you are disorganized."

"St-st-star s-s-s-salutations," Lady Cordial said, already halfway out the door. "And I don't think you're an ineffective leader."

"Understood," said Lady Stella as the door closed quietly. "Now let's go on with our exercise."

Everyone took turns giving and receiving compliments. And while the class ran longer than usual, the girls left feeling much better.

It's amazing how a little positivity can improve your outlook, Piper thought. She grinned at Leona. Who would have known Leona liked Piper's sleep masks so much she wanted to borrow some for a holo-vid she wanted to make with the band called "Star in Disguise"?

Libby whispered in Gemma's ear. Gemma nodded. "Hey!" said Libby as they all moved toward the door. "Is everyone up for a sleepover in our room tonight?"

It was rare for all twelve Star Darlings to get together outside the Celestial Café or SD class. "What a great idea," said Piper quickly. She knew what Libby was thinking: *We need time together, without any outside stresses, where we can be like any Starling Academy students, hanging out with friends.*

But the girls weren't really like other Starling Academy students. They had responsibilities and pressures no one else could imagine. When everyone agreed to go, Piper could only hope for the best.

CHAPTER
3

At lightfall, Piper was busily packing for the sleepover. "Let's see," she said, looking around. She wanted to take her dream diary, her toothlight, a few carefully selected pillows and sleep masks—in case anyone wanted to borrow one—and a star-shaped stone she'd found by Luminous Lake the first week of her first year at school. The stone was smooth and pleasing to hold. Whenever she slept somewhere new, Piper always took her "serenity stone." It made her feel better.

After she packed, she changed into her nightgown, because why wait? Then she tossed everything into a star sack, which started about the same size as a lunch bag but kept expanding the more it held. At the last moment, Piper threw in another pillow.

Finally, she took the Cosmic Transporter to Libby

and Gemma's room and arrived at the same starmin as a Bot-Bot delivering twelve snuggle sacks. Piper loved the sacks. The heavily quilted tubes immediately adjusted to a Starling's height and body shape, so they were star-mendously comfy when you slipped inside. It was like sleeping on a soft field of glowmoss, even if you were on a hard floor.

"Welcome!" Libby said. Piper noted the skylight, letting in beams of starlight, and felt her spirits rise higher—even when she realized she'd left her toothlight behind.

Meanwhile, the girls rushed to claim their snuggle sacks and a spot on the floor to sleep.

"Wait, everyone," said Libby. "There's plenty of room!" Then she took out her keytar. "Let's start the sleepover with a sing-along."

"You mean everyone sings at the same time?" said Leona, horrified. "This isn't some starcamp bonfire, you know."

Libby played a few chords. "Just give it a chance, Leona."

The girls sat in a circle and sang old favorites, like "Moonbeams and Rainbows" and "Stars in Your Eyes," then new hits, like "Lighten Up" and "Lightning Strikes Twice."

Afterward, they told stories about their first days at the academy. Piper admitted she'd gotten so lost she'd had to call for help on her Star-Zap—not once, not twice, but almost a hydrong times. Sage confided with a giggle that it had taken her starweeks to finally read the Student Manual.

The talk faded to a comfortable silence when Gemma suggested they give each other spa treatments. "It's always fun to do nails, but look." She held up her hands. "Our old polish has really held up."

"It's true," Tessa agreed. "No one needs new manicures."

"Well, we can still do our hair." Libby moved aside some sacks to clear space in a corner. "Who wants to be my first customer?"

"Not me," said Leona, marching over and plopping down on a cushion. She picked up a bottle of glitter spray. "Can you use this to highlight my extra-golden streaks?"

"Let me do it," said Astra, walking over. She took the spray and spritzed it all over Leona's hair. Immediately, the yellow curls turned bright magenta.

"How do I—"

"Look?" Piper interrupted Leona, shaking her head. "Here." She handed Leona a small hand mirror.

Smiling, Leona angled the mirror for the best view. "What?" she spluttered, angry sparks flying. "Astra, how could you make a mistake like that?"

"Star apologies, Leona!" Astra said. "It's just temporary. It will wash out."

Leona hurried off, and Astra started fiddling with Piper's hair. But Piper slid out from under her hands. She liked her hair color just fine.

It was a fun evening. After some hairstyle judging, snacking on starmores, a moonfeather pillow fight, and several rounds of starades, Cassie pointed to their hostess, who was already sound asleep.

"Looks like it's time to hit the sack," she said.

Gemma picked up the starstick that Astra had brought with her, walked over to the snuggle sacks, and smacked one of them.

"Really?" said her sister.

Soon they were all comfortably settled in their sacks, arranged in a star shape, with their heads in the center.

"You know," said Cassie, sitting up. "Have you noticed that there hasn't been a Wish Mission in a while?" She paused. "No offense, but maybe it's been postponed because mine went so startacularly well. . . ."

"Really, Cassie?" said Astra, picking up a stuffed twinkelope and tossing it at her.

As expected, it hit Cassie right in the middle of her forehead. Everyone laughed, Sage the longest and loudest. Cassie scowled (but goodnaturedly) and lay back down.

"So who do you think will go next?" Piper asked dreamily. Of course, Piper was convinced she knew the answer: she would! Hadn't her dream said as much?

"I don't know," said Vega. "Who here is wishin' to take on the next mission?"

Suddenly, Piper sat up in her sack and grinned. "I know! Maybe we can make a mission happen faster with a visualization. Let's hold hands and visualize our Wish Orbs."

She thought Leona or Scarlet might snicker. Neither one was particularly into mental imagery. Instead, they—along with every other Star Darling—reached out their hands. Even Libby seemed to sense something in her sleep and stretched out her arms.

"Close your eyes and imagine our special Wish Cavern," Piper began in a low voice. "See the remaining Wish Orbs. Smell the aroma—a little Starlandy, a little Wishworldly."

Sage sniffed the air and giggled.

"Each and every Wish Orb is glowing," Piper went on. She could sense the girls smiling. "Now look closely at just one. That's your Wish Orb. Watch it glow. Feel the intensity."

Piper's own Wish Orb glowed so strongly she felt its heat. Suddenly, she saw a rainbow of colors shoot from her orb and flow right into the center of the Star Darlings' circle like a fountain of sparkly hues.

All twelve Star Darlings sat up with a start. Their faces glowed with wonder. Piper gazed at her friends. "Did you see it, too?" she asked.

Tessa nodded. "It was beautiful. Like flareworks at the Festival of Illumination."

"And it started right in front of you, Piper!" Gemma added.

Piper snuggled deeper into her sack. All that powerful wish energy had come from *her* visualization . . . *her* Wish Orb had exploded with light and color. . . . She was definitely the next Star Darling to go on a mission.

But what else did it mean? If she succeeded in her mission, would she collect more energy than ever before? And if she failed? What then? The stakes were so high Piper's toes tingled. She reached for her stone and rubbed her thumb along its edge.

The visualization over, some girls still whispered about the burst of color and light. Others talked about the boys at the school across the lake. Vega tried to get everyone to play A Moonium Questions.

But Piper's eyes were closing. She took a deep, cleansing breath, enjoying the feeling of warmth and heaviness that was overtaking her. Within starsecs, she was fast asleep.

Piper was dreaming she was moving through a shadowy landscape. A dim shape moved with her—a Starling Piper couldn't make out, but a dark presence nonetheless. Piper could feel in every star inch of her being that this Starling could not be trusted. She tried to pull away from the Starling, but it was difficult. She pushed herself to run faster, to be stronger. But then she stumbled. And suddenly, she was falling . . . falling. . . .

Piper woke up, gasping. She could still see the Starling's indistinct form, feel the menace. The idea that someone was not the Starling he or she seemed was so powerful, and the dream was so frightening, that Piper was shaking.

And why was she on the floor? Nothing looked familiar. She shook harder.

"It's okay, Piper." A cool hand brushed her forehead.

"You had a bad dream. That's all. You're here with us, safe and sound."

Piper breathed easier. She was in Libby's room with the other Star Darlings, of course. She turned to Sage, who was crouching beside her, her lavender eyes filled with concern.

"Star apologies for waking you, Sage."

"You don't have to apologize. My little brothers wake me up all the time," she said with a laugh. "It's fine, Piper. You had a bad dream."

"Well, that's just it," Piper explained quietly. "I don't think it's just a bad dream. I think it meant something. Something important."

Next to them, Leona muttered in her sleep and smiled like she was modeling for a holo-photo.

"Let's go outside," Sage whispered, "so we can really talk." She looked toward the door and it opened without a sound.

Piper nodded, and the two crept quietly around the sleeping girls. They stepped onto the Cosmic Transporter and made their way outside, where the moon shone with a comforting yellow light and starlight illuminated the trees with a lovely brightness. The girls settled in a soft grassy spot and for a moment watched the flareflies buzz in looping circles.

PIPER'S PERFECT DREAM   53

"So can I tell you my dream?" Piper finally asked. "Sometimes it helps to talk."

"Of course," said Sage.

"It starts on the Wishworld Surveillance Deck. I'm waiting for a shooting star to take me to Wishworld when a shadow falls over me. It's a Starling, an evil one, but I can't tell who, and this cold, clammy feeling comes over me—"

Sage stifled a giggle.

Piper stopped talking.

Sage shook her head and said, "Go on, Piper. I'm really listening."

"Okay. So this Starling reaches out to me, but I run away, and I'm running faster and faster. I can't tell where I am now; all I see is shadows."

Sage giggled again. She waved at Piper to continue, but with every word Piper said, Sage laughed louder and longer.

Piper stood up to leave, brushing grass from her nightgown.

"Wait—" Sage choked out between giggles. But Piper had had enough. She turned on her heel. "Come on, Piper," Sage pleaded.

"Why don't you just laugh at me so hard and long you'll never have the wish energy to move a glimmerfeather, much less anything else?" Piper said. No one had stronger energy manipulation skills than Sage, and Piper knew it was her secret pride.

Sage sucked in her breath, finally silent.

Without another word, Piper strode into the dorm and back to Libby and Gemma's room. But outside their door, she realized she wouldn't be able to get in. The scanner would refuse her entrance. Only Libby and Gemma were allowed automatic entry. Piper groaned. She didn't want to disturb anyone. Just then she heard Sage's giggles floating through the air.

Well, at least Sage would be stuck outside, too.

Piper sighed. She didn't like having those negative thoughts. And she certainly hadn't wanted to lash out the way she had at Sage. But sometimes she couldn't help herself. Maybe that would change after her mission. Right then she felt like she was in limbo, just waiting to be chosen.

Back in her own room, lying on her water bed, Piper felt doubly worse. Of course she had overreacted to Sage's giggle fits. Sage was just trying to help. And she must have been overtired. If Piper had said anything, even good night, she would have collapsed with laughter. Piper understood. She was exhausted, too. She'd sleep late the next day, no matter what.

Sure enough, Piper slept so late the next morning that when she walked into the café, the rest of the Star Darlings were finishing their meal. As soon as they saw Piper, they stopped talking.

Quickly, Piper slid into the empty seat between Clover and Astra. "So what did I miss this morning?" She was trying for a cheerful tone, but the corners of her mouth turned down, and suddenly, she was afraid she might cry. Sage must have told all the Star Darlings how sarcastic Piper had been the night before. Clover hugged her, which made Piper feel better for a starsec—until Clover stood up and hugged a first year walking by, a girl Piper doubted Clover even knew.

Pointedly, Sage moved a cloth napkin through the air, then onto Piper's lap. "See, Piper?" she said lightly. "I haven't used all my wish energy laughing." She giggled loudly and clapped a hand over her mouth. "Sorry," she said.

Sage didn't sound angry at her, and Piper sighed with relief.

"I was a little star-crazed myself last night, Sage. The sleepover helped us connect. Let's try to hold on to that feeling."

Piper waved to a Bot-Bot waiter to take her order. She wasn't very hungry, and she still felt a little tired. Clearly, Libby did, too. At some point during breakfast, she had put her head on the table and dozed off.

"I'll just have a large cup of Zing," Piper told the Bot-Bot. *That should help*, she thought as it zoomed off.

Vega's eyes widened in shock. "I can't believe you're only having Zing. You know it's not the healthiest thing."

Piper nodded. "I know, I know. But I really need to wake up," she explained. Her stomach grumbled. "Where is that Bot-Bot waiter?" she said. "Maybe I will order something."

Astra handed her a plate of astromuffins. "Go ahead, Piper, take one," she said. "Tessa will be back in a minute, but she won't mind."

Piper bit into the soft muffin. "Hot! Hot!" she cried, waving a hand in front of her mouth.

"Oh, sorry," said Tessa, who had just returned to the table. "I slathered them in starpepper jelly to cover up the moonberry taste."

Luckily, a Bot-Bot waiter had just brought over Piper's Zing. Gratefully, she took a long, deep gulp. "What?" she sputtered, spraying the drink everywhere. "That's not Zing!"

Clover leaned over to take a tentative sip. She made a face. "It's hot-spring tonic. Nobody likes it except—"

"Astra!" Piper finished.

Astra burst out laughing. "Okay, okay, Piper. I switched our drinks." She passed over the real cup of Zing. "I thought it would be funny."

Sage giggled.

"See? Sage thinks so."

"Sage thinks everything—and everyone—is funny," Leona said.

Piper took a sip of Zing. Nothing had been making much sense lately. But Piper tuned everything out, took a few deep breaths, and felt her shoulders relax. It was still early. What better incentive was there to stay centered when her Wish Mission could begin at any moment?

CHAPTER
4

For Piper, the starday passed slowly and peacefully. She took a long quiet walk and an afternoon nap that stretched till dinnertime. Still, she had a slightly fidgety feeling, a sense that something was about to happen.

During Star Darlings class, Piper had trouble paying attention to their guest lecturer, Professor Eugenia Bright. Professor Eugenia Bright taught Wish Granting. She stressed the importance of understanding the emotions behind a wish. Normally, Piper hung on her every word. Now she forced herself to focus as Professor Bright said, "You need to be sensitive to your Wisher to pick up on feeling and—"

"Desire," Piper interrupted automatically. The other girls seemed distracted, too. Sage kept giggling to herself.

Cassie took a lot of holo-selfies. Once again, Libby had her head on her desk. The class seemed to go on and on.

But time did pass, and by lightfall, Piper was already in her nightgown, studying her holo-books.

Stars crossed, she'd get enough done that she wouldn't have to listen to lectures while she slept. She wanted to keep her mind open, ready to receive the next dream message. Still, interpreting dreams could be tricky.

One time, while Piper was living with her parents, her mom had dreamed their door scanner kept announcing, "Guest! Guest!" She thought they'd wind up having hydrongs of Starlings for dinner that night. So she'd asked Bot-Bots to deliver star sack after star sack of sparklecorn to serve. Unfortunately, the dream merely meant their scanner was broken. Piper had sparklecorn sandwiches, sparklecorn salads, and just plain sparklecorn for starweeks.

She still didn't like sparklecorn, after all those staryears! As Piper smiled to herself, her Star-Zap buzzed. Piper felt a tingle. Could this be it? Could this be her mission?

Of course, every time her Star-Zap had gone off lately, she had wondered the same thing. But this time it was different: SD WISH ORB IDENTIFIED, read the holo-text. PROCEED TO LADY STELLA'S OFFICE IMMEDIATELY.

Piper moved as if she was in a dream, as if the Cosmic Transporter wasn't real, as if Halo Hall was just in her mind. When she reached Lady Stella's office, she had no real memory of getting there. But apparently, she had gotten there quickly. Piper was the first to arrive.

"Oh, Piper." Lady Stella smiled, standing at the doorway and ushering her inside. "You could have taken a few starsecs to change." She gestured at Piper's clothes.

Piper looked down. She was still wearing her night-gown.

One by one, the other girls came through the door. Some looked sleepy. Some looked wide-awake. Scarlet skipped in, as if she was in Physical Energy class, ready to go.

Everyone sat at Lady Stella's round silver table. Starlight streamed through the large windows, flashing on the Star Darlings' sparkly skin. Each girl twinkled with energy—except for Libby, who snored lightly.

Lady Stella walked around the table and leaned down to place her hands on Libby's shoulders. "Libby," she said with a gentle tap, "you need to stay awake." She squeezed her shoulders lightly.

"I know," Libby said without opening her eyes. "I'm just so tired."

"Let's assume Libby is listening and continue with

our meeting," Lady Stella continued, pacing around the table. Each girl twisted in her seat to follow the head-mistress's graceful movements.

Lady Stella sounded as calm as ever, Piper thought. But why didn't she just stop and speak to them from her usual spot? She held herself a little stiffly, too, as if she was trying to contain some nervous energy.

"Soon we will head down to the Wish Cavern to see who will be going on the next Wish Mission," she said. "Please remember that we still haven't determined what happened to Leona's Wish Pendant. Although this will most likely not happen again, whoever is chosen for this mission should proceed with caution."

Up till then, Piper had just assumed it wouldn't hap-pen again. Leona had had a scary trip home. Her star had stalled and Vega had had to pick her up along the way. But now Piper didn't feel so sure. Quickly, she pushed away the negative thoughts. She wanted to relish this part of being a Star Darling. The starhours before a mis-sion were filled with anticipation and optimism, a time before anything went wrong.

And if Piper concentrated on this mission . . . really concentrated . . . if she kept thinking positive thoughts and stayed alert . . . the stars were the limit.

Lady Stella pressed a secret button in her desk

drawer. A hidden door slid open to reveal the passage to the Star Darlings' own Wish Cavern.

Piper took a deep breath and pushed back her chair. Sage pulled Libby to her feet. "It's time to get serious," she said with a giggle. Gemma moved slowly, too. And when her sister told her to "hop to it," Gemma jumped on one foot all the way to the door.

Piper barely noticed. She paused to breathe deeply. Then she followed everyone down the winding stairs to the underground cavern.

Piper loved going around and around, down and down along the stairway, catching sight of bitbat creatures hanging by their feet. Maybe one day she'd try that pose for meditation. Being upside down would bring a new angle, a different way of looking at the world.

But those thoughts were fleeting, too. Piper's focus narrowed to one vision: riding a shooting star to Wishworld.

In the Star Darlings' Wish Cavern, a deeply magical place underground, the glass ceiling looked out on the dazzling night sky. Piper could make out the planet Trilight, its three circling moons casting yellow, blue, and red light.

Everyone was silent as they gathered around the

grassy platform. Each time, the ceremony happened a little differently. *How will it be for me?* Piper wondered.

Trilight's moons beamed three different-colored rays directly into the cavern. They joined together just above the platform to create one startlingly white light. The platform opened silently and a Wish Orb floated into the spotlight.

To Piper, it seemed the orb glowed brighter than any she'd seen before. It reflected all the colors of the rainbow as it spun around the Star Darlings, swooping in front of each one. Piper closed her eyes, its image burned in her mind. She knew when her eyes opened, the orb would be directly in front of her, waiting.

And it was.

"The Wish Orb has chosen," Lady Stella announced. "Congratulations, Piper."

CHAPTER
5

Piper slept a deep dreamless sleep that night. She woke up late, feeling refreshed. She had special permission to skip classes. So she took her time choosing Wishling clothes from her Wishworld Outfit Selector. Then she went for a long, leisurely hover-canoe ride around the Serenity Islands. While she leaned back in her seat and let the boat drift, her Star-Zap buzzed. A picture flashed on-screen: her mother. She always knew when something big was happening in Piper's life.

Piper wished she could confide in her mother, tell her everything about the Star Darlings and their missions. For now, though, she had to keep it all inside.

"Hello, Mom," Piper said as a hologram of her

mother appeared. She wore loose, flowing clothes and sat with her legs crossed on a colorful starmat.

"Hello, Pippy," her mom replied. "I had a starmazing dream about you last night. . . ." Her mother spoke about travel and journeys, and Piper nodded at every sentence. By the time she finished the holo-call, lights were flashing in Halo Hall, indicating regular classes were over. Star Darlings class wasn't being held. Instead, everyone was meeting on the Wishworld Surveillance Deck—the takeoff spot for Wishworld—to wish her well.

"Hi, Piper," Astra said in a low voice as she and Piper arrived at the Flash Vertical Mover at the same time. "It's a big—"

"Starday for me, isn't it? Yes!" Piper nodded quickly as more Star Darlings joined them.

Lady Stella, along with Lady Cordial, was already waiting on the deck. She beckoned Piper closer. "The Star Wranglers are still monitoring the skies," she explained. She smiled warmly at Piper. "You'll be on the first star they—"

"Catch," finished Piper.

Lady Stella gave her a funny look. "Is everything okay, Piper? It seems—"

"I've been interrupting a lot lately." Piper nodded.

"Everything's fine," said Piper. She smiled at the head-mistress. "Any last-minute advice?"

Piper managed to hold her tongue while Lady Stella ticked off some items: "Keep checking energy levels on your Wish Pendant. While you should be aware of time passing, don't rush through wish iden-tification. Use your emotions. And be careful not to lose anything."

With that, Lady Cordial passed Piper her special backpack and dangling keychain. "Y-y-y-y-yes," she added. "Keep these items close by at all t-t-t-times."

That reminded Piper: she wanted to place some spe-cial things of her own in the backpack: two sleep masks and her serenity stone. Who knew what would happen to them when her outfit changed in space?

She reached into one dress pocket and removed the sleep masks. But the other pocket was empty. She'd forgotten the stone. In her mind, she could see it, still resting on a pillow in her room. *Starf!*

By then a wrangler had caught a star and was hold-ing it steady, waiting. Vega hurried over to take both of Piper's hands and say, "You'll be good, you'll be great. You'll tell me about it later; can't wait."

Clover hugged her tightly, then hugged Lady Cordial,

standing next to her. "Well," said Lady Cordial, backing away slightly, "that was s-s-s-sweet."

Everyone else said good-bye quickly, and before Piper knew it, she was rushing through space, starlight flashing, colors flying.

The ride was not smooth. In fact, it was much rougher than Piper had expected. She tried not to worry. But it was frightening to think she was out there in the universe, traveling alone.

"Stop that, Piper!" she told herself. "No negative emotions." Of course, there was always her Mirror Mantra. Even without a mirror, it could provide reassurance. But Piper needed a different phrase, one rooted in the here and now.

Even bumpy journeys could end with smooth landings, she knew. "Bumpy journey, smooth landing. Bumpy journey, smooth landing," she repeated to herself again and again until she believed it.

Piper kept saying the phrase even as she accessed her Wishworld Outfit Selector. But soon she had to stop to recite, "Star light, star bright, the first star I see tonight: I wish I may, I wish I might, have the wish I wish tonight," to transform her skin and hair to Wishworld plain.

Then, just as her Star-Zap flashed PREPARE FOR

LANDING, she saw Wishworld hurtling closer. She closed her eyes tight. "Bumpy journey, smooth landing."

And her feet touched the ground with barely a bounce.

Piper opened her eyes. She was facing a brown wall made, it seemed, out of logs. She turned to her right. There was another wall of logs. She turned to her left and saw another wall and still another. Clearly, she was in some sort of room—an empty room, with no ceiling. Clouds and sky were visible overhead. Piper's heart thudded at the strangeness of it all. Then she heard voices.

"Okay, we're just about set to put the roof on."

"This is going to be one amazing playhouse."

Then there was a much younger voice: "Did you see that bright light, Mommy?"

Suddenly, Piper heard *vrooom* sounds and chains clanking. A pointy roof came down atop the walls, leaving the room in darkness.

Piper's heart beat even faster. Without her serenity stone, Piper rubbed her Wish Pendant bracelets, hoping the smooth jewels would help keep her calm.

With nowhere else to look, Piper gazed at the walls. Then, amazingly, she was gazing *through* the walls! She could see outside! She had sunray vision! That must be her special talent, the ability to see through walls, logs, and who knew what else! She'd discovered it so quickly, without even trying. Surely that was a sign of good things to come.

Piper saw a group of Wishlings, young and old, smiling delightedly outside the walls.

"This is just what this playground needs!" said one female Wishling, holding the hand of a toddler. "Won't this be fun, Sophie?"

A playhouse for little Wishlings! Nothing to be scared of at all. But still, Piper needed to get out. She folded up her star and placed it in the backpack's front pocket just as the door opened and light streamed into the room.

A man stood across from Piper, staring at her in surprise.

"Why, there's a girl in here!" he exclaimed.

"Hello!" Piper said pleasantly. "I was actually just leaving." Before anyone could say anything else, she slipped outside, past the Wishlings' astonished faces, and briskly walked away.

The play space was big and busy, and Piper soon blended in. She paused at the edge to get her bearings.

On a long ramp-like structure, a small Wishling

whooshed down. "Not headfirst!" shrieked a female Wishling—the mom, Piper guessed. Meanwhile, a girl rode past on a very small two-wheeled vehicle, pushing on pedals that moved in circles. "Chloe!" the dad called out. "Where is your helmet?"

Wishlings are very focused on small Wishlings' heads, Piper noted.

She retreated behind a tree and felt her spirits soar. What a great place to land! She'd learned about those areas. What had those Wishlings called it? A playground? She could have sworn Professor Illumia Wickes had called them play-arounds during one of her Star Darlings guest lectures. But really, what difference did it make? She was there, with lots of adorable Wishlings who came up to her waist. They were all too young to be her Wisher, though. Just to make sure, she glanced at her Wish Pendant. The bracelets were still dark. But maybe there'd be older Wishlings nearby, and she wouldn't have far to go.

Piper checked her Star-Zap for directions. It showed the exact route, and it seemed to lead quite far away. Piper sighed. She enjoyed exercise as much as the next Starling—as long as it involved stretching—but right then her Wishling sandal straps were digging into her feet. Made from Wishling material, the sandals didn't mold to her feet like comfy Starling ones. Her long, swirly skirt was nice, though. And her cropped T-shirt, a vibrant emerald color with a rainbow by her heart, was cute and perfect.

The sun was perfect, too, shining brightly with just the right degree of warmth. And Piper felt a tingle all around her, an air of expectancy.

She heard one Wishling mom say to a dad, "I'm so happy spring is finally here!"

The male nodded. "We'll be spending a lot more time here now that the weather is nice." He glanced at the Wishling equivalent of a Star-Zap. *A cell phone*, Piper thought. "Oops. Almost three o'clock. Time for pickup."

Piper watched as the play-around emptied out.

It was the end of the school year, Piper realized, putting together the adults' comments and her tingly feeling. That mix of sadness and excitement, with one staryear ending and a long, lazy vacation ahead. The feeling was the same no matter where someone lived.

Piper moved on, following the coordinates of her Star-Zap. She edged toward the far corner of the play-around, where she saw a gate. She pushed against it. Nothing happened. The gate was locked in some way, and she couldn't find a scanner, of course.

"Excuse me," said a little girl who couldn't have been

more than three Wishworld years old. She lifted a hook-like handle and the gate swung open easily.

"Well!" said Piper. "Star sal—I mean, thank you!" She hoped she wouldn't get locked in somewhere else. There might not be a little Wishling around to help.

Piper continued down a treelined street with small cozy-looking houses. Each one had a wide porch that wrapped around to the back. In front of one, Piper stooped to pick up something from the sidewalk. It was shaped like a tube, about the length of her arm, and wrapped in a clear sleeve. She could read words through the wrapper, although it clearly wasn't a book: *Greenfield Crier.* Greenfield was most likely the town's name, Piper thought. And it was fitting. The town had wide yards and grassy plots along the walkways. But what did *Crier* mean?

Piper pinched the tube to see if it would actually cry. It stayed silent. Then she noticed a man walking up to another house and picking up a tube.

"Late delivery today," he said to Piper, taking off the wrapper and unfurling the tube into flat paper. "I missed it before I left for work. Still, it's nice to look over the newspaper in the afternoon, too!"

A newspaper! She'd learned about that in her Wishers 101 class last year and Professor Elara Ursa had gotten it exactly right. It was exciting to actually hold a newspaper in her very own hands. The professor had said that more and more news was being delivered electronically—like it was on Starland—but many Wishlings still had papers delivered to their homes.

"Are you visiting the Trunks?" the man asked, interrupting her thoughts.

"Trunks?" she repeated. Was he asking if she was visiting trees? "Yes, the Trunks," he repeated, pointing to the house behind her.

"Ah!" Piper said, remembering that Wishlings might be referred to by their last names. The house, and the newspaper, must belong to a family called the Trunks.

"No. I'm just picking up the newspaper for them. There!" She placed it carefully on the front steps and kept walking.

Soon small stores replaced the small homes. Piper walked past a brick building with signs that read GREENFIELD STATION, TICKETS, and TRAIN PLATFORM, THIS WAY. Beside the platform, Piper saw what looked like a ladder running on the ground, with yet another sign: BE CAREFUL ON TRACKS.

Two identical little buildings with windows all in a row and wheels at the bottom were parked on the side. *Greenfield Local* was painted on one, *Greenfield Express* on the other. *Can these houses actually move?* Piper wondered. It seemed doubtful.

Piper kept walking, and the sidewalk grew more crowded. Some Wishlings hurried into and out of stores, carrying sacks. Others walked more slowly while chatting with friends. She passed the Coffee Corner. Peeking inside, she saw everyone drinking out of mugs and cups. Coffee, she remembered reading in a holo-textbook, was a staple of the adult Wishling diet. But she had never realized it was a drink!

Then she stopped in front of a place called the Big Dipper. Her heart skipped at the words. *Home*, she thought. The older Starlings' dorm. It gave her a pang just thinking of Starling Academy while she was here, in a place where she couldn't even leave a children's play-around without help. But what was this place? A line snaked out the door, so it must be popular. People were leaving, gripping cone-shaped holders with scoops of brightly colored food inside.

"Yummy ice cream!" said a Wishling boy walking outside with his mom. *Ice cream!* She'd heard about the frosty dessert, too. Maybe it was called the Big Dipper after an ice cream scooper, not the constellation.

Next Piper passed the Greenfield Library and a

flower shop. Finally, the Star-Zap led Piper to a place called Big Rosie's Diner. It was marked with a glowing star on her Star-Zap screen. She was there. The spot where she would meet her Wisher.

The diner looked a little like one of those vehicles she'd walked by earlier. Only, this one appeared to be stuck in the ground. Pretty flower boxes hung just below its windows. The diner was sweet-looking and inviting, with bells above the door. They jingled when customers came in or went out.

A diner, mused Piper. *That sounds like* dinner. *It must be some sort of restaurant.* Casually, she strolled closer. A few Wishlings stepped outside. One held the door open, assuming Piper wanted to go inside. She decided she might as well. Her Wisher might already be there.

Nodding her thanks, Piper walked in and smiled. Yes, it was a restaurant! Tables with red-checked tablecloths stood in the center, while booths with red cushions lined the walls. There was a long counter directly in front of her, with lots of activity behind it. Wishling workers— not Bot-Bots!—bustled here and there, busily doing things Piper could only guess at. One sprayed some kind of liquid into glasses from a long hose. Another yelled into a window in the wall, where Wishlings appeared to be cooking in a separate room. "Two number fours, one with everything, one with everything hold the mustard," a cook cried, plopping plates on the window's shelf.

Odd, thought Piper. None of her friends had mentioned that Wishlings used numbers, not names, for food.

Then she noticed a separate counter—more of a desk, really—with a woman seated behind some kind of metal machine.

The woman had short curly hair and a nice smile. She reached for a long flat book and stood up. Obviously, she was going to the library down the street.

Instead of leaving, though, the woman carried the book over to Piper and asked, "Seat at the counter?"

"Yes," Piper agreed. "There are seats at the counter." To demonstrate, she moved closer to a stool and tried to pick it up. It didn't budge. But it did spin around.

"Oh!" said Piper. She couldn't resist sitting on it, pushing off from the counter as it twirled squeakily. "Starmendous!" she said. It reminded her of the starry-go-round rides back home. Of course, those rides flew through the air, too.

The woman held up the book. "Would you like to look at—"

"Your book?" Piper said.

"A menu," the woman answered. She handed it to Piper, who saw it was a list of food choices. "Or are you waiting for—"

"A bus?" finished Piper.

"No," said the woman, looking puzzled. "Friends."

Piper gulped. Her first decision. "Oh, I am waiting," she tried to explain, "but not for friends. Not really. But maybe I will find a friend here. Why else am I here, unless it's to make some sort of connection with a . . ." Her voice trailed off.

She was babbling, she knew, and while the woman waited patiently for Piper to stop talking, she was also giving her a slightly funny look.

"I'll just go outside," Piper finished. Her Wish Pendant was dark, so there really was no reason to stay inside, anyway.

"You do that, honey. There's a nice comfy bench right under the oak tree."

Piper headed outside for the big leafy tree and the bench. A shiny silver plaque was nailed onto the back slats. Piper read the inscription out loud: " 'In memory of Rose MacDonald. Thanks for the great food and the even better company.' "

"In memory of" must mean Rose had completed her Cycle of Life. Big Rosie's must have been her diner. Piper gazed up at the clouds, wondering if Rose's star beamed its light right at that spot. Was the star twinkling right then, unseen, in approval of this mission? Piper's mind was wandering, considering the cosmos and its connection to all life-forms, when a boy and girl walked past.

Piper snapped to attention. Could one of those Wishlings be her Wisher? They both had light hair and similar-shaped noses and lopsided grins. Brother and sister, Piper thought. The two laughed and pushed each other playfully. It was the kind of relationship she'd always wanted with her own brother. She glanced hopefully at her pendant. Nope, it wasn't either of them.

Another girl hurried past, her nose in a book. The pendant stayed dark.

Wishling after Wishling walked by while Piper sat on the bench. Still, there was no sign of her Wisher. "Patience, Piper," she counseled herself. This was such a different, new, and exciting experience. She couldn't quite hold on to her calm. So much could go wrong; so much depended on her.

But she'd been waiting on that bench for a long time. What if there was a problem with her pendant and that was why it wasn't lighting up? She shook the bracelets lightly, then harder and harder.

Stop it, Piper! she ordered. It was time for her Mirror Mantra. She crisscrossed her legs in her favorite meditation pose. "Dreams can come true," she said out loud. "It's your time to shine!" The pane revealed Piper's shimmery skin and hair, but just for an instant, and just for her to see. Immediately, she felt energized.

A moment later, Piper felt a tingle at her wrist. *Finally!* she thought, glancing at her pendant. The bracelets were glowing faintly. Smiling, Piper peered down the street. A group of girls was approaching, and with each step they took, the pendant lit up brighter and brighter.

The girls stopped directly in front of Piper. Her pendant flashed even stronger; the jewels sparkled fiercely. One of these Wishlings was definitely her Wisher.

There were four girls, huddled together so closely Piper couldn't see their faces or hear their words. It didn't seem like happy chatter to Piper, though, with the girls talking about the cute boy in class or the latest fashion. Something was up.

The group broke apart, and three of the girls drew away, leaving one girl standing alone. "Bye, Olivia," the shortest one of the three called back in a commanding way. "Everything will be fine." She tugged at the other two, and they walked quickly away.

Maybe the short girl was the Wisher. Piper thought it was a definite possibility. But she wasn't thrilled. The girl seemed a little bossy.

Meanwhile, the girl left behind—Olivia—stood still for a long moment, lost in thought. Piper gazed at her. She was sweet-looking, with a round face and long dark brown hair pulled into a high ponytail. Her blue eyes were large and searching. Surely, Olivia was a deep thinker. But her eyes had dark circles beneath them, as if she was losing sleep. Piper liked her immediately.

By then the other girls were down the block. Olivia stepped past Piper, heading into the diner, and the pendant glowed with extra intensity.

Piper straightened her shoulders. She had found her Wisher.

CHAPTER
6

Now what? Piper wondered. Should she follow the Wisher and go inside the diner, too? She felt hesitant. The woman at the desk already thought she was strange. And while Piper never minded when other Starlings thought she was a little weird—let's face it, not everyone liked to do downward-facing glion poses while meditating in P.E. class—this seemed different.

Piper cared what these Wishlings thought, and she wanted to make a good impression. Maybe because they were the first Wishlings she'd ever met. And maybe, just maybe, it might help her complete her mission.

Through the glass door, Piper saw Olivia drop her backpack behind the front desk. She gave the curly-haired woman a kiss on the cheek. Then she walked around the long counter and slipped behind it to the other side. She waved hello to a woman wiping up a spill at the other end—a "waitress," Piper had learned—and tied on an apron. It seemed that people, not Bot-Bots, served food on Wishworld.

Olivia works at the diner! Piper realized. Now she had no choice but to go in again. This time, she would think carefully before she spoke.

"Hello," Piper said cautiously to the woman at the desk. Now she saw the woman wore a name tag. "Alice," Piper added.

"Hello again," said Alice. "Have you figured out if you want to—"

"Eat?" said Piper.

"Stay," said Alice.

"Yes, I do." Piper leaned over, closer to Alice. She didn't say anything; she just concentrated on connecting.

A funny expression crossed Alice's face. It was a wistful look, like she was remembering something from long ago. She sniffed deeply. "Rhubarb pie. Strawberry-rhubarb pie with crumb topping." She smiled at Piper. "It smells just like the pie my mom, Rosie, used to make. I didn't even know we were serving it today! Or that anyone else could make it the same way!"

Rosie . . . the plaque on the bench . . . the diner name . . . Piper wanted to ask her more, but she had to focus on the task at hand. Adult Wishlings always smelled favorite desserts from childhood when they got close to Starlings. And those memories made them open to suggestion—and to believing whatever the Starlings told them.

Piper stared into Alice's eyes. "I am Piper, and I am here to help out."

Alice nodded solemnly. Then she called, "Everyone! This is Piper, and she is here to help out."

The cook came from the kitchen, wiping his hands on a dishcloth. "I think I'll whip up a coconut cake. For some reason, there's a smell around here that reminds me of coming home from school and finding a thick slice of cake waiting for me on the kitchen table." He stuck out his hand for Piper to shake. She touched his fingers, unsure what to do. "I'm Pete," he said. "Now, what is your name again?"

"I am Piper," she repeated. "And I am here to help."

"Of course you are," Pete said, slightly dazed. Then he smiled. "We can always use an extra pair of hands around here." He turned to the counter. "Olivia! Come meet our new employee." He stopped, looking confused. "Wait a minute. Not an employee. A helper, I guess."

Olivia walked over. "Just a helper?" she asked Piper. "Why would you want to help without getting a—"

"Star payment," finished Piper. *Oh, Starf!* she thought. That can't be right.

"Um . . . a paycheck," said Olivia.

"It's for a school assignment," Piper told Olivia as the two girls moved off to the side to talk.

"You don't go to the Lincoln School, do you? Where do you go?" Olivia sounded curious, not accusing. But Piper felt angry—at herself: why hadn't she thought about that earlier? Walking over, she had come up with a pretend last name: Smith. She had read somewhere it was a common Wishling name. She had even thought of a pretend address: 123 Main Street, again very common. But her school? She had no idea. And she couldn't very well whip out her Star-Zap to request information about common Wishling school names. Not that it would work anyway!

Her gaze lit on a passing truck that said MAIL DELIVERY. "Uh, the Mail School?"

"Male School?" Olivia said, puzzled. "You go to a school for boys?"

"No!" Piper said quickly. "It's Mayle . . . M-a-y-l-e, for the name of my town . . . Mayfield!" The name sounded kind of lame, Piper knew. Too much like

Greenfield. But it was the best she could do with hardly any time to think.

"Maylefield," mused Olivia. She shook her head. "I've never heard of it."

Piper smiled. She had this part covered. "Oh, it's floozels . . . I mean miles . . . away. And we're on vacation this week so I'm visiting my grandmother. I'm doing a work-study program for extra credit," she said.

Olivia nodded. "Extra credit is good," she said thoughtfully. "It could bring up your grade so you don't get anxious when you take a test. It's kind of like being thrown one of those rescue rings lifeguards use to save people from drowning."

Piper had just studied beach recreation in Wishling Ways, and she could picture the safety device—like a floating doughnut. Then, just as Olivia started talking again, she had another vision. It was from a bad dream. She was trying to swim to shore at Luminous Lake, but that same evil presence she'd felt before was trying to pull her down . . . down.

"So if you have that sinking feeling during a test, you—" Olivia was saying with a laugh.

"Go underwater," Piper finished for her. "You don't scream, you don't breathe, you don't even think."

Olivia took a step back, startled by the dark image.

"No . . . I was going to say that you can just relax. It would make you feel better knowing you had help—like a rescue ring."

Relaxation! Piper, of all Starlings on Starland, knew about relaxation. Why hadn't she gotten that right away? And now she'd scared poor Olivia on top of everything else. Not the best way to connect!

"So did Olivia tell you that anyone who works here is part of our family? Just like Big Rosie used to say?" Alice came over to put an arm around Piper.

"No, I didn't," Olivia said, taking another step away from Piper.

"Well, we're one big family here," Alice went on. "Pete is my husband, and Olivia is our daughter. Rosie was my mom, Olivia's grandmother. She started the diner."

"Wow," said Piper. "That's so nice that you're all together. And it's nice that you're keeping the diner in the family."

Olivia smiled but stayed where she was. "It is nice!" she agreed. "Big Rosie started a great tradition. But she wasn't really very big," Olivia confided, clearly happy to have someone to talk to about her grandmother. "She was actually shorter than you, Piper—and even shorter than my friend Morgan. And she was really skinny, especially for someone who spent so much time in kitchens! But she had a big, big personality!" She paused. "I really—"

"Miss her," Piper finished. "I'm sure you do," she added quietly as Alice went to help a customer. "My granddad left us, too, and it's sad. But I think of him so often and imagine conversations. So sometimes I really feel like he's here with me. Star apologies for your loss."

Piper ended her speech with such warmth and understanding that Olivia's eyes filled. Later, Piper realized she'd used the Starland saying. Luckily, Olivia was more focused on the meaning than the actual words.

Piper sighed. Olivia's family was making her think of her own. Her brother, Finn, never very talkative, could still be a comfort. They were related, after all, and she never had to explain little things to him, let alone big things.

"Do you have brothers or sisters?" she asked Olivia.

Olivia brightened. "Yes, a sister. And she's coming home from college for the summer in May."

A grown-up Wishling, coming up to the counter, overheard. "Oh, your sister Isabel!" she said. "My son was in class with her all through elementary school, middle school, and high school. She was always an amazing student. Straight As in every class. I heard she never got a grade below that, in fact!" She turned to Alice, a hint of jealousy in her eyes. "You must be very proud."

"Yes, we are," said Alice. Piper was watching Olivia. While the woman was speaking, she had seemed to freeze, barely moving a muscle. But when Alice reached over to squeeze her arm and say, "And we're just as proud of Olivia," she grinned, and Piper thought maybe she had imagined it.

Anyway, it was time to get to know Olivia—to see her in action and figure out her wish. "Do you want to show me around so I can start helping?" she asked.

"Of course," Olivia said happily. "We're not some big fancy restaurant. My mom likes to run everything the old-fashioned way, just like Grandma Rosie did. Anyway, there's the cash register." She pointed to the machine on Alice's desk, and Piper nodded like she understood what it meant.

Next Olivia led Piper behind the counter and showed her different workstations. The front station directly behind the counter held ice cream freezers, coffee machines, and a small refrigerator to store juice and milk.

Ice cream! Coffee! Piper knew the words. She'd even seen ice cream and coffee for herself. But she still needed to study them—and everything else!—to truly under-stand. Piper took out her Star-Zap, hoping Olivia would think it was just a regular cell phone. She pretended to hold it casually, the way she'd seen Wishlings do, when really she was taking holo-vids and recording Olivia's voice.

Olivia gestured for Piper to follow her into the kitchen, then stopped by another workstation. "This area is for roll-ups," Olivia explained.

Hmmm, roll-ups. Piper knew about push-ups and pull-ups from Physical Energy class. Perhaps roll-ups were another form of exercise. But truth be told, she'd never paid much attention. She'd discovered a starmat hidden behind some equipment in the gym, and if she wandered slowly to that corner, no one noticed. So while everyone else jumped and ran, she just meditated quietly. She was pretty sure Coach Geeta knew what she was up to but never called her on it. Most likely, the coach understood that Piper got more energy from meditating than from playing star ball.

"So," Piper said to Olivia, "you keep in shape while you're working by rolling up?"

"No!" Olivia giggled. She grabbed a napkin. And before Piper could even blink, she had rolled a knife, fork, and spoon inside the napkin in such a way that it stayed wrapped even when she flipped it in the air. It was almost like magic.

"This is part of side work, and for now you should just focus on this kind of stuff. Roll-ups, refilling ketchup"—she pointed to squeezable containers that came to a point, filled with an unappetizing red liquid mixture—"and sugar dispensers. No waiting on tables. Not yet, anyway."

"Okay." Piper kept nodding as if she understood. Hopefully, it would all make sense when she studied everything later. It turned out, though, there wasn't time.

"You can start right now and refill the sugar dispensers," Olivia said. She took out a tray of empty dispensers. Then she waved toward a high shelf where a dozen large containers stood in a line.

Piper opened her mouth, about to explain how clueless she was, when the phone in front rang. Olivia backed away to answer it. "Okay, you're on your own," she told Piper.

Piper paced in front of the containers. Which one held the sugar? She glanced around helplessly and looked straight through the cabinet door above the containers. There were unopened jars labeled MUSTARD and PICKLES,

plus bags labeled SALT, PEPPER, and—Piper grinned—
SUGAR!

She took out the bag, then used her sunray vision to
see what sugar actually looked like. Okay, now she realized the sugar dispenser was the third from the right.
When she lifted the container off the shelf, though, she
had to laugh. It was labeled on the lid!

Now Piper had the dispenser. She had the sugar.
She'd even found a scooper. She mentally patted herself
on the back for that one.

It should be simple from here on, she thought. The
dispenser had a hole on top, and the sugar should slide
right in.

She ladled out a heaping scoop from the container
and poured the sugar over the dispenser. Sugar granules
bounced off the top with a *ping ping ping* and scattered
all over the floor. Only a few granules actually made it
into the dispenser. Piper tried again and again with the
same results.

"This is going to take a starday and a half," she told
herself. But she had to do it. She would acknowledge
these negative feelings so they would pass like drifting
clouds; then she'd get back to work.

She reached once again for the scooper. But then

Pete walked in, holding another sugar dispenser—this one with its top screwed off. "Here's one more for you," he said.

After that, it was easy to fill the dispensers. She just took off each lid, poured in the sugar, then closed it up. A short time later, she was done. But the table and floor were still covered with sugar. Piper gazed down, dismayed. Why couldn't the floor be self-cleaning?

"That's okay, honey," Alice said, coming over to inspect the mess. "But it always makes me me feel better to leave a workstation as clean—"

"As you found it," Piper finished.

"You too?" said Alice. "Good. Just use the broom and dustpan in the corner."

Another confusing task! Piper eyed the long stick with bristles on one end in the corner. It didn't look like any kind of pan, so that must be the broom. Experimenting, she pushed it along the floor. To her surprise, it moved the sugar granules into a neat pile, almost by itself! Then she swept it all into the flat pan-thing that had been next to it.

She gazed at the pan a moment, half expecting the sugar to disappear into thin air. But of course, she was on Wishworld, not Starland, and the pan stayed full. *Next step: find a garbage can.* She spied one in the opposite corner and hurried over. *Ewww!* She wrinkled her nose. It was stuffed with actual garbage that smelled. No vanishing garbage cans here! *Disgusting!* Quickly, she dumped the sugar on top, then turned on her heel.

"Nice work," said Alice, returning. "Olivia is in a booth in the back, doing homework. Why don't you join her, and in a little while you two can have dinner here? The least we can do is feed you!"

Olivia grinned. Her first Wishling compliment—it felt almost like Star Kindness Day. Now to find Olivia. She walked around the diner tables, all the way to the back and the very last booth.

Schoolbooks were spread across the table, along with pencils and pens and notebooks. But there was no sign of Olivia.

Piper's heart sank. She'd spent way too much time filling sugar dispensers. And now look what had happened. She'd lost her Wisher!

CHAPTER
7

Piper had no idea what to do next. So she sat down in the booth and idly leafed through the books, thinking. Wishling books were so heavy and cumbersome. How did students carry them around, much less hold them up to read?

"Concentrate, Piper," she told herself. "Focus on Olivia!"

Where could she be? Why had she left so suddenly? Would she return?

Piper pushed aside *Our Nation's History Through the Centuries* to clear space to put her head down. She always thought better that way. But the history textbook bumped the math book, which nudged something called

Advanced Reading Material for the Young Scholar, and they all fell onto the seat across the table.

"Ouch!" Olivia popped up, rubbing her shoulder. The books thudded to the floor.

"You were resting here the whole time?" Piper was amazed. "I'm so sorry I interrupted your time of rejuvenation."

"Huh?" Olivia sounded confused. She blinked and shook her head. "I must have fallen asleep."

Piper nodded encouragingly. It certainly made sense to sleep in the late afternoon. Although, as a general rule, she preferred an earlier naptime.

Olivia yawned. "I've been so tired lately."

Piper leaned closer, a tingle of excitement running down her spine. Clearly, Olivia wasn't getting enough sleep. Most likely, she was anxious about a problem; worrying could keep anyone awake. And her wish must revolve around solving the problem.

But what was the problem?

Piper could almost feel the wish dangling in front of her, tantalizingly, as if she could reach out and touch it.

"Sometimes I have trouble sleeping, too," Piper told Olivia in a way meant to encourage her to tell more. That was stretching the truth. So Piper crossed her legs at the ankles the way Starlings did if they told a fib.

"You do?" Olivia took a deep breath. "Usually I fall asleep as soon as my head hits the pillow and I don't wake up until my alarm goes off. But lately I've been—"

"Sensing an evil presence lurking in your dreams. Dark and threatening. You can almost see it in your mind's eye whenever you close your eyes. . . ."

Piper's voice trailed off when she caught sight of Olivia's put-off expression. "Uh, no," Olivia said, leaning back against the bench, farther away from Piper.

"Oh, *starf*," Piper muttered to herself. Now she had really freaked out her Wisher. And she really needed to gain Olivia's trust. It was so important in pinpointing the correct wish.

"Don't mind me," she said airily, as if didn't matter that much. "That whole 'evil presence' stuff? It was just part of a bad dream I had the other night."

Olivia smiled sadly. "I've been having bad dreams, too," she confided. But then she seemed to pull back once more and shrugged. "It's really no big deal. Everyone has bad dreams. I'm sure they'll just go away."

She didn't sound like she believed it. And Piper didn't believe it, either. Bad dreams had a way of sticking around until you figured out what they meant.

"Girls!" Alice called from behind the counter. "Come and get your dinner."

Reluctantly, Piper stood when Olivia did. They made their way to the front of the diner, where two heaping plates of food were waiting. Piper stared at her dish. She didn't recognize a thing. So she grabbed a nearby menu and leafed through the pages. There were tons of choices. How could she figure out what she was eating?

Her eyes stopped at the entry HOT DOG. She gasped. Wasn't that a Wishling pet? But right next to the words was a picture of a cylinder-shaped food in a bun. It looked nothing at all like those cute four-legged creatures. Luckily, there were other pictures, too. Piper identified her food as a veggie burger, sweet potato fries, one of those long green and bumpy things called a pickle, and coleslaw. She couldn't guess what that was, even squinting at the photo.

Partial to greens, she started with the pickle. It reminded her of cukumbrella, a crunchy vegetable that didn't need much light to grow. There were always lots to be found in the Flats.

Piper picked up her knife and fork to cut the pickle. But Olivia was just holding hers in one hand, so Piper did the same. *When on Wishworld, do as Wishlings do,* she thought. That was one of the sayings professors were always spouting. She took a big bite. Sour! Everything else was delicious, though. Piper decided she'd have this for every meal on Wishworld if she could.

In record time, Piper finished her dinner. Traveling to Wishworld used up so much energy! She had definitely needed to replenish. Meanwhile, Olivia just pushed her food around the plate. Piper was sure she was still thinking about her bad dream. If only she could get Olivia to open up again. She had to try. And this time, she'd take it slow.

"Maybe you'd like something else to eat?" she asked gently. "Some kind of comfort food?" Eating garble greens always made Piper feel better. "I can get it for you."

"Good idea, Piper. Comfort food! But I'll take care of it myself." Olivia jumped off her stool, went around the counter, and started working by the fountain area.

Piper grinned.

Olivia smiled back as she grabbed two tall glasses. In each, she put a spoonful of chocolate syrup and some milk. Then she filled the glasses with cold seltzer from the fountain tap. Olivia named everything as she went, so it was easy to follow.

Piper could barely contain her excitement when she heard *chocolate*. Even though she'd eaten a big dinner, she still had to try the tasty treat she'd heard about from other Star Darlings. But she did have to ask about the seltzer.

"Oh, it's just bubbly water," Olivia explained, adding a bit more.

The drinks foamed to the brim, without one drop spilling over. Olivia mixed the glasses with a long spoon and plopped in straws. Then she pushed one across to Piper.

"Try it!" she said.

Piper sipped. "Startast—I mean fantastic!" The drink was starmazingly refreshing, with a yummy chocolate sweetness to it. But it had a fizz and pop, too, and might just have been the best thing Piper had ever tasted. Other Star Darlings had talked about soda and chocolate milk, but she doubted anyone else had had one of these on her mission. "What is it called?"

"It's a chocolate egg cream. I know, I know," Olivia added quickly. "It doesn't have eggs or cream. So don't ask me why it's called an egg cream. And I'm not surprised you don't know it. Hardly anyone outside of New York City has heard about it."

New York City? The place name meant nothing to Piper. She supposed it was a very small town in the middle of nowhere. It had to be, for hardly anyone to know about this wonderful drink.

Piper reached for her trusty menu to find the listing. "Oh, you won't find it there," Olivia said. "People wouldn't order it, anyway. It's just a New York thing. You know my parents are from there."

"Okay, girls," said Alice, reaching to clear Piper's empty glass. "It's getting late. Time for you to head out." She looked at Piper. "Is someone coming to pick you up?"

Piper concentrated. Staring into Alice's eyes, she said solemnly, "Why don't I sleep over at your house?"

Alice sniffed the air. "There's that rhubarb pie smell again. How strange. Pete isn't even baking today!" Then she looked at Piper. "Why don't you sleep over at our house?"

Olivia looked surprised but not upset. A favorable sign, Piper thought.

"Sounds good," said Piper. "I'm sure my grandma won't mind." Holding in her laughter, she pretended to place a call on her Star-Zap. Her family had no idea she was on Wishworld. But she felt sure that if they had, they'd have been fine with her spending the night with this nice family.

The two girls cleared the rest of their dishes, then made their way to Olivia's home. It was just around the corner from the diner, on a street very much like the one she'd walked down earlier, with snug little houses and big leafy trees.

To open the front door, Olivia used a metal tool, twisting it into a hole below a knob. The inside of the house was just like the outside, Piper thought: cozy and colorful, with shaggy rugs covering brightly polished hardwood floors, small rooms, and lots of knickknacks spread on shelves and cabinet tops. In one alcove, framed photos and awards covered the wall. Piper examined them all closely.

In most pictures, Olivia posed with an older girl who had the same deep blue eyes. "Is this your sister?" Piper asked.

"Yup," said Olivia. "Isabel."

Isabel's awards took up more space than Olivia's, Piper noticed. But that was probably because she was older. She'd finished more school years. "You both are excellent students," Piper observed.

Piper meant it as a compliment. She expected Olivia to say thank you or at least acknowledge the comment in some way. But Olivia leaned over her backpack as if she didn't want to continue the conversation. She pulled out some textbooks and said, "I'll do my homework now if you don't—"

"Mind," Piper finished for her. "Why would I mind? You feel like I'm a real guest, I know, and like you're responsible for me. But I basically invited myself. Do your homework."

Olivia finished her homework at the dining room table while Piper browsed through her schoolbooks. She couldn't get over the feel of them. They were heavy, true, but wonderful, too. The textbook pages were so smooth and shiny and fun to turn. After about an hour, Alice came home from the diner and announced, "Bedtime!"

Olivia pushed aside dozens of stuffed animals on her bedroom floor and set up a blow-up bed for Piper. She opened a drawer to show Piper pair after pair of pajamas. Piper lifted a gauzy scoop-necked nightgown, the color of Luminous Lake. "Could I wear this one?" she asked.

"Of course," said Olivia. Without even looking, she took the first pair of pajamas from the pile and went to the bathroom to change. It always amazed Piper that most Starlings paid so little attention to their nightwear. She guessed Wishlings did the same.

The girls settled into their beds quietly. *That has to change; we need to connect*, Piper thought. And really, it was the perfect time. There was something about talking in the dark, right before you fell asleep, that was tailor-made for confidences.

"So," Piper said, pulling the blanket up to her chin, "tell me about a typical day here in Greenfield. Then I'll tell you about my days in Ladyfield."

"Ladyfield?" Olivia repeated. "I thought you were from Maylefield!"

Piper groaned to herself. Why couldn't she keep these things straight? Sometimes she was too dreamy for her own good. "Just testing you," Piper said. "You passed."

"Oh, okay. Well"—Olivia fluffed up her pillow—"about my day. I set my alarm for six-fifteen. It's early. I know. We don't have to be in school until nine, but I have to—"

"Give yourself plenty of time, in case you have more bad dreams and need to shake off that feeling of impending doom."

"Ummm. No. I have to go to the diner to eat breakfast."

Piper considered this. Olivia went to the diner before school and after school. That was a lot of time spent away from home. Could that have something to do with her wish? Most likely, yes. She should definitely look into this more.

"Okay, breakfast. So then what?" Piper prompted her.

"Then my friends meet me in front of the diner and we—"

"Discuss any disturbing dreams you may have had the night before," Piper finished.

"Walk to school together," Olivia said, moving closer to the wall, putting more and more distance between them.

But Piper had to keep trying.

"And then school?"

"School is just plain old school." Now Olivia actually turned her back on Piper. "And then I head back to the diner after."

The diner again! Olivia was there way too often, and it was obviously stressing her out. It sounded like she was working an awful lot. Maybe she wanted to be home instead. Maybe she wanted to join an after-school club or play a sport. Although Piper didn't see the appeal, many Starlings did, and it was really good for them! But once again, Piper was getting off track. *Olivia, Olivia,* she told herself.

"Well, I'm here now," she said to Olivia. "I can cover for you at the diner so you don't have to work so much. Wouldn't that be great?"

"Oh, no! I love working there," Olivia told her, sounding annoyed. "I don't *have* to go. I go because I *want* to." She yawned. "I'm getting kind of tired," she said pointedly.

Uh-oh. All Olivia wanted to do was sleep, but Piper kept asking irritating questions. Suddenly, a thought popped into her head, and she sat up.

"What?" Olivia said, sounding even more annoyed.

"Don't worry," said Piper. "I won't ask you any more questions. I just had an idea. If you like, I could show you some ways to relax. I know some techniques that may help you sleep."

"Really?" said Olivia, interested. She sat up, too.

Piper nodded.

"Okay," Olivia agreed. "Let's do it."

"First, let's both lie back down." It wouldn't hurt Piper to de-stress, too. "Now we close our eyes and focus on breathing. Deep breath in. Deep breath out. Deep breath in. Deep breath out."

Together, the girls breathed, keeping their eyes shut tight.

"Now we're going to focus on each part of our body, to help it relax. Start with the toes on your right foot. Tense those toe muscles for a count of ten. One, two, three . . ." Piper spoke slowly and softly. "Now relax those same muscles for another count of ten."

Of course, Piper couldn't see Olivia with her own eyes closed. But as they worked from the toes to the legs, to the arms and up, she could sense a peace coming over the Wishling. By the end, Piper was as loose as a rag doll. She felt herself drifting off to sleep. *I hope this helps Olivia*, she thought.

Piper was dreaming. She was floating on her back in a warm stream. Her skin tingled in the fresh air, and all was right with the cosmos. She gazed up at the starry sky, listening to the peaceful sound of water lapping against the shore. Suddenly, the calm gurgles turned into frenzied gasps.

It wasn't the sound of the stream. It was someone struggling to breathe.

Piper shot up, wide-awake. Her heart was beating quickly. She could see Olivia in the dim light, shaking and heaving, trying to catch her breath.

"Are you okay?" Piper climbed into bed beside Olivia.

Olivia nodded, her eyes half closed. She held up a finger, the universal sign for *Wait*, and slowly her breathing returned to normal. Piper brushed a strand of hair from Olivia's eyes. Her forehead felt damp and cold with sweat. Piper wished she could make that scared feeling disappear like a puff of stardust.

"I had another nightmare," Olivia finally said.

Piper held her close, murmuring words her mother used to say after she and her brother had bad dreams. "Hush, hush, I'm right here. It's over now. It will be all right."

And it would be all right. Piper just had to identify the correct wish and help Olivia make it come true. Then everything would be fine. And Piper felt sure she was on the right track. Olivia might not be working too hard, but Piper was sure her wish had to do with the diner. She'd barely mentioned anything else!

Still, Piper thought ruefully, she'd felt sure the relaxation exercise would help Olivia get a good night's sleep. And look how that had turned out. It hadn't done a star-blessed thing.

CHAPTER
8

True to her word, Olivia's cell phone alarm went off at 6:15 the next morning. That was way too early for Piper, who liked to sleep as late as possible and still make it to breakfast in time.

Olivia didn't seem particularly happy to get up, either. But she trudged around the room, grabbing clothes.

Meanwhile, Piper stretched lazily on her bed. Maybe she didn't actually have to get up now. True, it was a school day, but only for Olivia. Piper's pretend school was on vacation this week. She really didn't need to spend the day in class. While she was curious about Wishling schools (Did the students really take notes by hand, writing down everything the teachers said, without recording a thing? How quaint!), she was more interested in completing her mission. And Piper felt positive that

Olivia's wish had to do with Big Rosie's.

"I really should spend another day at the diner for my assignment," she told Olivia. "Do you mind if I don't go to school with you?"

Olivia laughed. "I didn't expect you to go with me! Why would you think that? You're on vacation!"

Piper laughed, too. It was because all the other Star Darlings had gone to school so far. "Oh, I was just kidding," she said.

Olivia nodded distractedly as she tried to fit all her books in her backpack. "I've got to hurry now. I'll tell my parents you'll go to the diner when you're ready. You can eat there. Just close the front door of the house on your way out."

Olivia was certainly organized when she needed to be! "Sounds like a plan." Piper yawned and pulled the blanket over her head. Just a few more starmins of rest and she'd be raring to go. She didn't even hear Olivia leave. She was already sound asleep.

ZZZZZZ! ZZZZZZZ! A loud startling noise, like the biggest swarm of glitterbees imaginable, woke up Piper. She glanced at the clock. *Hmmm.* That was a bit more than a few starmins.

ZZZZZZ! ZZZZZZZ!

Moon and stars! What was that sound? If Olivia heard that every morning, no wonder she was having nightmares. Piper rolled off her cot and shuffled to the window.

A grown-up Wishling was riding some sort of machine. Grass and dirt spurted out one side, and the grass seemed to shorten as he rode over it.

Starland's grass always looked immaculate but never actually needed cutting. These poor Wishlings had so many chores it was no wonder they looked harried.

Anyway, it was time to start her starday; her last on Wishworld, Piper felt sure. Now that she'd figured out that Olivia's wish concerned the diner, she just had to get to Big Rosie's to discover the details.

A little while later, Alice met Piper at the diner door, swinging it open and waving her inside. "Piper! I am so glad you're here! Usually we have two waitresses working the morning shift. But Donna called in sick. It would be great if you could take care of customers today." She paused. "Only if you're comfortable waiting tables, of course."

Piper's eyes opened wide. The previous day, all she had done was fill some sugar dispensers, and that hadn't gone well at all. Could she possibly be a waitress? And keep all the orders straight?

Piper breathed deeply. Of course she could. She just had to stay calm and focused. Besides, how could she say no? Big Rosie's Diner needed her help!

"Sure," Piper said gamely. "Where do I start?"

Alice beamed. "Diane will show you the ropes."

Now there were ropes involved. Waiting tables sounded complicated already.

"This is Diane," Alice went on as a woman walked by holding a tray of dirty glasses. Diane paused but didn't smile.

"Don't worry. Diane's just a little grouchy this morning. She'll warm up to you." Alice nudged Piper toward the kitchen. "Go on. Follow her. She'll show you what to do."

In the kitchen, Diane eyed Piper's outfit: loose bright green drawstring pants that swept the floor, a flowery top with long bell sleeves, and delicate-looking sandals. All suitable for lounging, but not really for waitressing. "Do you have anything else to wear?" she asked.

Piper looked at Diane. She wore a knee-length black skirt, a button-down white shirt, and sensible black lace-up shoes.

"Be right back," Piper said. She ducked into the bathroom, accessed her Wishworld Outfit Selector, and emerged wearing ankle-length black pants and a neat white shirt, with just one small flower on the front pocket. Her black shoes looked just like Diane's.

Diane nodded at the outfit then spent the next half hour explaining how to set tables and write up orders on the pad, when to pick up food, and, it seemed to Piper, about a moonium other things.

For once, Piper didn't interrupt. She just listened intently. She was excited to write on paper with a writing utensil.

Diane checked the clock. "It's time for the morning rush," she said, "so get ready." Then she disappeared into the back just as the doorbells jingled. A mom carrying a baby walked in, followed a few starmins later by an elderly man. Alice led them to their tables. But then other customers were coming in, too.

Piper took a deep breath and glanced in the mirror. "Dreams can come true," she said. "It's your time to shine!"

She could do this.

Smiling steadily, Piper walked to the older man. He had silvery hair that circled his head, with a large bald spot right in the center, and a big bushy mustache that matched.

Piper placed a glass of water on the table. Then she flipped open her pad and stood poised, pen in hand, to take his order. "What would you like, sir?" she asked in a pleasant voice.

"What?" he said, clearly surprised. "Don't you know?"

"Ummm . . ." Piper hedged. Was she supposed to read customers' minds, too? She tried, concentrating her energy on his thoughts. And while she picked up that he was feeling impatient and a little put out, she couldn't for the starlife of her figure out what he wanted to eat.

"I have the same thing every morning," the man said. "Haven't you—"

"Waited on you before?" Piper shook her head. "No, I'm new."

"Okay, here's what I get. Three egg whites scrambled, omelet-style, a whole-wheat bagel with the center scooped out, an extra plate to put the bagel on, no home fries, and two low-fat cream cheeses."

Piper wrote furiously to take it all down.

"And a cup of—"

"Zing?" Piper asked.

"No, coffee," he replied. "What in the world is Zing?"

Oops, thought Piper. *There I go again.*

"Let me handle Lou," Diane said on her way to the kitchen. "He can get a little grumpy if you don't get everything exactly right."

"No, no," Piper insisted. The diner was filling up.

Other people were taking seats. And Piper wanted to prove herself. "I want to do this," she told Diane. Then she paused. "Just tell me what a bagel is."

Time passed in a haze. After an hour, Piper found an elastic band and loosely tied back her hair so it wouldn't get in the way. After another hour, she retied it in a high, severe ponytail.

No doubt about it, waitressing was hard work—always hurrying from customer to customer, from kitchen to table. But it wasn't only physical. It took mental energy, too.

At one point, Piper was turning the corner carrying a tray of dirty dishes back to the kitchen. She heard Diane say, "Corner." Piper had no idea what that meant until Diane flew around the corner and the two bumped. They were both carrying loaded trays, and plates crashed to the floor, shattering into little pieces. Now the floor had to be cleaned and Diane's food prepared again.

"Next time I yell 'corner,'" Diane said through gritted teeth, "stop if you're nearby. It means I'm coming around it."

Another time, Pete shouted from the kitchen, "Burgers, eighty-six!" So Piper helpfully, or so she thought, began to carefully count eighty-six plates for the eighty-six burgers. But Pete had only frowned when she brought them over. "That means we're out of burgers," he explained in a tense voice. A little while later, he called out that the lunch special was "on the fly." Piper ducked to avoid the flying chicken potpie. Only later did she learn that *on the fly* meant Pete was cooking something quickly.

Each of those times, Piper had almost lost control. She'd felt tears slip out of her eyes, a burning sensation in her cheeks, and a knot forming in her stomach. But then she had retreated to a quiet spot in the back and visualized herself floating carefree in Luminous Lake. Moments later, she'd been ready for more customers.

By the time lunch was in full swing, Piper didn't feel frazzled at all. She glided around the diner, quickly but smoothly, pausing to take deep breaths every once in a while but managing to stay unruffled. If only the Star Darlings could see her now, she thought—especially practical Vega, who always had everything under control. Dreamy, absentminded Piper was holding down a complicated Wishling job!

Piper considered it a minor victory when Lou came back for lunch and asked for her specifically. Maybe it was because she smiled at him. She smiled at everyone. But not every customer smiled back. In a job like this, she realized, you saw the best and worst of Wishlings.

"Busy day," Diane said to Piper when there was a lull in customer traffic. Diane had definitely warmed up to her. She lowered her voice to add, "And that's unusual lately. You know. . . ." She nodded across the street, to a restaurant with a big yellow-and-black BB on its sign. "'Your local Busy Bee,'" Piper read from the sign, "'the buzz-iest place in town. Five billion served.'"

"Ever since that fast food place opened," Diane continued, "business has been slower than usual."

Piper understood the slow business part. But fast food? She pictured hamburgers and French fries with little legs, racing around a restaurant.

"Lots of customers have started eating across the street." Diane shook her head. "The prices may be cheaper, but you can't compare the quality. This right here"—she tapped the counter—"is real home cooking. Just like—"

"Bot-Bot cooks used to make," Piper finished.

"Huh?" said Diane. "I was going to say 'Mom.' Like my mom used to make."

"Of course," Piper agreed. "That's what I call my mom. Bot-Bot. It's from when I was a baby." Of course, *mom* and *Bot-Bot* sounded nothing at all alike. But it was the best Piper could do. "I have no idea why."

Diane shrugged at the explanation. "Alice and Pete will never admit it. But they're feeling stressed about the business."

Piper's heart thumped at the word *stressed*. *Aha*, she thought. *If Alice and Pete are stressed about customers, then Olivia must be, too.* That was the problem.

I've identified the wish! she thought. She didn't feel any energy, but she knew not all Starlings did. Well, hopefully she had identified it. Piper knew not to count her stars just yet. Fifty percent of wishes were misidentified, after all.

Still, Olivia's wish seemed clear enough: she wanted the diner to have more customers! If the diner did more business, Olivia would feel better and her bad dreams would end.

"Waitress!" someone called out to Piper, interrupting her thoughts. Piper had seen Diane flinch when a customer called her "waitress," though most knew her by name. Greenfield was a small town, after all. But being called "waitress" made Piper feel proud. She looked out the diner window to see a dad lifting his son out of the backseat of a car. He slammed the door shut and the two walked into the diner. The boy didn't look happy. His face was streaked with dirt, and tears had left clean little trails down to his chin.

Before Piper could say a word, the boy started to wail. "Where Harvey?" he cried. "Where Harvey?"

"I'm sorry," said the man. "Harvey is my son's—"

"Best friend?" Piper suggested.

"No, his bunny," he explained.

"I'm sorry, sir," Piper said to the father. Her heart went out to the little boy, but she was proud to know that a bunny was a Wishworld animal with long floppy ears. "We don't allow pets in the diner."

"No, no," the father said. "Harvey is his stuffed animal." He turned to his son. "It's okay, Sammy. We'll find that lost bunny. I promise. But right now, we're going to order you a special treat."

But Sammy didn't want ice cream, pie, rice pudding, or Jell-O. He just wanted Harvey back. Piper's own mind flashed back to the day before and how a special treat seemed to cheer up Olivia—if only momentarily. "I know just the thing," she said.

She disappeared behind the counter. Then she set to work making two chocolate egg creams. "Chocolate syrup," she told herself, "milk, and seltzer. No eggs. No cream."

"Are you making egg creams?" Alice asked, moving closer. "We don't sell them; they're not even on the menu. Why would a customer even order it?"

Piper flushed, hoping she hadn't made a mistake. "They didn't," she said. "I just made it for them. Is that okay?"

Alice thought a moment. "Yes, I guess it is. It's already made, anyway. So just go ahead and serve it. I'll figure out how much to charge."

"Thanks!" said Piper, relieved she wouldn't have to disappoint the father. His son had settled down a bit and was just sniffling. But anything could set him off again.

A starsec later, she placed two tall glasses on their table. "Here!"

Sammy slurped through his straw while his father watched. "Yummy!" the boy said, grinning ear to ear.

Then the dad sipped his own egg cream and smiled. "It *is* good!" he exclaimed. "What do you call this?"

"It's a chocolate egg cream," Piper told him. "And you can't get it at any fast food restaurant." Piper tapped her elbows three times for luck. At least she hoped you couldn't get it at any fast food restaurant. What about places in that small town called New York City?

"Well, that's for sure," Alice said from across the room, and Piper felt better.

"Sweet," said the dad, who took out his phone and, oddly enough to Piper, took a photo of the egg cream.

"Hey, Alice!" a customer at the counter called out. "Can I get one of those egg dreams?"

"Egg creams," Alice corrected. "And yes!"

"Me too," someone else shouted "They look really good!"

Just then a wail echoed through the diner. "My bunny," Sammy cried again. The egg cream finished, he'd remembered his lost stuffed animal.

All of a sudden, a picture appeared in Piper's mind: a raggedy stuffed bunny on a Wishling car floor. Every once in a while she'd get a hunch or instinct—she didn't know what to call it. But she'd learned to trust it.

She peered through the diner window, into the car they had exited. She looked through the car doors. Like magic, the metal melted away to reveal the floor, covered by books, toys, and a blanket. And underneath the blanket, Piper could see the missing bunny. "Hey," she said, as casually as she could. "Did you check the backseat?"

The dad sighed. "I already looked."

Then he sniffed the air and got a wistful look on his face. "Mmm," he said. "Apple cobbler. Just like my aunt Kitty used to make." He smiled. "I'll go check again right now." He hurried outside with Sammy. Starmins later they were back, Sammy clutching his precious bunny tightly.

"Thank you, thank you," his father said to Piper. "I

don't know how you knew where to look. You're a life-saver." Sammy hugged her, which made Piper glow for a split starsec, too quick for anyone to notice. Then the dad left an extra-big tip.

It had taken a while for Piper to figure out the tip business. First of all, there was no physical money on Starland so the bills and coins themselves were odd to her. And it seemed strange that Wishlings would just leave money lying on tables. But when she realized it was like a thank-you present to the waitstaff, she'd slipped all her tips into the tip jar when Alice wasn't looking.

She didn't think she'd contributed enough to turn business around. But maybe it was a start.

The rest of the day passed uneventfully. Olivia came by after school, with the same friends dropping her off outside. The four held another whispered conference before she went inside.

That night, Piper was exhausted. All she wanted to do was sleep. But even in the dark, she could tell Olivia's eyes were wide open and staring at the ceiling. The girl was afraid to fall asleep.

"Do you think you can talk me through that relaxation technique again?" Olivia asked almost shyly.

"I could," Piper agreed, "but there's another approach we can try, too." *And maybe this one will work better*, she added to herself. "Close your eyes, and imagine you're at the ocean." She stopped. "Wait a minute," she said to Olivia. "Do you even like the beach?"

"Love it," Olivia murmured.

"Okay, so you're standing on warm, smooth sand, looking out over the water. A light breeze ruffles your hair."

Piper thought she saw Olivia's hair lift slightly from her pillow.

"It's perfect," Piper went on, "except that you're holding a heavy backpack you can't put down, because you're afraid the tide will wash it away."

Olivia's shoulders hunched.

"Now each time a wave rolls onto the sand, one item disappears from your backpack. After it leaves, you feel stronger, less worried. Here comes the first wave . . . in . . . and . . . out."

Olivia's shoulders rose the slightest bit.

"And another wave . . . in . . . and . . . out, coming a little closer to your feet."

Each wave seemed to make Olivia's load lighter. Each wave came a little closer. Finally, Piper told Olivia she was carrying nothing at all, and the water lapped at her feet, cleansing and purifying her mind.

Olivia sighed happily. "Thank you, Piper."

"You're welcome, Olivia. But I'll tell you something else that can make you feel better."

Olivia shifted to face her, still interested. "What?"

"Opening up to others." Piper held up a hand before Olivia could protest. "Opening up to people you trust can be a powerful force." She felt sure that was one reason Olivia had bad dreams: she was holding all her worries inside, not telling a soul. And they were finding their way into her dreams.

"There is strength in vulnerability," Piper went on, "and communicating emotions. It gives me so much energy I glow. . . . I mean, I feel like I'm glowing. It would make you feel energized and strong."

Piper waited patiently. She knew Olivia was mulling this over. And maybe, just maybe, she'd confide in Piper. She'd talk about her concerns about the diner. Then they could come up with a solution together.

When Olivia stayed quiet, Piper decided to change direction a bit. Maybe Olivia wanted to talk about the nightmares first.

"And you know what else? Dreams are amazing windows into feelings," she began. "They seem so real, because the emotions that drive them are real."

"And the feelings are intense!" Olivia put in. "They're even stronger than when I'm awake, because—"

"Your dream is so much more intense!"

"That's it exactly!" Olivia said. "I mean, I can dream I'm in school, but the next moment I'm climbing Mount Everest. In real life, when I'm in school, I'm in school, and I can't blink and find myself anywhere else."

Piper thought a moment. With enough wish energy manipulation practice, she could probably teleport from Halo Hall to the Crystal Mountains in the middle of Astral Accounting class. But it didn't seem right to mention it to Olivia. Besides, she understood exactly what Olivia meant.

"Dreams make the impossible possible," she said. "So they can be amazing and crazy and scary and wonderful all at the same time. Believe me, I know how powerful dreams can be. But you're going to wake up. They can never really hurt you. In fact, they may be able to help you. They have meaning and can guide you."

"Grandma Rosie used to say something like that, that dreams are the windows to the soul."

"She did?" Piper said, delighted. "I really wish I knew her."

A tear slid down Olivia's cheek. "I really miss her. My parents are great and everything, obviously. But they work crazy hours and in their downtime they have so many things to take care of, like taking me to the doctor, buying me shoes, helping me with my homework. . . ."

This didn't seem to have much to do with diner business. Still, Piper thought it could lead to a revelation. So she nodded, interested.

"My grandma and I would just talk and talk, especially once Isabel left for college and I was on my own so much. I could tell her anything. Good, bad, it didn't matter. She always understood." Olivia lowered her voice. "If she were here right now, I'd talk to her. I'd tell her—" She paused. Piper knew she was about to say something important, something revealing—something that would confirm Olivia's wish.

But for some reason, Piper had to finish Olivia's sentence: "'That you're flailing around, worried about everything, trying to get through the nights when everything around you seems so dark and unforgiving.'"

Piper felt Olivia stiffen. And even in the darkness, she could see her face draw closed.

"I'm going to sleep now, Piper. Good night."

Piper groaned softly. She wished she hadn't been quite so gloomy and bleak. But sometimes she just couldn't help it.

CHAPTER
9

By the time Piper woke up, the sun was high in the sky. Olivia's bed was neatly made, the blanket stretched tight and tucked into the corners.

Piper wiggled her toes, then raised her arms over her head for an easy stretch. The clock on the nightstand read 11:19, late even by her standards. She heard some thumps and bumps and light steps coming down the hall.

That must be Olivia, she thought. *Good, I'm not alone.*

She hoped Olivia had been able to sleep late, too. It was Saturday. And as far as she knew, her Wisher hadn't needed to be anywhere early. Of course, there was the not-so-small matter of the Countdown Clock and starmins ticking away. The wish had to be granted by that evening. Still, Piper felt confident.

A nagging doubt tugged at the far corner of her mind. . . . Those feelings Olivia was about to talk about when Piper interrupted . . . they could have been important. Maybe they wouldn't have confirmed the wish. Maybe they would have pointed in an entirely different direction. But Piper shook away those negative thoughts. She had nailed down Olivia's wish: improving business. And they had all day at the diner to make it happen.

Moving a little more quickly than usual, Piper dressed with the help of her Wishworld Outfit Selector. She settled on stretchy black leggings and a shimmery seafoam green blouse that fell to her hips. Not her usual look, but it was both pretty and comfortable.

"Oh, good. You're ready," Olivia said, walking into the room just as Piper was letting the air out of the blow-up bed. "I told my parents we'd be at the diner around lunchtime to help."

Olivia was quiet as they walked to work. But it was a companionable silence. Piper was pleased. Clearly, Olivia had gotten past the previous night's irritation.

As they neared Big Rosie's, the two girls gasped.

"Oh, my stars!" Piper said. A line of customers stretched out the door. "What's going on?"

"I have no idea," Olivia answered. "Let's find out."

She led Piper to the entrance, skirting people she

knew. "Excuse us, Mr. Raymond. Hi, Thomas. Could you let us past?"

Inside, they saw some people waiting for tables, but many more were by the takeout counter.

"Two chocolate egg creams to go, and throw in a blueberry muffin," one woman said to Donna, the waitress who had called in sick the other day.

"Egg creams!" Olivia repeated. "How does she know about egg creams?"

Just then a customer sitting at a table flagged down Diane. "We'd like egg creams, too," he said.

"This is beyond weird," Olivia said as the next customer in line ordered an egg cream with a bagel.

Alice hurried to the girls. "Everyone wants egg creams!" she said excitedly. "Some are just ordering them at the counter. But lots are staying for full meals."

She put her hand on Piper's shoulder. "We're doing incredible business. Just look at all these people. Apparently one of our customers tweeted about our amazing egg creams with a photo."

"It must have been Sammy's dad," said Piper.

"It's all thanks to you," Alice told her.

"No, it wasn't me. It was really Olivia. She made it for me the other day, remember? Then I just suggested it to a customer." Piper gazed around the diner. Practically everybody had an egg cream. "It's really caught on."

"You know, I think we'll add it to the menu," Alice said. "In fact, we should come up with other new drinks. And maybe desserts." She smiled. "First on the list is that rhubarb pie I keep thinking about!"

"Yeah, but we don't have to stop there," Olivia said. "We can add dinner entrees and appetizers and—"

"The sky's the limit!" Piper broke in.

"Now hurry up and grab some aprons," Alice said. "Things will move more quickly with you two here."

"This is so amazing!" Olivia told Piper as they rushed to the back room. "All this business is really going to help my parents out."

Piper looked at Olivia. Her shoulders were relaxed and the furrow between her eyebrows was gone. This was it. She'd helped Olivia get her wish. She stood still, waiting for the wish energy to flow.

"What?" said Olivia. "Come on! Get moving! We have work to do!"

Still, Piper just stood there, staring at Olivia. Any starsec now a colorful wave would stream from her Wisher straight to her bracelet pendants.

Where were the sparks she had heard about? The rainbow of lights and flashes shooting out from Olivia to Piper? Piper was confused. But maybe the wish wasn't entirely granted yet. Maybe the energy would come later, when they waited on their fiftieth customer or reached a certain dollar amount.

"Okay, let's get cracking!" said Piper. This would be her very last shift. She wanted to make it a good—no, great!—one.

Hours passed in a blur. Customers kept coming and Piper kept working. But still no wish energy. Her shoulders sagged. What was the problem?

"Something wrong?" asked Olivia, stepping around her with a tray full of chocolate egg creams.

"Olivia," Piper said slowly. "Do you think business is booming? That you guys have enough customers now?"

"Of course!" Olivia said happily. "We've never been so busy!"

"So you're not thinking to yourself, 'Oh, it would be great if we reached nine hundred ninety-nine customers. Or if we made a million dollars'?" Piper wasn't actually sure if a million was a lot of dollars, but it sounded good.

"Uh, no. I think this is perfect!"

Olivia was thrilled with the business now. So, clearly, that hadn't been her wish at all.

Piper stared at Olivia despairingly. What could her wish be? She had wasted all that time on the wrong wish! Now she was running out of time. Wish identification was much more difficult than Piper had ever dreamed.

The crowd was thinning out. Piper began wiping down tables. Then the bell above the door jangled. She looked up to see Olivia's friends walking into the diner. When Piper stepped behind the counter, she could see straight to the door. Olivia's friends were just walking through.

Olivia walked in carrying a tray of ketchup dispensers she had just filled. When she spotted her friends, a shadow passed over Olivia's face. Oh, no, another blunder. Piper must have hurt Olivia's feelings, saying the girls were there for the food, not their friend. "No! I bet they're here just for you!"

Olivia watched as the girls took a table at the far end, her mouth tugging down at the corners. "I'll wait on them," she said, grabbing some menus. Seconds later, she stood at their table, whispering. Then she actually sat down next to the short girl, the one named Morgan. Piper had never seen her do that before!

"Olivia!" her dad called loudly. "Your sixteen with SPF and MG is ready."

Part of Piper couldn't help identifying what that meant—cheeseburger with sweet potato fries and mixed greens—even while she was concentrating on Olivia.

Reluctantly, Olivia got up, then walked slowly away from her friends.

Friends! The word hit Piper like a bolt of white-hot lightning.

Friendship must be as important to Olivia as the diner, maybe even more. Piper remembered her first wish identification guess, that Olivia was spending too much time at the diner. Maybe she'd been half right. Olivia loved working at the diner. But it still got in the way of her being with her friends.

Okay, Piper was sure she had it right this time: Olivia wished she could spend more time with her friends.

Without waiting another starmin, Piper grabbed a bag of candy, then refilled the FREE MINTS bowl by the cash register. "You know," she said to Alice, looking deep into her eyes, "Olivia should have the night off, and have those friends"—she pointed to the table—"plus me, over for a sleepover."

"You know," Alice said thoughtfully, "I think Olivia should have the night off, and have those friends—plus you—over for a sleepover. Diane can stay late."

"I'll tell Olivia!" Piper said. She grabbed the girl's hand and pulled her back to the table. "Hey!" she said to the girls. Morgan, the short one who Piper thought might be bossy, looked up. The girl sitting next to her was Ruby. She nodded hello, her shoulder-length hair bouncing. The third girl was Chase and she had bright green braces that showed when she smiled at Piper. "Alice said we can all have a slumber party at Olivia's tonight."

"And who are you?" asked Morgan, sounding just shy of rude.

"This is Piper," said Olivia. "I told you, she's been staying with us while she works on a school project."

Everyone seemed to wait for Morgan to respond. Finally, she shrugged, saying, "Sure, sounds like fun."

"It will be!" Piper assured her. "We can have a dream slumber party! We'll decorate notebooks with glitter or stickers or any way we like to make dream journals! Then in the morning we can write down our dreams. Any dreams," she hastened to add. "From the night before or the week before, good or bad."

Piper plowed on, not waiting for a reaction. "Maybe I can help you guys figure out what your dreams mean." She looked down modestly. "I have a knack for dream interpretation."

Again, everyone waited for Morgan, Piper with bated breath. She had to like the idea. It was nothing short of brilliant, if Piper did say so herself. The sleepover activity could help grant Olivia's wish *and* serve as a healing session, to clear Olivia's mind of any disturbing thoughts. All at the same time!

Morgan tilted her head, thinking it over. "That's cool," she finally said.

Immediately, the two other girls agreed, and the three began chattering about what to bring.

"No!" Olivia interrupted them, her voice rising above the others. Everyone stopped talking and looked at her, surprised. "I mean, it sounds great. Really. But we can't do it. I have to—"

"Work tonight? Don't worry!" Piper said gleefully. "I already spoke to your mom. She's totally fine with it. Diane's going to fill in."

Morgan, Ruby, and Chase started talking again and took out their cell phones to ask permission. Meanwhile, Piper gazed anxiously at Olivia. She had thought Olivia would be thrilled her friends were coming over. Instead, she didn't seem any happier than she had earlier. In fact, her expression was downright glum.

Olivia edged away from her friends to talk to Diane. "I'm sorry you have to take my shift," she told her.

Oh, so that was it. Olivia felt bad that Diane was working extra hours. That was why she wasn't excited— yet. Piper felt sure that once the girls actually came to her house, everything would change.

According to the Countdown Clock, the wish had to be granted that evening, by eight o'clock. Piper's pulse quickened. She'd have to return to Starland—with or without Olivia's wish energy. Already she could feel her own energy level sinking. She'd been there so long and accomplished so little. . . .

Piper shook her head to clear it and envisioned a smiling Olivia radiating a rainbow of colored light. It could happen. It *would* happen. If only Piper didn't feel so tired . . .

"Table number two is wobbly," Diane said, hurrying past. "Do you think you could fix it?"

"Of course," said Piper, straightening up. She was putting a piece of cardboard under one table leg to keep it steady when the bells above the door jingled, signaling another customer. Piper felt a tingle run down her spine. She froze, her head still under the table. Something was about to change. She heard a familiar voice: "Oh, so this is a diner."

It was Astra! In her haste to actually see a fellow Star Darling, Piper stood up without thinking. "Ouch!" she said, banging her head.

Piper sighed. This wouldn't do at all. She had to center herself, concentrate on unhurried action and calm movement.

She took a breath and came out from under the table in one fluid motion. "Astra!" she called, beaming happily as she saw her friend in her glittery glory. She knew that she looked sparkly to Astra, too, and that made her feel good. She felt so glad to see someone who knew all about her, even if it meant Lady Stella thought she needed help. And while Piper thought she had matters well in hand, another Star Darling could only be helpful.

Astra was wearing a sporty outfit, cutoffs, red sneakers, and a T-shirt with a red star on it. Her hair, now a flaming auburn, was pulled into two pigtails. She looked friendly and confident, a girl any Wishling would want as a friend.

Alice stood by the cash register, smiling at the girls. "Hi . . . Astra?" she said questioningly. Piper nodded. "Are you a friend of Piper's?"

"Yes," said Astra. "We go to the same school." She was looking around, soaking in all the sights and sounds and smells. It was a little mind-blowing when you first got there, Piper knew. So much was similar to Starland, but so much was different. "Your world is amazing," she told Alice.

Luckily, Alice said, "Yes, the diner is my world, along with my family, of course. You must be from Maylefield, too."

"Maylefield," repeated Astra, sounding as if she'd never heard of it before, which, of course, she hadn't.

"Yup," said Piper, linking her arm through Astra's. "She just came for a visit."

Astra nodded, finally realizing she had to be more careful. "Let me fill you in on what's been going on in . . . uh . . . Maylefield, Piper."

She pulled Piper aside, adding, "Star apologies for being a little dense. There's just so much to take in." She turned toward the cash register, fascinated when the cash drawer sprung open.

"Is everything okay at home?" Piper asked as they found two empty seats at the counter.

"Things haven't gotten any better," Astra told her. "There've been more power flickers. I'm not sure anyone outside Starling Academy has been paying attention, though. But, Piper, you must know why I'm here. Lady Stella thought you could use some help."

"I do know." Piper was actually quite glad Astra was there. Her presence gave Piper a personal energy lift. "Let me introduce you to Olivia, my Wisher."

Of course Astra made a good impression; she even made Olivia smile when she asked about her favorite item at the diner.

"Well, you won't find it on the menu yet, but it's the chocolate egg cream."

While Olivia performed her magic roll-ups, Piper

made Astra an egg cream and quickly filled her in on Olivia, the diner, and the sleepover.

Astra listened, picking up a nearby saltshaker. "What is this thing?" she asked.

"Wishlings use it to season their food," said Piper. "Dishes don't come out perfectly like the food at home."

Astra sipped her egg cream. "Starmazing!" she proclaimed. "And totally worth the trip."

Just then the customer sitting next to Astra picked up the saltshaker and shook it over her French fries. The shaker top fell off, and all the salt rained down on her food.

"Oh, no!" she gasped.

Piper took the plate from the customer. "I'll just get you another serving," she said. "On the house."

While Piper was getting more fries, she stopped to talk to Alice and get Astra invited to the sleepover, too. When she returned, Astra was spinning on the stool.

"You are officially invited to Olivia's sleepover," she told her. "To watch me collect my wish energy!"

"I can't wait," said Astra. "But do you really think it's going to be that easy? I mean, why am I here?"

Piper shook her head. "It's all under control, Astra," she said.

CHAPTER
18

Olivia still wasn't excited about the sleepover, but Alice certainly was. For the first time in a long while, she left the diner early. "Just to get a few things for the party," she told the girls.

By the time Piper, Astra, and Olivia got to the house, it was filled with slumber party supplies. "It's not every day we host a party at home," Alice told Olivia. "I want to make it special for you."

Olivia scanned the food, crafts, balloons, and decorations. "This is all for tonight?" she asked. "Or are we starting a party business?"

"No business tonight," Alice said. "You've been working too hard—at the diner and at school. And you just did so well on that history test. I'm proud of you, honey. Consider this a reward."

Olivia flushed. "I'm going to change," she said, hurrying out of the room.

Alice frowned. "I just want to make this a fun night," she said. "I want Olivia to have a good time." She sighed, looking down at a stack of plain white pillowcases, ready to be decorated with fabric markers. "And I might have gone a little overboard."

Piper glanced around the room. She was glad to see that Alice remembered the dream journals, too.

"Piper and I can set all this up," Astra offered.

"Thanks," said Alice. "That will give me time to make dinner and dessert."

Alice left for the kitchen, and Piper and Astra sorted through the stuff.

The two agreed that play stations, kind of like work-stations at the diner, would be fun. So they pushed tables here and there, made signs, and artfully arranged the supplies.

When Olivia returned, she looked no more enthu-siastic than she had earlier. Piper gazed at her anxiously as Olivia took stock of the living room. There was a mani/pedi station and a decorate-your-own-pillowcase table next to a spot with mason jars and glow-in-the-dark paint. When they were done painting the jars, they'd look like colorful lanterns. All perfect for a slumber party, Piper thought.

"We're not done decorating yet," she told Olivia. "Let's make glitter balloons to hang around the room."

The three girls blew up balloons and dipped them in glue, followed by glitter.

"They look like sparkly disco balls," Olivia said, looking pleased. Standing on chairs, the girls hung them upside down from the ceiling.

Inspired, Olivia ran to the attic and returned with twinkle lights. Working together, the girls strung them from room to room.

Olivia's spirits seemed to be rising. Piper took this as a good sign that she had identified the right wish. But she wanted to make sure. "Isn't this great, that you get to spend so much time with friends? Like a wish come true?"

Olivia shrugged, twisting a lightbulb so it turned on. The light cast a rosy glow over her face. "Yeah, it's okay they're coming over. It'll be nice. But a wish come true? I wouldn't go quite that far."

Piper felt a sinking feeling in her stomach, as if she'd taken an express ride in the Flash Vertical Mover. She slid over to whisper the news to Astra: she had the wrong wish again! And the girls exchanged worried glances just as the doorbell rang.

Piper stole a glance at the Countdown Clock. Three hours and fourteen minutes remaining! Could she figure it out in time? Morgan, Ruby, and Chase tumbled in all at once, laughing and talking, oohing and aahing over the decorations and party ideas. Piper moved to the music station and picked out music to play. With Astra's help, she figured out how to work the device. Soon a soothing instrumental piece filled the room.

Piper snuck away to a mirror in the front hall and chanted her Mirror Mantra one more time. "You can do it, Piper," she said to her reflection. And somehow, it boosted her mood.

Smiling, she rejoined the group.

The evening was filled with activities. They had breakfast for dinner, with the girls throwing their own veggies and fillings into an omelet pan while Alice flipped the eggs. They played Truth or Dare, a game in which they had to answer an embarrassing question or take on a dare. Piper laughed when Astra wound up standing outside with a sign reading HONK IF YOU THINK I'M CUTE. She stopped laughing when she saw Astra tape the sign to the back of the shirt Morgan was planning to wear the next day. Chances were Morgan would see it before she wore it outside. But to be on the safe side, Piper tore it off.

Then Morgan suggested they give each other mani/pedis. She actually looked to Piper for confirmation, and Piper nodded, pleased.

Piper picked up a bottle of nail polish. It was a deeper green than the seafoam color she was wearing, and she thought she'd give it a try.

She glanced around for a nail polish remover machine, then realized the other girls were removing their old polish with liquid from a bottle. She, too, soaked a ball of fluff in the harsh liquid and rubbed her nails. Astra joined her. "It's cold," said Piper.

"It's not coming off," Astra said.

"It is really sticking," Piper agreed. "We'll just have to scrub harder."

The girls rubbed furiously. Finally, the color lightened a bit. "Keep at it," Piper urged. By the time the polish had come off completely, Piper's wrists ached from the effort. But it was worth it once she had the new polish on. The new green color looked lovely. She felt a bit lighter, too; with just a little more energy than before, she was ready for the next part of the plan. Would it help make the wish come true? Only time would tell.

She had the girls put on pajamas, then set up their

sleeping bags in the center of Olivia's room. They were spread in a star shape, with their heads in the center, just like the Star Darlings had been at Libby's.

They all looked at Piper expectantly. "Let's do some happy daydreaming," she said. Maybe it would lead to Olivia's revealing the real wish.

"What's that?" asked Morgan.

"You just close your eyes and picture a place in your mind—a place that makes you happier than any other. It can be somewhere you'd like to go or a place you'd like to visit, real or not. It could be your room, just like it is, or made entirely of candy." She searched her brain for Wishling examples. "Marshmallow pillows, fruit strips for blankets, candy bar chairs . . ."

"My happy place is on the playing field," said Astra.

"Really?" Morgan humphed.

"Come on," Piper gently admonished. "There is no wrong place to set a happy daydream. Astra's may be different from yours, but the point is to open yourself to positive feelings. It's very personal." She thought a moment. "My happy place is a sparkling stream, a place I can do the back float, with stars twinkling above."

"I like to swim, too," Ruby said. "But my happy place is the ocean, where I can dive down deep to meet dolphins and ride on their backs and"—she stood with a little pirouette—"maybe perform water ballet with them, too."

"My happy place is my grandma's kitchen," Olivia said quietly. "With the smell of freshly baked cookies and my grandma about to pour a big cold glass of milk for me. All the smells are mixing together: the cookies, the flowers she always kept in a blue vase, her perfume . . ." Her voice trailed off as she closed her eyes and smiled dreamily.

Piper closed her eyes, too. "Isn't that wonderful? And you can go to these places anytime you want. You just have to picture it and feel the joy."

Piper felt more relaxed than she had all day, and she sensed the girls felt the same. Now was the time to uncover Olivia's real wish.

"You know," Piper continued, "happy daydreaming can carry over into your nighttime dreams. They can help make them sweet and pleasant. But even bad dreams have their place."

"I don't like bad dreams," Olivia said, shaking her head. "And I don't see why anyone would."

"Well, bad dreams have meaning. And they're not necessarily literal. If you're dreaming you're stuck in a glion's—I mean, lion's—cage, of course you aren't really there. But you can discover something from the dream, like maybe you're afraid of your neighbor's pet."

"Tell us one of your nightmares," Morgan suggested.

"Okay." Piper thought a moment. "Once I dreamed I was on a Flash Vertical . . . I mean, elevator . . . and I kept going up and up and up, which was fine. I wanted to get to the top floor. But each time I looked, the floor numbers changed—they kept going higher, and so I had to go higher and higher, too, or I would never get off. It was scary, sure. But I realized what it meant: I was waiting to hear if I got accepted to the school where Astra and I go, and if I didn't get in—reach the top—I'd be stuck forever. Or at least that's how I felt. It made me realize how important school was to me."

At the word *school*, Piper noticed Olivia sneaking a furtive look at her desk. Maybe it meant something; maybe it didn't. But Piper decided to use her special sunray vision talent to look inside.

All she saw were pencils, old gum wrapped in tissues, and a crumpled-up paper. It looked like a test, with questions and answers and, in the corner, a grade: A. *That must be a terrible grade*, she thought, *for Olivia to crumple it up like that.*

But then she remembered the customer talking about Isabel's As and how great they were. So A was good. Why did Olivia have a problem with that?

"I understand what you mean, Piper," Olivia was saying softly. "I have this same dream again and again where I'm chewing gum or eating candy, and at first it's great. But then the gum—or whatever—keeps getting bigger and bigger and fills my whole mouth. I want to scream or shout for help, but I can't talk, and I can't tell anyone what's wrong. I feel like I can't breathe, and then I wake up shaking."

Again, she stole a look at the drawer.

"It probably doesn't sound so awful. I mean, I'm eating candy! But it is. When I wake up, I have this sickeningly sweet taste in my—"

"Mouth," said Piper. She swallowed in sympathy. She could almost taste it, too, a cloying sugary sensation clogging up her throat. "When did you start having this dream?" she asked gently. Olivia was finally opening up. And if they could figure out more about the dream, it might just reveal the wish.

"Two weeks ago. I remember it was a Thursday night, because I was so rattled I forgot to wear sneakers to school the next morning. And that's when we have gym."

"That was just after we saw Another World," Morgan added.

"You traveled to another world?" Astra asked unbelievingly. She shot a look at Piper to say, *And we thought Wishlings were so primitive!*

"I know, it's unbelievable! But we didn't have to go far. They were playing in the next town over."

Ruby sighed. "That band is the best thing I've ever seen."

"Oh," Piper couldn't help saying. Another World was a group, and the girls had gone to their concert.

"I was exhausted at school the next day," Ruby went on. "And we had that test!"

"But it all worked out," Morgan said.

Piper thought hard. Olivia kept having nightmares in which she couldn't talk. And she'd stayed out late the night before that history test. That had to be connected to her wish.

She reached over and pulled open the desk drawer. "Don't!" Olivia cried. But before she could stop her, Piper took out the test. " 'Great job, Olivia,' " she read from the top. "Has this test been on your mind?" she asked.

Olivia sighed and slowly nodded. "Yes, we had this big history test scheduled for the day after the concert.

I never told my parents about it. They wouldn't have let me go if they knew."

"And we didn't have time to study," Chase added.

The four girls looked at each other in silence. They seemed miserable. Finally, Morgan nodded. "We didn't know what to do," Olivia started. "We knew we'd fail the test and we were scared. So we wrote up cheat sheets the day before," she said slowly. "And we all got As."

Olivia looked down. "I hate to disappoint my parents about grades. They expect me to do as well as Isabel! Still, I wish I hadn't cheated. It feels—"

"Awful," said Piper, nodding.

The wish! Her heartbeat quickened. But she couldn't grant that wish. She couldn't go back in time. But that dream where Olivia couldn't speak . . .

"I bet you'd feel better if you told your mother the truth," she said to Olivia.

"I wish I could!" Olivia said quickly. "But I'd get everyone else in trouble, too. And these guys don't want to get in trouble!" She shrugged. "So it's done."

So that was what the four had been whispering about, and why Olivia wasn't thrilled to be spending time with them now.

"You know, it must be bothering me, too," said Ruby.

"I've been having weird dreams about Ms. Stadler following me home from school."

"Me three," said Chase. "I had a nightmare that I had to go to a special summer school for cheaters."

The girls turned to Morgan. Piper knew she was the one holding the others back. "Just imagine how much better you'd all feel after talking about this," Piper said. "You'd be able to connect to your happy daydreams without a pesky nightmare getting in the way."

Morgan jumped up. "Okay! I'm sorry I've been such an idiot about the whole thing. I was just scared. Let's tell the whole world we cheated!"

"Well, I don't know if you have to do that." Piper grinned. "Olivia, why don't we start with your mom?"

Morgan, Chase, and Ruby followed Olivia to the kitchen. "Mom," Olivia said, "I have something to tell you."

Piper stood around the corner. She held out her wrist just as the wish energy whipped around the wall, straight into her pendant. And just in time, too. She and Astra grinned at each other.

Astra and Piper decided they'd leave in the morning. Exhausted, the girls all climbed back into their sleeping bags.

Alice had been disappointed, but proud of the girls for telling the truth. Piper could feel the relief coming from Olivia. She squeezed Piper's hand. "Thank you for helping me tell the truth," she said. Piper squeezed back.

The next morning, Piper was the last to wake up—again. She found the girls and Astra eating waffles in the kitchen. Morgan, Chase, and Ruby decided they would tell their parents later that day and they would go to their teacher together on Monday morning.

Piper was pleased to note that everyone looked well rested. "I slept like a baby," Olivia said delightedly.

It was almost time to leave. But Piper wanted to do one more sleepover activity. "Let's write in our dream journals!" she told the girls.

As the Wishlings bent their heads over their notebooks, recording their dreams, Piper and Astra smiled and nodded at each other.

A little while later, Morgan glanced at her phone and slammed her book shut. "My mom is picking us up in ten minutes," she announced.

"Astra and I have to leave, too," Piper told Olivia. "I've certainly been here long enough!"

Olivia grinned. "It's been great, Piper. And you can visit anytime. My mom said you could even work at the diner over the summer!"

The girls gathered their things and headed outside. Piper took a long last look at Olivia, who was chatting happily to her friends. It would have been fun to hang out with Olivia and work at the diner. But she had another job to finish.

"Well, good-bye, Olivia," she said, feeling her eyes fill with tears.

"Don't look so sad," said Olivia. "We'll see each other soon."

She hugged Piper close, and when she pulled away, she looked at her blankly. The hug had erased all memories of the Star Darlings.

"Oh, hi!" said Piper. "Can you give my friend and me directions to the train station? I have to catch the next train home."

"Sure," said Olivia, pointing. "Walk two blocks, then turn left." Just then a minivan pulled up to the curb, and Olivia disappeared into a happy huddle with her friends.

"Are you ready to head home?" Astra asked Piper as they walked away. "We need to find an out-of-the-way place to unfold our stars and shoot back home."

Piper nodded. She was ready.

Epilogue

It was a smooth ride home from Wishworld, much easier than the trip there. Piper somehow landed on the shore of Luminous Lake, where she took a few moments to close her eyes, relive her journey, and put herself back in the Starland mind-set.

Just as Piper opened her eyes, her Star-Zap flashed. "I landed right behind the dorms," Astra holo-texted. "So everyone knows about your mission already. Come to Lady Stella's office right now for a meeting."

Even though she'd hurried about the diner, Piper still didn't like to rush. But she did put a little energy into moving quickly. She had successfully completed her mission, after all. And the ceremony was special. She couldn't wait to see if her Wish Blossom had a gemstone inside.

Everyone was already at the office when Piper got there. When she walked in, the Star Darlings stood and clapped.

"Congratulations!" Vega cried. "You did great. And here you are, not even late!"

Clover quickly stepped up, giving Piper a hug. Then she went from Starling to Starling, hugging each one, including Scarlet, who couldn't pull away fast enough.

Still, Scarlet smiled, skipping over to Piper to offer her own congratulations.

Libby said nothing. As soon as she'd sat down, she'd fallen asleep.

Lady Stella entered the room. "Welcome back, Piper," she said. "You did a startastic job!"

Piper smiled broadly and shimmered with pride.

"Now you should all take a seat," the headmistress continued.

Gemma lifted a chair. "Um . . . where should I take it?"

Piper suddenly felt very tired. There was a weird tension in the air that left her feeling uneasy. She looked over at Astra, who had a puzzled expression on her face.

Then Lady Stella stepped forward, Piper's Wish Blossom cupped in her hands. As Piper reached to accept it, it began to glow brighter and brighter. Piper gasped as it started to transform. "Why, it's a sleepibelle!" Piper whispered, delighted. She loved the way its hanging petals swung in a soothing motion, back and forth like a pendulum. It's soothing glow warmed her right to her toes. Then, one by one, its drooping petals rose and unfurled. And there was her Power Crystal. "Dreamalite," Lady Stella declared.

Gingerly, Piper picked up the stone, sparkling green with hidden depths. Holding it felt right. It touched Piper's very essence. This was a stone she would never, ever lose.

Lady Stella nodded seriously, then continued. "I know it's been an unsettling few days here."

Sage giggled.

"So it's extra nice to have Piper—and Astra—back safely from a mission well done."

Once again, the Star Darlings applauded.

As Sage tried to pull Libby to her feet and everyone started to leave, Astra edged closer to Piper. "Is it me," she asked, "or is something different?"

"It's not you," Piper said. "I think so, too. Maybe it took us going away to see it."

Something was not quite right. But what in the stars was it?

Astra's Mixed-Up Mission

Prologue

STAR MEMORANDUM, Astra typed on her holo-keyboard.

TO: Cassie and Piper, was the next line.

Then: *FROM: Astra*

She paused for a moment as she considered the subject line. She needed to get Cassie's attention. The question was, how?

Something strange was going on at Starling Academy. Astra was almost sure of it, and Piper was pretty convinced, too. They wanted to discuss it with one of the other Star Darlings, but Astra couldn't decide whom to approach. Piper suggested talking to Cassie, mentioning her thoughtfulness and perceptiveness. And Astra was, despite her initial hesitation, learning to trust Piper's instincts. To be completely honest, when she first met Piper, she had found her slow dreaminess annoying and her occasional dark side ridiculous. But now Astra had a new respect for both the hidden messages that dreams could hold and the strength of Piper's intuitive powers.

But even though Cassie had been so concerned about the flowers, she was now completely focused on herself. She spoke about her starmazing mission, about how startacularly it had gone. She continued by praising her own wish energy manipulation skills. She even went on to discuss her eyelashes, calling them "dusky, luxurious, and starmazingly sooty." Astra could barely even see them behind those large star-shaped glasses Cassie wore, so she told her she'd have to take her word for it.

Perhaps she had snorted as she said it? Because Cassie had stormed off. Possibly to go look in a mirror. Or to find someone with a finer appreciation of eyelashes. Who knew?

So Astra decided it might be best to send both Cassie and Piper a holo-message. Something short, direct, and to the point. But what should the subject be? She thought and thought and then smiled as she came up with the perfect idea. Astra's fingers practically flew over the holo-keyboard. So many odd things had happened since the beginning of the starmester!

STAR MEMORANDUM

TO: Cassie and Piper
FROM: Astra
SUBJECT: Top ten weird things that have been going on at Starling Academy

10) MESSED-UP MISSIONS. EVERYONE.
    (Think about it: each and every Star Darling who has been sent down to Wishworld has had great difficulty identifying her Wisher or figuring out the wish.)

9) SCARLET'S OUSTER. (One day she was a Star Darling; the next she was kicked out. Then the Wish Orb picked her to save a mission that was going badly and she was back in the fold again. Startastically strange.)

8) POWER WENT OUT. (We've been taught since we were in Wee Constellation School that we have massive wish energy reserves. How in Starland could the lights have gone out?)

7)   THE RANKER. (Somehow the whole school got invited to try out for Leona's band. The Ranker was brought in to choose the band members and their name, and it chose an all-SD band and the name of our secret group for the band. Coincidence? Perhaps not.)

6)   FIGHTING FLOWERS. (Each of our rooms had a vase of these. We all fought like rats and hogs, or whatever that Wishling expression is. Now that they are gone—thanks, Cassie—we are getting along again. Something to think about.)

5)   PIPER'S FOREBODING DREAMS. (No offense, Piper, but I used to think you were way creepy. Now I know you've got some stellar prediction skills.)

4)   ONE WORD: OPHELIA. (It makes entirely no sense that someone so clueless could have been a real Star Darling. Then you got suspicious of her, Cassie, and she disappeared.)

3)   LEONA'S FAILED MISSION. (She's self-absorbed—star apologies, Cassie—but even I felt bad when she didn't collect wish energy and her Wish Pendant got all burnt-looking. What an embarrassment.)

2) STAR KINDNESS DAY MESSAGES WERE
    THE EXACT OPPOSITE OF WHAT WAS
    INTENDED. (Because I know that neither of
    you think I am a bad sportswoman, or that I
    have slow reflexes. And no, I am not holding
    any grudges.)

1) EVERYONE IS ACTING LIKE A WEIRDO!
    (Star apologies again, Cassie, but it's true. Piper
    and I can't put our finger on exactly what it is,
    but we'll get to the bottom of this soon. . . .)

Astra smiled, read it through one more time, and pressed SEND. To her disbelief, the entire holo-document disappeared into thin air. "*Starf!*" she yelled.

The sparkle shower turned off and her roommate, Clover, stepped into the room. "Are you okay?" she asked Astra. Her eyes lit up. "Do you need a hug?" Not waiting for an answer, Clover headed her way, arms wide.

"See you at breakfast!" Astra called as she expertly dodged away from her roommate's embrace. She picked up her starstick, slid the door open smoothly using energy manipulation, and was gone.

"Piper! Piper!" called Astra, waving urgently at the girl sitting across the cafeteria table from her. Astra's red-and-silver-striped fingernails caught the light and she noticed with dismay that the polish she had applied on Wishworld was already starting to chip. She knew it wouldn't last through Physical Energy class later that afternoon. What a difference from her Starland manicure, which had taken *forever* to remove!

Piper looked up from her dream holo-diary, flipping a lock of hair the color of ocean foam over her shoulder. "Is someone on the way?" she asked.

"I think Tessa is heading over," Astra told her. After striking out with Cassie, they had tried to talk to some of the other Star Darlings and had begun to notice that something seemed off with each and every one of them. But they couldn't figure out exactly what was going on. So they decided they'd study their roommates first and report to each other.

Back in their room, after Clover had hugged Astra tightly for the tenth time, she realized that no one could possibly have missed her that much. So she sent Piper a holo-text:

 Clover is a mad hugger! What about Vega?

After a while she received a holo-text:

 To figure it out took me some time. But Vega only talks in rhyme!

They made plans to study the rest of the Star Darlings the next starday, starting at breakfast. So there they sat, awaiting their arrival.

Piper shut off the dream diary with a swipe of her hand. "Star apologies, Astra," she said. "I just thought I'd skim through some of my latest dream entries to see if I could come up with any clues about what's going on. You know, any themes or symbols that might have deeper meaning."

Just a few stardays earlier, Astra would have scoffed at such a statement. But now she totally got it.

"Find anything?" Astra asked hopefully.

Piper sighed. "Not yet," she said.

They both watched as Tessa, her brilliant green eyes flashing, made a glitterbeeline for the table near the windows that the Star Darlings had claimed as their own. All the Star Darlings knew how much Tessa loved food and looked forward to each meal. "Star greetings," she said pleasantly. She plopped down in a chair. "I'm starving!" she announced.

A Bot-Bot waiter zoomed up to drop off Piper's and Astra's breakfasts and take Tessa's order. She thought for a moment, then nodded. "I'll take a pastry basket and a cup of Zing, please," she said.

Her breakfast arrived shortly thereafter. Tessa's hand hovered over the baked treats, and she licked her lips as she made her choice. She pulled out an ozzief-ruit croissant and took a big bite. "Moonberry," she said when she was done chewing. She made quick work of the flaky pastry, then, dabbing the corners of her mouth with a cloth napkin for any errant crumbs, reached in again. This time she grabbed a mini astromuffin, which Astra could see was liberally studded with lolofruit. She popped the entire thing into her mouth and chewed.

"Moonberry again!" she said. "What are the chances?"

Astra's Star-Zap, which was sitting in her lap in silent mode, flickered. She flipped it open and read the message.

 Tessa = Everything tastes like moonberries?

 Sure looks that way!

Cassie and Sage strolled in next. Cassie sat next to Piper and smiled at her as she flicked open her napkin.

"Starkudos on your mission, Piper," she said.

"Star salutations, Cassie," Piper said, digging into her bowl of Quasar Krispies with sliced starberries.

"It probably didn't . . ." Cassie began, obviously trying to figure out the best way to phrase her statement. "It probably didn't go quite as seamlessly as mine, did it?" She thought for a moment and laughed, placing a hand on Piper's arm. "Of course it didn't," she said. "What was I thinking? My mission was such a stellar success!"

Piper looked stricken for a moment. But her expression changed to a knowing grin when she received Astra's holo-text:

 Cassie = Braggy! Now her weird behavior yesterday makes sense!

The rest of the Star Darlings began to arrive at the table. Astra and Piper watched as Sage giggled when Clover shamefacedly confessed to getting a D (for *dim*) on her Chronicle Class examination and then guffawed when the Bot-Bot waiter informed her that the kitchen was out of the Sparkle-O's she had ordered.

 Sage = Can't stop laughing.

Piper nodded and began to compose a holo-message in response.

 Libby = Can't stay awake.

Astra looked at the girl, whose cheek was resting on her plate of tinsel toast. *My stars,* she thought. She reached for her mug, drank the last gulp of twinkle tea, and began to compose a reply.

"Hey," said Cassie, noticing. "Are you writing a message about me?" She looked down at her silver dress and lace tights and smiled. "I did pick a startastically fashionable outfit this morning, didn't I?"

Astra wanted to roll her eyes but instead replied (as pleasantly as she could), "You *do* look nice today."

They don't know that they are acting odd, do they?

 I don't think so. Let's see. . . .

"Vega," Piper said, "have you noticed that everything you say is in rhyme?"

Ten Star Darlings swiveled around to look at Piper, curious expressions on their faces.

Cassie cocked her head to the side. "Really?" she said. "I don't hear it."

Gemma turned to Tessa. "Imagine if I talked in rhyme all the time. That would be so annoying!"

Tessa laughed. "My stars!" she said to her sister. "Bite your tongue!"

"Ouch!" said Gemma.

Astra made a mental note, to be verified later. *Gemma = Takes things literally?*

Vega stared at Piper like she had three auras. "Piper, do you need some schooling? Talking in rhyme? You must be fooling!"

With a quick glance at Astra, Piper asked, "You really didn't just hear that?"

"I think it is completely clear," Vega replied. "There isn't anything to hear."

Does that answer your question?

 It certainly does!

Soon it was time to head to class. Piper and Astra lingered at the table as the rest of the Star Darlings gathered their Star-Zaps and stood up to leave. Their Bot-Bot waiter collected the breakfast utensils and dishes around them.

"Star salutations, SL-D9," said Astra. When he zoomed off, she turned to Piper. "It's just so startastically strange that no one knows they are acting odd."

Piper nodded. "Or that anyone else is, either," she added.

The two girls headed out of the cafeteria, down the steps, and toward Halo Hall.

Suddenly, Piper grabbed Astra's arm and jerked her backward. "Watch out!" she cried. Astra realized that she had almost been knocked down by a Starling rushing to class.

Astra stared after her. "Was that Scarlet?" she said. Piper nodded.

"And was she *skipping*?" Astra asked incredulously.

"She was skipping," said Piper.

"Well, now I've seen everything," said Astra. "We've got to figure this weirdness out, and fast."

"So why aren't *we* acting odd?" asked Piper.

"Great question," said Astra. "I think when we sort out that part, we'll be able to get to the bottom of this."

Piper sighed. "Let's figure it out soon," she said. "If I have to listen to Vega's rhymes for much longer, I think I'll scream!"

CHAPTER
2

"*Ahhhhhhhhhhhhhhhhhhhhhhhhhhhhhhhhh!*"
shrieked Piper.

Vega jumped, then turned to Piper, her brow furrowed in concern. "Piper, are you quite all right?" she asked. "Your screaming gave me such a fright."

Piper's mouth opened as if she might yelp again, and Astra put a steadying hand on her arm. Vega, who had just bumped into the two girls on her way to class, shook her head in consternation and headed down the hallway, glancing back over her shoulder worriedly at Piper.

Piper turned to Astra and gave her a shaky smile. "My sincerest star apologies," she said. "But I just can't stand the rhyming anymore."

"No star apologies necessary," said Astra. "Really. I get it. Everyone's behavior is not just weird, it is startastically annoying. We'll figure it out after SD class this afternoon," she told Piper, more confidently than she felt. "I'll see you later. I'm off to Aspirational Art."

Piper brightened. "Maybe it will spark some creative ideas," she said hopefully.

Astra shrugged. "Doubtful. I don't even know why I have to take Aspirational Art, anyway," she said. "I'd much rather do a double P.E. class." Astra ignored Piper's shudder. She knew that while Piper loved stretching and meditating, she was no fan of team sports.

Astra walked into the classroom, a huge airy space with beautiful light pouring through the floor-to-ceiling windows. Giant holo-canvases, one for each student, were set up around the room. Each had an artist's station furnished with brushes of all sizes and tubs of glowing paintlight in every color of the rainbow. Astra selected a canvas positioned in the corner, which overlooked the lush ozziefruit orchard.

The rest of the students began choosing their canvases, ready to begin. But where was their professor?

"Should we just start?" asked Fioney, a girl with bright blue curls. She picked up a brush and positioned it over her jar of purple paintlight, eager to get started.

Astra grinned as she observed the empty doorway. "Maybe he's not coming and we'll get a free period!" she said hopefully.

Gaila, a serious girl with a turquoise aura, gasped. "We need to stay, Astra," she gently chided. "Imagine if he came in and we were all gone!"

Astra eyed the holo-clock. "If he's not here by eleven-eighty, I say we make our starry way elsewhere," she said. "We could all go for a run. Or play a game of Poses!"

"Or take a nap!" said a girl named Smilla, who had a bright green buzz cut. The rest of the class laughed.

Half the class stared at the holo-clock and the other half stared at the door as the starmins ticked by. With ten starsecs to go before eleven-eighty, the door slid open with a bang and Professor Findley Claxworth stood there, his tall frame filling the doorway. Astra sighed. "Sorry I'm late!" he said, his purple hair in even more disarray than usual. "But I couldn't find my favorite pair of purple socks! And you know how much I love to match." He indicated his purple-and-turquoise striped shirt.

"Did you find them?" asked Smilla.

"Yes, to my great relief!" he said with a grin as he lifted his pant leg to show everyone his violet socks.

The door slid shut behind him as he stepped inside

the classroom. "I hope you girls are ready to let your creativity soar today," he announced. "Today is going to be all about letting go of your inhibitions and shining like the creative geniuses I know you are. Today you should all just go crazy!"

Astra gave him a look. Go crazy? That was what she did on the playing field. Not in art class. She wasn't even quite sure where to start.

It was even more frustrating to her because the rest of the students immediately started to paint. One girl sang to herself as she covered her canvas with bold strokes of blue and yellow. Another closed her eyes and simply let the paint fly. Astra stood in front of her blank canvas, uncharacteristically hesitant.

"Astra!" said the professor as he stepped up behind her. "Don't think, just do."

Astra put down her brush, turning to face him. "I'm just not creative," she told him, shaking her head. Then, catching his sympathetic look, she added hastily, "It doesn't bother me! I'm an athlete! I just don't have time to work on my creative side. No offense."

His eyes crinkled behind his round magenta glasses. "None taken, Starling," he said. "But we all have creativity inside of us. It's just that in some it is closer to the surface than others. We need to give ourselves permission to be open to it and then let ourselves go. No self-consciousness, no embarrassment. You must embrace it and then you'll really soar. Trust me, there's no other feeling quite like it."

Astra nodded and smiled agreeably, but when he moved on to the next student, she rolled her eyes. No other feeling like it? That was easy to say if you hadn't scored the winning basket in a tied game of star ball as the holo-clock was counting down, or broken a school record in the quarter-floozel dash. She couldn't imagine that spreading some paintlight on a holo-canvas could even come close to that feeling.

Having this enormous blank canvas in front of her was daunting. She felt unsure of herself, and that was unfamiliar and unpleasant. She dipped a large brush in her favorite color, bright red, which was sparkly.

"Don't think, just feel," the professor said in her ear. She hadn't realized he had returned, and his voice startled her. She jumped, her arm moved forward, and a big splash of shimmery red paintlight landed on the canvas.

"There you go," said Professor Claxworth encouragingly.

The red splatter might not have been intentional, but it did look good against the blank canvas. Encouraged,

Astra picked up another brush and coated it in sparkling yellow paintlight. She flicked the brush at the canvas, and splatters of sunshine covered the right side of the painting on top of the red. She started to feel bolder. Orange was next, then green, then purple. She decided she needed more red. She stepped back and took a look. The entire canvas was covered in overlapping strokes and splatters of paint. It was very bright and colorful. Cheerful, even. She tilted her head for another look. Then she frowned. Something was clearly missing.

"Nice work," said the professor, who had made his rounds and was back at Astra's side. He stared at the picture. "It's very pretty." He shook his head. "But I think it needs more of you in it."

Astra considered this. More of her? What exactly did that mean? She liked sports, action, movement. Maybe she should be more athletic in her approach to the canvas. She dipped her brush in orange paintlight, then jumped in the air, spun, and made a bold stroke on the canvas, layering on more color. That felt good! She did it again, this time with green. Even better. Then she had an idea. Was it crazy or was it brilliant? She'd find out in a moment. She looked around. Her professor was deep in conversation with a girl named Oola, who had covered her canvas with huge flower shapes in purple and pink. The other students were concentrating on their paintings. So no one saw Astra walk to the other side of the room and pour a large container of white paintlight over her head. She took a deep breath, ran across the room, did a flying leap and a double flip, and launched herself right at the painting. The springy canvas acted like a trampoline and she bounced back onto the floor, landing on her feet. She was now completely covered in paintlight—not just white, but every color of the rainbow. The rest of the students stared at her in shock.

Astra stood there, dripping. The colorful canvas now had a life-size Astra shape in the middle. She looked at it and grinned. It was totally strange, unique, and decidedly her.

Professor Findley Claxworth stood in the middle of the room in silence. Astra stared at him. Had she taken things too far?

"My heavens!" he finally exclaimed. "It's brilliant!" He turned to Astra. "What do you want to call it?"

"Um . . . *Athlete in Motion*?" she suggested, wiping paint from her eyebrows. She felt happy—exhilarated, even. Maybe there really was something to this creativity thing!

Oola gave her a look. "Um . . . you do know that if you leave paintlight on yourself for longer than twenty starmins, it totally stains, right?"

Astra turned to her professor. "Is that true?" she asked him. "It doesn't just disappear?"

He glanced down at his paintlight-splattered clothes, then at Astra. "Oh, yes!" he said. "Isn't it great? It is the one substance on Starland that will permanently stain fabric if you leave it on long enough."

"Um, then may I be excused to take a sparkle shower before next class?" Astra asked. As she spoke, she felt a drip slide down her cheek.

He looked starprised. "Well, certainly," he said. "But are you sure? I think you look great!"

Astra passed by a holo-trophy case and stole a glance at her paintlight-splattered reflection as she walked down the hallway. She was drenched! Still, she gave a little skip, then glanced around quickly to make sure no one had seen it. Maybe Aspirational Art wasn't so bad after all.

She was rounding the corner, heading toward the front door, when she heard Lady Stella's voice. She wasn't quite sure why, but she found herself ducking back into the shadows and pausing to listen. *Astra, what are you doing?* she thought. *Spying on the headmistress—what is wrong with you?* She peered around the corner. A woman wearing a dark cloak, the hood pulled over her head, was speaking earnestly with Lady Stella.

Astra holo-texted Piper:

 Hey! I'm out of class and outside Lady Stella's office. She's here. Do you think I should ask her if she's noticed what's been going on with everyone?

She pressed SEND.

The immediate response: HOLO-TEXT FAILURE.

"Thank you *mumble* for coming by. . . . I'm glad that you called the energy *mumble* to my attention. . . ." Astra's head jerked up. Had one of the women said the word *shortage*? But then again, it could have been *sport edge* or possibly even *report ledge*. She wasn't exactly sure. She strained to hear more, but the voices drifted into gibberish. Then she suddenly realized there were footfalls heading her way. She stepped forward and, most unfortunately, bumped right into the hooded woman. Some spy she was.

"Star apologies," said Astra, noticing that the woman's soft plum cloak was now streaked with white, purple, and red paintlight. "But you'll want to wash that in the next twenty starmins or it will be stained forever."

The woman stepped back when she saw Astra, and gathered her hood more tightly around her face. But not before Astra caught a glimpse of her delicate pointed chin and deep lavender eyes. She looked so familiar. Did Astra know her from somewhere? Perhaps she was an actress on holo-vison? "Star salutations," the woman said softly, and hurried down the hallway. Astra stared after her retreating back. Something about that woman seemed so familiar. . . .

But it wasn't coming to her.

She looked up. Lady Stella was standing in the doorway, watching her. "Star greetings, Astra," she said with a smile. "Looks like you had a good time in Aspirational Art class."

"I did," said Astra. "It was totally starprising, but I really did."

"It's about time," Lady Stella remarked. Astra shifted in her shiny red boots, feeling a bit uncomfortable that the headmistress knew she had been struggling with the class. Was Lady Stella keeping tabs on her? Maybe as a Star Darling she should have expected it. But it was still disconcerting.

"Who was that?" Astra asked the headmistress, pointing to the hooded woman, who was by then a small figure at the end of the long starmarble hallway.

"Oh, just someone . . . interviewing for a position," said Lady Stella vaguely.

"But she seemed so famil—" Astra said.

"So how have you been, Astra?" Lady Stella interrupted. Her piercing eyes, a kaleidoscope of colors, seemed to be staring right into her. Astra looked away.

"Okay," she replied. Should she bring up her concerns about the other Star Darlings? She desperately wanted to, but without Piper's input, she didn't feel like she should do it. So she changed the subject herself. "So what's going on with Ophelia?" she asked. "I heard she left Starling Academy. Kind of abruptly."

"Yes, sh-sh-sh-she did," said someone behind them. Lady Stella and Astra both spun around. Lady Cordial stood in the middle of the hallway, her purple hair escaping from her bun, and her cheeks flushed in an unbecoming shade of violet.

She caught her breath and continued. "We received some good news from the orphanage where Ophelia was from. They found a family who wanted to adopt her and sh-sh-she needed to return immediately to s-s-s-start the proceedings."

Lady Stella nodded. "Such wonderful news," she said.

So Cassie had been wrong. Ophelia *was* an orphan.

"Well, that's great," said Astra. "I'm really happy for her." She thought for a moment. "Maybe we could all send her a holo-card. Does she still have her Star-Zap?"

Lady Cordial shook her head.

"I guess we could send it to the orphanage," Astra said, pressing on. "What is it called?"

Lady Cordial frowned. "I think it was called the S-s-s-starland C-c-c-city Home for Orphaned S-s-s-starling Children."

Lady Stella shook her head. "Are you sure? I seem to recall it was called the Starland Memorial Institute."

"We'll let you know," said Lady Cordial. She stared at Astra. "Hadn't you better get back to your room to rinse off before the paintlight s-s-s-sets in and you're stained forever?"

Astra looked down. "Oh, that's right!" she said. With a quick farewell to the two faculty members, she hurried down the hall and to her dorm. She glanced at her Star-Zap and quickened her pace. She liked her aura red, not rainbow, thank you very much.

CHAPTER
3

freshly sparkled and paintlight-free, Astra jumped onto the Cosmic Transporter, her starstick in hand. It was time for SD class and she didn't want to be late. She started to jog on the moving sidewalk, passing students who preferred a more leisurely ride, were upperclass-men with a free star period for their last class, or simply didn't care about their attendance records. She spotted a cluster of students chatting together on the transporter and, about to overtake them, shouted, "On your left!" so they would get out of her way. Suddenly, the floor stopped moving underneath her. The students she was about to pass all bumped into each other and began to fall like a bunch of stardominoes. To her great starprise, Astra found herself hurtling through the air, about to crash into the girls. Thinking quickly, she jammed her starstick down, lifted her body up, and vaulted right over them.

She landed neatly on her feet on the other side of the fallen girls. Brushing herself off, she stretched out her hand to the students, who had tumbled on top of each other in a very untidy pile.

"What happened?" a girl with shoulder-length bright yellow hair asked as Astra helped her to her feet.

"The Cosmic Transporter just stopped moving," said Astra. "How startacularly strange."

Once she had determined that the girls were not hurt, just shaken up, she headed to Star Darlings class.

The students, ensconced in the soundproof room they used for their private classes, were all chattering excitedly about the power outage. "The Cosmic Transporter just ground to a halt!" Astra informed them dramatically. "I'm lucky I didn't get hurt!"

"Nothing is working," said Piper. "It's like when the lights went out after Cassie's mission."

"Very strange," said Adora.

"What?" said Astra. She shook her head. Adora and her low talking! Adora opened her mouth to speak again.

"It's okay," said Astra. "Never mind."

The girls' Star-Zaps chimed and flickered. They all

had received a holo-message. Tessa read it first. "Oh, no, Professor Illumia Wickes is trapped in the Flash Vertical Mover!" she said. "No class today."

"Every cloud has a sparkly lining," said Scarlet, who then skipped right out the door. She almost knocked into Libby, who appeared in the doorway with a large bandage on her forehead.

"What happened?" asked Adora.

"What happened?" asked Astra.

Libby yawned, covering her mouth with her hand. "I was on the Cosmic Transporter on my way to class. The next thing I knew, I was under a pile of students!" She sat in her seat and put her head down on the desk.

Astra exchanged glances with Piper. They both realized that Libby must have fallen asleep standing up.

"Since we're all here—well, everyone but Scarlet, that is—I have some news to share," said Astra. "I ran into Lady Stella and Lady Cordial earlier today and they told me that Ophelia really *is* an orphan. And that she's getting adopted. That's why she left Starling Academy so abruptly. I'm just not sure which orphanage she is at," Astra continued. "Lady Cordial said it was called the Starland City Home for Orphaned Starling Children and Lady Stella thought it was Starland Memorial Institute."

She looked to Cassie for her reaction, but Cassie was too engrossed in posing for starselfies.

"So, Cassie," she said loudly, "it looks like your theory was totally wrong."

Cassie put down her Star-Zap for a moment and smiled distractedly. "Yes, I do have many theories," she said. "In fact, I shared seventeen of them today in my classes. Everyone was very impressed, I could tell."

"Really," said Astra. "Seventeen, you say."

"Really," said Cassie. "I have a fascinating way of looking at things, and I enjoy sharing my perspective with my fellow students."

Vega spoke up. "Now this may truly sound absurd," she said. "But should we take Lady Stella's word?"

Astra paused, digesting Vega's rhyme. "So you think she isn't telling the truth?" she finally said.

"The answer is I'm just not sure," Vega replied. "But maybe we should find out more."

"That's a good point," said Astra. "I'll try to get in touch with the orphanage and verify that information."

Piper nodded. "Good plan."

"Well, I'm going to call the orphanage right this very starmin," said Leona. She walked across the room and proceeded to photobomb Cassie's starselfies. Astra sighed and looked around the room. Adora was moving her lips, but no sound came out. Libby snored gently, her head resting on her desk. Vega opened her mouth to speak. Piper, seeing this, put her hands over her ears.

Astra had reached her limit. Enough was enough. "That's it!" she shouted. Everyone stopped talking and stared at her.

"Something really strange is going on, and none of you can see it," she said. "And it's driving me and Piper crazy!"

Tessa stared at Astra. "Maybe you two actually *are* crazy," she said, "if none of us can see it but you."

Astra looked around wildly, then noticed that Vega was holo-vidding her. "Vega, give that to me," she said brusquely. Vega scowled and opened her mouth, about to retort. "Please," Astra added. "I just want to look at some of your holo-vids." You never knew when Vega was going to start holo-vidding. Luckily, once Astra said the magic word, Vega handed it over without rhyming.

Astra began to quickly scan through the holo-vids. She found what she was looking for—breakfast that morning—and pressed the projector option. The cafeteria scene sprang to life in the middle of the room.

"Do you really think this is going to work?" whispered Piper.

Astra shrugged. "It's worth a try," she said.

Slowly, the Star Darlings began to drift over and watch. After a couple of moments, Cassie's mouth fell open in shock. Leona shook her head. "Oh, my stars," said Sage. She giggled, looked mortified, and slapped her hand over her mouth. Adora said something; no one knew what. Only Libby, still snoozing, did not react.

"Moonberries," whispered Tessa.

"Did I really just . . . skip?" asked someone in a horrified-sounding voice.

Astra spun around. Scarlet was standing in the open doorway.

"I forgot my Star-Zap," she explained. "Is that holo-vid for real?"

Astra nodded grimly. "It's for real."

"Well, then we have to do something about this!" Scarlet said, her cheeks bright pink with embarrassment. "Right now!"

Vega nodded. She opened her mouth, then shut it. It was clear that she didn't want to talk because she knew she would start rhyming again. Finally, with a look of resignation on her face, she said, "I thought that you were being cruel. But I really am a rhyming fool."

CHAPTER
4

Now that everyone was aware of their strange behavior, they wanted it fixed, and fast. The problem was that nobody had any idea how to fix it.

Later that night, after they had attended their various meetings and clubs and had an unusually quiet dinner, the girls gathered in Astra and Clover's room, where they could talk freely.

After everyone was settled on couches, chairs, and the floor, Astra started the conversation. "I know it was kind of shocking to watch Vega's holo-vid today and be able to see how you all have been acting. Piper and I think the key to finding out why it is happening has to do with the fact that the two of us are acting normally."

Leona snorted.

"Very funny, Leona," said Astra. She smiled. "Well, acting as normally as we usually act, anyway."

Adora typed into her Star-Zap and passed it to Piper, who sat next to her. This had become her new way of communicating since she had been informed that her voice was inaudible. CLEARLY IT WAS YOUR TRIP TO WISHWORLD, she'd written.

Piper considered this and shook her head. "Oh, I don't think so," she said.

"Yeah, I'm pretty sure that's just a coincidence," Astra informed her.

"What makes you think that?" asked Gemma.

"Because Piper and I never acted odd, even before we went to Wishworld," Astra explained. "So it must be something else."

Piper nodded in agreement, but the only response from the other Star Darlings was laughter. And it wasn't just from Sage.

"What's going on?" Astra asked, feeling irritated.

Vega looked up from her Star-Zap guiltily. "I found a holo-vid of you. You will not like it, this is true." She held up her Star-Zap and projected the image. It was of the Star Darlings sitting around their table in the Celestial Café a starweek earlier, eating lunch. Astra and

Piper watched in disbelief as Piper finished everyone's sentences, sometimes quite incorrectly, and Astra pulled one silly practical joke after another—pulling out a chair as Scarlet was about to sit down, switching Gemma's iced Zing with Tessa's ozziefruit juice, gluing a fork to the table . . .

"Ohhhhh," said Astra, feeling completely mortified. Piper blushed and looked at the floor.

"So since you two were acting odd *before* the mission and then stopped once you got back, clearly something happened on the trip to reverse it," said Tessa.

"Maybe it has something to do with traveling through the atmosphere?" suggested Clover.

Astra frowned. "I don't think that's it," she said. She began to pace the room, thinking.

"Did you do anything out of the ordinary on Wishworld?" asked Gemma.

Tessa perked up. "Did you eat something different?" she suggested.

"Oh! Maybe it was the chocolate egg creams!" Piper said.

"What's that?" Tessa wanted to know.

"A delicious Wishling concoction of seltzer, chocolate syrup, and milk!" Piper explained. "We each drank one."

"That must be it!" said Tessa, licking her lips. "How do we get one?"

Astra was not convinced. "I just don't think that's it," she said. "But what could it be?" Absentmindedly, she put her hands on the ground and flipped her legs into the air. There! That was much better. She did her best thinking upside down; she was sure of it. As she roamed the room, walking on her hands, she saw Cassie's silver slippers, Clover's purple boots, and the star ball she had been looking for for a double starweek. Then she spotted a pair of bare feet, the toes sinking into the thick carpet. They had to belong to Piper, who often remarked that walking barefoot helped her relax. Astra noticed that Piper's toenails were a deep sparkly blue, which reminded her of her mission and the slumber party they had attended, where they had given each other . . .

Astra toppled over. "That's it!" she said from the floor. She was so excited she couldn't even wait until she stood up to speak. "It's the nail polish! Piper and I went to a sleepover and everyone gave each other manicures and pedicures. We had to take off our Starland polish first. And then, when we got back home, we could see that the rest of you were acting odd. All we have to do is remove your polish, and everything will be back to normal!"

The Star Darlings headed straight to the starbeauty-chambers in the Lightning Lounge where they had put on the polish in the first place. They eagerly sat down and accessed the polish removal function. But when their hands emerged from the pods, the polish was as shiny and perfect as ever. Adora tried over and over, to no avail.

"It's no use, Adora," Cassie told her.

"I can't believe none of you can hear me!" Adora said.

Cassie nodded. "You're right, this color does look great on me," she said. "But pretty as it is, we've still got to figure out how to remove it." She looked around at the group. "Moons and stars," she said. "Was I just bragging again?"

They next tried to scrape it off with the scratchiest materials they could find—leaves from the ruffruff tree, pieces of eternium wool, and prickly buds—but nothing worked. Adora ran off to her room and returned with vanisholine, which smelled so terrible the girls down the hall came by to complain, but it didn't make a dent in the polish. As a last resort, they tried to scrape it off with Sage's crystal from the Crystal Mountains, the hardest substance on Starland, but even that didn't work. The nail polish was impervious to everything. The girls stared at their colorful nails in disbelief.

"So how did you get yours off?" Leona finally asked.

"With this magical Wishworld potion that they use at slumber parties," said Piper.

"That's right," said Astra. "It's called the polish of removal. Whoever goes down to Wishworld next has to bring this magic elixir back with them. Apparently it's the only way to take this crazy polish off."

"I am furious!" Leona said. "So we have to wait, knowing we're acting like weirdos, and there's nothing we can do about it." She saw everyone staring at her. "I'm smiling, aren't I?" she asked.

Astra sighed. She hoped someone would get sent down to Wishworld and fast, to collect wish energy and also to bring back the magical polish of removal. Because now not only was everyone still doing the weird stuff, but they were annoyed with themselves for not being able to stop doing it.

After everyone had left for their rooms, looking disappointed, and Clover had hugged her tightly before heading off to take a sparkle shower, apologizing as she did so, Astra picked up her Star-Zap. In all the excitement, she had completely forgotten to call the orphanage! She was eager to verify that Lady Stella was correct. There was enough going on without the Star Darlings distrusting their leader, too.

Astra flipped open her Star-Zap. "Give me the numbers of all the orphanages in Starland City," she said. It turned out there was just one.

A pleasant-looking woman with turquoise hair in a neat bun answered the call. "Starland City Home for Orphaned Starling Children," she said. "Star greetings. How may I help you?"

"I wanted to verify the name of one of your, um . . . orphans," Astra said awkwardly. "Her name is—"

"I'm sorry," the woman interrupted. "Our students' privacy is very strictly maintained. We don't give out information about anyone over a communication device. If you want to request information on someone here, you must come in person."

"How about I say her name and you nod if she's there?" Astra suggested—rather cunningly, she thought. "Her name is O—"

The woman shook her head emphatically. "I'm sorry, but that is against the rules. Good night." The screen went black.

Astra scowled, then consulted her star schedule. Her Chronicle Class professor was out, so she had third and fourth periods free the next day. If she hurried, that was probably enough time to take a quick trip into Starland City. She holo-texted Piper:

 You free third and fourth periods to take a little field trip tomorrow?

 Sure. I've got study hall, and Professor Roberta Elsa never takes attendance.

Astra smiled. Piper didn't ask questions; she knew that if Astra asked, it must be important. Astra's Star-Zap beeped and she realized that a holo-message had come in while she had been talking to the unhelpful orphanage lady. She glanced down and saw that it was a holo-card from her family. She opened it. Instantly, her mom, dad, and two younger siblings appeared in a small 3-D holographic image, which beamed into the air in front of her. They sat around the dinner table, one chair noticeably empty. She could even smell the food they were having— flug and beans, her favorite.

Everyone immediately began talking over each other, as they always did.

"Hope you are having fun at Starling Academy!" her mom said tearfully.

"I'm redecorating our room!" shouted her little sister, Asia. Their dad gave her a look. "Well, I'm trying to convince Mom and Dad, anyway," she said. "More stuffed animals, fewer holo-trophies."

"She's kidding, Astra," her mom hurriedly interjected. "Your trophies and medals aren't going anywhere!"

"We miss you!" they shouted, waving at her.

Ajax threw a napkin at the camera. And then they were gone.

Astra smiled. Her nice, normal, boring family. They didn't quite understand Astra and her relentless quest for greatness both on the field and off. Maybe someday they would.

Directly after second period, Astra headed for the hover bus stop, right outside the main entrance to Starling Academy. She stood under the canopy of kaleidoscope trees, the blooms slowly shifting from bright orange to sunny yellow above her head. She pulled out her Star-Zap and accessed the bus schedule. It would be arriving in a starmin and a half. Where was Piper? Just then, she heard footfalls and looked up to see her rushing across the street. Or Piper's version of rushing, which to anyone else looked like a leisurely stroll. Her seafoam hair fluttered around her shoulders, and she was wearing a long flowing dress, as usual, plus a floppy hat. It wasn't a look Astra thought she could pull off—not that she par-ticularly wanted to, mind you—but it seemed right on Piper.

As the bus appeared in the distance, Astra filled Piper in. "We're going to the orphanage to locate Ophelia," she said, "and confirm the story. If all goes as planned, we'll be back in time for fifth period."

"Good," said Piper. "We wouldn't want to miss Color Catching."

The hover bus pulled up silently and the side lifted to let them in, revealing Starlings relaxing in comfort-able chaises. The two girls stepped on board and settled into their seats. A Bot-Bot conductor zoomed up to reg-ister their destination and collect their payment. They flashed their Star-Zaps. "You will reach your destination in eleven starmins," the Bot-Bot said. "Have a pleasant ride."

The bus had two rows of seats on either side, sepa-rated by an aisle. All the seats faced the windows so the riders could enjoy the scenery. Piper took off her hat, placed it on the seat next to her, and turned to Astra. "I'm actually looking forward to seeing Ophelia," she said. "She may have been a terrible Star Darling but she really is a sweet girl."

"Yeah," said Astra. "She is. It will be nice to see her, see how she's doing." She thought for a moment. "I really hope the news about her adoption is true." *For Ophelia's sake as well as Lady Stella's,* she thought.

Piper didn't answer. Astra looked at her. She had started meditating, sitting cross-legged with her hands, palms up, on her knees. Astra looked around at her fellow passengers: an elderly lady, cyber-knitting what looked like the world's longest scarf; a woman napping in the sunlight; two parents with a baby; and a boy, about Astra's age, engrossed in a holo-book. His hair was deep indigo and his skin a sparkly golden brown. He was wearing a school uniform, possibly from Star Preparatory, the all-boys school across Luminous Lake. Just then, to her dismay, he looked up, and their eyes met. He smiled at Astra, and she realized that her face was inexplicably getting warm. *What is wrong with you, Astra?* she thought. Her life, until that very moment, had been completely focused on sports, school, and, recently, the Star Darlings. Boys had never been a consideration; she simply didn't have the time or the interest.

She looked away quickly and faced forward, staring out at the scenery. The rural surroundings of the Starling Academy campus gave way to suburban houses with big lawns and then to city blocks tightly packed with stores and apartment buildings. The number of people—and vehicles—increased dramatically.

What was she supposed to be focusing on? Oh, yes—Ophelia. Astra had bigger things to think about than boys from across the lake. Even very cute boys from across the lake. She snuck another look at him and immediately looked away. He was looking right back at her, a broad smile on his face.

"He's cute," said Piper, her eyes still closed.

"Piper!" said Astra. "What are you talking about? You didn't even look."

"I can just tell," she said with a secret smile.

Piper could be spooky that way sometimes. "Whatever," said Astra irritably. "Our stop is coming up."

The Bot-Bot conductor zoomed over. "Your destination is approaching," it confirmed.

The bus rolled to a stop on a busy street corner and the door slid up. The two girls disembarked and consulted their Star-Zaps for directions.

"Excuse me," someone said. Astra and Piper turned around. Moons and stars! It was the boy from the hover bus.

"You left this behind," he said, holding out Piper's hat.

"Star salutations!" said Piper. "How kind of you. I hope you didn't have to get off the bus early."

"Oh, it's okay," he said gallantly. "I only had a few more stops to go. I'm going to the Abramowicz Center to check out their interactive holo-exhibit on wish energy kineticism." He suddenly looked bashful. "Besides . . . I wanted to introduce myself."

Oh, he wanted to meet *Piper*. Astra felt a rush of disappointment.

He turned to her. "You're Astra, right?" he asked.

She started. "Yes! How did you know?"

He gave her a big grin. "I'm a huge star ball fan and you're one of the best players on Starland, that's how. I follow your stats. They're totally startacular," he said. "My name is Leebeau," he added.

"Nice to meet you, Leebeau," said Astra. "This is Piper, by the way."

Piper and Leebeau exchanged pleasantries. Then Leebeau turned back to Astra.

"Well, see you around," he said. He waved to them both and was on his way.

"Well, he *was* pretty cute," said Piper. "And he certainly has a crush on you, that's for sure."

"Shut your stars," said Astra quickly. But she was secretly pleased.

The two girls walked a couple of blocks to the orphanage and were soon standing in front of a building from a bygone era, made entirely of glimmering star-marble and complete with intricate holo-glass windows in brilliant colors. "They don't make them like they used to," Piper remarked. It was such an old lady thing to say that Astra laughed. Piper gave her a look. "What's so funny?" she asked.

At the top of the steep stairs was another old-fashioned touch—a wish energy bell pull. Astra concentrated on ringing it, and after a while, when she got the hang of it, the door slid open. They stepped inside a dark yet cheerful room. It was comfortable and cozy, with a large rug of old Starlandian design in the middle of the floor, overstuffed armchairs, and colorful pillows. On the walls were holo-photos of smiling kids and shelves full of holo-books.

The receptionist, whom Astra had spoken to the day before, sat in front of a holo-screen, typing away on a holo-keyboard.

"Star apologies," she said. "I'm under a deadline and need to file this report immediately. I'll be with you in a starmin."

Piper grew more anxious and Astra more agitated as a quarter starhour ticked by. Worriedly, Piper checked her Star-Zap. Third period was over and fourth was about to begin. Piper shifted nervously in her seat.

"Um, are you almost done?" Astra asked the woman.

"Almost," she replied distractedly as she frowned at the screen and began rearranging her text with a few carefully placed swipes.

"There," said the woman as she typed the final line and pressed SEND. She turned to the girls. "Star greetings," she said. "Star apologies for the delay. How can I help you?"

"We're here from Starling Academy," Astra said. "We need to talk to a student named Ophelia."

"Oh, Starling Academy!" said the woman, appearing impressed. She took a closer look at Astra. "You look familiar. Did you holo-call yesterday?"

"I did," said Astra. "You told me to come in person, so here we are."

The woman's turquoise bun bobbed as she accessed the student schedules. "Ophelia is in Moonematics class right now. Let me see if she can be interrupted." She stood up and walked to a tall doorway. She paused before opening it. "Who should I say is here to see her?" she asked.

"Astra and Piper," Astra said.

"Astra and Piper from Starling Academy," said the receptionist. "I'll be right back."

Several starmins later the door slid open and the woman stepped back into the room. The door shut behind her. She was frowning. "I found Ophelia, but she says she doesn't know you, or anyone from Starling Academy."

"No," said Astra stubbornly. "She definitely knows us. If we could just see her for one starmin . . ."

The door began to slide open again behind the receptionist. Astra caught a quick glimpse of overalls and sneakers.

"Ophelia!" Astra said.

The door fully opened. There stood a girl of medium height with bright pink hair.

"You're not Ophelia," said Astra.

"I most certainly am," said the girl with a laugh. "I'm just not *your* Ophelia."

"Star apologies," said Piper quickly.

"Not necessary," said the girl. "Can I get back to class?" she asked the receptionist. "We're in the middle of discussing infinite integers."

"Of course," said the woman. She turned to Astra and Piper. "I'm afraid that she's the only Ophelia in the whole place."

Piper pulled out her Star-Zap. "Can you just take a quick look at her holo-photo?" she said. She projected a picture of Ophelia, taken during a game of Poses they had played one evening after dinner. Ophelia was balancing on one leg, looking sweetly serious. Astra could be seen in the background in the middle of one of her famous up-and-over starflips.

The woman peered at the holo-photo and shook her head. "No, she doesn't look familiar at all," she said. "Star apologies, Starlings. I wish I could have been of help."

Astra and Piper headed down the front steps dejectedly. "Maybe she's lying," Astra muttered.

Piper gave her a quizzical look. "What reason would she have to lie?" she asked. "Somebody is lying, that's for sure. And her name is Ophelia."

CHAPTER
5

As they trudged back to the bus stop, Astra tried to look on the bright side of things. "Well, at least we'll be back in time for Color Catching cla—" She broke off as their Star-Zaps began to chime and flicker.

SD WISH ORB IDENTIFIED. PROCEED TO LADY STELLA'S OFFICE IMMEDIATELY.

"Moons and stars!" Astra and Piper exclaimed at the same time. But they didn't laugh; they were too panicked. They were going to be late for the Wish Orb reveal! That had never happened before, and this was the one event Astra did not want to come first in.

"Let's go!" said Astra. The two girls raced down the street, Astra accessing the holo–bus schedule as she ran. "We might just make it if we hurry!" she shouted. She rounded the corner to see the bus sitting at the stop. "It's still here!" she shouted, and put on a burst of speed, reasoning that she could hold the bus for her slower friend. But even with her stellar track skills, by the time she arrived at the stop, the bus was gone.

"*Oh, starf!*" she yelled, stamping her foot. "There isn't another hover bus for fifteen starmins," she told Piper, once the girl had caught up. "We're never going to make it."

Piper peered down the street. "Hey!" she shouted. "It looks like the hover bus is stopping up ahead!"

"Startacular!" said Astra.

The two girls hurried. The door lifted up and they clambered on, Piper completely out of breath.

"Thank you," Astra said to the Bot-Bot conductor.

"Don't thank me. Thank him," said the Bot-Bot. "He's the one who saw you."

What in the stars? Astra turned around and there he was—Leebeau, a sunny grin on his sparkly face.

"Fancy seeing you two again," he said.

Neither girl was able to respond: Piper because she was panting so hard, unaccustomed as she was to quarter-floozel dashes or running up and down a star ball field; Astra because she was overwhelmed by the overpowering and unfamiliar feeling in the pit of her stomach. It was like she was going down the biggest drop on a giant star coaster. Wearing a blindfold.

What was going on?

"How was your trip?" Leebeau asked as they all took their seats.

"Okay," Astra managed to squeak out at the same time Piper caught her breath and answered, "Not so good."

"You've got to get your stories straight," he said with a laugh. "In any event, I bet it was better than mine. Turns out the Abramowicz Center is closed today. That's what I get for not checking first."

Astra nodded, glancing down at her Star-Zap anxiously.

"Are you late for class or something?" he asked her.

Astra nodded. "Or something," she said.

Leebeau got a mischevious twinkle in his eye. "Listen, I know just the thing. Since we're the only ones on this bus, I'm going to let you in on a little trick. We can access the hyper-speed function on this bus with a few swipes on my communicator."

"Are you sure it's safe?" asked Piper.

"I'm positive," he said.

"Do it!" said Astra.

Leebeau flipped open his communicator, swiped a

few times, and—*whoosh!*—they were in front of the black curlicued gates of Starling Academy. The Bot-Bot conductor raced down the aisle, its eyes flashing in alarm. "This is highly unusual!" it said.

The door lifted and Astra stood and turned to Leebeau, a happy smile on her face. "Star salutations!" she cried. "We owe you one!"

"Just wave to me at your next game," he said. He made a fist and pumped it in the air. "Go, Glowin' Glions!"

The two girls waved good-bye and hurried through the campus gates.

Piper spoke first. "If I didn't know any better, I'd think that maybe you were starting to have a crush on Leboy," she said.

"Leebeau!" Astra said, correcting her.

"I knew it!" said Piper with satisfaction.

"You don't know anything," said Astra dismissively. But the truth was that *she* was the one who didn't know what was going on. Luckily, she had the Wish Orb reveal to concentrate on instead.

"Thank the stars you're here!" said Lady Stella as Astra and Piper burst into her office moments later. "We were starting to worry!" Everyone was seated around the silver table in the middle of the headmistress's cavernous office. Astra and Piper silently slipped into the two empty seats.

Leona leaned over and whispered in Astra's ear. "Where were you guys?"

"I'll tell you later," Astra whispered back. Now that she was seated, she started to feel the buzz of excitement. With all the strange things going on, she hadn't focused on the fact that the next mission could actually finally be hers. She counted in her head. Sage, Libby, Leona, Vega, Ophelia—make that Scarlet—Cassie, and Piper had all gone on their missions already. That left her, Tessa, Gemma, Clover, and Adora. The odds were in her favor. And she was ready to go.

On her right side sat Libby. It looked like her eyelids were getting heavy. Astra poked her in the side, perhaps a bit too roughly.

"Mom, I told you, I'm awake!" Libby shouted. Then she looked around at everyone at the table, embarrassed. "My stars, was I drifting off again?" she asked. Astra nodded.

Gemma looked around the room. "No Wish Cavern this time?" she asked.

"No, the Wish Orb has something else in mind

today," said Lady Stella. She was suddenly holding a tray with five golden cups on it. Astra blinked. That tray had not been anywhere in sight a starsec ago; she was sure of it.

"The five remaining Starlings who have not yet gone on their missions—and I'm certain you all know who you are—need to keep their eye on the cups as they move about the table," Lady Stella said, smiling at the group. "One by one you will have a chance to select a cup and lift it. The Star Darling who is intended to go on this mission will be the one to find the orb."

Well, that was different. As Lady Stella placed the golden cups on the table, Astra's fingers moved involuntarily, eager to choose.

Before their amazed eyes, the golden cups began to slide around the table, moved by an unseen force. They flew by, faster and faster, until they were just a blur. Finally, they came to a stop in the middle of the table. Five identical golden cups. Which one could be hiding the orb?

Tessa went first. She stood up, took a deep breath, reached across the table for one cup, changed her mind, and placed her hands on another. She lifted it, letting her breath out all in a rush. Nothing.

"Moonberries!" she said in disgust. That this was her

new expletive would have made Astra laugh out loud, but she was too keyed up at the moment to crack a smile.

"Now it's your turn, Adora," said Lady Stella.

"Star salutations," said Adora.

"Excuse me?" said Lady Stella.

Adora shook her head as if to say that it didn't matter. She then placed her hands on the cup directly in front of her and closed her eyes. She picked up the cup and opened them. Astra couldn't hear her, but she could clearly read her lips. *"Starf!"* Adora said. Actually, thought Astra, it was a good thing it wasn't Adora's turn to go to Wishworld. Her Wisher would not have been able to hear a thing she said! Adora flipped the cup to peer inside, as if to see if the orb was hiding from her, playing tricks.

"Your turn," Lady Stella said to Astra.

And suddenly, Astra knew exactly which cup to lift. She reached over and placed her hand on top of it.

"No!" said Leona. "Tessa already picked that one!" But Astra shook her head. She knew she was right, the same as she knew that you never, ever threw a lolopitch when the runner was on her first leg in starshoot and that you always bobbled in the final three starsecs of a tenth. She smiled at Lady Stella and lifted the cup off the table.

"Ohhhhhh!" breathed the Star Darlings. For under the cup a brilliant orb was floating in midair, looking exactly like a miniature star ball. Astra tossed it into the air and cradled it in her hands. "It's mine, it's finally mine," she said.

"The Wish Orb has chosen," Lady Stella pronounced. "Starkudos, Astra."

A blur of activity followed. Once everyone had left, congratulating Astra (though she could tell that four Star Darlings—Adora, Tessa, Gemma, and Clover—were perhaps not as pleased for her as the others, and who could blame them?), she met with Lady Stella and received her instructions, then got a briefing on shooting star travel and the trip to Wishworld, an upgrade to her Star-Zap, and a quick lesson on the Wishworld Outfit Selector.

When she left the headmistress's office, she let out a sigh of relief. There had been no inquiry into why she and Piper had been late, for which she was very grateful. Until she knew for sure what was going on, she didn't want to make any accusations or show her hand. However, as she had stared into the brilliant kaleidoscope eyes of her headmistress, Astra couldn't help wondering: *Is she who she says she is?* Truth be told, she was finding it almost impossible to believe that Lady Stella could be anything but a stellarly trustworthy leader, but there was still a small glimmer of doubt she couldn't shake.

The meeting ran late, so by the time she made it to the Celestial Café, there was just time for a quick star sandwich. She wolfed it down and headed to her room. She would leave for Wishworld early the next morning. The rest of the evening was hers.

Astra bounded into her room to find her room-mate, Clover, sitting cross-legged on her bed, playing her keyboard and jotting down lyrics. "Astra!" she said delightedly. Clearly she had gotten over her disappointment at not being chosen. Astra could see that the girl was struggling not to stand up and rush over to her. Astra was feeling generous. "That's okay," she said. "Get over here." She held her arms open.

"Sorry," Clover said into Astra's hair as she squeezed her tightly for a moment. She broke the hug and stood back, staring at her.

"This is so exciting, Astra," she said.

Astra couldn't contain herself. "It is!" she shouted. She hopped onto her bed and started jumping up and down.

"No flips!" said Clover in a warning tone. "Remember

what happened last time? You almost flew right out the window!"

"All right, all right," said Astra. She dropped to the bed and bounced a few times.

"So let me see your Star-Zap!" said Clover excitedly. "Should we flip through some Wishworld fashions? Cassie told me that's what she and Sage did the night before their missions."

Astra looked down at her clothes. She dressed sporty. Very sporty. Hair pulled back, knee-length shorts, a T-shirt, tube socks, and sneakers. "Do I look like I want to make a fashion statement?" she asked her roommate.

Clover, who picked out her own outfits with great care, looked disappointed.

"So what do you think the wish will be?" she asked, changing the subject.

Astra reached her arms above her head and stretched. "I don't know," she said. "I'm hoping it has to do with sports, or some kind of competition."

Clover nodded. "That would make sense," she said. She thought for a minute. "But will it be confusing, since Wishworld sports are so different from ours?"

Astra shrugged. "How different could they be?" she asked. "From what I've seen of Wishworld sports from the Wishworld Surveillance Deck, the movements are all the same—throwing, hitting, tagging, kicking, catching, flipping, leaping, jumping, tumbling, sliding, tackling. It's just the rules that are different. That's easy enough to figure out."

"I'm dying to see how the Cyber Journal works," Clover said. "Can you make a mental observation?"

Astra considered this and smiled. "Well, we're only supposed to use it on Wishworld, but I guess once won't hurt," she said. She accessed her Cyber Journal, pushed the record button, handed Clover the Star-Zap, and made her observation.

And before Clover's amazed eyes appeared: *Star Observation: Note to self, get new roommate.*

"Oh, Astra!" said Clover with a laugh. She threw a small star-shaped pillow at her roommate and it bounced off Astra's head.

"They don't call it a *throw* pillow for nothing," joked Astra.

Clover began getting ready for bed, but Astra found she was still full of excited energy. She headed to the Radiant Recreation Center and went for a run on the startrack, which helped relax her a bit. Then she returned to her dorm room and, in the dim light so as not to wake up her already-sleeping roommate, put on pajamas, slipped on her headphones so she could absorb her lessons, and finally fell into a deep sleep. In her dreams she played strange sports with unfamiliar equipment in a vast arena, and despite her confusion, she was presented with a medal in front of a roaring crowd—which happened to include a handsome boy with indigo hair and golden-brown skin. She didn't need Piper to interpret that dream. Clearly her subconscious was telling her that her mission was going to be a success. She just wasn't sure why Leebeau had been there. Why was she dreaming about someone she hadn't even known existed that morning at breakfast? That was startastically odd indeed.

"Good-bye, Astra!"

"Good luck!"

"Safe star travels!"

The Star Darlings were all clustered around Astra, getting a little too close for her personal comfort. "Back up, guys!" she said, waving them away. Still, it was nice that they were so excited for her. Piper pushed to the front and spoke softly. "I'll keep looking for Ophelia while you're gone," she said. "Do you think I should ask Leona for help? I know she was worried about her."

"That's a great idea," said Astra. "See if there's anything you two can find out." She paused. "But don't forget that she's going to say one thing and do the opposite. It could get confusing."

"I'll remember," said Piper.

Sage squeezed Astra's hand. "Think things through, try not to draw too much attention to yourself, and be careful," she said with a laugh. "I'll be sending you good thoughts."

Astra got an unexpected lump in her throat. She and Sage could be real competitors, so that meant a lot to her. "Star salutations, Sage," she said.

Tessa leaned in next and gave her a hug. "Can't argue with the Wish Orb," she said. "This one is all yours. Good luck to you."

Adora was the last Star Darling to see her off. "The best of luck, Astra," she said sincerely. "And just keep in mind that we're here for you if you need us."

"Huh?" said Astra. "I mean . . . uh, thanks!"

A star had been captured. The wranglers would only be able to hold on to it for so long and it was time for Astra to go. Lady Cordial handed Astra a red backpack with a star on it. Lady Stella turned to Astra. "I would wish you luck, but I don't think you need it. You are bold and strong and full of confidence. Never lose that."

She paused. "But you must also remember that there is strength in vulnerability, as well."

"There is?" asked Astra.

"There is," Lady Stella said.

Astra had had enough advice. She was done with good-byes. She motioned for the Star Wranglers to help her onto her star and release it, and she shot off into the ether. It was time to start her mission!

CHAPTER
6

After her relatively boring trip down to Wishworld to help Piper with her mission, Astra was hoping for a wilder ride this time. Sure, there were some bumps along the way and some stomach-scrambling spins, and she did narrowly avoid hitting an asteroid, but all in all it was a disappointment, in her opinion.

COMMENCE APPEARANCE CHANGE, her Star-Zap announced. Astra accessed her Wishworld Outfit Selector and put on a sporty yet sassy outfit. It wasn't very different from her Starland apparel, just a lot less sparkly. It was her signature style and practical, too, as you never knew when you'd have to sub in for someone on the playing field (or so Astra hoped).

Now it was time to make sure her skin and hair lost

their Starland sparkle, too. She began to recite: "Star light, star bright, the first star I see tonight: I wish I may, I wish I might, have the wish I wish tonight." She watched with amazement as her skin lost its glimmer, and from the corner of her eye she could see that her hair was no longer bright red but a dark reddish brown. Since clothes and hair and accessories were not her thing, she really did not mind at all.

APPROACHING WISHWORLD ATMOSPHERE, said the Star-Zap. That's when things livened up a little, as the star began to buck and bump.

"Whee!" yelled Astra with glee. But all too soon the ride was smooth again.

She was hoping the landing might be exciting, but it was completely uneventful, to her disappointment. She touched down gently in a stand of trees, well hidden from curious eyes. Astra stood and stretched her legs. She was pleased to note that the air was warm and the sun was shining. It was a beautiful Wishworld day. She waited patiently as the star finished sparking, then picked it up and folded it down to pocket size. She accessed the directions to Pine Brook School, where she would find her Wisher, and set off at a quick pace in a northwest direction.

But there was so much to see along the way! Astra's

last visit to Wishworld had been centered in a limited area in a small town, and she now found herself in a park, which was of much more interest to her. She passed a small body of water and admired some swimming creatures. She was shocked when one of them suddenly unfolded its wings, started flapping them, and then lifted itself out of the water and began to soar through the air! They made funny noises that she tried to copy. "Quack!" she cried, and she was pretty sure they quacked right back at her. She heard some chirpy whistling and looked up to find adorable feathered creatures hopping from branch to branch. The many trees were all shades of one color—green—but they were attractive nonetheless.

She had to tear herself away but finally headed out of the park and made her way to a busy road. She walked alongside it on a grassy embankment as the cars passed by. Next she came to a fenced-in field. A man was blowing a whistle and kids were running around kicking a black-and-white patterned ball. So Astra, even though she knew she should be hurrying along, had to rest her arms on the fence and watch. The game reminded her a lot of star ball—without the wish energy, of course—and, she realized, in this game you could only use your feet. Each team had to direct the ball to the other team's net, which was guarded by a player who, oddly enough, *could* use her hands. If it got past that player, the other team scored a throw, which there on Wishworld was quite obviously called a "gooooaaaal!" The game looked like a lot of fun (even without the use of wish energy), and she wished she could join in. That she was twice the height of any of the players kept her on the sidelines.

The whistle sounded. "Game is over!" the man shouted. "Time to get back to class!"

Starf! It was time for Astra to get to class, too. She glanced down at her Countdown Clock. She had wasted more than one of her precious Wishworld hours and she hadn't even arrived at her Wisher's school yet! *Correction*, she told herself. She hadn't wasted the time at all. She was observing Wishworld life. She hadn't recorded a single observation, though. She should get started on that.

I wish I was already at my Wisher's school, she thought. *WHOOSH!* There was an unexpected blast of air, a moment of blurry discombobulation, and as soon as Astra caught her breath she realized she was standing right in front of Clarkston Mills School. *My stars!* thought Astra. *My talent must be teleporting.* A woman with short dark hair and piercing blue eyes sat behind a desk.

"May I help you?" the woman asked.

"My name is Astra," she said, as she had been instructed. "I am a new student in school."

"Your name is Astra. You are a new student in school." The woman frowned and leaned forward. "You do know that this is the next-to-last week of school, don't you? Kind of an odd time to start!"

"Well, better late than never!" said Astra brightly.

Then the woman's expression changed as she sniffed the air. "Why, I do believe that is devil's food cake." She sniffed again. "With fudge frosting, if I'm not mistaken." Her eyes misted over. "My grandfather was a baker and I used to help him after school. That was my favorite cake of them all. I'll have to go to the cafeteria and get a slice later." She smiled. "Come right in, Astra. Do you know which classroom to go to?"

"I'll find my way," Astra told her.

The woman nodded. "You'll find your way."

Astra followed the directions her Star-Zap provided and was soon pushing open a set of double doors. She was back outside again, to her delight. And she was treated to a most welcoming sight. Dozens of Wishlings, all milling about, playing games in the sunshine. Was it P.E. class or a non-compulsory-between-class recreational break like they had on Starland? Not that it really mattered. There was a group of kids hitting a round white ball back and forth over a net. Some were kicking around the same type of black-and-white ball she had seen earlier. Others were bouncing a brown ball on the ground and taking turns tossing it into a net high above their heads. When they got it in, they slapped hands.

She loped over to that group, and without a second thought, she ran into the middle of the game and grabbed the ball. It was different from a star ball—larger, more solid—and it had a funny rubbery texture. She liked the way it felt in her hands. She pointed, aimed, and shot.

"Nothing but net," said a Wishling boy admiringly. "Hey. I'm Tony. Who are you?"

"I'm Astra," she answered. "The new girl. I enjoyed playing your netball game."

Tony laughed. "It's called basketball, you know."

Wish Mission 8, Wishworld Observation #1: Wishlings have funny names for their games. There is no basket in basketball!

She then glanced at her Wish Pendant wristbands. Nothing. That was too bad. None of the netball—make that basketball—players was her Wisher. Astra had been distracted—again—by another one of the wonderful sports there. Now it was time to get down to business.

She looked around the yard. *Aha!* A girl was holding one of those fluffy white wishing flowers Lady Stella had told them about. Imagine if she was Astra's Wisher and she was just about to make her wish again! Astra ran over as the girl took a deep breath, ready to scatter the seeds.

"Hey!" Astra said eagerly. "Are you wishing for something?"

The girl lowered the arm holding the flower and gave Astra a dubious look. "Um, yeah," she said. "Why else would I be holding this dandelion?"

Wish Mission 8, Wishworld Observation #2: The fluffy white flowers Wishers wish on are called Dandy Lions.

"What's your wish?" Astra asked eagerly. "Is it a good one?"

The girl smiled. "I'll say. I wish I had a million dollars!" she said.

Astra frowned. A million! That was like a moonium! "All for yourself?" she asked.

The girl nodded.

"You wouldn't even share it?" Astra asked, trying to give the girl the benefit of the doubt.

"Nope," said the girl.

Astra gave her a disgusted look. "Well, that's not a good wish at all!"

The girl looked insulted. "Mind your own business!" she said. Then she raised her arm, closed her eyes, and blew. Astra watched as the fluffy seeds danced through the air across the schoolyard.

"Good luck with that one," muttered Astra to herself. She scanned the yard, counting the kids. Well, that girl obviously wasn't the person Astra was looking for. So who among the twenty-four remaining students was her Wisher?

A bell rang and the students all dropped what they were doing to line up and head inside. A black-and-white ball rolled up to Astra and she sent it flying with a well-placed kick. She smiled. She had been itching to do that! She joined the line and followed her class inside.

A young woman with her dark hair pulled into a ponytail was standing in the doorway, watching everyone head inside. Astra realized she must be her teacher. "I am Astra Starling. I am your new student," she told her.

"You are Astra Starling. You are my new student," the teacher repeated, just as Astra had known she would. "I am Ms. Lopez," she told her. "Head inside, Astra, it's time for lunch!" She sniffed the air. "And if I am not mistaken, it smells like they're making banana cream pie, lucky you!"

Astra smiled. There was something really nice about reminding adults of their favorite treats from childhood. It seemed always to bring a wistful smile to their faces.

The class trooped in through the cafeteria doors and Astra followed close behind. She had been warned that cafeterias on Wishworld were not up to Starling Academy standards, but she wasn't prepared for what she saw once she was inside: a dingy room with scuffed floors lined with bare tables. She grabbed a beat-up orange plastic tray and waited in line as a lady handed out plates of weird-looking food. Limited choices. No cloth napkins. And certainly no Bot-Bot waiters.

"I wish . . ." a boy ahead of Astra said.

In her eagerness, Astra nearly knocked down a curly-haired girl who stood between them. "You wish what?" she asked him.

The boy grinned. "If I tell you, it won't come true."

Astra shook her head. "Huh? Where did you get a crazy idea like that? That is not true!"

He arrived at the counter and peered through the foggy glass at the lunch offerings. "Hey, look, I got my wish!" he said.

Astra's heart leaped. "You did?"

"Yeah—pizza bagels!" he said excitedly.

"Pizza bagels?" Astra repeated. She had learned about both pizza and bagels in school, and she was certain they were two different things. But he pointed to a round food item covered in red sauce and some melted cheese. Astra frowned. What a waste of a wish! Still, she ordered one for herself. Might as well see what all the fuss was about. Once she had her food she looked around the crowded cafeteria for a seat.

"Hey, new girl, over here!" someone called. Astra smiled, headed to Tony's table, and sat down. "This is Timmy, Sean, Roseanne, Eleni, Janice, and Stephen," he said.

"Star—I mean, hello," said Astra. She glanced at her wristbands, which, unfortunately, were still dark.

"Astra's new," he explained.

Rebecca gave her a funny look. "Who starts school two weeks before summer vacation?" she asked, peeling the top off a container of something pink and creamy and licking it.

"Did you just move here?" asked Timmy.

Astra smiled. "I just arrived!" she said.

Too many questions! As Astra ate her pizza bagel (which was surprisingly tasty), she steered the subject to basketball, which was a good choice, as the kids all had a lot of opinions on the subject. She was relieved when the bell rang for class. She dumped her tray and headed to her new classroom. She was relieved to see that her wristbands began to glow as soon as she passed through the doorway, so she knew she was in the right place.

Once Astra was settled at a desk and had been given a math book, they started their lessons. The other Star Darlings hadn't mentioned just how tedious Wishling classes were. Math was especially painful, as Wishlings were terribly slow at figuring out the answers. She thought she might scream. They didn't know anything! In English class she thought she'd get to read some Wishworld lighterature, but instead they diagrammed sentences, which seemed startacularly silly. Did Wishlings really need to know this stuff?

Suddenly, class was interrupted as a voice, loud and crackly, came over the loudspeaker: "ATTENTION, STUDENTS. We have two announcements to make this afternoon. There will be a gymnastics competition this Friday after school in the gymnasium. Don't forget to come and cheer on your fellow students as they tackle the parallel bars, floor routines, the vault, and the uneven bars!"

Competition! Astra perked up. She had no idea what gymnastics was, but she was certain she was going to find out.

The announcements continued. "And on Saturday morning at eleven a.m., please join us for an art show in the lunchroom. Support your fellow student artists and check out some really beautiful and inspiring art they've been working on!"

Out of the corner of her eye she could see a serious-looking girl with curly brown hair jotting something down in her notebook. Astra's pulse quickened. The gymnastics competition was the key to her mission; she was sure of it!

"Time for science," said Ms. Lopez. "Have a great rest of the day, guys." The class packed up their backpacks, pushed in their chairs with a maximum of noise and effort, and headed out the door.

In the science room, Astra walked up to the teacher, a tall thin man in a long white coat. Oddly, he was missing hair from the top of his head.

"I am Astra, the new student," she told him.

"You are Astra, the new student," he said. He smiled at her and sniffed the air, looking wistful.

The students all sat down at tables in pairs. Astra stood at the front of the room uncertainly, not sure where she should go.

"Astra," said the teacher, "it looks like Emma's partner is absent today. Emma, will you wave so Astra can join you?"

Emma waved. To Astra's delight, she was the

curly-haired girl from across the aisle—the one who had been writing in her notebook during the announcements. *This could be it*, Astra thought. She took a deep breath. She was ready.

"Hey, Astra," Emma said, holding out her hand. Astra stared at it, not sure what to do. Then she slapped it, as she had seen the basketball players do earlier.

Emma blinked at her in surprise. "Oh, okay," she said with a shrug. "So it's nice to meet you." Then she said, "Wow." Both she and Astra stared as Astra's wristbands began to glow brightly.

"And it is extremely great to meet you," Astra said. "You have no idea."

"So tell me all about your—" Astra began.

"Shhh!" said Emma. "Mr. Tedesco is about to start!"

"Greetings, students," said Mr. Tedesco. "Today we are going to learn how to build a catapult." He paused. "Can anyone tell me what a catapult is?"

Astra raised her hand. She knew that one and was eager to impress her Wisher with the knowledge she had gained in Wishers 101. "It's a magazine with pages full of things that you can purchase with paper money," she said confidently.

The class laughed. Astra scowled, but when she saw Emma grinning at her, she realized that the kids thought she was saying it to be funny. She laughed along, to show that she was a good sport.

Mr. Tedesco smiled. "Actually, that's a cata*log*. But that was a good guess, Astra." He looked around the room. "Has anyone heard of a catapult?"

Tony raised his hand. "It's a machine that launches things!" he said. "Like when you're attacking a castle. Flaming hot tar right over the walls!"

"That's exactly right, Tony," said Mr. Tedesco. He then projected an image of a strange machine on the whiteboard. "Catapults were widely used during medieval times. As you can see," he said, pointing to the different parts, "a catapult has a lever for pulling back and a fulcrum for rotation. When released, the catapult flings objects—or flaming liquids, in Tony's case—and they can go over walls and travel distances. We are going to build our own catapults in class today and then demonstrate them. We are going to learn all about force and its effect on speed and distance with this project. Plus it's a lot of fun to shoot things in class, isn't it?"

The class laughed.

"Very cool," said a girl with pale hair.

It was no wonder Astra had never heard of a catapult. Starland was a peaceful place and there was no need for weapons of any kind.

The teacher handed out shoe boxes, rulers, markers, tape measures, rubber bands, tape, plastic spoons, and a few small white objects to all the student pairs. Astra squeezed one of the small white things. It was soft. She smelled it. *Mmmmm.* Sweet, too. "Are these edible?" she asked Emma.

"Um, yeah," said the girl, giving her a funny look. "Marshmallows usually are."

While they began figuring out how to assemble their catapult, Astra tried to engage Emma in conversation. But she soon discovered that her partner was extremely single-minded when it came to schoolwork. While it was admirable, it was also pretty frustrating.

"Astra," Emma said. "Less talk, more . . . catapulting."

"As soon as you are done, you should try out your catapults," said Mr. Tedesco. "Shoot your marshmallow, measure the distance it travels, record the distance, and make any changes to your machines to see if you can shoot the marshmallows farther. Take careful notes on your work sheets. They are due tomorrow."

Suddenly, Astra had a great idea. If she worked super slowly and made lots of mistakes, she and Emma would have to work on the project that night after school. So she deliberately measured incorrectly, put the spoon on backward, and ate the marshmallows for good measure.

Emma looked frustrated. "Let's get this done," she said. "I have a lot going on after school today."

The bell rang. School was over for the day. And they still weren't close to finished. Astra was thrilled.

⭐

"I can't believe we have to finish that stupid catapult tonight," Emma moaned, shaking her head as they stood by her locker after school. "Like I don't have enough to do."

Astra leaned forward. "Sounds like you are very busy and wish for a more peaceful life of harmony and quietude," she said, stealing a few of Piper's phrases.

"Not really," said Emma. "That sounds kind of boring, actually."

Oh, well. Astra tried again. "So where are you going after school?" Astra asked. "Can I come?"

Emma shook her head. "Sorry," she said. "I've got gymnastics practice. Why don't I come to your house after I'm done? It's got to be quieter than my house!"

Astra had to think fast. "Um . . . my parents are working late tonight," she said.

"Isn't anyone going to be home? Do you have any brothers or sisters?" Emma asked.

"No, just me," said Astra. She had no idea why she had said that. But it sounded really appealing, actually. No little siblings getting in your stuff, stealing the attention from you and your accomplishments with their distracting cuteness. "Yeah," she went on. "It's just me and my parents. I have this whole huge room to myself. And my parents have all the time in the world for me. It's pretty great."

Emma smiled. "It sounds nice," she said. "I bet it's quiet, too. And that you never get compared to anyone. Nothing to live up to. You can just be yourself."

Astra nodded. "And since you're the only one, you never need to babysit or anything."

So Emma and Astra went their separate ways, promising to meet later at Emma's house. Astra teleported herself to town, popping into and out of shops. She could have spent all evening in the sporting goods store, trying out each piece of equipment while an extremely helpful salesperson explained how it all worked. Then she glanced at her Star-Zap and realized it was time to meet Emma. Her Star-Zap leading the way, she walked along the sidewalk, past homes with neat lawns and well-trimmed hedges, until she reached a cozy house with a swing on the porch and window boxes with pretty pink flowers cascading out of them. She walked up the steps and knocked on the door. Emma answered it.

"Hey, Astra," she said. "Come in." Astra stepped inside. The walls of the small entryway were jam-packed with photos of girls with medals and trophies, and it looked like the very same medals and trophies sat on the entryway table. Intrigued, Astra paused to take a look.

"Come on, we need to get started," said Emma, pulling her by the arm (a little forcefully, Astra thought) into the living room.

They walked into the kitchen, where Emma's mom was preparing dinner.

"Mom, this is Astra," said Emma. "She's new at school."

"Pleased to meet you," said Emma's mom, extending her hand. As before, Astra slapped it.

Emma's mom looked surprised for a moment, then laughed. "Oh, okay," she said. "So will you be joining us for dinner, Astra?"

"I'd love to," said Astra.

"We're having eggplant parmigiana," Emma's mom said. She paused for a moment. "Does anyone else smell cream puffs?" she asked. Emma and Astra both shook their heads.

Emma rooted around in the cupboard until she found a half-eaten bag of marshmallows. She shoved it under her arm and they headed upstairs to her bedroom to do their homework. The room was filled with colorful paintings, drawings, and sculptures. They knelt on the flowered rug, finished assembling their catapult, shot it, and measured the distance the marshmallow traveled. Then they learned that by tightening the rubber bands and adjusting the position of the spoon, they could make it go even farther. That time the marshmallow went so far it hit the opposite bedroom wall, knocking over a bottle that was sitting on a dresser. Astra walked over and picked up the bottle. She blinked. It was the polish of removal! Her eyes lit up. "Hey, can I have this?" she asked, holding up the bottle.

Emma shrugged. "Sure, I guess," she said.

"St—I mean thank you! Thank you!" Astra gushed, making sure the cap was on tightly before putting it carefully into her backpack. One bottle down, nine to go! They wrote down their observations.

"Cool," said Emma when they were done. "That wasn't so bad after all."

They had math homework, too, so they went straight to work on it. Astra watched as Emma stuck out her tongue in concentration as she worked. Astra knew all the answers, but she labored over them so Emma wouldn't get suspicious. She made sure that they finished at the same time.

Astra was ready to get to the bottom of the wish situation. "So tell me—" she started.

"Emma!" called her mom. "Have you finished your homework? Come help me with dinner! Your dad and sisters will be home soon!"

"Coming!" shouted Emma. She stood and turned to Astra. "Wanna help?"

Downstairs, Emma's mom pointed to a pile of vegetables and a white board. "Here, help me make the salad," she said.

Emma grinned. "My mom hates making salad," she told Astra.

"I do!" said her mom. "All that washing and chopping!"

"You can peel and slice those carrots," Emma said, pointing to the end of the counter, where two bowls sat. One was filled with yellow food and the other was filled with orange food. *Oh, starf!* she thought. *Which ones are the carrots?*

Wish Mission 8, Wishworld Observation #3: Add an "Identifying Wishworld Food" tutorial to avoid awkward situations like this!

Well, she had a fifty-fifty chance of getting it right. So Astra separated one of the yellow things from the rest. She pulled the stem on top and the peel began to separate from the inside pretty easily.

Emma glanced at what she was doing. "Astra, why

are you peeling a *banana*?" she asked. Then she started laughing. "You're so funny!"

"Ha-ha," Astra said. Yikes, she had to think fast! "Imagine mixing up a banana and a carrot. That is so silly!" She picked up the banana. "Mmmmm, what a tasty carrot," she said, taking a big bite. Emma and her mother exchanged amused glances. *Not bad*, thought Astra as she chewed. The banana had a soft interior and a mild, pleasant taste. Then she picked up a carrot and stared at it. She grabbed the green fronds at the top and gave them a tug, but it did not peel like the banana had. Now she was stumped. This was getting very uncomfortable.

Emma laughed and laughed. "That's so funny, pretending you don't know how to peel a carrot. Is that how you get out of helping in the kitchen at home?" She handed Astra a knife and a soft round reddish-orange food item. "Here, you can slice this tomato. I'll peel the carrots." She grabbed a utensil and began scraping the skin off them. *Whew! That was a close one!* Astra thought.

A bell dinged and Emma's mom put on some extremely large mittens, opened the oven door, and pulled out a bubbling dish. It looked pretty messy, all gooey and saucy, but it smelled startacularly good.

"Hello! I'm home!" someone called. A large man strode into the kitchen in a matching jacket and pants, a long strip of fabric tied around his neck. He was followed by a smallish girl in a zippered jacket with a hood and matching pants, her hair in a sleek bun.

"Hey, honey," Emma's mom said to the man, who was presumably her husband. "How was practice, Elizabeth?" she asked the little girl.

"It was great!" Elizabeth said. "I finally perfected my aerial!"

"Daddy!" cried Emma, lunging forward to hug him around his middle.

"Hello, sweetums, how was school today?" he asked, patting her head.

"Fine," she told him. "This is my new friend Astra."

Astra smiled. She liked that.

"Hello, new friend Astra," said Emma's dad. "Pleased to meet you."

Astra extended her hand. Oddly enough, Emma's dad didn't slap it. He engulfed it in his large one and shook it up and down. Astra made an observation: some Wishlings slap hands and other Wishlings shake them. Emma started to say something.

"Can it wait a minute?" he said. "I want to go upstairs and get changed out of this monkey suit." Without waiting for her answer, he left the kitchen, and Astra could hear the steps creak as he bounded upstairs.

Emma's mom took out plates and silverware, and the three girls set the dining room table, then headed back to the kitchen for napkins. The front door opened again with a burst of excited chattering.

Astra looked at Emma. "My big sisters," Emma explained. "Eva and Ellie. They're twins." Two girls who looked exactly alike, dressed just like Elizabeth, crowded into the kitchen, kissing their mother, tousling their sisters' hair, grabbing carrot sticks, dropping bags and jackets on the kitchen table, and talking, talking, talking. They talked almost as much as Gemma, for stars' sake! Astra caught a few phrases—straddle, press handstand, dive roll, pike. None of it made any sense to her. But she was entranced by their energy and enthusiasm. Elizabeth joined in and told her big sisters about her aerial. They cheered and hugged her.

When they finally paused to take a breath, Emma introduced Astra to them.

"We're the gymnastics champs of Greendale High," said Eva.

"And I'm the top gymnast at Greendale Elementary," offered Elizabeth.

Emma leaned over to whisper in Astra's ear. "They never stop talking," she said. "And it's only ever about one thing. My entire family is obsessed with gymnastics."

"What *is* gymnastics, anyway?" Astra asked her.

Emma grinned. "That's a good one. Oh, Astra, you make me laugh!"

Emma's dad came back downstairs, dressed in Wishling relaxing clothes, and there were more hugs and greetings. They sat down to dinner and Astra found that she was famished. Her plate of eggplant parmigiana and salad disappeared quite quickly, and she eagerly refilled her plate when offered seconds.

After the twins filled in the family on every move they had completed successfully at practice, Elizabeth told the story, in painstaking detail, of her aerial. Meanwhile, Astra polished off her second helping.

Emma's parents nodded happily. "All it takes is determination and practice," her father said. He turned to Emma. "Right, my girl?"

"Right, Dad," said Emma, her eyes on her plate.

"We're so excited to go to your competition on Friday, Emma," her mother said.

"Yeah," said Emma quietly.

"How about a little more enthusiasm, young lady!" her father said. "That floor routine isn't going to perfect itself, you know."

Astra listened to all this with great excitement. It made perfect sense to her now. Obviously, she had been chosen to go on this mission because of her love of sports. She wondered if Emma needed her help with the floor routine.

After dinner Elizabeth begged everyone to come outside to see her aerial. "And we can show you some of our moves," said Ellie.

Emma rolled her eyes. "How thrilling for you," she said.

But it *was* thrilling for Astra. It turned out that gymnastics was a variation of the advanced moves Astra did while playing a game of Poses—leaps and jumps and tumbles.

"Come join us!" said Eva.

Astra didn't need to be asked twice. Before she knew it, she was showing everyone her famous up-and-over starflip.

Someone started clapping. "You're good," said Emma's mom admiringly.

"Wow!" said Ellie. "You just did a perfect roundoff back-handspring back tuck. Emma!" she shouted. "You need to see this!"

But Emma was nowhere to be found.

"Oh, she's probably up in her room," said Elizabeth.

"She doesn't like gymnastics?" Astra asked, confused. "But I thought she was on the school team."

Eva lowered her voice. "Oh, she's just freaking out because she totally choked at the last meet."

Elizabeth did another perfect aerial and landed right in front of Astra. "Yeah, she blew it for her team. They lost because of her. She was really upset."

Ellie looked at her parents, who were talking to each other quietly. "My dad took it really hard."

"Well, he *was* the gymnastics champ in high school," said Eva. "He almost made it to nationals. But he lost out by one point. He doesn't want the same thing to happen to any of us."

Astra headed upstairs. She found Emma lying on her bed, staring up at the ceiling.

"Hi," said Astra.

"My dad is so proud of my sisters," Emma said sadly, "and I wish that . . ." Her voice trailed off.

"And you wish he was proud of you, too," Astra finished.

She felt a tingle of electricity down her spine. She had figured out the Wisher *and* the wish on the very same day! Things could not be going any better.

CHAPTER
8

Astra woke up, and for a brief moment she had no idea where she was. She looked around and saw that she was surrounded by paintings and drawings. *Oh, that's right.* She was in Emma's bedroom, wrapped up in something called a sleeping bag. Simply by saying "Hey, wouldn't it be a great idea if I slept over for the next three nights?" to Emma's mother, she had received an enthusiastic invitation. Emma's sisters had been confused ("You never let *my* friends stay over for three nights in a row!" Elizabeth had wailed. "And on a school night, too!"), and Emma had been delighted. Astra was certain she would be taking off right after Friday afternoon's meet and wouldn't need that third night, but she had added it just to be safe.

She yawned and stretched, feeling well rested and content. Her first day had gone extremely well. She'd made some interesting Wishworld observations, met her Wisher, and confirmed the wish. She knew that Emma's father would be incredibly proud of Emma when she helped her team to victory on Friday afternoon. Nobody knew more about competition, concentration, and training than Astra did. It was the perfect mission for her. They could just start creating that holo-statue in her likeness right now.

Emma was still asleep, so Astra considered her next steps. It seemed pretty simple: she'd just have to make sure that the girl went to all her practices, wasn't distracted, ate well, got plenty of sleep, worked hard, showed up at the meet, and did her best. Her father was sure to be impressed—and, most important, *proud* of his daughter.

School that day was pretty uneventful. Astra was just going through the motions, waiting for gymnastics practice that afternoon, where her real work would begin. At last the final bell rang. Astra and Emma grabbed their backpacks and headed to the locker room to change for practice.

"So I can't wait to see that floor routine of yours,"

Astra was saying as they walked down the hallway. Just then, a classroom door opened and an adult Wishling stepped out. She was a tall, thin woman with long, curly brown hair. Emma stopped right in her tracks.

"Well, hello there!" the woman said pleasantly. "I'm so happy to see you, Emma."

"Hi, Ms. Gonzales," Emma said—somewhat nervously, Astra noted. She looked both happy and a little apprehensive at the same time.

"Are you coming to art club this afternoon?" Ms. Gonzales asked. "There's still time to—"

"Sorry," Astra interrupted. She had this covered. Emma didn't need any distractions. "Emma has gymnastics practice today. There's a big meet coming up on Friday. Maybe she can come to your club after it's over."

Ms. Gonzales frowned. "But the . . ."

Astra grabbed Emma's arm and began to steer her down the hall. Who was that woman, and why was she trying to interfere with Emma's wish? "We're late for practice," Astra called over her shoulder. "See you later!"

There were other girls milling about in the locker room, already dressed in various uniforms, when they arrived. Astra wanted to use the Wishworld Outfit Selector, but she had no idea what to wear. Rather than make Emma suspicious, she pretended she needed to use the bathroom and wandered around the locker room trying to figure out what gymnasts wore.

"Is that a gymnastics uniform?" she asked a girl in a brimmed hat, striped pants, and a short-sleeved jersey. A large brown glove was tucked under her arm.

The girl gave Astra a funny look. "Softball," she said. "That's a joke, right?"

Astra moved on. "Do you play gymnastics?" she asked a girl in a tight-fitting outfit that covered only her torso, her hair tucked under a tight rubber hat. The girl gawked at her.

"No, I play swimming," the girl finally answered. "Are you for real?"

Another girl took pity on Astra. "I'm on the gymnastics team," she said. "Can I help you?"

Astra took in her one-piece outfit with long sleeves and bare legs. "You already have," she told her.

Astra ducked into a bathroom stall and flipped through the outfits on her Wishworld Outfit Selector until she found what she was looking for. She picked a red one with a pretty multicolored star on the front. She stepped up to the mirror and took a look. Perfect.

She found Emma, who was similarly dressed, shoving

her school clothes and books into a locker. "Cute leotard," Emma told her.

"It *is* a cute leotard," Astra said.

They walked into the gym and Astra was instantly in heaven. The room was filled with all sorts of equipment. There were girls flipping and spinning and vaulting and jumping. Astra introduced herself to the coach ("I am Astra. I am the new girl on your team.") and found out that her favorite childhood dessert was something called brownies. Before the coach could blink, Astra was on the mat, showing off her up-and-over starflip. Make that her roundoff back-handspring back tuck. This was amazing. Not only was she making a wish come true; she was learning a new sport, which just happened to be one she had a natural talent for. She kept an eye on Emma, who was working on her floor routine. Astra learned how to do an aerial. It was going to come in very handy during her next game of Poses; that was for sure.

She especially enjoyed when she was able to take a break and shout encouragement at Emma, who looked like she could use some. When practice ended for the day, they pulled sweatpants on over their leotards (Emma loaned her a pair), laced up their sneakers, grabbed their backpacks, and headed out the exit door.

"Surprise!" said someone from the curb. The girls spun around.

Emma's face lit up. "Daddy!" she cried. "What are you doing here?"

"I thought I would take you girls out to dinner," he said.

"Can we go to Chewsy Cheese?" Emma asked excitedly.

"Of course," he said. "Grilled cheese and a root beer float, am I right?"

"You know it," Emma said. She slipped her hand into his. "Come on, Astra, my dad is taking us out to dinner!"

They drove to a nearby restaurant, which was lit up with multicolored blinking lights. Inside it was crowded and loud. Astra loved it immediately.

Astra stared at the menu. There were cheeseburgers, cheese sticks, cheese omelets, cheese fries, cheesecake, and twenty different kinds of grilled cheese.

The waitress came over. "May I take your order?" she asked. Astra stared at her hat, which looked like a large block of cheese.

"Is that made of real cheese?" Astra asked, her eyes wide. This warranted an observation.

Everyone laughed. "Oh, Astra," said Emma's dad,

shaking his head. "You're too funny." He ordered a cheeseburger, fries, and coffee.

"I'll have a grilled cheese with tomato on rye and a root beer float," said Emma.

Hmmm. Sounded good. "Me too," said Astra.

The waitress returned with a steaming mug of coffee. Emma's father ripped open a paper package and poured some grainy stuff into it, stirring it with a spoon. Meanwhile, Emma pulled some colored pencils out of her schoolbag, flipped over her menu, and began drawing on it.

Her dad took a sip of his coffee, pronounced it quite tasty, and began peppering his daughter with questions.

Had she tried her best that day? Yes, she had.

Was she perfecting her floor routine? She was working on it.

What did the coach have to say? Nothing much.

Did she think she was ready for Friday's meet? Sure.

Emma's dad sighed and ran his hand through his hair. Emma's answers were apparently not satisfactory. Astra noticed that she seemed pretty distracted. Emma's dad turned to Astra, clearly frustrated.

"What do you think, Astra? Is she working hard?" he asked.

"She is," said Astra. "I think she is going to do great on Friday, actually. You're coming, right?" she asked worriedly.

"Of course," said Emma's dad. "The whole family is going to be there. I just want to make sure that Emma is ready."

Emma continued sketching, as if she hadn't heard herself being discussed.

There was an uncomfortable silence. Luckily, the food came very quickly. "Here you go," said the waitress, setting the tray down on the edge of the table. "Grilled cheese with tomato on rye," she said, setting it before Astra.

Astra picked up one of the melty sandwich halves and took a tentative bite. Then another. It was positively delicious. She next took a sip of the root beer float, and it was sweet creamy goodness. *Almost as delicious as an egg cream*, she thought.

They ate their food in silence. When the plates were cleared, Emma went back to drawing.

"I had an idea, sweetheart," Emma's dad said.

Emma looked up expectantly. "Yes?" she said.

"Astra is really good at roundoff back-handspring back tucks. Maybe she could teach it to you. You could add it to your floor routine," he suggested. "That might really put you over the edge."

"Maybe," said Emma quietly. She went back to her paper.

Emma's dad sighed again. "Can you stop doodling for a minute and talk to me?" he asked. "I don't think that you are taking this meet as seriously as you should. Your sisters seem to understand how important it is. Heck, Elizabeth is already doing—"

"Dad, I need to ask you . . ." Emma interrupted.

Just then, the waitress came over with the check. Emma's dad stood up.

"In a minute, sweetheart. I'm going to go pay the bill."

Emma scowled and crumpled the menu. Astra put a hand on her friend's arm. Emma shook her off.

"He just doesn't get it," she complained. "I want to win the meet, of course, but there's something else that's more important. . . ."

"Yes, I understand," said Astra. "You want to make him proud of you."

"Yes, but . . ."

"But nothing," said Astra. "You have to believe in yourself, Emma. You have to focus on what is most important to you and not be distracted by the things that are not. Everything is going to work out great if you can just do that."

Emma sighed. "Fine," she said. She slid out of the booth and walked over to her dad. They spoke for a moment and he gave her a quick hug.

Astra gathered her backpack and, before she got up, leaned over and smoothed out the menu. She gasped. Emma had drawn Astra. She had gotten her hair, her upturned nose, the shape of her face, and the mischievous gleam in her eyes just right. It was a perfect likeness.

CHAPTER
9

Astra woke up, her eyes gleaming. It was Friday! How was she going to survive a full day of classes before the big meet? She was so excited about making Emma's wish come true and collecting the wish energy, and she was thrilled that she was going to be the first Star Darling who didn't need help on her mission. She wondered if that meant she would collect double the wish energy or something.

Emma's parents each gave her a big hug as she headed out the door. "Good luck!" they called. "We'll see you in the gym!"

Emma turned to wave from the sidewalk. "See you in the gym!" she called. She waited until they got to the end of the block, then turned to Astra. "Tell me again it's all going to be okay," she said.

Oh, no! Why was Emma so nervous? That wasn't helpful at all!

"It's all going to be okay," Astra said soothingly. But when Emma was looking the other way, she tapped her elbows together three times for good luck. With an attitude like that, she was pretty sure they needed it.

"Astra, are you paying attention?" Ms. Lopez asked during English class. "Can you please tell me which word in this sentence is the adjective?"

Astra blinked at her slowly, then stared at the board. "Um, roundoff?" she said. She had been running Emma's routine through her head step-by-step instead of paying attention.

The class laughed. Everyone, that is, but Emma. The very word seemed to make her ill.

"Do you mean rounded?" Ms. Lopez asked. She looked at Astra sympathetically. "I know you are excited about the gymnastics competition," she said, "but please try to pay attention for the rest of the day. It's not that much longer, I promise."

Astra nodded. She was a little disappointed that she wasn't going to be competing. How exciting would that have been! But there simply hadn't been enough time to teach her all of the events. So instead she had memorized Emma's floor exercise. She would show everyone when she got back home, which hopefully would be very soon.

Astra waved excitedly when Emma's family entered the gym. She wanted to sit with them so she could make sure that Emma's dad didn't miss a thing. She was counting on wrapping up the wish that day.

Astra sat between Emma's dad and Eva. She looked around the gymnasium. There were a couple of kids from her and Emma's class there. She gave them a wave. She was pleased to note that Ms. Lopez was there, too. The teacher looked at Astra and raised her thumb. Astra gasped. Back on Starland that was an extremely rude gesture, one that would certainly get you a detention, if not a suspension, especially if you did it to a teacher. But Ms. Lopez was looking back at her expectantly. So Astra gulped and returned the gesture. She burst into laughter. Wait till she told the rest of the Star Darlings that she had given a teacher a thumbs-up!

Eva explained how the meet worked. The teams each competed in four events—uneven bars, floor exercise, vault, and balance beam. The team with the highest overall score would be the winner. "I'm worried about Emma's floor exercise," Eva said. "She didn't get enough height in her tumbling pass last time."

Emma did well on the vault, balance beam, and uneven bars. Astra watched her with admiration as she soared through the air, effortlessly catching the bar in both hands, extending, releasing, and pirouetting. How she wished they had that kind of equipment on Starland! It was like flying!

Astra stole a glance at the scoreboard. Emma's team was doing well—but so was another team. Their scores were uncomfortably close. The floor exercises would settle that. There were two girls left to go from the top two teams . . . and Emma was one of them.

Eva buried her head in her hands. "Poor Emma," she said. "The pressure is going to get to her!"

The other team went first. The music began to play and the girl began with a tumbling pass that included a series of cartwheels. Her routine was nearly flawless.

Astra had been keeping a running score in her head. If Emma didn't get at least a nine point six two five, her team would lose. Eva turned to Astra. "I know this is confusing at first," she said, "but if Emma doesn't get at least a nine point six two five, her team will lose. Just like last time."

"Thanks," said Astra, hiding her smile. "It's so confusing!"

Eva clutched Astra's arm as Emma went through her routine. Leaping, tumbling, turning, twisting—she did it all perfectly. "This is it," said Eva. "She just needs to do her final tumbling pass and stick her landing."

Astra watched as Emma took a deep breath and began. But instead of doing a series of cartwheels as usual, she did a dive cartwheel into a roundoff back-handspring ending with a double back tuck! It was Astra's move! She felt so proud. But with such momentum, would Emma be able to stay within bounds and stick her landing? The crowd gasped as Emma bobbled for a moment, then quickly regained her balance, feet firmly planted beneath her, toes barely inside the line. The crowd erupted. As Emma's family stood and cheered, Astra stared at the scoreboard, holding her breath.

Then the score: 9.9!

"She did it!" Eva shouted. "She did it!"

Emma's parents hugged each other. Her sisters clapped and cheered some more. Emma's coach and her teammates jumped up and down. Emma had a small smile on her face. *Why isn't she happier?* Astra wondered. *Her wish is coming true.*

Emma's dad ran onto the gym floor, and Astra jumped up to follow and collect her energy. He picked Emma up and spun her around. "I am so proud of you," he said.

Proud. The magic word. Astra turned to Emma, ready for the onslaught of wish energy. She held out her wrists, a smile of eager anticipation on her face. But there was nothing. What was going on?

She looked up at Emma, who wore a wistful smile. She didn't look happy at all. She actually looked kind of sad.

Astra shook her head. "What's wrong?" she asked. "Your wish came true!"

Emma frowned. "*My* wish?" She laughed. "Maybe my father's wish, but not mine."

"But you said you wanted to make your father proud of you," Astra argued.

"Not this way," said Emma. She opened her mouth to speak, then shut it firmly. She shook her head. "Listen, I've got to go."

Dumbfounded, Astra watched Emma walk across the gym floor and out the door.

Astra glanced down at her Countdown Clock. It was still ticking. She didn't know what to do. She knew that she was wasting precious time. *How did I mess this up so badly?* she wondered. She thought and she thought and she could not come up with an answer.

She waved good-bye to Emma's family and sat there as the teams packed up and everyone left. She sat as the custodian moved all the equipment back to the corner of the gym and started sweeping the floor. And when he turned out the lights, she sat in the faint gloomy glow that came through the high gymnasium windows. She had no idea what to do.

Suddenly, there was a big bang as the heavy gym door swung open. Astra whipped her head toward the sound.

"Need a little help?" said a very familiar voice.

Astra could have wept with joy when she realized just who was making her way toward her in the darkened gymnasium.

"I do," she said, standing up in the bleachers. "I really do."

It was Libby. "Lady Stella sent me," she said gently. "Your energy levels were dropping and she started to get worried. You're running out of time."

"Thanks for pointing that out," said Astra sarcastically.

"Don't get mad at me," said Libby. "I'm here to help you."

Astra sighed. "I know. Star apologies."

"Why don't you just fill me in on everything that's happened so far?" Libby suggested, sitting down on the bleachers. So Astra did.

When she was finished talking, Libby sat in silence, digesting the information. Finally, she spoke. "So you confirmed that her wish was to make her father proud of her?"

Astra sighed. "Yes, she was very clear about it," she said.

"Exactly how much time is left?"

"Eighteen hours," said Astra.

"So that takes us to . . ."

"A little after one o'clock tomorrow," said Astra.

Then she heard a delicate snore. "Stay right there!" she said to Libby, who clearly wasn't going anywhere. Astra ran to the girls' bathroom and grabbed a couple of paper towels. She returned to the gym and rooted around in her backpack until she found the polish of removal. She poured some on a paper towel and began to scrub Libby's nails. It was very slow going, but finally, when the last nail was polish-free, Libby sat up.

"Where were we?" she asked. Astra held up the

now-empty bottle. Libby gave her a huge smile and looked down at her nails. "Star salutations, Astra," she said happily. "I feel so awake!"

"That's great," said Astra. "But what isn't so great is that we only have eighteen hours left—until one o'clock tomorrow."

"That seems like an odd deadline," said Libby. "Does something important happen at one o'clock tomorrow?"

Astra shook her head. "I just don't know."

"Hmmm . . . should we try to find Emma and ask her?" Libby asked.

Astra sighed. "Sure," she said dejectedly.

They walked into the hallway. Astra tore down a poster advertising the gymnastics meet. She reached for the next poster and stopped. "Moons and stars!" she said. She pointed to it.

"Oooh, paper," said Libby. "Pretty cool."

Astra shook her head. "No. Look." She pointed to the words:

ART SHOW!

20,000 LEAGUES UNDER THE SEA

SCHOOL CAFETERIA

SATURDAY AT 11:00 AM

But it was the last line that was the most important:

WINNERS ANNOUNCED AT 1:00 PM

It all came to her in a rush. "Emma's a great artist," she explained to Libby. "Her room is full of beautiful paintings and drawings, and someone—I guess it was the art teacher—was trying to get her to work on a project." Astra's face got warm as she remembered how dismissive she had been to the teacher. She shook her head, recalling Emma's words: *Not this way.* "Emma wanted her father to be proud of her, all right. But it wasn't for gymnastics. It was for her artwork. Moons and stars! How did I miss that?"

"So all we have to do is find her and convince her to submit something for the art show?" Libby asked. "When's Saturday, by the way?"

"I think it's tomorrow!" Astra answered. "And that's got to be it!" she added. "I think I know where she is. Follow me."

Astra led Libby down a hallway, then up a flight of stairs. She paused in front of a classroom door, waiting for Libby to catch up. She put her hand on the doorknob and quietly opened the door. There was Emma, standing in front of a large sculpture. She was concentrating so hard she didn't hear the girls enter the room. She had an expression on her face that Astra did not recognize. She almost gasped when she realized what it was—pure happiness.

"Oh, Emma," she said. "It's beautiful."

And it was. Emma had created a large sculpture of a beautiful woman with wild, flowing hair. Astra took another look and blinked. Well, it was a beautiful woman from the waist up. From the waist down was a completely different story. It was some sort of odd creature.

"Wow," said Astra. "I really like your . . . sculpture."

"It's a mermaid," explained Emma. "I've been working on it for months, whenever I could find the time. I was hoping to have it done for the art show tomorrow." She shook her head. "But I never had time to finish."

Libby stepped up. "It's gorgeous," she said.

"This is my friend Libby," Astra explained. "From my old school."

"You're really talented," Libby said, studying the sculpture.

"Thank you," said Emma.

"What is it made out of?" Astra asked.

Emma's eyes were shining. "It's this special sand clay I made. The theme of the art show is 20,000 Leagues Under the Sea, and I remembered all the fun summers we had when I was little, building castles and digging in the sand. So I decided to do a sand sculpture." She paused and her shoulders sagged. "I didn't get it finished in time."

"Can't you finish your sculpture tonight and submit it tomorrow for the show?" Astra asked.

Emma shook her head. "No, I needed to go to the beach and gather rocks and shells and seaweed and stuff and decorate it. But with all the practices and meets, I could never get my parents to take me. I'm totally out of time. It's too late to finish it."

Astra's heart sank. If only she had truly listened to her Wisher, she might have been able to help her.

Suddenly, she had an idea. "Hey, Emma," she said. "What if I told you we could get you exactly what you need?"

Emma smirked. "I'd say you were crazy," she answered.

"Go home and have dinner with your family," said Astra. "Tell them about the art show and that they need to come. We'll take care of getting the stuff you need. You can finish it in the morning and enter it in the competition."

Emma looked like she was trying hard not to get excited. "You're sure? You're really sure? It sounds impossible."

"I'm sure," said Astra. "But don't wait up," she added. "This could take a while!"

"I think you're crazy, too," said Libby.

"That's because you don't know my special talent," said Astra. "It's teleporting!"

"Ooh," said Libby. "Now that's a good one to have."

The question was, would she be able to take Libby along with her? The two girls held hands as Astra wished. It did not work. They stood back to back and Astra tried again. No such luck. Astra was about to head off on her own when she had a sudden idea, inspired by her roommate. She engulfed Libby in a big hug. *I wish I was at the beach*, she thought. There was a *whoosh*, everything grew blurry, and there was a feeling of moving fast.

And suddenly, they were standing in the sand! They were surrounded by palm trees and crystal-blue waters. White foam flew as the surf crashed onto the shore. They took off their shoes and dug their toes into the soft, silky sand. Astra couldn't help herself: she did a cartwheel of joy. Then another.

"That's a new one," said Libby. "You're going to slay us all in Poses when you get back."

"As usual," said Astra cheekily. She looked around, taking it all in. "It really is amazing here," she said.

The girls raced to the water's edge, filling their pockets with all the treasures from the sea they could find—tiny whelk shells; bits of green and blue sea glass, their edges softened by the tides and the sand; driftwood weathered into interesting shapes and bleached by the sun. Libby gathered the edges of her skirt with one hand and filled the hollow with crab claws, sand dollars, and scallop shells.

Astra spotted something star-shaped in the surf and thought for a moment that her eyes were deceiving her. She reached down and cradled the creature in her palm. "Have you ever seen anything lovelier?" she asked.

"How startastic!" said Libby.

"Piper would love it," Astra said. The creature moved its legs gently in her hand. "I wish I could take it home." But she knew it needed to be returned to the sea. She waded out and gently placed the creature back in the water.

Then Astra got a sudden inspiration. She bent down and filled her arms with seaweed in all shapes and sizes—thin ribbons, wide sheets, curly bright green tendrils. They lay their treasures on the sand and began to fill Astra's backback. The sun was sinking, its golden pink rays settling over the horizon. "It's time to go back," Astra said.

"Hey," said Libby with a laugh. "One of my shells is making a run for it!" She pointed to a tiny spiral shell that was slowly sneaking away.

"That was a close one!" said Astra. "Let's make sure we're not taking anyone else for a ride!" They carefully checked their shells, then finished packing. They hugged each other and Astra wished that she was back at Emma's house. Luckily no one noticed two girls magically appearing in the middle of Emma's backyard.

As she walked up the stairs to Emma's room, Astra thought she would burst with excitement. She also felt hopeful. But worried, too. Time was running out. This was their only chance. Emma had to convince her father to go to the show, finish her sculpture, win the prize, and make her father proud.

This had to work; it just had to!

CHAPTER
11

When Astra woke up the next morning in her usual spot on the floor in the sleeping bag, she immediately sprang up to wake Emma.

But Emma was already gone.

On her pillow was a note.

Dear Astra & Libby,

I found the bag of sea stuff! I don't know how you did it, but thank you so so so much! I'm going straight to school to finish the sculpture, so meet me there.

Love, Emma

P.S.: I told my family about the art show last night. Fingers crossed that they make it!

"Good morning, Astra," said Emma's mom when Astra and Libby entered the dining room. "And nice to meet you, Libby. Emma told me you would be staying over. Is she sleeping in this morning?"

"She already left for the art show!" said Astra. She looked at the family, all eating bowls of cereal around the table. "So you all are going to come, right?"

Eva yawned. "Ellie and I have practice this morning," she said. "And, Mom and Dad, you promised you were going to come watch us."

"I did," Emma's dad said, nodding. "I guess I'll have to go see Emma's art another time."

Astra gulped. This wasn't exactly going the way she had imagined.

Emma's dad stood and headed into the kitchen to refill his coffee cup. Astra followed him. She knew how to make him come to the show. It wasn't ideal, but she couldn't be choosy at that point.

She cleared her throat and Emma's dad glanced at her. Looking deep into his eyes, she said: "You are going to Emma's art show this morning."

He frowned. "I don't think I'm going to be able to make it," he said. "You heard the girls. I promised to go to their gymnastics practice."

Astra stood there, blinking. The rules of hypnotizing adults were very confusing.

She followed him back into the dining room. Libby looked at her hopefully, and Astra shook her head. Libby grimaced.

Astra could feel herself getting angrier and angrier. This wasn't fair to Emma at all. Her family had all the time in the world for gymnastics, but they couldn't be bothered to go to her art show? That was wrong, wrong, wrong.

Before she realized what she was doing, she slammed her hand down on the dining room table.

"Listen up," she said.

Everyone stared at her, openmouthed. Elizabeth had been about to put some cereal into her mouth, and the spoon hovered in midair.

"This is really important to Emma. The most important thing in her life, believe it or not. She has given up so much to do what you guys like—gymnastics—and she did an amazing job yesterday. But art is her passion. And it would really mean so much to have you all there. You *have* to be there."

The family looked at each other. "I guess we could leave practice early," said Eva reluctantly.

"If it's that important to Emma, we'll be there," said her father.

"But Saturday mornings are my only days to watch cartoons!" whined Elizabeth.

"Too bad, short stuff," said Ellie. "Emma is always there for us. Now it's our turn to be there for her."

Emma's mom put her hand on top of Astra's. "Thank you, Astra," she said simply. "Now you can sit down and eat."

Whew. Astra felt relieved. After breakfast she and Libby ran upstairs to get dressed, then headed to the school. Now all that was left was to make sure Emma's sculpture was finished in time.

When they arrived, Ms. Gonzales, the art teacher, was there, as well. "Hello!" she said when she saw Astra and Libby. "I am so thrilled that Emma is going to enter the contest! I gather you two had something to do with it."

Astra smiled and nodded.

"Her sculpture is wonderful," the teacher continued. "So evocative of the sea and childhood diversions."

"Um, yeah," said Astra. "Exactly."

Emma turned to the two girls proudly. The mermaid

was nearly finished. She wore a necklace of crab claws. Two large scallop shells served as her bikini top. Her tail was covered with a stunning mosaic of shells, pieces of seaweed, and sea glass. It was startacularly beautiful.

Ms. Gonzales glanced at her watch. "I've got to go and welcome the judges," she said. "The show begins in ten minutes and all entries must be registered beforehand. So please don't be late."

"I'll be done in a minute," said Emma distractedly. She squinted at the sculpture. "Something is missing. . . ." She grabbed some of the ribbony seaweed and artfully entwined it in the mermaid's flowing hair.

Astra grinned. "That's it. Perfect!"

It took the three of them to lift the sculpture and carry it down the hallway toward the auditorium.

"Be careful! Don't drop her!" Astra said warningly. When they successfully reached the auditorium, she peered through the doors, where she could see Ms. Gonzales, chatting with the judges and looking around nervously for Emma.

"Here we come," said Astra. She leaned her back against the door and pushed it—but it wouldn't budge.

"Hurry, Astra, this is getting heavy!" said Libby.

Astra pushed again. Then, after making sure the two girls could hold the sculpture on their own, she let go of it and pulled. She tried the other door. "I can't open it!" she cried.

"This is the only way in," Emma said. "It's got to open!"

Emma looked at the clock on the wall. "We're running out of time!" she cried.

Libby took a step backward. There was a strange sickly gray mist surrounding the door handle. *What in the world—*

She touched the mist and shivered. "It's so cold!" she said, rubbing her hands on her skirt for warmth.

"What's going on?" asked Emma. "I can't see!"

Something very strange was going on. It was almost as if something—or someone—was deliberately trying to keep them out.

Emma was near tears. "We're going to miss registration!" she said. "We have to get in there!"

Just then, Libby got a funny look on her face. "I'm not quite sure why I am doing this," she said, "but reach into my pocket. . . ."

Astra did and her fingers closed around an angular pink stone—Libby's Power Crystal!

"Put it on the door," instructed Libby.

"Put what on the door?" asked Emma, her view blocked by the large sculpture. "What is going on?"

To Astra's and Libby's amazement, the gray mist shrank back and disappeared.

"What's happening?" Emma demanded. "What are you doing?"

Before they could figure out how to answer her, the door opened with a snap.

The Star Darlings looked at each other. They had no idea what had just happened, but they realized it was something very big indeed.

Would Emma's wish come true? Or was Astra destined to be a wish energy failure?

CHAPTER
12

Astra, Emma, and Libby raced to the registration table (well, as quickly as three girls carrying a very heavy sculpture could race), arriving just in time.

"A minute longer and you wouldn't have made it," said the judge.

Afterward, Emma placed her sculpture on a folding table. A crowd began to gather around it. But Emma didn't notice.

She scanned the room excitedly. "Where is my dad?" she asked. Astra looked around but couldn't find him. Emma's shoulders sagged. "He forgot," she said. "He only cares about gymnastics."

Emma moped in the corner while Astra and Libby

examined the rest of the entries. The judges roamed the room, taking notes and consulting each other. Astra tried to eavesdrop and briefly wished that her special talent was super hearing.

There were many visitors to the art show. But Emma's family was nowhere to be found.

Astra sighed.

"We tried. We couldn't have tried harder," Libby assured her.

A crowd began to gather around the judges' table. One of the judges stepped up to the microphone. She gave a speech about art and creativity and effort, which Astra didn't really listen to. She was too upset. Emma reached out and squeezed her hand. "Thanks for everything," she said.

"And the winner is . . ." The judge paused, holding up a shiny gold medal on a bright red ribbon.

"Emma Prendergast!"

Despite the fact that her Wish Mission was foiled, Astra squealed and jumped up and down with joy. Emma threw her arms around Astra and Libby.

"You won!" shouted Astra. "You did it!"

"*We* did it," said Emma, her eyes shining. "I couldn't have done it without you."

"Go up and get your medal!" Libby shouted.

Emma looked around the room and her face fell. "What's the point?" she said bitterly. "My family didn't come. All they care about is gymnastics. They just don't care about anything else."

"Emma! Emma!" someone called. Emma and Astra spun around. Emma's father was trying to fight his way through the crowd to his daughter. "That's my girl!" he shouted.

Emma's face broke into a huge grin. Her dad made his way to her side and scooped her up in a big hug. Suddenly, the rest of her family was there, too, hugging and kissing her.

"I had no idea how important this was to you," he said. "All I could ever think about was gymnastics."

"It's okay, Daddy," Emma said.

"No, it isn't," he said. "It wasn't fair to you at all." He took a deep breath. "Your mother and I were talking on the way here. Now that we know what is really important to you, if you want to quit gymnastics, that's fine with us."

"I'll never quit gymnastics," said Emma. "I like it. Just not as much as the rest of you. But maybe I'll cut back a bit so I can go to art club, too."

He tousled her hair. "I'm really proud of you, sweetheart. Really proud."

Astra and Libby both watched, openmouthed, as the rainbow arc of pure wish energy danced around the room joyously before being absorbed into Astra's wristbands.

Libby smiled gently at Astra. "Great job," she said. "But you know what happens now. We have to go."

Astra sighed. "I know," she said sadly. She had heard from other Star Darlings that it can be very difficult to leave once you get to know your Wisher so well. But it felt even worse than she expected it to.

Emma bounded over. "I got my wish!" she said. "My dad is so proud of me. For my art! I've never been so happy in my life. Thank you so much!"

"I'm so glad for you," said Astra. "I'm just sorry that it took me so long to figure out what you wanted. I was telling you to be a gymnast when you really wanted to be an artist. I'm sorry I wasn't more helpful."

"Don't be crazy," said Emma. "You told me to believe in myself. And to focus on what was most important to me and not be distracted by the things that were not important. I couldn't have done this without you. You helped me more than you'll ever know. How can I repay you?"

"Oh, don't be silly," said Astra.

Libby poked her in the back and pointed to her fingernails.

"Well, now that you mention it," said Astra, "could you give me some polish of removal? About nine bottles should do it."

Epilogue

Astra stood in the starmarble hallway, waiting to be summoned into Lady Stella's office. She knew she was mere starmins away from getting her very own Power Crystal, which—she had seen firsthand—had some pretty startastic powers. But why did she feel so nervous?

Only one thing would make her feel better. She flipped open her Star-Zap and placed a holo-call. Instantly, a holo-picture appeared in front of her.

"Astra!" her mother cried happily. "We were just talking about you. It's just not the same without you here."

"Hi, Mom," Astra said, her voice nearly breaking. "Hey, everyone."

Her family was sitting in the gathering room. Her brother and sister were playing a game of Aughts and

Naughts. They all paused what they were doing to wave to her.

"We really do miss you," said Asia. "And I was just kidding. I'm going to keep our room just the way you left it."

"So how is school?" asked her father. "Anything new and exciting?"

Astra smiled. "School is good. I'll tell you all about it. Someday."

Lady Stella's door slid open and the headmistress stood there, smiling kindly at Astra. "We're ready for you," she said.

"Who's that?" asked her brother. "Are you in trouble?"

"I'm not in trouble, don't worry," said Astra. "I've just got to go."

"Bye!" they shouted.

"Bye, everyone," she said. She suddenly felt glad that she wasn't an only child (today, at least), and even though her family didn't quite get her drive and ambition, she felt loved and appreciated. That was what really mattered anyway. She snapped her Star-Zap shut and followed Lady Stella through the door.

Astra walked to the Lightning Lounge with Piper, admiring her newly acquired Power Crystal, a quarrelite. It glowed with a red-hot intensity, and sparks of energy raced across the asteroid-shaped stone. She was starprised at how much she was enthralled by her jewel. Accessories were always just distractions before, things to get in the way, or possibly get lost, while she played her beloved sports. But this was different. The Power Crystal was breathtakingly beautiful, of course, but it was mostly, she thought, because she had earned it herself and because there was deep meaning behind it—an obstacle faced and overcome, a job well done.

Piper understood. "It's starmazing, isn't it?" she said simply. Astra nodded.

They stepped up to the door of a private room and slid it open. As soon as Astra stepped into the room the Star Darlings swarmed her. Everyone was desperate to take off the polish. Astra started handing out bottles.

"It smells terrible!" said Cassie as she unscrewed the top from the bottle of nail polish remover.

"It's so weirdly cold!" said Adora.

After a few minutes of rubbing and scrubbing . . .

"I feel so much better," said Adora.

"Me too," said Clover.

"You can hear me!" Adora cried.

"I'll never skip again," said Scarlet with a shudder. "How humiliating."

"Hey, where's Leona?" Tessa asked. She reached into the bowl of star snacks and pulled out a mooncheese crisp. She popped it into her mouth. "Mmmm, delicious," she said. "If I never eat another Moonberry, I'll be startastically content!"

"I have no idea," said Cassie. "Was she at the ceremony?"

Vega rewound her holo-vid and shook her head.

"Say something, Vega," Piper begged.

"What do you want me to say? I have no words upon this day," Vega said.

Piper's face fell.

"Just kidding!" Vega said. "Oh my stars, you should have seen your face! Was it really as bad as all that?"

"Worse," said Piper.

The door slid open forcefully and Leona ran inside, her golden curls wilder than ever. She had a broad smile on her face.

"I have terrible news!" she said. "We tracked down Ophelia while you were gone!"

"And this is terrible . . . how?" asked Cassie.

Astra glanced down at Leona's golden fingernails. *Of course!* She grabbed the girl's hands and scrubbed until her nails were bare.

Leona nodded and smiled. "Great news, huh?"

"How did you find her?" Cassie wanted to know. "And is she an orphan?"

Piper spoke up. "I remembered you had said that Lady Stella thought that the orphanage had a different name. So we went to Vega . . ."

Vega took up the story. "And I had holo-vidded the conversation, of course, so I rewound it and we got the name."

"Turns out it's a real school in Starland City," Leona broke in. "So we went there. We couldn't find Ophelia, but we left her a message. And she just sent me a holo-text saying that she's going to call any starmin now!"

Leona's Star-Zap began to flicker and chime. "It's her!" she cried, accepting the call. Ophelia's tiny self, with her ocher eyes huge and serious, appeared in the air.

"Hi, everyone!" she said.

Everyone waved to her as they clustered around Leona.

"I just wanted to say I am sorry," said Ophelia. "For misleading you and for pretending to be someone I wasn't."

"I knew it!" said Cassie and Scarlet at the same time.

"But why did you lie, Ophelia?" said Leona. "I thought we were friends."

"I had to," said Ophelia. "I had my stars set on going to Starling Academy. But my grades weren't so stellar."

"I'll say," said Scarlet.

"And I bombed the entrance exam. I somehow managed to get an interview, but that didn't go so well, either. I was devastated."

Ophelia continued. "Then I got a holo-communication from Starling Academy. There was a spot open. But I was told that it was intended for a special student, an orphan. But they couldn't find one. So I just needed to pretend I was an orphan if I wanted to go there. I thought it was strange, but I just did as I was told."

She took a deep breath. "Once I arrived at Starling Academy I got a message every morning that told me what to do. Act like a sad orphan. Report back on everything you all said and did. Make friends with Leona." She had the good grace to look ashamed. "Sorry, Leona," she said. "I really did like you as a roommate. You were very entertaining!"

Leona snorted. "Glad I could amuse you, Ophelia." She shook her head. "But I really liked you."

"You mean you felt sorry for me," said Ophelia. "And

I can't blame you. I was told to act pathetic so everyone would feel bad for me and open up to me." She smiled. "I'm a really good actress, huh?"

Scarlet sneered. "A regular Rancora," she said.

"Who?" asked Adora loudly. Clearly she had missed the sound of her own voice.

"My old roommate, Mira, told me all about her," Scarlet explained. "She was a Starling Academy student and apparently quite the actress back in the day."

"Are you serious, guys?" said Cassie. "We're discussing this now?" She addressed Ophelia. "Here's what I want to know. Who did the holo-communications come from?"

The room grew silent. Everyone leaned forward.

Ophelia gave a sharp laugh. "They came from Lady Stella, of course."

Tessa's Lost and Found

Prologue

Curled up in bed, Tessa gazed at her Star-Zap screen and yawned. Her roommate, Adora, had been sleeping for at least a starhour. But Tessa needed to get a holo-mail out on the school's zap-app 3C, otherwise known as the Cosmic Communication Center.

The system had mail, calendars, announcements, holo-textbooks, and grades that were constantly updating. Right then, Tessa was writing to her Wishworld Relations teacher, asking for an extension on a holo-paper.

Tessa added a few words, then abandoned the holo-mail once again to peek at her grades in a different class, Wish Fulfillment. Maybe the stars had aligned and Professor Eugenia Bright had changed her grade since the last time she'd checked, about fifteen starmins earlier. No, there it was, exactly the same as before: A for *almost glowing*, two grades below the perfect I for *illumination*. Definitely not what she was aiming for!

Really, though, Wish Fulfillment was the least of Tessa's concerns. She had to focus on Wishworld Relations. But first she decided to check the scores for the Glowin' Glions star ball team and see how Astra had fared in the latest game.

"Moonberries!" she moaned. They'd lost to the Twinkling Twinkelopes by half a hydrong. Next she scrolled through some announcements.

"That's interesting," Tessa said out loud. The Star Darlings band's biggest rival was holding another audition. *And no wonder*, she thought, a little gleefully. Another Starling must have quit the group. A girl named Vivica was its leader. And no Starling with even a flounce of talent would stick with her band. The way Vivica and her friends treated others was downright mean.

Now what? Tessa wondered. What should she click on next? *Oh! That Wishworld Relations holo-mail!*

This time, for sure, she wouldn't get distracted. She'd finish the letter. But first she read over what she'd already written.

Star greetings, Professor Margaret Dumarre,

Hmmm . . . She hadn't gotten as far she'd thought! She nibbled one of the astromuffins she kept by her bedside, and in a burst of energy continued:

I'm writing this holo-letter while everyone else is sleeping. I should be sleeping, too, but I'm staying up late trying to finish my holo-paper, "Being Human." Of course I know that Wishlings call themselves human! I've known that since I was in Wee Constellation School. And as a third-year student, I've recently learned many of these "teenage humans" put off homework and studying so they can watch a screen called "television" and constantly check their low-tech devices: computers, tablets, and cell phones.

I've absorbed this information so well I seem to have developed some of these traits myself. I've put off this paper, and now with star apologies, I must tell you it's going to be late. Would it be possible to have an extension? Maybe another starweek, until next Dododay?

I don't mean to make star excuses, but unlike my Wishworld counterparts, I have valid reasons for being so late.

First, there's that ~~super-secret Star Darlings class we take to prepare for our wish missions~~ special class I have to take for extra help. It requires a lot of outside-the-classroom work. And I can't always judge the timing. Often Lady Stella calls us together unexpectedly. And sometimes we meet on our own. Just the other starday, we talked about ~~all the strange happenings on campus and on Starland.~~ the basics of a successful Wish Mission.

Specifically, we discussed:

~~How Lady Stella tells us there's nothing to worry about, but Starland has had several blackouts.~~
How to recognize that you have correctly identified your Wisher.

~~How Scarlet was kicked out of the SD group and replaced by Ophelia. When it turned out Ophelia desperately needed Scarlet's help, Lady Stella explained that Scarlet was back in and Ophelia was out. And most shockingly, how~~

~~Ophelia later disappeared and just told us that she was lying the whole time and that Lady Stella put her up to it.~~
How to ask probing, yet innocent questions to determine your Wisher's wish.

~~How all the SD roommates were fighting because of the poisonous flowers someone mysteriously placed in our rooms.~~
How to keep an eye on your Countdown Clock so you don't miss your wish window.

~~How Star Kindness Day was ruined by negative energy when holo-texted compliments were replaced by insults.~~
How to erase your Wisher's memory once the wish is granted and wish energy successfully collected.

~~How all the Star Darlings were acting odd because we were wearing special nail polish, probably made with negative energy. My reaction: everything tasted like moonberries.~~
How to return to Starland safely when your mission is accomplished.

There's so much material to cover, in fact, the girls have an early-morning meeting in my room. ~~The future of the Star Darlings~~ Our grades may hang in the balance!

Starfully yours,
Tessa

And with those last words written and her real thoughts deleted, Tessa finally fell asleep.

CHAPTER
1

The next morning should have worked out perfectly for Tessa. All the Star Darlings were coming to her and Adora's room for an important meeting. And she was totally prepared.

Even though she'd stayed up late working on her holo-paper—and excuse note—Tessa had set the alarm on her Star-Zap for an extra-early wake-up time. Before morning, the alarm buzzed her favorite childhood tune, "Old MacStarlight Had a Farm."

She took her sparkle shower in record time, not losing track of starmins the way she usually did. She finished so quickly, in fact, Adora was still sleeping soundly when she went back to the room.

So Tessa tidied her ultra-plush bedcovers and smoothed her soft-as-a-cloud rug. Both came from Bed, Bath, and Beyond the Stars' exclusive line of luxury items, perfect for Tessa, who liked to surround herself with sumptuous comfort.

Then she pulled on the outfit she'd laid out the night before: an emerald-green and ocean-blue striped sweaterdress that swirled around her knees. It matched Tessa's long wavy hair perfectly.

Quickly, Tessa checked her Star-Zap to make sure she was still on schedule. Yes, she was doing great. She picked up her starbrush to sweep her bangs to the side. There was just one more thing to do before the Star Darlings came over. She had to—

Tessa caught sight of the headboard over her bed . . . and everything fell apart.

The headboard was really one big holo-screen, and Tessa was drawn to it like solar metal to a magnet.

Initially, Tessa had used the screen to care for virtual pets. She loved creatures of all sizes, shapes, and glows. But then she'd programmed the screen to show her family farm in real time—real creatures in real action.

Tessa and her younger sister, Gemma—also a Star Darling—were from Solar Springs, a tiny town of gently rolling hills. A small number of families lived on simple farms nestled in valleys. It was a lovely spot. But the town had just one general store that sold only basic items, like toothlights and starbrushes.

When Tessa wanted that starmazing luster-lotion for her skin, or the glitz gloves that felt soft as shimmer-butter, she had to put in a special order. Except for that, Tessa loved her farm life: the fresh fruits and vegetables she used for cooking, the farm creatures . . .

And that was why she couldn't turn away from the screen. Her favorite creature of all, a playful baby galliope named Jewel, was there in all her cuteness, nudging a round druderwomp bush across the ground like a ball.

The deep purple creature was all spindly legs and long neck, with a glowing feathery mane and tail. Tessa had seen holo-pictures of Wishworld ponies. She agreed they resembled galliopes. But she doubted they could hold a glowstick to Jewel in charm alone.

Tessa dropped her starbrush and edged closer to the holo-screen. "Jewel," she cooed softly. "Star greetings, little girl."

If Jewel was in the right mood, she could step out of the screen—or at least her image could—and be vir-tually close to Tessa. Hoping that would happen, Tessa tapped the bottom of the screen, and a virtual starapple floated into her hand. She held out the sparkling round fruit to Jewel. Back on the farm, it wouldn't be just an image; the starapple would be real and crunchy and sweet.

Jewel whinnied, stepped out of the screen, and nuzzled Tessa's neck. "I could do this all starday," Tessa said with a giggle.

"Maybe you could, but you really shouldn't," said Adora. Tessa looked across the room. Adora had gotten up and dressed without her even noticing.

"Everyone will be here in a starsec. So pick up your starbrush and finish getting ready."

Tessa ignored her, putting her arm around Jewel. "I don't like being told what to do," she whispered, as if the galliope could understand. "You'd think after rooming together for so long, Adora would know that."

Sighing, Adora picked up Tessa's starbrush and placed it on the nightstand. "Come on, Tessa, I put away all my test tubes and experiments—even that new lip-sparkle I'm working on. The one that actually shoots out sparks."

Adora spoke as calmly as ever; Tessa had rarely seen her ruffled or emotional. And they generally got along.

But Tessa had cleaned up! What was one little starbrush in the grand scheme of things? Still, the Star Darlings were coming over. . . .

Tessa waved good-bye to Jewel, and the galliope stepped back into the screen. "See you soon, little girl. Next time we'll play and we'll—"

"Starland to Tessa!" Adora snapped her fingers in front of Tessa's face. "The Star Darlings meeting is—"

"*Knock-knock,*" sang Leona from the other side of the door.

"Now!" Adora finished, nodding toward the door so it slid open quickly. The other ten Star Darlings walked into the room and settled on beds, chairs, and rugs.

"Oh, Tessa," Gemma said, disappointment in her voice. She eyed Tessa's cleared-off table. "I thought for sure you'd have a whole breakfast spread for us."

Tessa groaned. That was what she'd been planning to do! Before she was distracted by Jewel, she had been about to bake breakfast treats in the micro-zap!

Scarlet shook her head emphatically, her dark hood falling to her shoulders before she quickly pulled it back up. "Breakfast is not important," she said brusquely. "We'll have plenty of time to go to the Celestial Café after the meeting."

"Still, we could have met a little later," Piper said wistfully, covering up a yawn. Tessa knew Piper liked her rest more than the average Starling.

"No, meeting now makes the most sense," said Vega. "This way we take care of business and keep the rest of the starday free for studying."

"I would have voted for a bit later so I'd have had time to warm up my vocal cords." Leona's voice started out deep, then rose higher with every word: "Now I have to do my exercises in regular conversation."

"Please, spare us," Scarlet said.

Tessa sighed. Those roommates were a much bigger mismatch than she and Adora! She doubted they would ever get along.

Cassie held up a hand, and everyone quieted down. She was the smallest Starling of the group, but her words carried great weight. "The fact is, spies could be anywhere on campus. I don't know whom we can even trust! Not even Lady Stella."

Tessa laughed. "You don't really believe what that crazy Ophelia said, do you? She was clearly making it up."

Half the Star Darlings nodded in agreement. Others didn't look quite so convinced.

Libby stood up. "Okay, everybody, let's focus!"

Tessa nodded in agreement. It would also be great if they could move the meeting along so they could make it to breakfast in a timely fashion. Without her usual pre-breakfast snack, she was hungry.

"Fine." Cassie nodded. She took off her star-shaped glasses, polished them so they shone, and nodded again. "Someone is clearly trying to sabotage the Star Darlings. If it isn't Lady Stella, then who is it? And why? I mean, there have been so many crazy problems. . . ."

"Like our holo-text compliments coming out as insults," interrupted Piper indignantly.

"And every student invited to try out for my band," Leona added, "when it should have just been Star Darlings!"

"And those are just communication issues," Cassie continued. "What about everything else? The poisonous flowers? The strange nail polish that wouldn't come off? Who is responsible?"

Scarlet shook her head irritably. "It's so clearly Lady Stella," she said. "Why can't you all see it?"

The Star Darlings began to argue.

Lady Stella was the head of the school. She was revered in academic circles for her principles and forward thinking in education. She was held in highest regard all across Starland. Business Starlings, Starling scientists, and heads of state constantly consulted her, and wee Starlings wanted to grow up to be just like her.

Tessa had actually dressed as Lady Stella once for Light Giving Day, when young Starlings dressed in costume to hand out flowers and welcome the growing season. She guessed a couple of others may have, too.

Tessa thought back to one of her first days at the academy, well before the Star Darlings had been formed. She had been curled up in a chair in the Lightning Lounge, holo-texting Gemma back home and feeling homesick.

Lady Stella had come over and sat down next to her. She seemed to know all about Tessa without Tessa's saying a word, and she led her on a tour of the Celestial Café kitchen, where Bot-Bot cooks and waitstaff worked.

"You can come here any time you like," she had said, "and cook, bake, or just relax. The Bot-Bots will be informed."

Then they'd sat in a corner and munched on astromuffins together—moonberry for Lady Stella (she said they were her favorite) and lolofruit for Tessa.

Lady Stella couldn't be capable of any wrongdoing whatsoever!

"Scarlet, you're going galactic!" said Libby, apparently agreeing with Tessa. "The person or people responsible don't even have to be part of Starling Academy! He or she could be from outside the school."

"I doubt that," Cassie said nervously. "Whoever is doing this would need to be here full-time. And Lady Stella is here 36/8."

"You're *both* going galactic!" Sage said to Scarlet and Cassie. "Lady Stella has been starmendous to each and every one of us!"

"Well, count me out of that lucky stargroup," Scarlet shot back. "Here's a fact for you: my grades were switched with dimwit Ophelia's so I'd be kicked out of the Star Darlings. Who else would be able to do that? And why would Ophelia lie?"

The girls fell silent. It was hard to disagree with Scarlet; plus, she could so easily go supernova. Tessa looked at Leona, who stood up to Scarlet regularly. But Leona had been uncharacteristically quiet. Then Tessa glanced at Gemma. What was her sister thinking? She, too, had been quiet.

"Well, lots of Starlings could have access to records,"

Tessa finally said. "What about the Bot-Bot guards? They have access to every room on campus."

Gemma finally spoke up. "That's right! Once, when I was walking past the teachers' lounge, I was hurrying really fast down the hall. I can't even remember why I was there. Maybe because I had to go to the Radiant Rec Center and I was a little nervous because I had never—"

"Get to the point of the story," said Scarlet.

"Well, once there was a Bot-Bot repairman outside the lounge door, stooping over. He could have been trying to listen in!"

"Or fix the hand scanner," said Scarlet.

"Lady Cordial keeps close watch on all the comings and goings in that hall," Cassie noted, "because the admissions office is there. She'd notice anything strange. So forget about the Bot-Bot!" She sighed. "Lady Stella clearly set up the whole Scarlet-Ophelia switch. She told me Ophelia was an orphan. She lied. And as we all know, Ophelia was never even in an orphanage!"

Scarlet leaned closer to Sage with an almost compassionate expression. "I was fooled, too, for a long time." A shadow passed over her face. "But Lady Stella pulled the glimmersilk over my eyes."

Finally, Leona spoke up, as if she'd been weighing the information and had made up her mind. "Well,

I spent the most time with Ophelia of all of you, and frankly, I think she's telling the truth."

"But why would Lady Stella want to sabotage our missions?" Vega asked. "It doesn't make sense. The missions were her idea to begin with!"

The girls all spoke at once.

"Maybe she wants Starling Academy to fail so she can start a new school."

"Maybe she wants to move to Wishworld!"

"Maybe she's just a hologram, and the real Lady Stella is being held captive in one of the underground caves."

Tessa shivered. The last comment, which had come from Piper, was especially creepy.

"I don't know why she's doing it," said Scarlet. "But we have to confront her, and soon."

"I just don't believe it," said Tessa stubbornly. "I need real proof."

"I don't believe it, either," Sage said.

The room fell silent. The girls eyed each other nervously. No one knew what to say. But then Tessa's stomach rumbled loudly. Gemma laughed, breaking the tension.

"I say we've talked enough for now. It's time to eat," said Tessa.

Cassie nodded and stood up. "Before we confront

anyone," she said to Scarlet, "we should do more sleuth-ing." Then she turned to Tessa. "And you're right, of course. We should all go to breakfast."

Cassie is smart, Tessa thought as everyone left the room, *even if she does suspect Lady Stella. And she's read all those detective books her uncle wrote; she must know about sleuthing.* She'd stick close to Cassie, find out what was really going on, and put in her two stars to defend Lady Stella whenever she could.

Tessa stepped onto the Cosmic Transporter, careful to get in place right behind the younger Starling.

Cassie and Scarlet were standing side by side, whis-pering. Tessa edged closer, trying to listen. *It's not like I'm really eavesdropping,* she reasoned. *We're all just heading to the Celestial Café at the same time.*

But all she heard was: "Mumble mumble Lady Stella." "Mumble mumble Leona." "Mumble Ophelia." "Mumble mumble mumble."

Nothing new there.

Then Cassie said "Star Caves" loud and clear. Scarlet gave her a "shut your stars" look. "Later!" the older Starling whispered harshly.

Hmmm, thought Tessa. Now that was interesting. They must think the secret underground tunnels, where the special Star Darlings Wish Cavern was hidden, held clues. *Maybe—*

Suddenly, the star above the Celestial Café dimmed, signaling that breakfast was about to end. Tessa forgot about the caves. She took off past the other Starlings, thoughts of warm astromuffins and tinsel toast filling her head.

CHAPTER
2

After breakfast, Tessa's starday was basically back-to-back classes. Some flew by like a comet. Others seemed to last an entire Cycle of Life. So much of what the professors taught had already been covered in the special Star Darlings class.

Tessa's final class before Star Darlings lessons was Wish Fulfillment, taught by Professor Eugenia Bright. Usually, Tessa paid attention to Professor Bright's lessons; the teacher was warm and engaging and cared about each student. Besides, Tessa wanted to raise her grade.

That day Professor Bright was lecturing about wish fulfillment history: how Starlandians had first discovered their connection to Wishworld.

"During a space exploration trip," the teacher explained, "scientist Dusty Particulus forgot to transfer shooting stars. She wound up landing near a group of Wishling stargazers just as they wished on a different shooting star. One Wishling said, 'I wish I could come face-to-face with someone from another planet.' So Dusty stepped right in front of her, and suddenly a surge of energy. . ."

Yes, it was starmazingly interesting. But Tessa had heard the story so many times she found her mind wandering back to the Star Darlings meeting.

It was true: much had gone wrong for the Star Darlings. Right there on Starland, there had been the band tryouts, the flowers, the nail polish, the holo-texts, and, of course, the power failures that affected the whole planet. And they'd had trouble on Wishworld, too. There had been Leona's burnt-out Wish Pendant that lost wish energy; and her scary trip back, when she almost hadn't made it home; and all the Starlings' misidentifying of Wishers and wishes.

But Lady Stella? How could some of the Star Darlings think she was responsible?

"Star excuse me, Tessa." Tessa looked up. Professor Eugenia Bright was standing over her desk, smiling. They were the only two in the classroom.

"Is there something you'd like to discuss with me?" the teacher asked kindly.

Tessa eyed the professor. She had to say something, but she certainly couldn't say she'd been lost in thought, wondering if Lady Stella was sabotaging Starland.

"I like your earrings!" she sputtered. She turned deep green with embarrassment, but it was true—she did like them! The glittery cylinders hung almost to Professor Bright's shoulders and twirled when she moved, giving off sparks. They were exquisite and classic and must have come from Starland's most acclaimed jewelry store, Starrier's, where the rich and famous shopped.

Professor Eugenia Bright lowered her voice. "I found them at the Brilliant Bargain Basement in Old Prism. Sure, it's a tourist town, but you can still find starmazing deals there."

Tessa laughed and stopped worrying about Lady Stella and Star Darlings problems—at least for the moment.

That afternoon, Tessa joined the Future Farmers of Starland after-school club. They visited a new colony of glitterbees at the foot of the Crystal Mountains. And it was well worth the trip, Tessa thought on the way back. One delicatacomb in particular was starmendous, as big as a Starcar! Plus, she even managed to bring some of the sweet liquid back to campus. It was starrific for baking.

But now, standing in front of Halo Hall, saying good-bye to her fellow future farmers, Tessa felt restless. She paced back and forth, her mind returning again and again to Lady Stella. She thought fleetingly of her overdue Wishworld Relations paper. She even took a few tentative steps toward the library. But how could she settle down to work when her mind was in such a state?

Tessa's feet switched course and she found herself heading to the Celestial Café.

I'll just bake for a starhour or so, Tessa thought. *It will calm me down, help me focus, and then . . .* "On to my 'Being Human' paper!"

"You're still working on that?" Cassie asked. Tessa hadn't realized that she'd spoken out loud, or that Cassie was walking next to her. She shook her head to clear it. She really did need to bake!

"Yes, but cross my stars, I'll get an extension. I'm still waiting to hear from Professor Margaret Dumarre. Right now I'm going to the kitchen."

Cassie brightened, and her pale skin glittered, show-ing her interest. "Are you baking? Can I tag along? I promise I won't talk about Lady Stella. We can agree to disagree until more facts are in."

"Of course!" It would be an opportunity to find out about the caves with Cassie. Usually when she baked, every bit of her energy went into creating the per-fect dish. But this time, she'd multitask. Smiling, she motioned for Cassie to join her as she stepped off the Cosmic Transporter.

"I want to use fresh delicata," Tessa went on, "so I'm thinking about mini comet cakes. Only instead of sparkleberries, I might add cocomoons with a starburst of solar cream."

"Mmm-mmm," said Cassie as they entered the kitchen. "Sounds starmendous. What can I do to help?"

"For starters, set the micro-zap for a moonium and four degrees."

The two girls got to work, Tessa humming as she measured and mixed, crimped and coated, sometimes telling Cassie what to add.

"A flounce of milk."

"Two quax of sunflour."

"A zingspoon of sparklesugar."

Then she poured the batter and popped the tray

into the micro-zap. "Two point six seven starsecs," she instructed Cassie. She grinned happily. "Star salutations for your help!" Then she remembered: the whole time, she was supposed to have been getting more information!

Before she could say anything else, the comet cakes were ready. There were twelve mini comet cakes, one for each Star Darling. Tessa couldn't help admiring the treats, with their perfectly round shape and tapered tails made from starberries. The bright red fruit looked just like a comet's fiery stream.

Cassie sniffed. "They smell so good! Can I have mine now?"

Tessa grinned. "Tell you what. Let's have as many as we want. Then we can make another batch!"

Cassie stretched out her hand, but Tessa held the tray high over the small Starling's head. It was a little unfair, she knew, to hold back the treat. But she had to work fast now to get some information. And she knew from when Gemma was younger that this was the best way to get it.

"Tell me what you and Scarlet were whispering about on the Cosmic Transporter this morning."

"What? I don't know what you mean," Cassie said, turning away so she wouldn't have to look Tessa in the eye.

"Oh, I think you do." Tessa sounded more confident

than she felt. "I distinctly heard you say 'Star Caves.' And I bet you two are convinced those caves have something to do with your Lady Stella suspicions."

The caves were real, not a theory or an idea, and they were something Tessa could reach out and touch— something that could hold solid proof of Lady Stella's innocence. *Or guilt*, Tessa thought for a starsec, before she could help herself.

She lowered the tray and waved it tantalizingly under Cassie's nose.

"Oh, okay!" Cassie grabbed a cake.

She paused to take a bite. "Scarlet's explored the caves. She found another entrance, and she's gone down a bunch of times. I guess she likes the bitbats and the feel of the tunnels—the mystery and the isolation. But it's not as if she's found anything revealing there."

"Is that all?" Tessa asked, disappointed.

"Well, I have my own ideas about the caves," Cassie went on. "There are so many twists and turns. They could hold so many secrets, and they're so closely tied to our missions I just feel there could be clues down there— answers to what's been going on."

"Exactly!" Tessa exclaimed. "So what are you two going to do next? For your sleuthing?"

"Nothing," said Cassie, squirming a bit.

Was Cassie skirting the truth? She seemed uncomfortable, and Tessa guessed the Starling didn't really like to lie. So she didn't want to call her on it. But she needed to keep pressing her.

"The next time Scarlet explores the caves, we should go, too," Tessa said. "We may spot something she's missed."

Tessa gave a little shudder. Really, the last thing she wanted to do was trek through those damp, spooky tunnels. Going with the Star Darlings to their special Wish Cavern was one thing. But just roaming around—unescorted—was a galliope of an entirely different color.

Meanwhile, Cassie had polished off four comet cakes and was reaching for a fifth. "Well, I can ask her. I have no idea what she'll say, though, and there's no way we can go alone. We don't even know how to get in."

Cassie popped the round cake into her mouth and sighed. "These are really good, Tessa. I wish I could bake like you."

"You can!" said Tessa. "You already watched me once. So this time when I bake, holo-vid me with your Star-Zap and use it for reference."

"Can I borrow yours?" asked Cassie. "I brought

mine in for repairs. It's been weird lately, and I haven't been able to get holo-messages, or even send them."

"Uh-huh," Tessa murmured, not really listening. Already she was measuring sparklesugar and pouring it into a bowl. Maybe this time she'd add just a flicker more delicata. . . .

CHAPTER
3

The next starday Tessa was late for class. But why, oh, why did it have to be Wishworld Relations with Professor Margaret Dumarre?

After baking the comet cakes with Cassie, she'd felt so calm and productive she'd actually finished her "Being Human" paper. She'd sent it right off but hadn't heard back from the professor. Not a holo-note saying it was okay it was late. Not a message saying she was lowering the grade because Tessa had missed the due date. However her teacher felt, Tessa wasn't looking forward to walking into class after the lecture had already begun.

If only she hadn't tried to take a quick peek at Jewel! The "quick peek" had turned into a very long gaze. And then her mom had holo-texted a new recipe, and Tessa just had to holo-call to say star salutations, it sounded great, and the two had talked until her mom asked why she wasn't in class.

Now, racing along the Cosmic Transporter, she was tempted to go back to her room and grab a leftover comet cake to give to Professor Margaret Dumarre. Maybe that would somehow explain her tardiness, or at least give the teacher a reason to be more lenient. But Tessa doubted that would, in fact, help. Professor Margaret Dumarre would know she was being bribed.

"Oops!" Lost in thought, Tessa had almost gone right by her classroom.

"Hey, where's the starfire?" Scarlet stepped in front of her, blocking the classroom door.

"I'm late for class, Scarlet. So please star excuse me." Tessa started to walk around the other Starling, but then she remembered the caves. She stopped, turned back, and smiled encouragingly.

Scarlet almost smiled back. "I'm actually late, too. Since I've stopped skipping, it's taking me longer to get places than I think it should." She shrugged. "I didn't even know I was skipping, but I guess acting crazy can have its benefits. Anyway, it's okay with me if you and Cassie come with me next time."

"To the caves?" Tessa said loudly, not quite hiding her

surprise. It was all happening faster than she'd thought it would. She had imagined Cassie would have trouble convincing Scarlet, a notorious loner, to let them go along.

"Shhh!" Scarlet said, annoyed. Then she stomped away without saying another word, her boots thudding loudly.

Tessa took a deep breath and peered through the window of the classroom door. Professor Margaret Dumarre had her back to Tessa and was speaking to the students.

Now! thought Tessa. She quietly opened the door— just a bit—with her wish energy manipulation, then slipped inside.

"Today we will delve into one of the pillars of positivity: creating a peaceful space." Professor Margaret Dumarre paused, then, with her back still to Tessa, said, "Tessa, please take a seat and join us."

Tessa hurried to an empty desk, thinking, *That wasn't bad at all!* Professor Margaret Dumarre didn't sound angry in the least. Maybe she didn't care that Tessa was arriving after the bell.

A girl named Violetta, sitting next to Tessa, turned to her with a smirk. "Late again, Star Dope," she hissed.

If only she hadn't been in such a rush, Tessa would have noticed Violetta and found another empty desk. She would never, in a moonium staryears, purposely sit next to the girl. The purple-haired Starling was great friends with Vivica. Even though Violetta was two grades ahead, she fawned over the younger Starling as if she was the most starmazing thing since sliced tinsel toast.

Maybe Violetta liked the way their names sounded together, or maybe she was just afraid if she didn't flatter Vivica, she would turn on Violetta like she had done to so many others.

Violetta tapped the clock on her Star-Zap and shook her head sadly at Tessa. "Now you're slow to get to class, too? Poor, poor Tessa. You Slow Developers lag behind in everything."

Or maybe she was just plain mean.

Tessa shifted her attention to the front of the room. Professor Margaret Dumarre was gesturing at a small device. Instantly, a holo-picture of a lovely garden appeared. Flutterfocuses, their sparkly wings glowing, fluttered around delicate blushbelle flowers, their pink petals glimmering in the sun. Kaleidoscope trees ringed a clear blue pond, their ever-changing colors reflected in the still waters.

With a wave of the teacher's arm, the picture expanded, wrapping around the classroom and winding among desks so it seemed the girls were sitting right at its very center.

Professor Margaret Dumarre wrinkled her forehead in concentration, her magenta-and-blue-striped bangs swaying gently with the motion. Tessa's seat slowly transformed, shrinking, changing shape, texture, and color, until she realized she was sitting on a moss-covered stone as soft as her bed. She looked around and saw all the chairs had been replaced. A sweet fragrance filled the air. Someone sighed with contentment.

"To feel positive, to be trusting and open to experience and accepting of outcomes, to be in the moment . . ." Professor Margaret Dumarre spoke in a low soothing voice. "Be mindful of your surroundings. Feel a sense of place . . . real or imagined. And let that place bring a peaceful moment . . . a moment that will bring good vibrations to everything and everyone in sight. Gather and share that positive energy flow!"

Tessa's fingers grazed her velvety-smooth moss and, using all her senses, took in the scene.

She watched a gold-and-silver flutterfocus intently, studying and enjoying its grace and beauty. She felt loose and relaxed.

Is this for real? she wondered idly. *Or just a holo-illusion?* The girl on her other side slowly tipped her head up to the ceiling, now a bright sky. The entire class seemed lulled into a sunshiny, dreamy state. Even Violetta had a sweet smile on her face. So maybe it didn't matter.

What counted was the feeling, the positive emotion you took from a tranquil setting—the feeling that you could achieve the impossible. She felt the positive energy flow.

"Creating a peaceful space," Professor Margaret Dumarre said softly, "can bring with it power to shrug off negativity."

She turned to look steadily toward Tessa, an understanding smile on her lips. "One day, when you're on a Wishworld mission, things may not be going your way. You may not be able to find your Wisher." She paused for a moogle to stare directly at Tessa. "Or your Wisher may be late."

Tessa realized she hadn't really gotten away with anything. In her own way, Professor Margaret Dumarre was taking her to task for being late. But Tessa felt surprisingly okay about it; the calm feeling persisted.

"And in those cases," the professor continued, "you'll need to increase your positivity."

At the word *positivity*, Tessa heard a buzzing sound and looked for a nearby glitterbee among the flowers. But the garden scene was fading, the flutterfocuses and flowers disappearing, and the buzzing seemed more insistent.

Oh! Tessa realized with a start that it was her Star-Zap, set on low.

"Class dismissed. See you on Lunaday," the teacher said, smiling. "And don't forget to check 3C for your term paper grades. I'm sure you'll all be pleased. There were many Is."

Illumination! Tessa thought. Did she have a moon-shot at a grade like that? Violetta gave her one last sneer before she left class, saying, "If I were a Star Dope, I wouldn't be in a rush to find out my grades."

But Violetta spoke in such a soft, pleasant way the words barely stung. *Positivity at work!* Tessa thought. *A little more time spent in pleasant surroundings—minus Vivica—might be all that Starling needs.*

Buzzzz!

Oh, my Star-Zap, Tessa remembered. She checked the screen and saw a group holo-text from Scarlet, with Cassie included in the message.

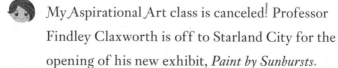 My Aspirational Art class is canceled! Professor Findley Claxworth is off to Starland City for the opening of his new exhibit, *Paint by Sunbursts.* Have free period next. Let's go exploring! Meet me at the fountain right now!

Tessa had to smile. Scarlet, usually so abrupt, was quite chatty by holo-text!

Luckily, Tessa had an independent study period next. She was supposed to go to the Illumination Library and report to the supervising librarian, Lady Floridia. But as a third year, she was allowed to skip study hall three times a term. She wasn't sure how many periods she'd missed already. Hadn't she used some study time to bake Bright Day cakes just recently?

But she didn't have time to check in at the Illumination Library, so she hurried directly to the fountain, in the Star Quad. As always, the water seemed to dance as it flowed, sparkling with all the colors of the rainbow. Scarlet was already there.

"Where's Cassie?" Scarlet said immediately, dispensing with any sort of greeting.

"*Moonberries!*" Tessa shook her head. "I totally forgot. Cassie brought her Star-Zap in for repairs. She didn't get the holo-text."

Tessa expected an angry retort from Scarlet, but maybe she'd come from a positivity class, too, because the Starling only shrugged. "Well, no rush. I have band practice after this period, but Leona won't mind if I skip it."

Scarlet was the Star Darlings band's drummer. She

was so talented maybe Leona allowed her flexibility. But no matter what, Leona most certainly *would* mind if Scarlet missed practice.

Then again, Scarlet probably found that appealing.

"Cassie has Wishers 101," Tessa told Scarlet. It was an introductory course, taught by Professor Elara Ursa. The class was held in the largest lecture hall, filled with row upon row of first years just figuring out Wishlings. Cassie had already met several in person and surely knew more than all the other students combined. It wouldn't be a big deal for her to miss it. "If we hurry, we can catch her before class starts."

The two Starlings ran along the Cosmic Transporter but weren't quite fast enough. Cassie's classroom door was just sliding shut as they approached. Through the door's window, they could see Cassie's pink hair falling over her desk as she readied her supplies.

"Come on," said Scarlet, pulling Tessa back outside. She stopped by the floor-to-ceiling window along one wall of the lecture hall. "We'll just wave to Cassie until she comes out."

"Uh, I don't think so."

The last teacher Tessa wanted to get in trouble with was Professor Elara Ursa. Well, no. The very last teacher was Professor Margaret Dumarre. But she needed to be on her best behavior around Professor Elara Ursa, too.

Tessa ducked behind a starmarble pillar.

"Listen, Tessa, you have to stop hiding," Scarlet told her. "You still haven't gone on a mission, so you may be chosen any starmin now. How will you be successful on Wishworld if you're too nervous to get a friend out of class right here on Starland?"

Tessa took a deep breath. Everyone knew Scarlet was fearless. And she, Tessa, was not—not by a moonshot. Still, Scarlet had a point. She had to learn to handle setbacks, just like Professor Margaret Dumarre was trying to teach them. For a moogle, she pictured the peaceful classroom garden.

"Okay," she said, stepping close to Scarlet.

Scarlet grinned, then waved her arms furiously at Cassie. She shielded her eyes like she was on some sort of search, then flapped her arms like a bitbat.

It was a good pantomime and would definitely give Cassie the idea of exploring the caves . . . if she was looking. Unfortunately, she wasn't.

Tessa waved tentatively just as Cassie turned her head and seemed to stare in her direction. So Tessa gestured widely with both arms, meaning, "Come out to us."

Cassie wrinkled her brow in a "Huh?" expression.

Now Tessa put her whole body into it, gesturing wildly at Cassie, then crouching low and holding her Star-Zap like a flashlight, as if she was exploring a dark tunnel. Tessa began to enjoy herself, thinking it was like star charades, a game she and Gemma would play for starhours on cold, snowy nights at the farm. She didn't even pause when Scarlet tapped her shoulder.

"Wait a moogle. I'm almost finished," she whispered.

"Finished doing what?" asked someone in an amused tone. It was a voice Tessa knew all too well. She straightened slowly, a bright green blush rising to her cheeks.

"Uh, nothing, Professor Elara Ursa," she said weakly. Scarlet was nowhere to be seen.

"Would you mind doing 'nothing' somewhere else, Tessa?" the professor said pleasantly. "It's a little distracting for the class."

"Of course," said Tessa, edging away and ducking her head in embarrassment. "Star apologies, Professor Elara Ursa."

When she found the courage to look at the teacher, it was too late. Professor Elara Ursa was already back in the classroom.

"Whew, that was close," said Scarlet, emerging from behind the pillar.

"Yes, for me," Tessa said testily. But really, she'd done

the same kind of thing to Gemma at home, thinking their parents would go easier on her little sister because she was younger. Of course, she and Scarlet were exactly the same star age. But what good did it do for both of them to get in trouble? "Now what?"

"We go to the caves!" said Cassie, coming out from behind the pillar, too. "While you were talking to Professor Elara Ursa, Scarlet snuck me out of class!"

"Wrong way, Tessa!"

"What?" Tessa was heading toward Lady Stella's office, where the Star Darlings always took a secret passage to the Star Caves.

"I said, wrong way," Scarlet repeated. Tugging on Tessa's arm, she led Tessa and Cassie out of the building, toward the dorms.

"Where exactly are we going?" asked Cassie.

"To the Big Dipper Dorm."

Cassie opened her mouth to ask another question, but Tessa shot her a look. Tessa was learning that sometimes with Scarlet, less was more. Not asking questions might get you all the info you needed.

"There's another entrance here," Scarlet continued,

leading them inside the dorm, then through the halls to a door marked STARLING ACADEMY STAFF ONLY.

"This is it?" Tessa asked. Her stomach rumbled, the way it did when she felt hungry—or anxious. She thought longingly of her room, only a few doors away, where a dish of garble green chips sat on her desk.

Without saying a word, Scarlet opened the door. Inside, Tessa saw a tiny room filled with baskets of glo-pong balls, sparkle-shower supplies, and disappearing garbage cans. The three girls stepped into the small space, and Scarlet shut the door behind them. They were in total darkness.

Tessa sucked in her breath and only released it when Scarlet switched her Star-Zap to flashlight mode. Scarlet flicked her wrist, and a trapdoor opened at their feet.

The supply closet filled with an eerie light. Tessa glimpsed winding metal stairs but nothing else. "Let's go," Scarlet whispered.

"Okay," Tessa whispered back. That was what she wanted, after all. She wanted to find something there that would clear Lady Stella or at least provide a clue.

Still, farm girl Tessa liked bright open spaces, not closed-in dimly lit tunnels. Of course she'd been in the caves many times and loved the light-filled Wish-House. But she'd never, ever enjoyed the trip there. And that was when Lady Stella had been leading the way. Now she and Cassie only had—*gulp!*—Scarlet.

As they made their way down the steps and into a passage, Tessa gazed at water dripping from the ceiling. Rocks hung like icicles, and stones rose from the ground in pointed shapes. Glowing gems, set deeply into walls, cast strange shadows. No, she really didn't want to be there.

But Scarlet seemed to know her way, walking quickly through corridor after corridor, stopping once to point the way to their secret Wish Cavern.

"I don't know what we're looking for." Cassie spoke for the first time in a quiet, calm voice.

"Me neither," said Scarlet almost happily. "But if Lady Stella is doing something in secret, it would probably be down here, in a spot the rest of us have never seen. Maybe there's a room full of poisonous flowers. Or a tech lab where she can mess with everyone's Star-Zaps.

"Besides," Scarlet went on, "isn't it a nice change of pace from being aboveground, surrounded by so many Starlings and their silly chatter? I feel like I can breathe here."

Tessa pulled out her Star-Zap. "I forgot to tell Gemma where I was going," she said.

Scarlet put her hand over the communicator. "Those don't work down here," she said.

Tessa didn't feel the way Scarlet did about being underground and was about to suggest they leave, when, suddenly, a bitbat swooped star inches from her face. Tessa jumped back, startled.

"Star greetings, little one," Scarlet said in a cooing voice Tessa had never heard her use before. The bitbat landed on Scarlet's outstretched finger, then swung upside down, folding its wings.

"Oh!" Tessa gasped. "She's so cute!" Tessa had never seen a bitbat so close before. She was silvery white and as small as a glowfur. Her big luminous green eyes seemed a little sad.

Tentatively, Tessa held out her hand, and the bitbat swung over to her finger.

"Ugh." Cassie pressed herself against the wall.

"She likes you, Tessa," said Scarlet approvingly.

Other bitbats flew past, and Tessa smiled. They were like tiny acrobats, somersaulting through the air and swaying upside down. "I like them, too!" she said.

Tessa felt her fears vanish into the air. She understood

now why Scarlet could spend starhours there.

They wandered the caves until it was time to go to their next class. The caves suddenly seemed enticing and mysterious to Tessa, and she felt like she understood Scarlet better after that. At least a little bit anyway.

But still, they didn't find a thing.

CHAPTER
4

The next morning, Tessa was the first to arrive at the Star Darlings' table in the Celestial Café. She turned to the door, and right on cue, Gemma walked in. The two were almost always the earliest for breakfast. Life on the farm began with the chickadoodles crowing at sunrise. And neither could manage to sleep even a bit past that—with few exceptions.

The sisters settled into seats facing the café's glass wall, with a glowrious view of the Crystal Mountains. Brilliant rays bounced off the mountain peaks. For a moogle, the two were silent. Even Gemma knew to sit quietly, soaking in the positive energy.

"So," Gemma said, finally breaking the silence, "I have to tell you what happened last starnight. Libby and

I were walking through the Serenity Gardens when we saw Piper meditating. So we . . ."

Tessa listened with one ear, a skill she'd developed at a young age when it became clear that Gemma could take starhours to tell a story that should be told in starmins. Their orders were taken and delivered. She finished her starcakes, then looked questioningly at Gemma and her half-eaten bowl of Sparkle-O's.

Nodding, Gemma pushed the bowl to her, saying, "So then Piper tells us this dream about driving a Starcar. I mean actually steering and braking it, with no auto feature that she can figure out, and . . ."

Meanwhile, more Star Darlings were arriving, and the café was filling with students eating, talking, and laughing. Leona, Piper, Astra, and the others sat down, with Scarlet slipping into a seat at the other end of the table. Only Cassie was missing then.

"Sage, did you see Cassie this morning?" Tessa asked.

Sage shook her head, tossing her long lavender hair. "No, she was already gone when I woke up."

Just then, Cassie hurried in, looking worried. She took the last seat, next to Scarlet.

"Is everything all right?" Tessa asked, her voice carrying across the table.

All talking stopped while everyone turned to Cassie. Even a few girls at the next table paused their conversation to listen. Tessa noted Vivica at the head of that table, Violetta at her side.

Cassie gave a funny sort of laugh. "Of course." She shot a look at the other table, and the girls reluctantly turned away. "I stopped by tech repair to pick up my Star-Zap. . . ." She trailed off as if she had more to say.

"And?" Sage asked impatiently.

"Well, it's fixed." Cassie leaned forward, lowering her voice. "But something strange may have happened to it."

"Something strange happened to your Star-Zap?" Tessa repeated to make sure she'd heard correctly. Heads turned in her direction. *Oh, starf.* She'd spoken way too loudly. Now everyone was interested.

So she raised her voice even louder. "I've heard about this new virus going around."

"Me too!" added Sage. "My mom was talking about it. The Star Bores bug. It just keeps replaying your old holo-texts."

"Oh, that's old news," Vivica called out loudly, not even caring that now everyone knew she'd been eavesdropping. "You Slow Developers are always behind the times. You should have a new special class, just for how to work a Star-Zap."

She and her friends giggled loudly, then flounced out of the café with superior looks at the Star Darlings.

"Don't let them dim your glow," Libby told Cassie. "Go on."

"Well," Cassie continued after taking a deep breath, "it turns out my messages were all being rerouted, stars know where. The technician said it might be a virus. Or a forwarding mechanism could have been—"

She whispered the rest of her sentence to Scarlet, who frowned and leaned over to whisper to Libby. Libby whispered to Sage, and the message went around the table until it reached Tessa.

"The forwarding mechanism could have been saving face on your jar cap?" Tessa giggled. "This is worse than a game of holo-phone!" she complained. "Let's find somewhere to talk."

So the entire group of Star Darlings got up and found a private relaxation room in the nearby Lightning Lounge. Immediately, the room started to play the theme song from a popular—and scary—weekly holo-vision program called *The Dark Files*. The show had been keeping viewers in suspense for eons. Tessa wasn't crazy about it; it was too spooky for her liking. Plus every starweek it focused on some strange conspiracy theory, such as all Starland leaders plotting with alien beings. For once she wished the room's sensors didn't pick up on mood.

But a few starmins later, Tessa finally understood what Cassie had been talking about: the technician thought someone might have sabotaged Cassie's Star-Zap, programming it to send her holo-texts to another device. Astra had a thoughtful look on her face. "Mine's been acting odd, too," she said.

"Remember when I accidentally left it in Lady Stella's office?" Cassie asked everyone. "She could have done something with it then."

"Oh, come on," Sage said, leaning back to gaze at the sky as the retractable roof opened. "First of all, Cassie, you're always losing your device. I can't count how many times you've had to use Find My Zap.

"Besides," she added offhandedly, "you always think people are taking it, too. Remember when you thought Lady Cordial, of all Starlings, stole it?"

All the Star Darlings giggled.

"When was that?" asked Libby. "Oh, right, during the first week of school."

Tessa remembered the Star Quad had been filled with first years who were having trouble getting acclimated to their Star-Zaps. Of course, poor Lady Cordial, the admissions director, had been in a panic. She was trying to explain how Star-Zaps worked to a large group. But her stuttering had been so severe no one could understand her.

"Yes," Cassie said, "somehow my device wound up with all her display Star-Zaps, and she was about to walk away with it! When I asked for it back, she was so distraught she tried to give me a different one! Then she offered to give me all the Star-Zaps!"

"Lady Cordial is always trying to do the right thing," Libby said. "Once she held the door open for Lady Stella using wish energy, but then Starlings kept coming and she didn't want to close it on anyone, so she stood there, concentrating on that door, for an entire starhour."

"I'm just saying it's possible," Cassie said, bringing the conversation back to Lady Stella's tampering with her Star-Zap. "Lady Stella isn't like Lady Cordial. She's so powerful. Everyone has to take her seriously."

"I certainly do," Scarlet agreed.

Tessa blinked. This was all just guesswork. There

wasn't one shred of real evidence against Lady Stella. But looking at the other girls' faces, she could tell some were wondering: was their beloved headmistress out to get them?

CHAPTER
5

"So what do you think?"

Tessa and Gemma were strolling through the Ozzie-fruit Orchard arm in arm, in the usual Starling fashion. It had been an uneventful day for Tessa; she hadn't once been late to class, and she'd been fully prepared for each. She'd even gone to the library to star apologize to Lady Floridia about missing independent study.

Now it was just after dinner at lightfall. Gemma had been chattering about going home for the Time of Lumiere and how they would spend their time: grooming the galliopes; taking care of the chickadoodles, the small winged creatures that couldn't fly; coaxing the fruit to grow.

But Tessa was wondering exactly what her sister

thought about the Lady Stella accusations. Earlier she'd just assumed that Gemma agreed with her that Lady Stella was innocent. But something about Gemma's expression in the Lightning Lounge made her want to find out for sure.

"I'm confused," Gemma answered. She stopped to twist an ozziefruit from its stem, then bit into the sweet indigo-colored fruit. Bright juice dribbled down her chin, and Tessa used wish energy to wipe it off. "I don't want to think Lady Stella is a bad Starling. But Cassie and Scarlet seem so sure. I mean, she did set up Ophelia to take Scarlet's place!"

"Well, I'm just as sure she's doing everything in her power to help us and Starland," said Tessa. "Maybe Ophelia made everything up about Lady Stella. Maybe she's star-crazed and just plain bitbatty."

Gemma took another bite of the ozziefruit. This time juice squirted down her dress. Tessa gazed at her sister and felt an urge to protect her. She seemed so young, so inexperienced. She was only a first year. How could she go on a mission when each one seemed more dangerous than the last?

"You know," Gemma said thoughtfully, as if reading Tessa's mind, "one of us could be chosen for the next mission."

Tessa nodded. At least she had already been to Wishworld, to help Sage with her mission. But that had been the very first one. It seemed like light-years had passed since that time.

Back then Tessa had thought the journey was an adventure—nothing more, nothing less. *If Sage doesn't manage to bring back wish energy, no big deal*, she'd thought. *There's always next time.* But things had gone wrong on most of the missions. And the trip itself could be dangerous. Just thinking of how Leona's shooting star had burned out made Tessa shiver. What if Vega hadn't been able to strap her onto her own star? She'd have been lost in space!

Tessa's Star-Zap went off suddenly, interrupting her thoughts. But it wasn't only her device buzzing; Gemma's was going off, too. And Tessa knew what that meant. They were getting the same holo-text from Lady Stella, telling the Star Darlings to report to her office immediately.

The sisters looked at each other. "The next mission!" they said in unison.

Lady Stella's office was so quiet you could hear a pin drop. Tessa and Gemma were the last to arrive. They took the only empty seats left: on either side of Lady Stella. Tessa glanced around the oval table.

Everyone wore serious expressions. The air seemed charged with excitement, and an undercurrent of anxiety swirled through the room. No one looked directly at Lady Stella.

The headmistress moved gracefully toward the window, her long gown sweeping the floor. As she had her back to the girls for a moment, they all exchanged nervous glances. When Lady Stella turned, Tessa was relieved to see her expression was as calm as ever.

"Star greetings," Lady Stella said warmly, letting her eyes linger on each girl for a moment. When she gazed at Tessa, Tessa felt her nervousness disappear like a puff of smoke.

Cassie was next, and Lady Stella rested her gaze on her longer than the others. Tessa saw Cassie smile at the headmistress—an open, admiring smile. Even Scarlet was moved, pulling down the hood of her black sweatshirt to soak in more warmth.

Lady Stella finally spoke. "I must star apologize to all of you. I've been so busy lately that I haven't spent enough time with any of you."

The girls murmured their agreement. Cassie nodded eagerly. Tessa felt her shoulders relax. She hadn't even realized how tense she'd been, worrying about Lady Stella and how the other Star Darlings felt about her. But now she felt so much brighter. She began to hope the next mission would be hers.

"Now let us see the new Wish Orb," Lady Stella said.

Linking arms and talking softly to one another, the group headed through the secret door, down the ladder, and into the dimly lit tunnels.

When they passed the spot where the bitbat had hung from Tessa's finger, she exchanged looks with Scarlet. There was nothing going on in those caves; no clues pointed to Lady Stella. Clearly the headmistress had nothing to hide.

The group reached the Wish Cavern. Tessa blinked in the bright sunlight, once again wondering how the sun could shine so far underground. The glittering waterfall cascaded to the ground like a moonium sparkle showers, and the grass felt as soft as a cloud beneath her feet. She sighed happily.

There was no evil plot spearheaded by Lady Stella, Tessa was sure of it. Maybe there wasn't a plot at all, just a random mix of mishaps. Tessa felt more relaxed than she had in a double starweek. It was the perfect frame of mind for a trip to Wishworld.

Only four girls had yet to go on a mission. Behind

her back, Tessa counted on her fingers: "Me, Gemma, Clover, and Adora. One of us will be chosen."

The girls grouped around the lush green platform and waited. Tessa squeezed between Gemma and Clover and took their hands. Then she leaned across Gemma to nod at Adora. All four girls leaned forward eagerly, hoping to see the Wish Orb as quickly as possible.

"Now," said Lady Stella, and the platform noiselessly parted. Four delicate Wish Orbs floated lazily into the air. *Four!*

"Are we all going?" asked Gemma breathlessly. "What kind of mission would be perfect for all four of us?"

But three of the orbs descended back into the platform as quietly as they had risen. "Guess not," said Gemma, sounding half glad, half disappointed. Tessa gave her a small smile; it would have been starmazing to go together.

The remaining Wish Orb swung this way and that in an almost hypnotic manner. Tessa followed the motion and, with every arc, felt her sleepy mind wander a bit farther. If only she'd eaten a bigger dinner, she would be wide-awake and ready for whatever the future might hold. She should have had another serving of noddlenoodle soup or more glorange juice or—

Suddenly, Clover elbowed her in the side. "Oh!" said Tessa. The Wish Orb had stopped right in front of her. She held out her hand, and the pulsing ball of energy settled gracefully in her palm.

"The orb has chosen," Lady Stella said, smiling. "As soon as you're ready, Tessa, you may leave."

Tessa grinned. "I can be ready in two shakes of a glion's tail."

"I do believe you can," said Lady Stella. "But I meant you can leave as soon as you're ready in the morning. You'll need a good starnight's rest."

CHAPTER 6

It was just as well Tessa hadn't hurried to Wishworld right after the orb had chosen. She hadn't realized just how much she had to do. First she needed to select a Wishling outfit. Something that would be comfortable and rugged, she thought, in case she wound up doing something outdoorsy like she hoped. After a starhour or so, she settled on cropped jeans that had a hint of green in the blue material and a tailored button-down shirt with sleeves that could be rolled up easily.

Next she called Jewel to come out and play. She needed to say good-bye. The young galliope—even in virtual form—seemed to have grown in just that day. How big would she be when Tessa came back from her mission? "I'll be away," she told Jewel, "but I'll be thinking of you."

In fact, Tessa would be more than "away." She'd be mooniums of floozels away. Did Jewel understand? And would she miss Tessa, too?

Quickly, Tessa holo-called Gemma. "Can you keep Jewel company while I'm gone?" she asked as Gemma's image hovered in front of her.

"Of course," Gemma said. "It will make me feel better, too."

Tessa gulped. She'd gotten used to seeing her sister every starday. It made being away from her parents and the farm much easier. "I'll be back before you know it," she said.

"In time for dinner?" Gemma asked teasingly.

"Oh my stars!" said Tessa. "You just gave me a brilliant idea. Gotta go! I have hydrongs of things to do!"

Early the next morning, Tessa was finally ready and, she feared, late for her mission. She rushed around on the Cosmic Transporter, juggling boxes and containers and skirting students. The packages were piled so high she could barely see.

"Star excuse me," she said again and again, bumping into girls with every step.

Right in front of Halo Hall, she pressed past Vivica and Violetta.

Vivica snickered to Violetta. "What would happen if I 'accidentally' bumped into her right now?"

Tessa concentrated, using her wish energy manipulation to hold everything together. And she didn't bother to star apologize when she accidentally stepped on Vivica's foot.

Finally, she reached the Flash Vertical Mover, and she used her nose to press the button.

When she got to the top, the door whooshed open. Tessa, peering over her packages, saw everyone else already waiting on the deck that stood high above Starland.

"What on Starland are you carrying?" Sage asked as the Star Darlings crowded around, excited.

"Just some provisions." Tessa dropped everything at her feet and felt her shimmer flare in her embarrassment. She hadn't realized anyone would think it was strange. Gemma rooted through the pile.

"Astromuffins," she called out. "Garble greens and jujufruits. Star sandwiches with glimmer butter. Jujufruit tarts." She stopped to count. "A baker's glowzen of them!" She grinned at her sister. "What *didn't* you bring, Tessa?"

"I didn't have time for breakfast," Tessa said a little defensively. "And what if I don't like the food on Wishworld? I want to be prepared."

"Preparation is key to a successful mission," Lady Stella said, joining the group, her eyes twinkling. Then a serious look crossed her face. "Are you prepared, Tessa?"

Tessa had gone over everything again and again; she knew the importance of the mission and could rattle off tasks in her sleep.

Find her Wisher. Figure out the wish. Keep an eye on the Countdown Clock and monitor her energy levels. Recite her Mirror Mantra—the special phrase that would bring her glimmer back—when she needed a boost. And figure out her special talent as soon as possible. That would surely help her succeed.

Tessa touched her Wish Pendant, a silvery star brooch pinned to her collar. "Yes, Lady Stella," she answered.

"Now we will just wait for Lady Cordial to bring your backpack so you can take your provisions. And the wranglers will capture you a star." Lady Stella moved toward the Flash Vertical Mover to wait for Lady Cordial. As soon as she left the group, the mood changed.

A moogle before, Tessa noted, the girls had been

excited for her, same as they'd been for the other missions. But now they wore worried expressions.

Cassie leaned in close to Tessa. "Are you sure you're okay?" she asked anxiously. "I really don't know what to think! If Lady Stella is working against us, anything could happen."

Tessa *had* been fine. Why did Cassie have to go and say something?

Scarlet edged over, and Tessa found herself backing away. She didn't want to feel any more negative energy, not right before she left for Wishworld.

"Don't say a word, Scarlet," she commanded.

Scarlet nodded mutely, then reached over to hug Tessa tight. Tessa looked at her in amazement.

Then she gazed at Gemma and all the Star Darlings. Suddenly, she didn't want to go. "Don't worry about Jewel!" Gemma said, squeezing her hand.

"Or anything here." Cassie forced a smile. "Just have a starmendous mission."

"Stars crossed, I will," Tessa said. She tamped down her apprehension, once again visualizing Professor Margaret Dumarre's garden.

"S-s-s-star greetings," Lady Cordial stuttered, hurrying up to her, her purple hair escaping from her bun. "I have your backpack and keychain, Tessa."

"Star salutations," Tessa said, reaching to steady Lady Cordial before she tripped over a container of Sparkle-O's. Her heart went out to the older Starling. Standing next to regal Lady Stella, Lady Cordial seemed even smaller and stouter than usual. Tessa took the backpack, smiling, then quickly packed her supplies.

By then, the Star Wranglers had caught a star. After one last hug from Gemma, Tessa was ready to go. She made sure her backpack was secure and her Star-Zap was within easy reach. Cassie nodded her approval.

"Good luck St-st-starling!" called Lady Cordial. "This energy crisis isn't going to fix itself!" Then the head of admissions looked stricken and slapped her hand over her mouth. Lady Stella turned to her, her face twisted in shock. Had Tessa heard correctly? The other Star Darlings were staring at the two women, looking very confused indeed. And that's when the wranglers released Tessa's star into the heavens. She would have to put this possible new information out of her mind and concentrate on her mission. Still, it wasn't going to be easy.

Lights and shapes streaked past, a starmazing mix of heavenly bodies, bright flashes, and colorful beams. Tessa twisted her head this way and that, taking in each new sight, until her Star-Zap buzzed, signaling her final descent.

This was it. She recited the wish poem to change her appearance, her shimmer fading to a dull Wishling shade. Next she switched clothes and, an instant later, tumbled lightly to the ground.

"Oh my stars!" Tessa had landed on her back and was staring directly at the Wishworld sun. It seemed a bit dimmer than the suns of Starland but still impressive, she thought. She sat up, looked around, and gasped.

Farm fields stretched in front of her for what seemed like floozels, with neat rows of crops that resembled lighttuce and sunbeans. She saw a barn with a galliope-like creature just coming out of its red doors.

Maybe her Wisher was on that very farm!

"Let's move the billboard to the corner for now," she heard a male Wishling shout. "It will go on top of this building. But it needs to be out of the way during rush hour."

A truck engine revved, and the entire scene moved, revealing crowds of Wishlings hurrying along a city street behind it.

The farm was just a painting, a giant sign placed on top of a flatbed truck. Now she noticed there was even writing on it: VISIT THE U-PICK FARM, WHERE U HAVE FUN!

Tessa sprang to her feet. She was really on a street corner, not a farm. People rushed around her, not giving her a second glance. Most Wishlings wore jackets that matched their pants and skirts—either dark blue or black. Tessa was pleased to see her button-down shirt fit right in.

"Big meeting," one Wishling was saying into her cell phone. Tessa couldn't help staring. The phone looked like an early Star-Zap knockoff, but much more primitive. "Today was the worst day to oversleep," the Wishling went on. "Got to go. I'm late."

Everyone seemed to be heading toward a cluster of tall office buildings. There wasn't a young Wishling in sight, and Tessa highly doubted her Wisher was one of the office workers—"busy-ness people," Professor Margaret Dumarre had called them. And Tessa agreed; they all looked very busy and harried.

Feeling uncomfortable, Tessa wondered why she had been chosen for that mission. She was definitely out of her element. There were concrete sidewalks, there were hardly any trees, and she was about as far from a farm as a Starling could get—at least thirty miles away, according to the billboard. Whatever that meant!

Somewhere, a bell rang nine times, and everyone walked even faster. Then, like magic, the street emptied. The only people left were Tessa and the two billboard workers.

Tessa glanced around and noticed a street sign: COMMERCE STREET. Of course! Tessa almost laughed at herself. Distracted by all the hustle and bustle, she'd forgotten how simple locating her Wisher could be. All she had to do was check her Star-Zap for directions.

Following the route on the screen map, Tessa took the next left, walked two more blocks, and found herself on a quiet street. She walked toward a small brick building set back from the sidewalk. It looked a bit like the school buildings she'd seen through a Wishworld Surveillance Deck telescope. But this wasn't a school. A sign in the front yard read HILLSBORO ANIMAL SHELTER.

Tessa's heart skipped a beat. "'Animal,'" she read out loud, just to make sure. This might be even better than a farm! A wide smile spread across her face.

She knew the word *animal* meant a creature of some sort, hopefully friendly, like all the creatures on Starland. And *shelter* meant to protect. Animal shelter. It was an awfully big place to protect just one creature, she thought, even if it was the smallest building she'd seen so far.

But maybe the animal was huge! As big as a house! She'd read about one creature called a smellephant, so named because of its long, stretched-out nose, which could bend and curve and even pick up objects!

She paused. Maybe the creature was dangerous. The word *shelter* might mean protection *from*, not *for*, an animal. The building could provide a safe place for Wishlings.

Tessa glanced anxiously down the street. She willed herself to think positive thoughts. Once again, she called up the garden vision, and she added a few glober-beems for good measure. Her heartbeat slowed. She felt calmer.

Of course there were no dangerous animals there. Tessa was being star-crazed. She was in a small city, after all. There wouldn't be wild animals roaming the streets. Even in Starland City, you wouldn't find a glion or twinkelope wandering along the transporters.

Feeling better, Tessa walked up the building's path and stopped at the double glass doors. She tried peering in but couldn't make out much. So, taking a deep breath, she stepped inside and entered a lobby with a desk facing the entrance. There wasn't a creature in sight—or a Wishling, for that matter.

Tessa wandered to a wall covered with flat, unmoving pictures. Wishling photographs, she knew.

The photos featured Wishling creatures, some cuddling with children, some with adults, all adorable—and none as big as a house. In fact, most of them were quite small.

Tessa had taken every Wishling creature class she could back home—and had gotten an I in every one—so she was familiar with many of the animals. But they looked different here than in holo–artist renderings—and much clearer than from the Wishworld Surveillance Deck.

Her heart expanded as she looked at the animals, probably all in need, she realized. Cats and dogs, and others she didn't recognize.

One was a long, sleek creature that looked like a striped tube. It had no legs, and its head was part of its body. Tessa shivered.

But right next to that creature was a picture of a tiny, adorable animal, a ball of fur with big round cheeks and a small nose, running on some sort of wheel.

Next to the picture wall was a table piled high with sale items labeled DOGGY TREATS and CAT TOYS. To the side stood a big jar, filled with flat round silver objects.

Tessa read the sign on it: DONATIONS APPRECIATED. ALL PROCEEDS BENEFIT THE SHELTER.

Just then a woman walked briskly into the lobby from a hallway off to the side. She bent over the desk, flipping open a large book. *The book is made from paper!* Tessa thought excitedly.

"May I help you, dear?" the woman asked Tessa. She had short wavy gray hair, and when she smiled at Tessa, her eyes crinkled in a friendly way.

"Um." The woman had called her *deer*. Did she actually think Tessa was a Wishling creature that lived in the woods? Confused, Tessa just stood there for a moment. The woman gazed at her patiently, and finally, Tessa stepped closer.

The woman nodded encouragingly. "Our receptionist isn't here," she explained. "But you must be one of the students who are volunteering this summer. Since this is the first week of our program, we haven't figured out schedules or responsibilities yet."

She held out her hand. "My name is Penny Loar. I'm the director here. Please call me Penny. What is your name, dear? I'll check you off the list."

Tessa tapped the woman's fingers in what she hoped was the correct Wishling way. *Student volunteer,* she thought quickly. *Summer program.*

Summer was a season, similar to the Time of Lumiere, the warmest part of the staryear. Did Wishlings have a school break then? And had lots signed up to help at the shelter? It sounded like it, she decided. So this was definitely the place she'd meet her Wisher. Plus she was talking to the director, the head of the program. That was a stroke of luck.

Tessa smiled at Penny. She concentrated hard, blocking out all distracting thoughts, and said, "My name is Tessa. I did sign up to volunteer. I'm not on the list. But it doesn't matter."

Penny sniffed the air. A dreamy expression crossed her face. "Your name is Tessa," she repeated. "It doesn't matter that you're not on the list." She scribbled in the book, then looked up.

"Do you smell that, too?" she asked Tessa. "Someone nearby must be baking my favorite pastry, raisin cinnamon buns. I had one every morning for breakfast growing up."

Tessa grinned. The mind-control trick really was starmazing! Too bad it only worked on adults.

"I'm so sorry I'm late, Penny!" another woman said, hurrying into the lobby. She pinned a name tag—DONNA—onto her shirt, also button-down, Tessa noted. "I can take over now."

"That's okay," said Penny. "This is Tessa, one of our summer volunteers. I'll take her in the back and get her started."

Tessa still wasn't entirely sure what the shelter did, but it looked like she had a job!

Penny was leading Tessa down a long hall, explaining what the shelter did.

"Most of our animals are strays, lost or abandoned pets people find in the streets. Sometimes owners bring them in, too, if they're moving to a place that doesn't allow animals, or they feel they can't care for them anymore. Here we give animals medical care, clean and feed them, and try to exercise them as much as possible. And of course, we try to find them homes!"

Tessa held in a gasp. Wishling creatures could be lost or abandoned—things that never really happened on Starland. Now she understood what the shelter was. It was there to help any local animal in trouble.

Penny stepped into a small room filled floor to ceiling with gray metal cabinets. "We're changing over to a computerized system for our files," she told Tessa, "but we're still holding on to our paper records, just in case there's a problem."

Paper again! And there must be hydrongs of sheets in those drawers. But why all the paper records? Hadn't she learned in Wishling History that records had something to do with music? Were those files filled with songs?

Tessa shook her head to clear it. Music probably had nothing to do with her mission. She needed to focus on the here and now. So she just nodded knowingly.

"Anyway, I'm sure you want to see the animals," Penny said. "After all, that's why you're here! Let's start with the dogs."

She took Tessa through another door, marked DOGGY DAY CARE. Tessa stepped into the huge space and tried to take everything in.

First there was the noise. Yips, yaps, and barks echoed loudly. Along one wall, little rooms stood side by side in a row. Each one had a gate in front, like a half door. And behind each gate, a dog stood, jumped, paced, or slept.

It was a little disturbing to see animals cooped up

like that, but Tessa wasn't really shocked. She'd heard about zoos and aquariums, and she supposed this was for the animals' own good, too. It would be pandemonium to let all those animals roam loose. Besides, the spaces were good-sized, neat, and clean, and every dog had a little bed, a food dish, and a water bowl.

"Each dog has its own kennel," Penny said. "The kennels have swinging doors that open to the outside, with separate yards."

"R-r-r-r-fffff!" A big sloppy-looking dog with floppy ears and curly hair rushed toward his door, barking loudly. Tessa bent over the gate to scratch him behind the ears.

"This is Tiny," Penny said with a laugh. "We name all the dogs that come in, if they don't have names already." She sighed. "Tiny has been with us about a year now. The big dogs have a tough time finding homes."

"You mean they can go out and look for houses, too?" Tessa asked, confused.

Penny laughed, as if she'd made a funny joke. "That would be something! Imagine if that was true. Instead of people coming here, looking at animals and picking one to take home, the animals did the choosing! Or bought their own houses!"

Penny explained further, and slowly Tessa was able

to piece together more about the shelter. As for Tiny, his family had brought him in because he barked and jumped on people, and they'd given up on training him. They just didn't want him around.

"How horrible!" said Tessa. She buried her face in Tiny's furry neck, trying to hide her tears.

Next Penny showed her the outside kennel yards, where dogs chewed on bones or nosed balls. Some puppies were grouped together. *They're the cutest things ever,* Tessa thought. They had paws that looked too big for their bodies and large soulful eyes.

Penny pointed out the dog run, a giant fenced-in area where dogs raced around, playing, while a volunteer sat at a nearby picnic table, overseeing them.

"The dogs come out here at least twice a day," Penny went on. "But we also walk them, so hopefully they do their business outside." She smiled at Tessa. "That should make it easier to clean the kennels. But you'll find out about that later."

Tessa frowned. What did *do their business* mean?

All in all, Tessa didn't like the sound of it. What exactly would she be cleaning? Spilled food? Something else? But maybe she'd finish her mission before it came time for any tidying up. Discreetly, she checked her Countdown Clock. Already a few Wishworld hours had passed. And her Wisher still hadn't appeared. Tessa's Wish Pendant hadn't so much as blinked, let alone glowed brightly to signal her Wisher was near.

"Now for the cats," said Penny, opening a door marked CAT CONDOS. Inside, large comfy cages housed the creatures, some singly, some in groups. A few cats were playing in the middle of the room, in a large open area filled with toys.

One volunteer sat on the floor, playing with a baby cat—a kitten, Tessa realized. The kitten had gray and black stripes, a tiny pink nose, and ears that stood straight up at attention.

The volunteer motioned for Tessa to come closer, then scooped up the small creature for Tessa to hold. The kitten nestled against her chest and purred. Tessa's heart flipped; she wanted to take the creature home with her right that starsec.

She imagined the kitten going to class with her, watching her bake, and then going to the farm on school breaks and playing with Jewel. Of course, it could never happen. But at that moment, Tessa wished for it.

"I like you," a soft voice murmured. Tessa turned to Penny and said, "I like you, too."

Penny smiled a little uncertainly, as if she didn't know why Tessa had blurted that out. "That's good," she said, "since we'll be working together."

Reluctantly, Tessa put the kitten down so Penny could show her more: visiting rooms for prospective owners, examination rooms, grooming rooms, and a storage room filled with bags and bags of animal food. Last, Penny showed her the room that housed a few snakes—those slippery creatures without legs—and some hamsters, the animal Tessa had seen pictured on a wheel. One hamster's expression reminded Tessa of a glowfur's, so she asked, "How many songs does she know?"

Once again, Penny gave her a funny look. Then she said, "I don't believe she knows any!"

There was also one adorable black creature with a white stripe down his back. Penny said most of the staff stayed away from him, and she added something about a bad odor, but Tessa wasn't really listening. She was still straining to hear the hamster, just in case she started to sing.

"Okay, that's the tour," Penny announced, taking Tessa back to the dog room. "How long will you be staying today?"

Tessa almost said, *Until I meet my Wisher and help*

grant her wish. But she stopped herself just in time. "As long as you need me."

"Good. Mostly you'll shadow a staff member or volunteer to learn how things work around here. But right now, I think Tiny needs a walk." She pulled down a long strap from a peg. "This is Tiny's leash. Just attach it to his collar."

A leash? A collar? Starland creatures had neither of those. Tessa looked at Penny helplessly.

"I'll show you," Penny said, "because it can be tricky getting it on, and getting Tiny out safely. You don't want him taking off."

Taking off? Like a shooting star? Now Tessa was really confused. She pictured wings unfolding from under Tiny's fur. "You mean Tiny can fly?"

Penny laughed. "He sure can. He runs so fast it is just like flying! But seriously, you need to be careful he doesn't run away."

Penny demonstrated how to lean over and snap on the leash before she opened the gate. Tessa immediately reached down to pet Tiny. She looked into his big brown eyes and felt a spark of recognition, a connection like they'd known each other for staryears.

"Hi," said a voice.

Tessa looked around. It was a deep male voice, and only Penny was standing nearby.

"I said hello. Are you going to walk me? I love walks. I love to sniff the air. I love to chase squirrels."

What? Was that Tiny talking? And what in the stars was a squirrel?

Tiny tilted his head, as if expecting answers, and it hit Tessa like a lightning bolt: she could understand his thoughts—the same way she had earlier with the kitten, she now realized. Penny hadn't said she liked her! It had been the tiny adorable creature. That must be Tessa's special talent—knowing animals' thoughts!

She looked at the other dogs but couldn't pick up any voices. Maybe she needed to feel a special closeness.

Meanwhile, Penny was still talking, unaware of what had just happened. "So stay away from busy sidewalks and the highway out back. But everywhere else is fine."

Tessa didn't want to ask what a highway was. She felt embarrassed enough, having blurted out that she liked Penny without the Wishling's saying she liked Tessa first!

Anyway, a highway was probably a street of some sort, Tessa figured. But how high did it reach? She grew a little excited, imagining walking Tiny up among the stars, even though Penny had said to stay away from it.

Now Penny was holding out the leash. As soon as

Tessa took it, Tiny raced out of the kennel, then straight out a side door, taking Tessa with him.

At least Tiny knows where he's going, Tessa thought as she tried to keep her balance. He was pulling her along, barking happily, and Tessa heard him thinking, *Good girl, you can do it. Just keep running!* He was encouraging her, almost as if she was his pet!

Together, they ran through a small wooded area behind the shelter, then right by a busy road, where cars zipped along as fast as comets.

Highway, highway! Tiny thought. *I love to chase cars!*

Tessa struggled to keep him under control. "Slow down, Tiny!" she shouted. Really, they should call the road a fastway, not a highway. She hoped Tiny wouldn't jump the guardrail on the side.

"Stop!" Tessa pleaded, and luckily, Tiny listened, settling down to stay by Tessa's heels. Together they watched the cars for a bit—really rather unpleasant, Tessa thought. All that noise and smoky exhaust. How did Wishlings stand it? Of course, there weren't any homes nearby, so maybe they didn't like it, either!

After a while, Tiny led her back through the woods and into the shelter. Inside, a staff member showed Tessa how to fill water bowls and food dishes and how to clean out the kennels while the dogs were outside.

Cleaning wasn't as bad as Tessa had feared. She put on protective gloves and used something called a pooper-scooper. But most everything had already been funneled down the sloping ground into a drain. All she really had to do was spray a soapy mixture all around the kennel and hose down the floor.

"Nice work," said Penny, passing by.

Tessa felt as pleased as if she'd earned all Is.

That afternoon, Tessa helped a couple choose a puppy to take home and gave two dogs baths. That wasn't fun at all. She almost suggested the dogs take sparkle showers instead. They were so resistant to getting into the big tub! Luckily, she remembered Wishlings didn't even have sparkle showers.

Meanwhile, a constant stream of visitors came into and went out of the shelter. But so far her Wisher was nowhere to be seen.

After the doggy baths, Penny asked Tessa to take some photos. Tessa held the camera gingerly as she walked through the cats' play area. How did it work, exactly? Starland's glamera was a small egg-shaped device you could hold in your palm. But this was a big bulky object that you strapped around your neck like some kind of fashion accessory.

Play with me! the striped kitten squeaked to her. So Tessa convinced a volunteer to take photos of her and the kitten together.

Later Tessa organized the sales table in the lobby with Penny. She was thinking that things on Wishworld were similar to Starland yet so different at the same time, when a big drop of water fell—*splat*—on her head. She moved a few star inches to her left, and more drops plopped around her.

"What's that?" she asked, wondering if somebody else had had the idea of showering the animals and this was some sort of a test run.

Penny sighed, reaching for buckets they kept under the front desk. "Remember it rained yesterday?"

The starday had been glowrious on Starland, but Tessa nodded.

"Whenever it rains, our roof starts leaking sometime the next day. The roof is so old it really needs to be replaced, or at least repaired. But we're low on funds as it is. We have just enough money to cover basic care of our animals. So that's on hold." She smiled at Tessa. "Thank goodness we have volunteers to help. I can't tell you how grateful I am that you worked all day. But we're closing up shop now."

Tessa could see the sunlight dimming outside. The whole Wishworld day had passed, and she hadn't even caught a glimpse of her Wisher.

"Is it okay if I come back tomorrow?" she asked Penny.

"Of course. But we should really nail down your schedule for the rest of the summer." Penny took out the volunteer book and looked at Tessa expectantly.

Oh, no, not again! Tessa looked into Penny's eyes and said, "You do not need my schedule."

Penny closed the book. "I do not need your schedule." She shook her head. "And there's that raisin cinnamon smell again. I think I'll stop off at the bakery on my way home."

CHAPTER
8

That night, Tessa unfolded her star tent and pitched it in the dog run, careful to find a clean, clear spot. The tent popped up easily, complete with everything Tessa could want—including a portable micro-zap.

Tessa knew the tent was invisible to Wishling eyes. But she wondered briefly if animals could spot it. Either way, she needed to be up and out before anyone came to the shelter in the morning. Good thing the bells she'd heard chiming when she first arrived continued to ring every hour on the hour. That was one way to keep track of Wishworld time.

Tessa eyed her Countdown Clock uneasily. She probably had two to three Wishworld days left, with so much still to do! But it wouldn't help to worry or let her mind wander back to problems on Starland.

Instead, she smoothed the deep plush rug that stretched across the floor. She plumped her luxurious pillows, chosen specially for the trip, and sank into her bed, between cool smooth sheets. There. It was almost like being home. She stretched, reaching for warmed-up tarts and sandwiches on the nightstand.

Now what? Tessa didn't feel tired at all! So she fiddled around with her Star-Zap and found a Wishling video called *Middle School Musical 2*. It followed students throughout a day at school. Tessa made a note in her Cyber Journal especially for Leona: *Sometimes Wishlings break out in song to express their feelings—even if glowfur-like creatures don't!*

Tessa must have been more tired than she realized. The next thing she knew, the bell sounded nine times. *Starf!* She'd better hurry. The shelter would open any starmin. As quickly as she could, she packed her things and rushed to the front entrance.

A Wishling girl was walking down the path just ahead. The girl had straight reddish hair, tied back in a short bobbing ponytail. If Tessa squinted, the red hair looked orange and she looked just like Gemma! Tessa felt a pang. *But wait*, she thought. Maybe the pang was really a tingle, a clue that her Wisher was nearby. She looked down at her brooch. Sure enough, Tessa's Wish Pendant was glowing brightly. This girl was her Wisher!

"Hey!" Tessa said, running a bit to catch up.

The girl stopped, then grinned. "Hey, yourself! Are you a new volunteer with the summer program? I've been volunteering here all year, so if you want, I can show you around. Do you love animals, too? I have a dog named Fiona, but I love all the animals here."

Did the girl talk as much as Gemma, too? That was starmendously perfect.

"My name is Tessa," said Tessa, smiling happily. "I—I mean, my family and I—just moved to Hillsboro. Otherwise I would have been working here all year!"

"I'm Lizzie," said the girl. Tessa thought she'd ask questions about Tessa's family, or where she lived, or where she was going to school. She had already prepared some answers. Instead, a shadow crossed Lizzie's face and she fell silent.

Together, the girls walked into the shelter and said good morning to Donna and Penny. Tessa heard barks and meows and some random thoughts.

I'm hungry!

That's my catnip!

Hope my walker comes soon!

But she tried to shut them out.

No distractions, she told herself firmly. *Now is the time to concentrate on Lizzie.*

First order of business: figuring out her wish. Tessa had to stick close to her, get her talking again.

"I'm supposed to be shadowing someone this morning, to learn more," Tessa said to Lizzie. "Can you be my person?"

"Sure!" Lizzie brightened. "I can teach you everything I know. It's good, really, because"—there was that shadow again—"today is my last day, and I'll feel better knowing you're here."

Before Tessa could ask a question or get more information, Lizzie turned away. "I usually feed the dogs their breakfast first thing."

"Okay," said Tessa, following Lizzie to the storage room, where they filled bowl after bowl. Lizzie would only be there that day! Tessa really had to act quickly.

When Tessa brought Tiny a bowl, he threw his body against the gate and wagged his tail harder than any other dog.

"Wow, that's some greeting," said Lizzie. "Tiny is usually very particular, so you must have a way with animals."

"I hope so," Tessa said with a laugh. "We used to live

on a farm." She slipped inside the kennel, careful to close the door quickly. Tiny jumped all around her, and it was all Tessa could do to put down the bowl without spilling any food.

Tiny swung his head back and forth, looking at the bowl, then Tessa. Clearly, he was torn. But in the end, food won. As he slurped his breakfast, Tessa quietly edged outside to rejoin Lizzie.

"You must miss the farm terribly," Lizzie said. "Just like I'm going to miss this shelter. We're moving away, too, in just a few days. That's why I won't be working here anymore."

Lizzie was moving away. This was important information. Maybe her wish had something to do with that.

Lizzie carried a bowl to the kennel next door. A little black-and-white dog backed into a corner and looked at her warily. "Here, Trixie," Lizzie called softly. The dog was so thin Tessa could see her ribs. She couldn't tell what Trixie was thinking at all.

"Come on, girl," Lizzie said encouragingly. "Come eat." She put down the bowl, then slowly pushed it closer. Trixie didn't move. Lizzie moved it a little closer, then closer still.

Tessa held her breath. Finally, Trixie bent her head over the bowl and began to nibble.

For a long moment, Lizzie stayed as still as a statue. Finally, she backed out of the kennel, barely making a sound. "I'll give her some space now. But I think we just made some progress. Yesterday she wouldn't eat at all."

"You really know what to do," Tessa said admiringly.

"Well, I've worked at a bunch of different shelters. My parents are both in the military, and they're always getting different assignments. We've lived all over the world, some places less than a year. Volunteering with animals makes me feel better each time we have to move." She took a breath.

That was Lizzie's longest speech since her hello, Tessa realized. She hoped Lizzie didn't regret telling her so much.

"Anyway, I'm here all day today," Lizzie added. "How about you?"

That scheduling question again! "I don't know. . . ." Tessa snuck a peek at the Countdown Clock in case anything had changed since she last checked.

"Oh, you have to call home and check?" Lizzie asked, misunderstanding.

"Uh, yes," said Tessa. "But I'm sure it will be fine." She swiped her Star-Zap a few times and got ready to have a pretend conversation. But a voice with a much different accent from Lizzie's answered.

"This is Regina Barnes at the London office of Barnes, Barnes, and Barnes. How may I help you?" The woman's voice was loud enough for Lizzie to hear.

"Oops! Wrong number!" Tessa hung up. "I'll just text later."

Lizzie looked at her sympathetically. "I know it's hard getting used to different home numbers—and everything else."

"It is hard!" said Tessa. "I can't believe I just called London instead of Hillsboro!" Tessa acted like she knew all about London. But for all she really knew, it could be the next town over.

"We actually lived in London for a while," said Lizzie. "And it wasn't so bad being out of the country. I had a great friend named Nola who lived next door. We still keep in touch." She smiled at Tessa. "I try to stay friends with people I like. You should give me your contact info before we say good-bye."

"Sure," said Tessa. If only she and Lizzie really could stay in touch. *Wouldn't that be starmazing?* she thought. Her mind wandered to scenes in which she and Lizzie were both grown-up, traveling back and forth . . . meeting each other's families . . . going to each other's weddings.

"Tessa?" said Lizzie. "Are you all right? You have a funny expression on your face."

"I'm fine," Tessa said firmly, blinking her eyes to shake away the thoughts. She *was* fine, as long as she kept her mind on the mission. No distractions. "What should we do next?"

A few starmins later, they were settled in a quiet area of the cat condos room, holding miniature baby bottles to feed milk to the kittens.

Me! Me! Tessa heard the thoughts of the kitten she'd cuddled the day before coming from one of the cages. Gently, she scooped her out from a pile of snuggling cats. "I'll call you Snuggles!" she said.

Lizzie showed her how to hold Snuggles in the crook of one arm and tip the tiny bottle by her mouth so she would start to drink. Then she took her own kitten and sat next to Tessa.

Tessa smiled as Snuggles drank. *Mmmmm,* the tiny creature thought. Tessa could have sat there all day, holding and looking at Snuggles. But she reminded herself that she was on Wishworld for a reason. She had to find out Lizzie's wish.

"So," she said softly, trying not to disturb Snuggles, "it must be really hard moving around so much."

For Tessa herself, it would be near impossible to leave the farm. Her family had owned the land for generations.

Every starnight, she'd look up at the sky, find her great-grandparents' and her great-great-grandparents' stars twinkling down at her, and know they were pleased.

Tessa knew that after she graduated and finished her Wishworld duties, she'd go back to Solar Springs. She wasn't so sure about Gemma, who liked to be more in the center of things. But at least Gemma would always have a place to call home.

"Do you have sisters or brothers? Or both?" Tessa asked Lizzie.

Lizzie shook her head. "It's just my parents and me—and my dog, Fiona, of course." She smiled. "She's almost like a sister! We've basically grown up together. I don't remember a time she wasn't with us."

Tessa smiled back. That was nice, and it sounded like Lizzie had a strong family. But maybe she wanted roots, just one place to call home.

Maybe Lizzie's wish was to stay right there in Hillsboro.

"Do you wish you weren't moving?"

Lizzie shrugged. "No, I'm really okay with it. And it's necessary for my family. It's all part of my parents' jobs."

Tessa mentally crossed that off the wish list.

Lizzie looked at Tessa a little anxiously. "Don't get me wrong. Hillsboro is a great place. I'm sure you'll like it here. I've made a ton of friends."

"Oh!" Tessa straightened. Maybe the wish had to do with friendship.

Snuggles looked at her questioningly, so Tessa relaxed a bit and waited for the kitten to get comfortable.

"I bet you wish you could make tons of friends at your new school."

"I think I will. Making friends has always been pretty easy for me. You know," Lizzie said with a laugh. "I've had lots of practice."

Okay, so making friends wasn't the wish, either.

"Would you want your friends to throw you a good-bye party?" Tessa asked.

"They already have," Lizzie told her, "the last day of school." She stood and carefully put her kitten back in the cage. "Let's walk some dogs now."

For the rest of the morning, Tessa and Lizzie worked together. They walked Tiny and a dog named Oliver. They watched over more dogs at the dog run and took some visitors around the shelter. Lizzie was welcoming and courteous to everyone, and Tessa could see she did indeed make friends quickly.

In fact, Tessa felt like she and Lizzie were becoming

friends. That was nice. But between taking care of the animals and talking, Tessa kept forgetting about her mission. So just to be on the safe side, she set her Star-Zap on reminder mode, to go off every Wishworld hour.

When it went off at lunchtime, Tessa asked, "Do you wish you were moving to a different place?"

"No," said Lizzie. "We're going to Australia, and I'm curious about it. I've never been there before."

When the alarm buzzed an hour after that, while they were cleaning litter boxes, Tessa asked, "Do you wish you could finish the summer program here?"

"Not really," Lizzie said. "Of course I'll miss the animals, but I'm planning to volunteer at an Australian shelter, too." She looked at Tessa curiously. "You sure like to ask a lot of questions."

Tessa blushed.

"Star apolo—I mean, I'm sorry if you think I'm a busybody. It's just time is running out . . . I mean, you'll be leaving soon and I have so many questions about moving and making friends."

The afternoon passed, with Tessa asking more questions and getting no real answers. At five o'clock Penny said, "That's it, girls. The shelter is closing."

Then she put her arm around Lizzie. "Thank you so much for all your help. Make sure you stay in touch. You have our shelter e-mail, my personal e-mail, and all our addresses?"

Lizzie nodded, a little teary. "My mom's outside waiting. I'd better go."

No! Tessa thought. *You can't leave.* But then she realized she had to go, too. Together, the two girls walked through the door. "Are you sure you can't come back tomorrow?" Tessa asked.

"Yes, I'm sure," Lizzie said. "There's too much to do. I have to run errands. Pack. We're leaving the day after." Then she smiled. "Hey, come home with me for dinner! And this way, you can keep asking me questions."

"That would be great!" said Tessa, pretending to text her mom as they stood outside. The sky was overcast, and the air felt damp and warm.

Down the path, Lizzie's mom was waiting in the car. "This is Tessa," Lizzie said. "She's new here, and I just invited her to dinner."

Lizzie's mom frowned. "Honey, our house is almost all packed up, and you need to take care of so many things!"

Tessa stepped closer to the car. Remembering how Wishling adults liked to be addressed, she said, "Hi, Mrs.—" Tessa paused, realizing she didn't even know Lizzie's last name.

"Bennett," said Lizzie.

"Mrs. Bennett," Tessa continued. "I can be a big help. I should come for dinner."

"You can be a big help," Mrs. Bennett said slowly. "You should come for dinner." She glanced across the street. "Is there a new bakery around here? I smell chocolate éclairs, just like I had growing up."

"That's great!" said Lizzie. "It will be nice to have company while I pack."

Tessa breathed a sigh of relief. At least now she would have more time with her Wisher. Still, she'd been on Wishworld two days already, and there was lots left to do. Besides figuring out the wish, she still had to help make it come true!

CHAPTER
9

Lizzie's house was bare yet full. All the furniture was pushed to the side, the tables cleared of any odds and ends and knickknacks. The walls and counters were bare, too. But boxes littered the floor, and Tessa had to move in a zigzag just to walk from room to room.

She was following Lizzie into the living room when she heard the *click-clack* of nails against the hardwood floor. Suddenly, a small shape hurled itself at Lizzie.

"Fiona!" cried Lizzie, squatting on the floor to hug the little dog close.

Tessa sat down next to her and oohed. "She's so tiny!"

"She's a miniature dachshund," Lizzie said.

"Bless you," said Tessa, thinking Lizzie had sneezed.

Tessa smiled, relieved she'd remembered the Wishworld response.

"No." Lizzie laughed. "She's a miniature dachshund! That's her breed!"

Tessa laughed, too, leaning closer to pat Fiona's tummy when she rolled over. The dog's whole body wriggled with joy.

The girls took Fiona for a walk, then packed Lizzie's books and games. "Let's leave the stuffed animals," Lizzie said. "I want to sleep with them tonight."

Mrs. Bennett, who had dropped off the girls and then gone to pick up Mr. Bennett and dinner, returned.

"I'm sorry you're not getting a home-cooked meal, but our kitchen is in boxes," Mr. Bennett said, carrying in drinks and paper cups. He was very tall, with the same reddish hair as Lizzie, and the same warm smile.

"No, no," said Tessa. "This is all fine." But she did feel a little disappointed. The kitchen was big and spacious, and for a starmin she daydreamed about learning to bake the Wishling way—right on Wishworld. But that would have to wait for another mission—if she ever completed this one!

"I just have sandwiches," Mrs. Bennett warned Tessa. "Nothing fancy. I hope that's okay."

Tessa took a big bite of one sandwich, which wasn't really a sandwich at all. It looked more like a long stuffed tube—a "wrap," she'd heard Mrs. Bennett call it before handing one to Lizzie. Specifically, a Caesar salad wrap.

Tessa had been afraid she'd actually have to make a grab for Lizzie's sandwich in order to eat. Why else would it be called a "seize her" salad? But it turned out there were enough sandwiches for everyone.

"This is delicious," Tessa told Mrs. Bennett enthusiastically.

Lizzie's mom beamed. "It is very nice to have you here, Tessa. Why don't you sleep over, too? It would be nice for Lizzie to have a friend close by. We all could use a little extra support right now." She reached out to squeeze Lizzie's hand.

"Moving isn't easy for any of us," Mr. Bennett added. "But these are the choices we've made, and I wouldn't want to do it with anyone other than you two."

Lizzie nodded seriously, squeezing her mom's hand back. Then she turned to Tessa. "Say yes!" she pleaded. "Stay over! Please!"

"Sure!" said Tessa, happy she didn't have to use her mind control power. That took energy, and to be honest, she was feeling a little tired. She knew exhaustion was a side effect of being on Wishworld too long without granting a wish.

Just before bedtime, Tessa excused herself to go to the bathroom. There she peered at her image in the mirror. A Tessa-like being, without the shine or sparkle and with dark circles under her eyes, gazed back at her. Clearly, it was time for her mantra. She needed more energy.

Still looking at her reflection, Tessa recited, "Let your heart lead the way." Immediately, she felt a lift.

In the mirror, the real, sparkly Tessa gazed back, making Tessa feel even better. Bit by bit, her shimmer faded. But the strength remained. She could do this! *Now, back to Lizzie*, she thought.

The girls talked long into the night. Tessa wasn't getting any closer to Lizzie's wish. Still, she felt optimistic. She felt sure she would find out the wish before the sun rose. But then she couldn't help it: stretched out in a sleeping bag on the floor, Tessa fell into a deep sleep. Lizzie was already snoring gently in another sleeping bag, Fiona by her side.

Boom! A crash of thunder sounded, waking both girls. For an instant, lightning lit the room as bright as daylight. Tessa could see Lizzie sitting up, holding a quivering Fiona.

"It's okay, girl," Tessa said, reaching to stroke Fiona's head. "It's over."

But another roll of thunder roared, followed by an even louder crack. Rain pounded the roof and lashed at the windows.

The room lit up again, and Tessa saw Lizzie brush a tear from her cheek.

"Don't cry, Lizzie," she said. "I know thunderstorms are scary. But it really will be over soon."

"No, it's not that." Lizzie carried Fiona with her to the windows, making sure they were all tightly closed.

"But you're upset," Tessa said. She looked at Lizzie's tear-streaked face, and her heart went out to the Wishling girl. "It must be the move, then," she said. "You really don't want to go, do you?"

"I shouldn't feel this way!" Lizzie said with a hiccup. "But you're right. I don't want to move."

She snuggled back into the sleeping bag with Fiona and turned to face Tessa. "I told you I was fine with it. But I was trying to convince myself! I kept saying, 'It's exciting . . . it's an adventure. . . .' But that's not how I feel at all."

She burrowed her nose into Fiona's soft neck. "I've moved so often I know I can handle it. I just don't want to."

"You can't help the way you feel," Tessa said encouragingly. This was it, she knew; she was getting close to the wish.

"It's hard always being the new kid. I always get lost. I have to figure out a new school. And if we're in a different country, there's strange money and food. And just when I start to feel comfortable, we have to get up and move again.

"I know I should be happy," Lizzie continued, as if the floodgates had opened on her feelings. "I mean, how many kids can say they've traveled from Alaska to Zimbabwe?"

Or from Starland to Wishworld, Tessa added to herself, realizing she was lucky, too. The difference was she could always go back.

"And I know my parents' work is important. I don't want them to worry about me. They have enough going on." She grabbed Tessa's hand. "I just wish I could find one good thing about it. Just one thing about the move that makes me happy."

Tessa had it! She had the wish!

Lizzie yawned. "I don't mean to burden you, Tessa. But I've been keeping it all inside for so long . . ." Her eyes began to close. "It will probably be fine. . . ." And she fell asleep.

Tessa, meanwhile, was still wide-awake. Lizzie's wish: figured out. Making Lizzie's wish come true? That was entirely different.

She had to find one good thing about Lizzie's move—just one. But it had to be important enough to outweigh all the drawbacks. And she had to get Lizzie to see it, too.

★

Both girls slept late the next morning. By the time they went downstairs, Lizzie's parents were already gone. "They left a note," Lizzie said. She read the message stuck to the refrigerator door. Then she groaned. "They left a to-do list, too." Quickly, she scanned the items. "It's so long!"

"I'm not going to the shelter today," Tessa said. "If you like, I can hang out with you and help."

Lizzie grinned. "That would be great. The first thing on the list is to go out for breakfast. So you can help me eat!"

Outside, the air had the clean, fresh smell that came

after a big storm, and sunshine dappled the sidewalk.

"Let's go into Hillsboro Square to my favorite diner," said Lizzie, linking arms with Tessa, just like a Starling would.

A diner! Tessa had been curious about diners ever since Piper had come back from her mission and reported that she'd worked in one.

They walked in the opposite direction of the shelter. After only a few blocks, they reached the square. Tessa gazed at the small shops and narrow streets. It was so different from the area with the big buildings near the animal shelter. People were strolling, taking their time. And there were more bicycles than cars.

The Square Diner was busy, but the girls took seats at the counter and were served quickly. Tessa followed Lizzie's lead and ordered the pancakes. They weren't much different from starcakes, she realized after eating a forkful. All her fears about strange Wishling food were definitely unfounded.

After they finished, Lizzie picked up a piece of paper the server had left by their plates. It was filled with scribbles and numbers in columns. "I'll pay the check," she said.

"Excuse me?" Tessa said, not understanding.

"No, I insist!" said Lizzie. She took out green slips of paper with men's faces in the middle and numbers in the corners.

This must be money! Tessa thought. She had only the vaguest idea of Wishworld economy. Turning away from Lizzie, Tessa noted in her Cyber Journal that it might be a good idea to have a Wishworld economics class. She added that geography would be helpful, too. All those Wishworld place names Lizzie had rattled off! It was all so confusing.

Just as Lizzie finished counting out the money, a man came over, wiping his hands on his apron. He whisked away the check and said, "Your breakfast is on me."

Tessa squinted up at the man's head. There was nothing on it, not even hair, let alone a batch of pancakes.

"You and your family have been wonderful customers all year long," he continued. "We'll miss you around here, Lizzie."

Next Lizzie took Tessa to the Hillsboro General Store. They bought heavy-duty tape, markers to label boxes, and some cleaning supplies. "Just one more thing and we're done," said Lizzie, checking the list. "Packing peanuts."

"Peanuts?" Tessa perked up. Wasn't that a tasty treat

she'd heard about during a Wishling Cuisine lesson? Of course, she knew many Wishlings had bad reactions to peanuts. What was the reaction called? Something that sounded like energy. But Tessa doubted a Starling would be affected.

When Lizzie passed her a bag, she opened it right up and popped a peanut into her mouth. Immediately, she spat it out. "That's horrible!" she exclaimed.

"Of course it is," Lizzie said. "It's Styrofoam."

Tessa had no idea where Styrofoam grew, but she certainly wouldn't recommend any Star Darling try it while on a mission.

They moved to the counter to pay, and the owner smiled sadly at Lizzie. "I hear you're leaving us," she said. "We're all going to miss you." She rang up Lizzie's purchases on a big machine. Then she said, "Wait right here!"

The owner hurried to something called the deli section and returned with a big bone. "For Fiona," she explained. "A good-bye gift."

All day, everywhere they went, it seemed, shop owners were wishing Lizzie well and sometimes throwing in a farewell present. People stopped her on the street to say good-bye.

Tessa thought it all would make Lizzie happy. *Could*

that be the one good thing? she wondered. Instead, Lizzie's eyes filled with tears again and again. Sometimes, Tessa supposed, acts of kindness could make you cry more than anything else.

By the time they got back to the house, the sun was setting. Tessa worried that Lizzie would send her home, since it was getting late. But instead, Lizzie asked for more help packing.

Together, Tessa and Lizzie poured the packing peanuts into half-filled boxes of vases and glass bowls so the fragile objects wouldn't break in the moving truck.

So that's what they're for, thought Tessa. "Hey," she shouted to Lizzie. "Try to catch this!" And she tossed a lighter-than-air peanut in Lizzie's direction.

Lizzie lunged for it but missed—by a floozel. Tessa laughed. Then Lizzie grabbed a handful and threw them at Tessa. "Peanut fight!" she cried. She giggled loudly and emptied an entire bag over Tessa's head.

Abruptly, Tessa stopped laughing.

"I'm sorry!" Lizzie said. "Did I go overboard with the packing peanuts?"

"Huh?" said Tessa. She was staring into space, confused.

"What's going on?"

"Shhh! Just give me a starmin." Tessa didn't bother to correct herself and say *minute*. She was too busy concentrating. Just before Lizzie had poured the peanuts, she'd picked up some sort of signal. It was a cry for help that sounded strangely like a bark. She was hearing other thoughts, too: a kitten mewling in panic, another dog shouting for someone, anyone, to get her.

"Tessa?"

Tessa blocked out Lizzie and all the sights and sounds around her. She was not going to be distracted—not now, when it was so important. She heard more—*roof, danger, help*—again and again, and realized it was Tiny. No, not only Tiny—it was all the animals at the shelter. They were in trouble.

Tessa grabbed Lizzie's arm. "There's some sort of emergency at the animal shelter. Don't ask me how I know. I just do."

"Let's go," said Lizzie without hesitation. "I'll let Penny know so she can get over there, too." She paused. "And I'm calling 911. Just in case."

Who is Nina Wonwon? Tessa wondered. *And what does she have to do with anything?* But it didn't matter. They just had to get to the shelter.

The girls raced down block after block. Tessa had no

idea where they were going, but Lizzie led her through back alleys and side streets to save time. "My mom hates when I take these shortcuts," Lizzie panted, "especially when it's getting dark. But it's the quickest way."

Tessa nodded, trying to save her breath.

They reached the shelter just as Penny's car squealed into the driveway. Tessa saw a large red vehicle with ladders on the sides pull up beside her, lights flashing and sirens squealing.

It's chaos here, Tessa thought, trying to take it all in. People jumped off the truck, wearing funny hats and heavy black raincoats and boots. Tessa was too concerned about the animals to pay those people much mind. She started to run to the door, but Penny leaped out of the car and pulled her back. "No! We can't go in yet."

"We have to," Tessa cried. "The poor animals!"

She turned to Lizzie, beside her, pale with concern. "Tiny! Snuggles!"

"I know," Lizzie said.

Just then a man came over. "I'm the fire captain," he said.

Fire captain? Tessa blinked. There wasn't a fire. That was clear.

"Everyone needs to stay outside until we make sure it's safe," the captain said. "I'm sending my crew in now."

More than anything, Tessa wanted to go, too. The thoughts in her head had quieted, and she didn't know what was going on. She stared at the animal shelter building. Part of the roof had caved in, right in the middle. It looked like someone had taken a giant shovel and scooped out the shingles. Again, she started forward. This time, the fire captain held her back.

"Stay here, young lady."

"It looks like most of the damage is over the lobby," Penny said. "That's good." She sighed. "That darn roof. I should have known there'd be trouble after the storm last night."

The captain's communication device squawked. He listened, then said, "The animals are okay. The place seems secure. But we can't be sure."

"We still need to get the animals out," Penny said determinedly. "There are other shelters nearby. We can divide them up until we decide what to do."

Yes, Tessa thought. *Yes, a plan.*

Penny turned to Tessa and Lizzie. "You two call volunteers and staff and organize a car- and vanpool." She handed her phone over with the contact list on the screen.

Tessa whipped out her Star-Zap, ready. While she and Lizzie made calls, the firefighters began to bring out the animals.

Then she heard Tiny's voice. He was thinking, *Watch out!* She couldn't take it anymore!

Tessa raced through the door, then stopped short. The lobby was flooded. Beams had fallen across the desk and the donation table. Bits of plaster sprinkled down. Looking up, she could see the sky.

A firefighter was just stepping into the room, carrying Tiny. The big dog squirmed out of his arms and raced to Tessa, almost knocking her over. Quickly, she took him outside. "You stay right here," she said, leading him down the path. Then she went again to the door, where another firefighter handed over a small puppy. She held him tightly, carrying him away.

"We should bring them to the dog run," she told the captain, "and get the leashes, too." Penny agreed. And as other volunteers and staff arrived, along with Lizzie's parents, they formed an animal-rescue brigade, passing dogs, cats, and cages from one pair of arms to another in a relay to safety.

Hours passed. Someone brought over pizza for dinner. By then, most of the animals had been delivered to other shelters. Only Tiny and Snuggles remained, refusing to budge from Tessa's side. "I want to take them home so badly," Lizzie whispered to her. "But we're leaving tomorrow. I just can't."

TESSA'S LOST AND FOUND   411

Tessa's heart sped. She had to complete her mission before time ran out. But she had to take care of Tiny and Snuggles, too. She turned to Penny and said, "You should take Tiny and Snuggles home with you."

"I should take Tiny and Snuggles home with me," Penny dutifully repeated. Then she added, "You and Lizzie, her parents, and anyone else who wants to should come to my place. We can discuss more plans. Yesterday I bought lots of raisin cinnamon buns. So we can have dessert, too."

CHAPTER
10

A small group was gathered at Penny's apartment. They were snacking on buns, making lists, and figuring things out. Penny was calculating the shelter's budget on her laptop, hoping to find money somewhere to fix the roof.

"Do you have an emergency fund?" Mrs. Bennett asked.

"We used that a few months ago to replace the wiring. Remember, Lizzie, when we had the power outage?"

Immediately, Tessa's thoughts flashed to the power outages at Starling Academy and the odd thing she thought she had heard Lady Cordial say. She had to make this wish come true so she could return home to find out what in the stars was going on.

Me, me. Tiny sent the thought straight to Tessa as he nosed her palm.

Tessa wished she had a treat for Tiny, a doggy snack or a bone. Maybe they could stop off at the general store again and pick up some things. The shop owner had been so nice, giving Lizzie a bone for Fiona. Tessa felt sure she'd be happy to help Tiny.

Suddenly, Tessa jumped to her feet. Maybe she would even donate to the shelter!

"We should let people know about the roof," she said. "Shopkeepers, neighbors. They'd probably want to help."

Penny snapped her fingers. "You're right! We can do a fund-raiser. Something quick and easy, online."

Lizzie leaned forward eagerly. "Yes! We can reach out to so many more people that way, not only in Hillsboro!"

"I'm going to set it up right now," said Penny. Tessa and Lizzie peeked over her shoulder as she pulled it all together, adding a link to the website and a donation tracker with a thermometer chart to measure incoming pledges. A green bar would rise with every donation until they reached their goal.

"We can post about it, too," Lizzie suggested, "and tell people to check the site."

"That's a good idea, honey," said her dad. "But we

really need to get going. I'm sorry we can't stay longer," he told Penny. "We have to be ready to leave by tomorrow afternoon."

It was late, so everyone went their separate ways, promising to meet back at Penny's apartment early the next morning.

"I'll stop by, too, first thing." Lizzie glanced at her parents to make sure it was okay. "So I can say good-bye—again!—before we go. And I'll write those donation posts when I get home."

That night, Tessa again set up her tent in the shelter's dog run. It made her feel better to be nearby, just in case something else happened to the shelter. She spent a restless night. And the next morning—after a quick breakfast of slightly stale astromuffins and mushy starberries—she hurried over to Penny's, hoping it wasn't too early.

Luckily, the shelter director was up and dressed and happy to see her. "You're the first one here," she told Tessa. "The last time I checked the donations thermometer, we hadn't raised much. But let's look right now."

She tapped a few keys on her laptop and gasped.

"What?" said Tessa, straining to see the screen.

Penny turned the laptop to face her, and then Tessa gasped, too. The donations had topped their goal!

"Let's see where all these came from," Penny said,

hitting some more keys. She looked over the page. "Hmmm. There are some local donations. But most of the pledges are from places I've never heard of, and lots from out of the country, too."

"Really?" Tessa peered at the laptop. London, England. Bridgetown, Barbados. Victoria Falls, Zimbabwe. Zurich, Switzerland. The names sounded vaguely familiar. Why would she even know them? Then she realized they were places Lizzie had lived.

Lizzie's friends had come through! Excited, Tessa read some of their posts: "Remembering our good times volunteering at the Zurich shelter, and your friendship. Love, Sonja." "This is for you, Lizzie. Come back to Barbados soon. Pamela." And one from Lizzie's dear friend Nola: "London isn't the same without you. Happy to help any way I can. xx Nola."

This was starmazing! The shelter would get a new roof. The animals could move back to a safe place. And even more starmendous? This could make Lizzie's wish come true. Once Lizzie realized she had loyal friends around the world, she'd see that moving so often was a blessing in disguise. That was the one good thing!

She wanted to tell Lizzie in person, so she texted: COME TO PENNY'S PLACE QUICK! GOOD NEWS!

In the meantime, other shelter workers arrived. The

room buzzed with excitement. *Where is Lizzie?* Tessa
wondered, growing anxious. If she didn't come soon, she
wouldn't be able to come at all. It was almost afternoon,
and Lizzie had a flight to catch.

Just then the doorbell rang. "I'll get it!" Tessa cried,
rushing for the door. She swung it open.

"Oh," she said, disappointed. "It's you."

"Gee," said Adora, standing on the other side, her
hand on her hip. "Star greetings to you, too."

Tessa pulled Adora inside and gave her a quick hug.
"I was just expecting my Wisher, that's all. And if you
had waited a starhour or so, I would have finished my
mission—successfully, I might add—and been on my
merry way."

"Well," Adora noted, "we can't actually see what's
happening here. We just know when a mission is in trouble. Lady Cordial wasn't kidding. Lady Stella admitted
to us that there is a wish energy crisis. She said she didn't
want to worry us, that's why she kept it a secret. But now
everyone is going supernova, thinking Lady Stella is hiding something. And frankly, it seemed like you could use
all the help you could get. Besides, maybe I can still make
a difference."

"Maybe," Tessa said doubtfully. Adora looked like
a muted version of herself, but her eyes were still an

exquisite shade of sky blue, and really, Tessa was thrilled to see her.

How funny to see the Starling she basically shared a home with there when her Wisher was upset about leaving *her* home.

Quickly, she filled Adora in on Lizzie, the shelter, and the situation.

Adora shook her head. "Your Wisher sounds like a very emotional Wishling. I hope this isn't clouding your judgment, Tessa. Are you sure you have all the facts?"

"Yes, I have the facts!" Tessa said forcefully. "And once Lizzie gets here, you can analyze the situation yourself." *Hopefully*, she added to herself, *that will be soon.*

The Starlings were still standing just inside the door, not quite arguing, when the bell rang again. This time it was Lizzie.

"Lizzie!" Tessa cried. "Listen—" She stopped. Lizzie's eyes were swollen. Her skin was blotchy and her mouth quivered. Clearly, she'd been crying.

"Don't be upset! You don't have to worry anymore!" Tessa told her excitedly.

"Ahem," Adora said.

"Oh, this is my room—I mean, my friend Adora. She came to surprise me from . . . from my old hometown. After she heard about the shelter."

"Hi," said Lizzie, trying to smile. "It's nice that you came to help."

"See?" said Adora, turning to Tessa. "Everyone knows why I'm here!"

"But that's just it!" Tessa exclaimed. "I don't need—I mean, we don't need—any more help. We've gotten enough donations to build a new roof!"

"Really?" Lizzie's smile turned genuine. "That's incredible." Then she burst into tears.

"Are you okay?" Adora asked. She shot a look at Tessa.

"No!" Lizzie shook her head furiously. "Fiona is missing. We can't find her anywhere. And we're leaving soon! What are we going to do?" She flung her arms around Tessa, then reached into her pocket. "Look!" She pulled out Fiona's favorite chew toy, a squishy pink pig that oinked when you pressed it. "She doesn't even have Mr. Piggy!" she wailed.

Tessa reached out to hold hands with Lizzie. Then she asked Lizzie to recite a mantra with her. Lizzie looked at her through her tears, thoroughly confused.

"I think it will make us both feel better," Tessa told her.

A moment later, the two girls said, "Let your heart lead the way."

Almost immediately, Lizzie calmed down.

"We'll find Fiona," Tessa promised, feeling energized.

She quickly told Penny and the others, and soon everyone was working to find the lost dog. They made LOST DOG posters. They called friends. They set up search parties.

When they went back for a break, they saw Lizzie in the corner, talking on her phone. "Any news?" asked Tessa.

"No! And I have to go!" she told them. "My parents just told me the moving truck is here."

Tiny bounded over just then, wanting attention. Absentmindedly, Tessa scratched him behind one ear. She looked at him a moment and said, "Oh, the other ear is itchy." She paused. "And your tummy, too?" Tiny wagged his tail and rolled on the floor.

Meanwhile, Penny took Lizzie to the kitchen for a cup of soup before she left.

"How did you know the—what is it? a dog?—wanted to be petted that way?" Adora whispered to Tessa. "It seemed like you knew what he was thinking."

"I can get glimpses of his thoughts, and some other animals', too," Tessa explained. "It's my special talent."

"Can you do it with Fiona?" Adora asked.

Tessa grabbed her arm. "Adora! I am starmendously glad you're here. I don't know if it will work, but I can try. Maybe if I had something of hers . . ." Her voice trailed off; then she raced into the kitchen.

Lizzie sat at the table, oblivious to everything around her, spooning up her soup. Mr. Piggy was propped up next to the cup. Tessa picked up the toy and held it tightly, picturing Fiona as clearly as she could. *Where are you?* she thought, trying to send a message.

There was no answer.

Tessa moved Mr. Piggy closer to her heart. She poured her love of animals into the little pig. Suddenly, she felt a jolt of energy course through her body, out her tingling fingertips, and straight to Mr. Piggy. For a moment, his pink nose glowed.

Tessa closed her eyes and felt something. Fiona was safe, waiting patiently for Lizzie to find her. But where?

Tessa concentrated harder. A small slit of light was falling on Fiona's head. Soft, warm material surrounded her tiny body.

And that was all. Tessa groaned. It wasn't enough.

"We'll keep looking," Penny was telling Lizzie. "And I'll find a way to get her to your new home. But right now, you really need to go."

"Come on," said Tessa. "Adora and I will take you"— she almost said home but stopped herself—"back to your parents."

Outside Lizzie's house, a huge moving truck was parked at the curb. Workers carried boxes and hefted furniture, taking everything up a ramp to the rear of the truck. Lizzie peeked in. "It's full already!"

She rushed inside, shouting, "Mom! Dad! I'm not going without Fiona!"

"Oh, honey." Mr. Bennett wrapped his arms around her. "We can't stay much longer. Our flight leaves in a few hours."

"We're so sorry, Lizzie." Her mom wiped away her own tears. "We'd wait if we could."

Tessa felt terrible. Lizzie didn't want to go to begin with, but to move without her best friend must be unthinkable.

"I know I'm acting like a baby," Lizzie said, sniffling, "but I can't do this without Fiona."

The name Fiona echoed in Tessa's head, and suddenly, she could hear Fiona's thoughts: *I don't want to be left behind. I don't want to be left behind.* She saw more of Fiona's surroundings, too: something that looked like a book . . . a brush . . . a soft, fuzzy sweater . . .

"It's hard for all of us," Mrs. Bennett said. "But the truck is ready. Do you have everything?"

"Yes," Lizzie said in a trembling voice. "There's just my travel suitcase left. And I'm taking that on the plane."

"That's it!" Tessa cried. "Fiona is in your suitcase!"

Everyone raced up to Lizzie's room. The suitcase was on the floor, the top opened just a bit. Lizzie reached in, cried out in delight, and held up a wriggling, joyful Fiona.

"She was waiting in the suitcase," Tessa said, "to make sure you took her with you!"

"You silly dog," Lizzie gently scolded. "I would never leave you."

Lizzie's parents stroked Fiona, too, then left to talk to the movers. Grinning, Lizzie reached over to hug Tessa. "I am so happy! Thank you for being such a good friend."

Friend! With all the excitement about Fiona, Tessa had forgotten about Lizzie's friends' donations.

"I'm not your only good friend," she told Lizzie. "Do you know why the shelter raised so much money?"

Lizzie shook her head. "Because of you—and your friends from all over the world!" Tessa said, pulling up a screen on her Star-Zap showing all the messages from every corner of the planet. "Isn't it incredible? And you wouldn't have these friendships—not any of them!—if you hadn't moved around so much."

"It all adds up," Adora said in her cool, clear way.

"These friends are an important part of your life. A part you'd never want to miss out on."

Slowly, Lizzie nodded.

They were so close to granting the wish.

"And your friends in Hillsboro will never forget you, either," Tessa added. "You've done so much for the shelter! Penny is going to put a plaque in the new lobby, thanking you. And it's all because you moved here to Hillsboro!"

"Really?" Lizzie grinned.

A rainbow of colored lights flew from Lizzie, arcing through the air, then whooshing straight into Tessa's Wish Pendant. Lizzie's wish had come true! And Tessa had the wish energy to prove it.

She and Adora were grinning at each other like idiots when Lizzie's phone beeped. It was Penny, texting a special good-bye. Unbelievably, it seemed to Tessa, she wanted to let her know something else: she had decided to keep Tiny and Snuggles for her very own.

Now Tessa was feeling pretty emotional herself! Still, she wanted to do one more thing for Lizzie before she forgot. She grabbed a pen and wrote out some tips she'd come up with earlier for creating a homey space wherever you are: *Make sure you have the softest, most luxurious blanket. Your sheets should have the highest thread count. Put framed photos everywhere.*

"I envy you," she told Lizzie. "You get to make your room up all over again!" Then she winked at Adora and whispered softly, "But I wouldn't change mine for all the Zing on Starland." In fact, just thinking about their room—a jumble of cooking utensils and science equipment—made Tessa long for home.

Still, her mission had been starmazing. "Oh, Lizzie! I'll never forget you—or Fiona!"

Adora lifted her eyebrows and pointedly looked at at Tessa.

"Okay," said Tessa. "You have to go." She hugged Lizzie one last time. When they pulled apart, Lizzie looked at her a little strangely.

"Are you with the movers?" she asked. "I didn't know it was a family company."

Tessa thought of Gemma—and the other Star Darlings—and another wave of homesickness swept over her. "Yes," she said. "We are definitely a family that works together."

Then she added in a businesslike voice, "Just thought I'd come upstairs to make sure you have everything you need."

Lizzie hugged Fiona. "I sure do."

Tessa smiled and picked up one last thought as she and Adora left: *Bye, Tessa.*

It was sad that Lizzie would never remember her, but maybe Fiona would.

Epilogue

In no time at all, it seemed, she and Adora were back on Starland. At least, she assumed Adora was, too. Their stars had taken different courses. Just to be sure, she holo-texted: WHERE ARE YOU?

RIGHT OUTSIDE THE DORM! Adora responded in a starsec. ARE YOU COMING BACK TO THE ROOM?

I'M IN FRONT OF ILLUMINATION LIBRARY, Tessa holo-texted back. She was, in fact, in one of her favorite places: the sunlit library courtyard. It was a secluded, quiet place, filled with bluebeezle flowers and humming glitterbees. I'LL SEE YOU IN A LITTLE BIT, she added.

It felt nice to be alone, to run through everything that had happened in her mind and get her thoughts in order.

Unfortunately, someone else was rushing toward the courtyard. Then she grinned. It was Gemma!

"Tessa!" exclaimed Gemma. "I had a feeling I'd find you here!"

Tessa hugged her sister tightly. "For once, don't talk!" she warned. "I want to tell you about my mission. My Wisher made me think of you, and—"

Before she could say another word, their Star-Zaps buzzed.

"Wish Orb presentation time!" Gemma crowed. The girls linked arms and walked quickly to Lady Stella's office.

The ceremony was brief yet satisfying. The Star Darlings still looked uncomfortable around Lady Stella. But the headmistress was as warm as ever, even if she seemed a little distracted.

Tessa didn't want a lot of speeches or applause. At least, that's what she told herself. It was just nice to be acknowledged—and to see the orb transform into a Wish Blossom and then a Power Crystal. When the lovely ver-tessema spun its golden wheel, Tessa's Power Crystal fell right into her hand. It was a delicate gossamer crystal.

"How could someone so sweet be evil?" she whispered to Scarlet.

"To throw you off," Scarlet whispered back harshly.

Lady Stella cleared her throat, then glided out of the room. The girls rose, too, saying their last star congratulations to Tessa. Soon she was alone.

Well, that's that, thought Tessa, stepping out of the office and rounding a corner.

"Pssssst!" An arm shot out from a doorway and pulled her into a dark, empty room.

"What in the stars?" said Tessa.

"Hush, Tessa," someone said. Tessa recognized the voice. It was Cassie. Tessa's eyes adjusted to the gloom and she realized Scarlet was standing there, too.

"We're going down to the caves again," Scarlet said. "We tried to explore more while you were gone, but something always came up."

"One time Lady Stella called an extra SD class at the last starmin," explained Cassie. "It was like she knew what we were planning and wanted to stop us."

"And another time we were already in the supply closet, about to open the trapdoor, when Lady Cordial poked her head in to ask us to move furniture from the Lightning Lounge to the library," Scarlet added. "Why she couldn't just ask some Bot-Bots, I haven't the starriest."

"Still," Cassie said, "it was fun to practice wish

energy manipulation with heavy objects." She held back a giggle. "I just wish Lady Cordial hadn't told me to put that chair down right when it was hovering over her foot!"

Scarlet pulled up her hood and started for the door. "Enough chitchat. Let's go."

The three girls made their way to the supply closet, down the trapdoor steps, then into the cool, damp tunnels.

"I just know these caves hold some clues," Cassie whispered. "Stars crossed, this time we'll get lucky."

Tessa nodded, even though she really wanted to go to her room and take a sparkle shower. She had just come back from Wishworld, for star's sake, and here she was traipsing around these dim tunnels like she had all the startime in the worlds.

But still, she had to be there. Who else would be on the lookout for clues that proved Lady Stella innocent? Not that she didn't trust Cassie and Scarlet . . . well, at least Cassie.

Just a little way in, a bitbat swooped directly in front of them, and the Starlings stopped short.

"Why, hello there, little one," Scarlet said softly.

Tessa recognized the bitbat—or thought she did,

anyway—as the one who had met them the last time. Scarlet's special pet.

The bitbat fluttered her wings a star inch from Scarlet's nose, then seemed to beckon with one wing.

"Let's follow her," said Scarlet. "It's better than wandering around aimlessly."

Tessa and Cassie agreed. They walked single file through one tunnel after another, then another still, the bitbat leading the way. The tunnels grew narrower and more twisting as they sloped deeper underground. Tessa shivered. The air was colder, too.

She wasn't sure they could ever find their way out.

"I'm not enjoying this," she said. She thought of her cozy dorm room, where the temperature was always set at a perfect ten degrees Starrius. This definitely had none of the comforts of home.

Finally, the bitbat stopped, hovering in front of a sheer stone wall.

Tessa squinted. "This looks like any other part of the tunnels," she said as the bitbat dipped her head in farewell and disappeared into the darkness. "Why did she bring us here?" Her voice rose a bit in panic. "And how are we going to get out?"

"Let's take things one step at a time," Cassie said calmly.

"Yes, Tessa," said Scarlet testily. "Don't overreact here."

Tessa had to laugh. Scarlet was usually the one to act without thinking.

Just laughing made Tessa feel better. So she took her time, peering closely at the wall. "There's a crack here," she told the others. "It doesn't look like erosion or just some random break. It forms a perfect rectangle."

She traced her finger along the line, and the gray stone faded away to reveal a screen.

"A hidden holo-screen!" Cassie breathed.

The screen lit up suddenly, and Tessa blinked in the bright light. "Moons and stars!" she exclaimed.

"Password denied," said a Bot-Bot as the same words appeared on-screen.

Tessa gasped and pulled the others a little farther away. "Don't say anything too loudly," she warned. "It can hear us."

"There must be a secret room behind this wall. We have to come up with the password," Scarlet whispered excitedly. "I just know this could lead to answers!"

"We need to be careful, though," Cassie said in a low voice. "What if it's like one of those old stories, and we only get three tries? And if we're wrong, a stinkberry grows on our nose?"

"Oh, don't be such a scaredy-bitbat." Scarlet scoffed quietly. Then she faced the screen and, before Tessa or Cassie could stop her, shouted, "Lady Stella!"

"Password denied." The screen blinked.

"If it's three tries and we're out, we're already done here," Cassie said. "Should we chance it?"

"We have no choice." Tessa suddenly felt determined to see it through. "How about 'Star Darlings'?"

"I'll take this one." Scarlet edged to the holo-screen. "Star Darlings!"

Tessa tensed, expecting bells and alarms and stars knew what. Instead, the Bot-Bot just repeated, "Password denied."

"Well, at least we can keep trying," said Cassie.

The girls shouted out random words, willing to try anything.

"Wishlings. Bot-Bots!" "Wishworld!" Scarlet even tried "Secret password." But nothing worked.

Tessa's stomach rumbled. Not only had she gone straight from Wishworld to Lady Stella's office to the caves, but she hadn't even had time for a real meal.

"Moonberries!" she cried in annoyance.

The wall slid open. Tessa giggled. But then she grew sober as she recalled how much Lady Stella loved moonberries. Did that mean she had set up this secret room? And what would they find inside?

Holding hands, the girls edged inside the dark room. As soon as they crossed the threshold, the walls lit up brightly.

It was a small space, filled floor to ceiling with holo-books neatly placed on shelves. "Maybe it's just a storeroom for the library," Tessa said hopefully. Neither Scarlet nor Cassie bothered to reply.

Scarlet stepped up to a shelf and pulled out a holo-book. It looked extremely faded and worn. "This must be really, really old. Look—it's called *A History of Prism*. The town isn't even called Old Prism here."

"And look at this one," Cassie said, pulling another book from a shelf. "This one has all these old maps." She flipped the pages. "Here's the area around the Crystal Mountains. There's no Starling Academy!"

Tessa leaned closer. "The writing is so strange. All squiggly and hard to read." She reached for another book. "Most of these must be ancient!"

They browsed more shelves, and finally, Tessa pulled out a thick, heavy tome. Its deep purple cover had a glowing star, and Tessa sensed its power. If there had ever been a title, it had faded long before. She undid the heavy clasp.

Cassie and Scarlet watched as she thumbed through the pages. She stopped toward the end as a holo-picture came to life.

Twelve figures, clearly girls, posed in a circle. Glowing Wish Blossoms formed at their fingertips, swirling to meet in a burst of light. Dim words, difficult to read, were projected in the air.

"It says something about an oracle, a prophecy about the future," Cassie said, deciphering the text.

Haltingly, Tessa read phrases out loud: "'Twelve star-charmed Starlings' . . . 'Girls with a unique ability to grant wishes' . . . 'and so release wish energy so powerful' . . . 'save Starland' . . ." Her voice trailed off.

"The rest is a blur," Cassie said. Then she looked at Tessa and Scarlet. They gazed at one another in shock as understanding dawned on each of them.

"Oh my stars," said Tessa. "There are twelve girls in the prophecy. And there are twelve Star Darlings. The prophecy must be about us!"

Scarlet grinned. "I knew I was—I mean, we were—special!"

Just then the door closed with a whoosh.

The girls rushed to it. There was no screen on that side of the door. No hand scanner to slide it open. The stone was as smooth as polished glass.

With all her wish energy, Tessa willed the stone to crack, the door to open. Cassie and Scarlet did the same. It wouldn't budge.

They were trapped.

Glossary

Afterglow: The Starling afterlife. When Starlings die, it is said that they have "begun their afterglow."

Age of Fulfillment: The age at which a Starling is considered mature enough to begin to study wish granting.

Astromuffin: A delicious baked breakfast treat.

Bad Wish Orbs: Orbs that are the result of bad or selfish wishes made on Wishworld. These grow dark and warped and are quickly sent to the Negative Energy Facility.

Ballum blossom tree: A Starland tree with cherry blossom–like flowers that light up at night.

Big Dipper Dormitory: Where third- and fourth-year students live.

Bitbat: A small winged nocturnal creature.

Bluebeezle: Delicate bright blue flowers that emit a scent that only glitterbees can detect.

Blushbelle: A pink flower with a sweetly spicy scent.

Bot-Bot: A Starland robot. There are Bot-Bot guards, waiters, deliverers, and guides on Starland.

Bright Day: The date a Starling is born, celebrated each year like a Wishling birthday.

Celestial Café: Starling Academy's outstanding cafeteria.

Chickadoodle: A fluffy feathered farm creature that crows at sunrise and is similar to a Wishworld rooster.

Cocomoon: A sweet and creamy fruit with an iridescent glow.

Comet cake: A sweet Starland cake decorated to look like a comet, with a tail made of starberries.

Cosmic Transporter: The moving sidewalk system that transports students through dorms and across the Starling Academy campus.

Countdown Clock: A timing device on a Starling's Star-Zap. It lets them know how much time is left on a Wish Mission, which coincides with when the Wish Orb will fade.

Crystal Mountains: The most beautiful mountains on Starland. They are located across the lake from Starling Academy.

Cycle of Life: A Starling's life span. When Starlings die, they are said to have "completed their Cycle of Life."

Delicata: A sweet and fragrant liquid made by glitterbees and often used in baking.

Dramboozle: A natural herb that promotes sweet dreams and comforting sleep.

Druderwomp: An edible barrel-like bush capable of pulling up its own roots and rolling like a tumbleweed, then planting itself again.

Eternium wool: Fine strands of a strong, hard thread matted into a ball and used to scrub things clean. A bit like Wishworld steel wool.

Flareworks: Colorful displays at the Festival of Illumination.

Floozel: The Starland equivalent of a Wishworld mile.

Flutterfocus: A Starland creature similar to a Wishworld butterfly but with illuminated wings.

Galliope: A sparkly Starland creature similar to a Wishworld horse.

Garble greens: A Starland vegetable similar to spinach.

Glamera: A holographic image-recording device.

Glimmerwillow tree: A Starland tree with hanging branches called glimmervines that create a space at its base resembling a closed-off leafy room.

Glimmerworm: The larval stage of the glimmerbug. It spins a beautiful sparkly cocoon from its silk. "Pulling the glimmersilk over your eyes" is an expression meaning that someone is hiding something or is being deceptive.

Glion: A gentle Starland creature similar in appearance to a Wishworld lion but with a multicolored glowing mane.

Glitterbees: Blue-and-orange-striped bugs that pollinate Starland flowers and produce a sweet substance called delicata.

Glitterberries: A sweet Starland fruit.

Gloak tree: A Starland tree known for its strength and beauty.

Globerbeem: Large, friendly lightning bug–type insects that are sparkly and lay eggs.

Gloom flats: A rural, sparsely populated, dimly illuminated area of Starland and home to Piper's family.

Glorange: A glowing orange fruit. Its juice is often enjoyed at breakfast time.

Glowfur: A small, furry Starland creature with gossamer wings that eats flowers and glows.

Glowjay: A small flying animal with shimmering feathers.

Glowmoss: A soft vegetation that covers fields on Starland.

Goldenella: A tall slender tree with golden blossoms that pop off the branches.

Good Wish Orbs: Orbs that are the result of positive wishes made on Wishworld. They are planted in Wish-Houses.

Halo Hall: The building where Starling Academy classes are held.

Holo-text: A message received on a Star-Zap and projected into the air. There are also holo-albums, holo-billboards, holo-books, holo-cards, holo-communications, holo-diaries, holo-flyers, holo-letters, holo-papers, holo-pictures, and holo–place cards. Anything that would be made of paper or contain writing or images on Wishworld is a hologram on Starland.

Hydrong: The equivalent of a Wishworld hundred.

Illumination Library: The impressive library at Starling Academy.

Impossible Wish Orbs: Orbs that are the result of wishes made on Wishworld that are beyond the power of Starlings to grant.

Isle of Misera: A barren rocky island off the coast of New Prism.

Lightku: A spare and simple poem with only three lines of verse and seventeen syllables total.

Lightku Isle: An isolated part of Starland with sandy, sparkling beaches, where local Starlings speak solely in lightkus.

Lightning Lounge: A place on the Starling Academy campus where students relax and socialize.

Little Dipper Dormitory: Where first- and second-year students live.

Lolofruit: A large round fruit with a thick skin and juicy, aromatic flesh.

Luminous Lake: A serene and lovely lake next to the Starling Academy campus.

Mirror Mantra: A saying specific to each Star Darling that when recited gives her (and her Wisher) reassurance and strength. When a Starling recites her Mirror Mantra while looking in a mirror, she will see her true appearance reflected.

Moogle: A very short but unspecific amount of time. The word is used in expressions like "Wait just a moogle!"

Moonberry: A fruit that is a lot like a blueberry, but with a more intense flavor.

Mooncheese crisp: A crunchy, savory Starland snack.

Moonium: An amount similar to a Wishworld million.

Old Prism: A medium-sized historical city about an hour from Starling Academy.

Ozziefruit: Sweet plum-sized indigo fruit that grows on pink-leaved trees. It is usually eaten raw, made into jam, or cooked into pies. Starling Academy has an ozziefruit orchard.

Plinking: A delicious striped fruit that bounces like a ball.

Power Crystal: The powerful stone that each Star Darling receives once she has granted her first wish.

Prickly buds. Buds from a Starland plant that are covered in a rough, prickly casing before they open.

Quax: A unit of measurement used in cooking, similar to a cup.

Radiant Recreation Center: The building at Starling Academy where students take Physical Energy, health, and fitness classes. The rec center has a large gymnasium for exercising, a running track, areas for games, and a sparkling star-pool.

Ruffruff tree: A Starland tree with rough, scratchy leaves.

Serenity Islands: A Starland recreation area. Starlings sometimes take paddleboat rides around it.

Shimmer-butter: A delectable creamy spread that is often used on baked goods.

Shooting stars: Speeding stars that Starlings can latch on to and ride to Wishworld.

Silver Blossom: The final manifestation of a Good Wish Orb. This glimmering metallic bloom is placed in the Hall of Granted Wishes.

Sleepibelle: Piper's Wish Blossom. Its blue-green petals hang down and swing in a soothing motion, like a pendulum.

Snuggle sack: A heavily quilted tube that immediately adjusts to a Starling's height and body shape for extreme comfort.

Solar Springs: A hilly small town in the countryside where Tessa and Gemma are from.

Sparkleberries: A Starland fruit that is used in baking and often included as an ingredient in comet cakes.

Sparklecorn: A versatile Starland food.

Sparkle shower: An energy shower Starlings take every day to get clean and refresh their sparkling glow.

Sparklesugar: An ingredient used to sweeten baked goods.

Starapple: A large crunchy and sweet Starland fruit that grows on Tessa and Gemma's farm.

Star ball: An intramural sport that shares similarities with soccer on Wishworld, but star ball players use energy manipulation to control the ball.

Starberries: Bright red berries that grow on Starland and are used to create the tails on comet cakes.

Starcar: The primary mode of transportation for most Starlings. These ultrasafe vehicles drive themselves on cushions of wish energy.

Star Caves: The caverns underneath Starling Academy where the Star Darlings' secret Wish Cavern is located.

Stardominoes: Starland rectangular holo–game pieces that can be set up for a chain reaction in which they all knock each other over when one stardomino is knocked over.

Starf!: A Starling expression of dismay.

Star flash: News bulletin, often used sarcastically.

Star Kindness Day: A special Starland holiday that celebrates spreading kindness, compliments, and good cheer.

Starland City: The largest city on Starland, also its capital.

Starlicious: Tasty, delicious.

Starlings: The glowing beings with sparkly skin who live on Starland.

Starmarble: An attractive stone used for surfaces in Starland architecture.

Starpepper jelly: A condiment that adds spice and flavor to Starland foods.

Star Quad: The center of the Starling Academy campus. The dancing fountain, band shell, and hedge maze are located there.

Star sack: A Starland tote bag. This container starts about the size of a lunch bag, but it expands to hold whatever is stored inside.

Star salutations: The Starling way to say "thank you."

Starshoot: A Starland sport similar to Wishworld baseball, but players make use of energy manipulation techniques to move the ball.

Starweek: The Starland week, which is made up of eight star-days. The stardays in order are Sweetday, Shineday, Dododay, Yumday, Lunaday, Bopday, Reliquaday, and Babsday.

Staryear: A period of 365 days on Starland, the equivalent of a Wishworld year.

Star-Zap: The ultimate smartphone that Starlings use for all communications. It has myriad features.

Stellar School: A rival of Starling Academy in star ball.

Stellation: The point of a star. Halo Hall has five stellations, each housing a different department.

Sunflour: A baking ingredient made from ground-up plants. It is a basic ingredient of cakes and breads.

Sunnet: A rhyming poem that can be any length and meter but must include a source of light.

Supernova: A stellar explosion. Also used colloquially, meaning "really angry," as in "She went supernova when she found out the bad news."

Time of Letting Go: One of the four seasons on Starland. It falls between the warmest season and the coldest, similar to fall on Wishworld.

Time of Lumiere: The warmest season on Starland, similar to summer on Wishworld.

Time of New Beginnings: Similar to spring on Wishworld, this is the season that follows the coldest time of year; it's when plants and trees come into bloom.

Time of Shadows: The coldest season of the year on Starland, similar to winter on Wishworld.

Toothlight: A high-tech gadget that Starlings use to clean their teeth.

Trilight: A planet with three moons that is visible from Starland.

Twinkelopes: Majestic herd animals. Males have imposing antlers with star-shaped horns, and females have iridescent manes and flowing tails.

Vanisholine: A Starland natural substance used for cleaning.

Vertessema: Tessa's Wish Blossom. A wheel-shaped flower made of golden stars.

Wish Blossom: The bloom that appears from a Wish Orb after its wish is granted.

Wish energy: The positive energy that is released when a wish is granted. Wish energy powers everything on Starland.

Wisher: The Wishling who has made the wish that is being granted.

Wish-Granters: Starlings whose job is to travel down to Wishworld to help make wishes come true and collect wish energy.

Wish-House: The place where Wish Orbs are planted and cared for until they sparkle. Once the orb's wish is granted, it becomes a Wish Blossom.

Wishlings: The inhabitants of Wishworld.

Wish Mission: The task a Starling undertakes when she travels to Wishworld to help grant a wish.

Wish Orb: The form a wish takes on Wishworld before traveling to Starland. There it will grow and sparkle when it's time to grant the wish.

Wish Pendant: A gadget that absorbs and transports wish energy, helps Starlings locate their Wishers, and changes a Starling's appearance. Each Wish Pendant holds a different special power for its Star Darling.

Wishworld: The planet Starland relies on for wish energy. The beings on Wishworld know it by another name—Earth.

Wishworld Outfit Selector: A program on each Star-Zap that accesses Wishworld fashions for Starlings to wear to blend in on their Wish Missions.

Wishworld Surveillance Deck: A platform located high above the campus where Starling Academy students go to observe Wishlings through high-powered telescopes.

Zing: A traditional Starling breakfast drink. It can be enjoyed hot or iced.

Zingspoon: A small unit of measurement often used when baking, roughly equivalent to a Wishworld teaspoon.

Acknowledgments

It is impossible to list all of our gratitude, but we will try.

Our most precious gift and greatest teacher, Halo; we love you more than there are stars in the sky . . . punashaku. To the rest of our crazy, awesome, unique tribe—thank you for teaching us to go for our dreams. Integrity. Strength. Love. Foundation. Family. Grateful. Mimi Muldoon—from your star doodling to naming our Star Darlings, your artistry, unconditional love, and inspiration is infinite. Didi Muldoon—your belief and support in us is only matched by your fierce protection and massive-hearted guidance. Gail. Queen G. Your business sense and witchy wisdom are legendary. Frank—you are missed and we know you are watching over us all. Along with Tutu, Nana, and Deda, who are always present, gently guiding us in spirit. To our colorful, totally genius, and bananas siblings: Patrick, Moon, Diva, and Dweezil—there is more creativity and humor in those four names than most people experience in a lifetime. Blessed. To our magical nieces—Mathilda, Zola, Ceylon, and Mia—the Star Darlings adore you and so do we. Our witchy cuzzie fairy godmothers—Ane and Gina. Our fairy fashion godfather, Paris. Our sweet Panay. Teeta and Freddy—we love you so much. And our four-legged fur babies—Sandwich, Luna, Figgy, and Pinky Star.

The incredible Barry Waldo. Our SD partner. Sent to us from above in perfect timing. Your expertise and friendship are beyond words. We love you and Gary to the moon and back. Long live the manifestation room!

Catherine Daly—the stars shined brightly upon us the day we aligned with you. Your talent and inspiration are otherworldly; our appreciation cannot be expressed in words. Many heartfelt hugs for you and the adorable Oonagh.

To our beloved Disney family. Thank you for believing in us. Wendy Lefkon, our master guide and friend through this entire journey. Stephanie Lurie, for being the first to believe in Star Darlings. Suzanne Murphy, who helped every step of the way. Jeanne Mosure, we fell in love with you the first time we met, and Star Darlings wouldn't be what it is without you. Andrew Sugerman, thank you so much for all your support.

Our team . . . Devon (pony pants) and our Monsterfoot crew—so grateful. Richard Scheltinga—our angel and protector. Chris Abramson—thank you! Special appreciation to Richard Thompson, John LaViolette, Swanna, Mario, and Sam.

To our friends old and new—we are so grateful to be on this rad journey that is life with you all. Fay. Jorja. Chandra. Sananda. Sandy. Kathryn. Louise. What wisdom and strength you share. Ruth, Mike, and the rest of our magical Wagon Wheel bunch—how lucky we are. How inspiring you are. We love you.

Last—we have immeasurable gratitude for every person we've met along our journey, for all the good and the bad; it is all a gift. From the bottom of our hearts we thank you for touching our lives.

Shana Muldoon Zappa is a jewelry designer and writer who was born and raised in Los Angeles. With an endless imagination, a passion to inspire positivity through her many artistic endeavors, and her background in fashion, Shana created Star Darlings. She and her husband, Ahmet Zappa, collaborated on Star Darlings especially for their magical little girl and biggest inspiration, Halo Violetta Zappa.

Ahmet Zappa is the *New York Times* best-selling author of *Because I'm Your Dad* and *The Monstrous Memoirs of a Mighty McFearless*. He writes and produces films and television shows and loves pancakes, unicorns, and making funny faces for Halo and Shana.

Adora
finds a friend

"*Mmmmmm, hmmmm,* mmmm, hmmmm." Adora hummed tunelessly, alone in her dorm room.

It felt nice to have the room all to herself. Still, it was a little strange that Tessa, her roommate, wasn't there.

The two had just come back from a Wish Mission. It was Tessa's mission; Adora had yet to be chosen for her own mission to Wishworld. But Adora had been sent to help when the situation looked dim. Really, Tessa had been so caught up in her Wisher's emotions that she hadn't been able to see the orchard for the ozziefruit trees. Luckily, Adora had set her straight. So thank the stars, the trip had been successful and quite exciting.

After the Star Darlings ceremony, where Tessa had

gotten her Power Crystal, Adora had expected her to come straight back to their room. Tessa was quite the homebody, after all. And there were her virtual galliope, Jewel, to feed and her micro-zap waiting to bake yummy astromuffins.

But Tessa hadn't so much as stopped off at the room as far as Adora could tell. She was probably catching up with her younger sister, Gemma. And Adora planned to take full advantage of her alone time.

She had been right in the middle of an experiment when she'd been called on to help Tessa. She'd been itching to get back to it for over a starday now. It combined her two biggest passions: science and fashion—specifically sequins.

Adora wanted the sequins to be extra twinkly. That alone wouldn't be so difficult. But she wanted that new-found sparkle to bring out each sequin's color, too, to make the shades themselves brighter, warmer, and more radiant.

The gold sequins Leona favored had to become even more brightly golden; Cassie's silvery pink ones even more silvery pink; Clover's an even deeper, more brilliant purple. And Adora's goal was to do it with just one formula.

She wanted the formula to work with every shade under the suns, and that was twelve in the Star Darlings group alone. Add all the different tones at Starling Academy, or, furthermore, all of Starland itself, and the numbers were starmazing!

Adora had already removed natural elements from glittery yellow calliope flowers, fiery red florafierces, and other plants and trees. Now she needed to add twinkle-oxide—with a spark of glowzene for good measure—to each mixture. The combination had to be just right so the formula would react with any Starling shade.

Luckily, it was Reliquaday, the first starday of the weekend, which gave her plenty of time to test her ideas. Adora would be logical and methodical, as always. But she wanted to get it done sooner rather than later so the sequins could be sewn onto outfits the Star Darlings band members planned to wear for the upcoming Battle of the Bands on Starshine Day.

"*Mmmmm, hmmm, mmmmm.*" Adora hummed, pouring 5.6 lumins of twinkle-oxide into a beaker. "*Mmmm, hmmmmm.*" She turned on her personal bright-burner to 179 degrees Starrius and waited for the mixture to heat. "*Mmmm.*"

Alone in the room, Adora felt free to sing to her heart's content. Her music skills were nothing to brag about, but Adora wasn't much into the arts, anyway. For her, it was science, science, science—and fashion, fashion, fashion.

Adora planned to be a style scientist, maybe the first on all of Starland. And she'd show everyone she could be the brightest in both style and science.

Adora's parents owned a trendy clothing store in Radiant Hills, the ultraexclusive community in Starland City where Libby had grown up alongside glimmerous celebrighties and famous Starlandians.

Adora herself had lived in a perfectly nice neighborhood of modest, comfortable homes. She couldn't complain. She and her parents had shared a simple one-level house where they each had their own workspace to create designs to sell in the store. Even as a wee Starling, she'd had a microscope and a star-sewing machine and had come up with lustrous new fabrics for her parents to use in their clothing designs.

Adora pushed back sky-blue strands of hair that had fallen out of her loose bun, and adjusted her knee-length glittery lab coat and gloves. She checked her pockets, making sure the extra test tubes she always carried around were closed up tight.

Finally, with great care, she straightened her safety starglasses. Safety first, she knew from prior experience.

Just this staryear, Tessa had mixed a batch of glorange smoothies. Adora, meanwhile, had been working on special fabric that would sparkle extra brightly when it got wet. She'd combined orangey lightning in a bottle with starfuric acid and was ready to soak the fabric. The mixture did look a bit like the smoothies, Adora had to admit. So it was no wonder Tessa had reached for the wrong container and lifted it to her lips, about to take a sip. Adora had to make a running dive to knock the liquid out of her hands.

Right after that, Adora had established rules, including clearly separating food from experiments and wearing safety starglasses. The second one was particularly important, Adora realized a starsec later, when—

Bang! Her sequin mixture fizzled and sparked, overflowing from the beaker and spilling onto her workspace. Immediately, the smoking liquid disappeared, thanks to the self-cleaning technology featured in all Starland dwellings.

She wanted the formula to work with every shade under the suns, and that was twelve in the Star Darlings group alone. Add all the different tones at Starling Academy, or, furthermore, all of Starland itself, and the numbers were starmazing!

Adora had already removed natural elements from glittery yellow calliope flowers, fiery red florafierces, and other plants and trees. Now she needed to add twinkle-oxide—with a spark of glowzene for good measure—to each mixture. The combination had to be just right so the formula would react with any Starling shade.

Luckily, it was Reliquaday, the first starday of the weekend, which gave her plenty of time to test her ideas. Adora would be logical and methodical, as always. But she wanted to get it done sooner rather than later so the sequins could be sewn onto outfits the Star Darlings band members planned to wear for the upcoming Battle of the Bands on Starshine Day.

"*Mmmmm, hmmm, mmmmm.*" Adora hummed, pouring 5.6 lumins of twinkle-oxide into a beaker. "*Mmmm, hmmmmm.*" She turned on her personal bright-burner to 179 degrees Starrius and waited for the mixture to heat. "*Mmmm.*"

Alone in the room, Adora felt free to sing to her heart's content. Her music skills were nothing to brag about, but Adora wasn't much into the arts, anyway. For her, it was science, science, science—and fashion, fashion, fashion.

Adora planned to be a style scientist, maybe the first on all of Starland. And she'd show everyone she could be the brightest in both style and science.

Adora's parents owned a trendy clothing store in Radiant Hills, the ultraexclusive community in Starland City where Libby had grown up alongside glimmerous celebrighties and famous Starlandians.

Adora herself had lived in a perfectly nice neighborhood of modest, comfortable homes. She couldn't complain. She and her parents had shared a simple one-level house where they each had their own workspace to create designs to sell in the store. Even as a wee Starling, she'd had a microscope and a star-sewing machine and had come up with lustrous new fabrics for her parents to use in their clothing designs.

Adora pushed back sky-blue strands of hair that had fallen out of her loose bun, and adjusted her knee-length glittery lab coat and gloves. She checked her pockets, making sure the extra test tubes she always carried around were closed up tight.

Finally, with great care, she straightened her safety starglasses. Safety first, she knew from prior experience.

Just this staryear, Tessa had mixed a batch of glorange smoothies. Adora, meanwhile, had been working on special fabric that would sparkle extra brightly when it got wet. She'd combined orangey lightning in a bottle with starfuric acid and was ready to soak the fabric. The mixture did look a bit like the smoothies, Adora had to admit. So it was no wonder Tessa had reached for the wrong container and lifted it to her lips, about to take a sip. Adora had to make a running dive to knock the liquid out of her hands.

Right after that, Adora had established rules, including clearly separating food from experiments and wearing safety starglasses. The second one was particularly important, Adora realized a starsec later, when—

Bang! Her sequin mixture fizzled and sparked, overflowing from the beaker and spilling onto her workspace. Immediately, the smoking liquid disappeared, thanks to the self-cleaning technology featured in all Starland dwellings.